I0687296

WINTER FALLS

A Science Fiction Case Study in Artificial Intelligence

Author
Leif J. Erickson

Cover & Interior Design
Cosmo Publishing

ISBN: 978-0-9962804-9-5

Chapter #1

There is no better gauge of measurement for a civilization than the technology it creates. The masters of technology are the masters of the world. The civilizations and governments that embrace technology are the ones that thrive and expand, creating empires and dynasties for the ages. Technology always ebbs and flows though, sometimes increasing while other times decreasing. From the discoveries of fire and the wheel that allowed our ancestors to usher in new ages, to the computer and wireless networks of today, technology has always broken barriers, pushed boundaries, and begs the question, 'what if?'

Always fiercely debated, technology, inherently neutral, can be used for good or evil. The splitting of the atom that led to the deaths of millions of people in the blink of an eye or the engineering of a virus that could wipe out swaths of people before being brought under control, in the wrong hands, technology can and has spelled certain doom for those not intelligent enough to respect it's awesome, raw power. Throughout history, technology in the wrong hands has led to disastrous results for those not prepared to accept the consequences of breaking the limits.

As the computer race ramped up, with new computer technology being released almost daily, with new computer systems taking out the old standards, it's no surprise that companies like Everyday Computers, led by Allen Day, and Madison Software Labs, founded by Doctor Jack Hall, both of Palo Alto California, would attempt something which most thought was a dream. Even ten years prior, no one would have believed either man's attempt at controlling the systems that humans rely on every day. Using hardware from Everyday Computers and software from Madison Software Labs the small metropolitan of Winter Falls decided to run the entire city systems with a networked computer system that promised to make life for everyone easier.

Barely fifty years since desktop computers and the Internet became household names in the 1990s, Winter Falls attempted one of the most ambitious computer systems ever tested. Thousands of processors, untold amounts of storage, and the latest and greatest networking and RFID systems known to man. The people behind this said it was the promise of a new age—a better age. But what very few realized was that technology needed to be monitored, but not nearly as much as the people running it. Technology is wonderful until it is turned against those it is meant to help...

Outside the Winter Falls City Hall, a sweeping, ultra-modern building stretching into the sky with steel and glass, a crowd of over one thousand people gathered before the steps, waiting for the promised announcement. There was an air of excitement in the crowd, a heightened anticipation that was boarding on turning into a frenzy. For months the people of the city had heard about the new system that was going to make their lives easier, going to stop crime and increase productivity. A system that would improve health and increase free time. The crowd waited at the steps, eagerly chatting, discussing the rumors and legends about what was to come.

Beyond the steps, being held back by police barricades and a grouping of armed police officers, was an assembly of about a hundred protestors. The protestors, calling themselves the Neo-Luddites, held signs and chanted about the computer takeover of the world. They screamed at the crowd of onlookers, mocking their welcoming of the downfall of civilization. Most of the members of the crowd ignored the Neo-Luddites, having heard the warnings every time a new technology came out. The crowd was numb to the technology warnings that had been increasing in recent years. Ever since the glasses computer became commonplace, computers had become a permanent part of human life, no matter how badly the Neo-Luddites wanted to go back to the past.

The crowd began wildly cheering when a familiar face walked out of city hall; Mayor Theodor Kamp. All the newswire services turned their cameras and microphones toward Mayor Kamp as he made his way to a podium at the top of the stairs. Security guards kept the crowd at the base of the steps as they tried to push themselves closer to the mayor. Mayor Kamp smiled as he looked over the crowd. He was pleased with the turnout and knew that the newsfeeds would be sending these videos all over the world. He'd rehearsed this speech hundreds of times. This would be the speech that would thrust Mayor Theodor Kamp into the national spotlight. His regard for technology would be what carried him from small-town mayor to President of the United States, or so he hoped.

Mayor Kamp spared no expense for this outing. He'd purchased a custom-made, gray, three-piece suit. He had the best stylists work on his thinning black hair, lightly applied makeup to hide some of the stress wrinkles that were starting to show in his fifty-year-old face, and hired a personal trainer for the past six months to help him drop forty pounds and get him into a stunning physique for when the cameras were all pointed at him.

Mayor Kamp had thought of everything. His blockish, flat face was held in a warm, inviting smile, a smile he'd been practicing with trainers. Every accessory he wore, from his tie clip, to Rolex watch, to gold rings, had been carefully selected to present the best image possible for this moment. His Italian leather shoes were polished to shine. Mayor Kamp approached the microphone, taking a moment to soak in the crowd before confirming what they already knew.

"Ladies and gentlemen, welcome to the new world!" Mayor Kamp's voice boomed through the speaker system and the crowd cheered. Mayor Kamp waited for the cheering of the crowd to die down before speaking again. "Welcome to this most historic day. Years from now the world will look back and see that today, here in our little metropolis of Winter Falls history was made. A history that will change the world forever.

"I asked you, the voting public, to get behind me on this. I asked for your support, I asked for your patience, and I asked for your money. Hundreds of millions of dollars spent to set this system up and you didn't have a complete idea the extent it would cover. Well, today I'm here to tell you that the system will be better than imagined, better than could have ever been predicted. I guarantee this system will make history.

"I'm sure you've heard the rumors that have been floating around the Internet newsfeeds. We created a new computer. This isn't exactly accurate. What we've created is a system that will connect the functions of everyday life and make everything run together. This is beyond the current networks that monitor your refrigerator and order you milk when you are getting low. This is beyond the wearable computers we have today. This is a system that will network and control an entire city.

"It would take days to explain everything this new system does. Some of the high points, the most exciting points, are the traffic and health benefits. Traffic jams are now a thing of the past. Using the global positioning system in all cars, simply type in your destination and the system will factor everything; traffic flow, traffic lights, train schedules, and the like, give you the quickest route to your destination, making sure that gridlock traffic is obsolete.

"Thinking about going swimming at one of the local beaches on our river? With the right app, you can see real-time temperature and quality of the water at each of the beaches. Even find out how many people are there. Concerned about drinking water? Another app will tell you the exact composition of the water coming from any drinking fountain in the city, or even the quality of the water coming from your tap.

"Using the system's load-balancing software, we'll be able to better regulate power and water. Our energy usage will drop. We can better manage water flows in the spring to help with the yearly challenge of flooding on the river. This system will make our limited resources stretch further with no more of the waste that normally occurs.

"But beyond all of that, beyond everything else this system can do, the biggest part will be the medical implants. Voluntary now, but soon to be offered to everyone, these implants will alert the hospital at the first signs of heart attack or stroke. It will send an ambulance if any form of serious trauma occurs. These medical implants have already shown to be massive game-changers in the field of medicine. If you have a fall the ambulance will be on its way before you hit the floor.

"I couldn't have done this alone though. I have many people to thank for working on this with me. I have each and every one of you to thank for voting—not just for me, but for this system. With me, on stage, are two of the software engineers who made this possible, Doctor Jack Hall, founder of Madison Software Labs, and his top engineer, Doctor Holly Porter, both of whom have been working non-stop the past few weeks to bring this system online."

The crowd cheered as Mayor Kamp pointed to the man and woman behind him. Standing two paces behind, the confident and collected mayor appeared to be Mayor Kamp's polar opposite; Dr. Jack Hall. Dr. Hall was wearing an off-the-rack, ugly brown suit that was a size too big for his slender frame. His dress shirt was wrinkled. His tie, aside from not being tied right, didn't match anything else he was wearing. Dr. Hall's blonde hair needed a trim, or at the very least, a combing, as it blew around in the wind. The forty-year-old doctor looked out of place and uncomfortable on the stage. In his fidgety hands were a pair of glasses, thick black frames, and heavy glass; the control computer for the system they were about to turn on.

Next to Jack stood a poised and confident woman, Dr. Holly Porter. Dr. Porter was a tall and exceedingly lank woman whose round, pale face betrayed her recent lack of sleep. Her chestnut colored hair was pulled into a sloppy ponytail and she wore an unbuttoned lab coat over her black tights and sleeveless black blouse. Dr. Porter stood close to Dr. Hall, not bothered by the crowd, but obviously wanting to be somewhere else, somewhere that involved a dark room, a bed, and no distractions.

"And although we try," Mayor Kamp continued, "we can't forget...just a joke among friends there, folks. Help me welcome a voice of reason and a critical thinker, City Council Chairman, Jerry Bosen!"

Swaggering onto the stage behind the doctors was a smug, tall man, dressed all in black. Jerry Bosen, the City

Council Chairman stood near the front of the stage, his feet a little more than shoulder width apart, his thumbs hooked into his front pockets with his fingers hanging out. Jerry wore black pants, a button-up black shirt with the sleeves rolled to his mid-forearms and the top three buttons of the shirt unbuttoned, exposing a small part of his tanned chest that was covered with black hair. Atop his narrow and predatory face was shiny, wavy black hair that dropped to his shoulders. His eyes were hidden behind thick-rimmed black sunglasses and his thin lips were curled into a snarky grin. As Mayor Kamp introduced Jerry, Jerry lifted his arms above his head, flashing a peace sign with his fingers before moving his hands back down, hooking the thumbs in the pockets and letting his fingers rest against his legs.

"Very good, very good," Mayor Kamp said, looking back out over the crowd. "Doctor Hall, if you please, now is the time. Turn on the system!"

Dr. Hall nervously took the glasses from his hands and placed them on his head. Dr. Hall started waving his hand in front of him, pointing, sliding, and making other motions, using the computer implant in his finger to operate the computer in front of his eyes. The glasses computer, designed by Allen Day, was all the rage and the only way to use a computer. No more keyboards and mice, just the screen on the glasses and your hands in the air. After a moment of stillness from the doctor, a smile washed over his face for the first time, "All systems are operational, Mayor Kamp."

"The system is up and running," Mayor Kamp yelled into the microphone. "Today we enter the future!"

The crowd cheered wildly as upbeat, bright music blasted through the sound system and ticker tape started to fall from the roof of the city hall. Mayor Kamp moved in front of the podium he spoke from, pulled the doctors close to him as newsfeed photographers took picture after picture of the trio. Jerry remained away from them, aloof as the only members of the crowd that were addressing him were members of the Neo-Luddites. Jerry waved to them as he set his eyes on a stunning blonde reporter who was in the back of the flock of reporters, not able to get a decent picture or soundbite of Mayor Kamp.

A seductive grin crossed Jerry's face as the reporter noticed that he was looking at her. She smiled a warm and inviting smile and offered a slight wave. Jerry walked to the front of the stage and tapped one of the security guards on the shoulder, whispering in his ear while pointing at the reporter. The security guard walked over to the female, motioning her to come with him. The security guard helped the woman onto the stage where Jerry was waiting to shake her hand.

"Jerry Bosen," Jerry said, keeping a light but firm grip on her hand, making the handshake go much longer than appropriate, considering their surroundings. "City Council Chairman."

"Nevaeh Crick," Nevaeh said, blushing. "Reporter for Winter Falls Minor Newsfeed."

Jerry looked Neveah over. She was a short woman, standing not much more than five feet tall with curly blonde hair that cascaded down to her mid-back. A willowy body beneath a slender, pale face with bird-bright, ocean blue eyes behind a pair of thin-rimmed computer glasses. Her plump, ruby lips were pulled into a smile as she tried to make out Jerry's eyes behind his dark glasses.

"How would you like an exclusive look at Seth?" Jerry asked.

"Who's Seth?" Nevaeh asked.

"Seth is the name of the system," Jerry said. "Dr. Hall named it after his father. There haven't been any reporters inside yet, but I think I can work something out with Teddy to get you in there."

"Are you serious?" Nevaeh asked. "I need something big to get my name known in the newsfeeds."

"Stick with me kid," Jerry said, as he transitioned from shaking her hand to putting his arm around her shoulder and walking toward Mayor Kamp. "I'll get you all the stories you need."

Mayor Kamp and the doctors waved to the media for a final time before turning and heading into the city hall building with Jerry and Nevaeh a step behind them. Jerry smiled as he looked at Nevaeh, knowing that he was going to get her the story of a lifetime.

Chapter #2

The interior of Winter Falls City Hall was as grand as the exterior, a marvel of modern construction blended with a symphony of design. The entrance foyer, with sweeping mosaic cathedral ceilings, ornate support pillars, and swirled Italian marble floors shimmered from the magnificent sun beaming through the polished glass windows. For a government office, the entrance felt warm and inviting, like an entrance to a theater or museum. People were rushing about though, not bothering to take in the grandeur of the building, numbed to the sights by years of working there. Nevaeh on the other hand, since It was her first time in the city hall, was overwhelmed by it as Jerry guided her while attempting to catch up to Mayor Kamp and the Doctors.

Nevaeh almost couldn't believe where she was. For years she'd been a line reporter for the Winter Falls Minor Newsfeed, getting simple stories to run on the website, never getting a major break but always trying. Always on the lookout for something big that would be her breakout story. She had been assigned to cover the announcement of the system, figuring it would be a routine story. But now, with Jerry's arm around her shoulder, she felt an excitement that something amazing was coming her way.

"Mayor Kamp," Jerry shouted out as he caught up to the mayor, getting the group to stop. "This is Nevaeh Crick, a reporter for the Winter Falls Minor. She was the one you were going to give an interview to."

"I don't remember agreeing to an interview," Mayor Kamp said. "Jerry, what are you trying to pull?"

"Nothing," Jerry said. "Think about it, though, you want the story of this system told. You want everyone to know how great it will be, give Nevaeh a teaser interview and throughout the week we'll show her the full extent of the system and she can report it."

Mayor Kamp chewed at his lower lip as he looked Nevaeh over. She was a stunningly beautiful lady, but young, no older than her late twenties. Theodor wanted an interview, but he wanted the interview to be conducted by a reporter with gray hair; someone dignified and respected. Mayor Kamp knew Jerry's motive in all this, and smiled, shaking his head at how quickly Jerry could work over any woman.

"An interview, eh?" Mayor Kamp asked. "Alright Nevaeh, I'll grant you a short interview now for the evening newsfeed and I'll go more in depth later this week. What do you want to know?"

Nevaeh adjusted her glasses, turning the recorder on to film the interview, "how did this system come about?"

"Dr. Hall," Mayor Kamp said, deferring to the doctor. "You field that one."

"There have always been controlled systems," Dr. Hall said, fidgeting with his hands. "The problem is that none of them worked together. We had so many apps to control things, but they were all independent. I envisioned a system where everything would work together in unison. Each independent system would be part of a whole, complementing the whole, while at the same time functioning independently. I wanted a defined role and function for every player in the game space."

"I'm sorry," Nevaeh interrupted. "Player in the game space?"

"Sorry," Dr. Hall continued. "That's the term I use for this system, game space. Players are everything that it controls. Each independent system is a player. This is the culmination of computers and processing power."

11

"One hanging point that a lot of voters had with the system was the cost versus the benefits. Can you speak...?"

"The return will be amazing," Mayor Kamp interrupted Nevaeh before her question was finished. "Moneywise, there isn't even anything to think about. The savings this system will create will be staggering. Then when you factor in the time savings, the return is to the sky. Just fuel and time alone from never having to sit in traffic will be worth the cost."

"Can you explain that system in a little more detail to me please?" Nevaeh asked.

"Simple, really," Mayor Kamp said. "Although, I think Dr. Porter can explain that system better than I."

"Every modern car has GPS systems," Dr. Porter said. "Along with auto-drive. When you input your destination, the system looks at all the other cars on the road, the buses, train schedules, traffic lights, and all the other factors that could slow the car down. It computes the fastest, most direct route and takes the vehicle on that path. People can enter their commuting routes as city and school buses have entered their daily routes. You can even input a trip you're planning weeks in advance to claim the quickest route.

"The reason this has never been done before is the sheer amount of information needed to run this system. Sure, we've got GPS that tracks and operates every car so there are no accidents but to get all the GPS to work together, to get a logistics program that could figure out routes and balance them with the conditions of no traffic jams, that's where we needed more computing power and the fastest access memory to run it."

"How much storage is required for this system?" Nevaeh asked. "How much computing power is needed?"

"Millions of terabytes," Dr. Hall said. "Within the substructure of city hall, there is a secure room that houses hard drives, rows and rows of LBMs."

"LBM?"

"Light-based memory," Dr. Hall said. "This is a new design. This was the only way we could create a system of memory large enough to hold all the information needed while at the same time being fast enough to operate in real time. Everyday Computers built the system, Dr. Porter and myself led the teams that created the software. I can't bore you with the details of how light-based memory works. It's a classified trade secret."

"And the system is safe?"

"Perfectly safe," Mayor Kamp said. "What could go wrong?"

"Everything," Jerry said, flatly. "But no one listens to me."

"Don't get him started," Mayor Kamp said.

"I'm only trying to..."

"You'd have us living in the Stone-Age," Mayor Kamp scoffed. "You've never sufficiently explained your concerns, nor have you given any proof at all that your theories are correct."

"I've more than explained them," Jerry said, with a smug grin. "It's just that you refuse to listen."

"What are you talking about?" Nevaeh asked. "What do you mean? Are you a member of the Neo-Luddites, Jerry?"

"By all means, no," Jerry said. "The Neo-Luddites really do want us living with no modern technology. Their stated goal is to revert civilization to a point before electricity. Interestingly, they will allow the use of steam power. But no, I am not associated with them. I'm simply promoting The Shrinking Mind Theory. It's my theory that I presented in my last book of the same name."

"I saw a review but never read it," Nevaeh said.

"You should," Jerry replied. "I detail how so many simple tasks that every person used to know how to do are being forgotten. The human mind is shrinking because we are not using them to think anymore. Schools don't teach math, they teach how to use a computer to do math. They don't teach history, they teach how to use a computer to search history. Humans aren't pushing their minds anymore and as a result, the mind is shrinking."

"Of all the garbage I've ever heard in my life," Mayor Kamp scoffed.

"Let me ask you, Nevaeh," Jerry continued, ignoring Theodor, "do you know how to grow your own food?"

"No."

"What about hunting? Do you think you could hunt, kill, process, and cook an animal to survive?"

"No."

"What about building a shelter? Do you think you could create something to protect yourself from the elements?"

"No."

Jerry looked Nevaeh's outfit over from top to bottom. She was wearing black tights with a black and sapphire, sleeveless, formfitting top.

"Your top is very lovely," Jerry said. "Accentuates your eyes."

"Thank you," Nevaeh replied, blushing.

"What's it made of?"

"Satin spandex blend."

"May I?" Jerry asked, holding his hand out.

14

Nevaeh nodded as Jerry's hand reached out and felt the top at the side of Nevaeh's abdomen. He rubbed her side a moment longer than appropriate as he looked into her eyes. Although Jerry still had his sunglasses on, Nevaeh could feel his eyes on her, his electric eyes that were causing butterflies to flutter in her stomach. Jerry moved his hand from her side to her hand, holding her hand as they continued to talk.

"Very lovely," Jerry said. "Soft and beautiful...but could you make any clothing, Nevaeh?"

"No...but that's what we have stores for. For all of that stuff you asked about."

"We do now but less than one hundred and fifty years ago most of the population would have answered 'yes' to all those questions I just asked you. The human population could survive on its own. People didn't need stores. They complimented and helped but now they are a necessity. Every new technology that comes out destroys part of the necessity to practice the things that really matter. Think about it, if the power grid fails I would be willing to bet that within one year, over seventy-five percent of the population of this country would perish from starvation and exposure. They don't have the means to deal with it."

"See," Mayor Kamp interrupted. "He wants us to live in caves wearing animals."

"I said nothing of the sort," Jerry retorted. "It's pathetic that you're so afraid of my intellect that you resort to cheap sound bites for the media."

"Then what are you saying?" Mayor Kamp asked.

"That if we give our lives to the machines they will enslave us."

"We're not enslaved by machines," Nevaeh said.

"Really?" Jerry asked, laughing. "How many hours a day do you spend on a computer? If the computer didn't alert you that a word was spelled wrong or that the grammar was off, would you know about it? Could you even write stories for the newsfeeds without auto-correct?"

"In school, they teach us to use computers," Nevaeh said, looking at the floor. "I didn't have to take English classes or grammar classes, I simply tell the computer what format the story will be presented in and the computer takes care of the rest."

"The schools teach you to be slaves to computers," Jerry said. "Instead of supplementing and enhancing our lives, computers are controlling it. And now that humans don't have to think anymore, guess what? They won't. People will allow the computers to take over and there will be one of two outcomes. People with computers will enslave and control those who can't think anymore, or the computers will fall into disrepair because soon, no one will remember or be able to repair them. The computers will fail. When that day comes I'll be glad I remembered what our ancestors did."

"Of all the rubbish I've ever heard in my life," Mayor Kamp said. "That has to be the biggest scam I've ever witnessed."

"How did you become the chairman of a city council that voted to spend billions of dollars to create a computer system to control everything, Chairman Bosen?" Nevaeh asked.

"Please, call me Jerry," Jerry said, with a smile. "That's an interesting story, Nevaeh. I'd formed a company called Longfellow Consulting upon graduating university. I have multiple degrees, a doctorate in mathematics and statistics, bachelor's degrees in computer sciences, programming, and history. I've always been obsessed with large systems and their stability. I look at the countless factors that keep a system stable and what happens when those factors fall apart.

"My firm was constantly employed in two different areas, reconstruction and risk analysis. When a large system would fail, be it a stock market crash, the implosion of a government, or a structural failure, my team would come in and analyze how the failure happened. We could detail in a math formula what happened and why. What parts lead from stability to chaos. The risk analysis was where companies or governments would hire us to model what they were doing and show them where the inherent weak points or errors would come. We could show them what to watch for, how far out of tolerance things could get before a complete collapse, and what to do to prevent it.

"My company was very successful. We've worked closely with Everyday Computers and Madison Software Labs to keep their systems running. I was the first one to model Dr. Hall's idea for a computer system to control everything. I even presented a very detailed report explaining what would happen, but Mayor Kamp didn't read that report. He saw what this system could do and hired Dr. Hall instantly to test the system here.

"I tried to be the voice of reason, tried to explain that this system will fail, and it will cause irreversible damage to the people involved and to the people who are using this system. No one would listen to me, so I used some of the vast amounts of money I'd earned from my business to run for city council. I ran on the platform that I would stop this from being implemented. I won by a landslide even though I had no prior political experience. In a cruel twist of fate, however, the night before I was sworn into office, Mayor Kamp and the city council voted to approve the system. I swore I would do everything in my power to prevent this day from coming, prevent this system from coming online."

"So, not only are you a nut job," Mayor Kamp said, with a smug grin, "you're a failure as well."

Jerry grinned at Theodor, "I will be proved correct, Teddy."

"This is absurd. You're a joke, Bosen. And a bad one at that. You couldn't possibly..."

"Careful, Mayor," Jerry interrupted, pointing at Nevaeh. "You wouldn't want to say anything that would hurt your chances when you run for president."

Theodor's face froze in disbelief. He wanted to ream Jerry out for the slip but couldn't say anything in front of the reporter. Nevaeh's eyes were wide with what she'd just heard. She had heard rumors that Theodor was gearing up for a presidential run, but she hadn't believed them.

"So, the rumors are true?" Nevaeh asked. "You are going to run for president?"

"No comment," Mayor Kamp replied. "And if one word of that finds its way into your report you will have no more access around here. Jack, tell her about the hardware of the system."

"Okay," Dr. Hall replied, confused by the flow of the conversation. "All the hardware was built by Everyday Computers. Everyday Computers was the first to create the glasses computer. Allen Day, my best friend since elementary school designed the glasses and I wrote the software for him. We built the prototypes in his parents' basement. We took different paths, Allen and I. He's the CEO of Everyday Computers, a very vocal and visual leader where I hired someone to run Madison Software Labs. I'm a creator. I don't know how to run a company, I know how to create software. We are still close friends but neither of us have time for anything beyond business anymore."

"For argument's sake," Nevaeh said, "What would happen if someone was able to hack the system?"

"Impossible," Mayor Kamp said. "We have the strongest safeguards and a new little secret security system that no one knows about."

"And that is?"

"Nice try but no dice, Nevaeh," Mayor Kamp said. "Let's just say that if someone tries to hack this system they are in for a big surprise."

Nevaeh was about to ask another question when Dr. Hall's glasses started to ring. Dr. Hall put his glasses on his face and adjusted the band so the speaker was properly fitted in his ear. "Answer," Dr. Hall called out in a strong voice.

"Hello?" Jack said, looking at no one in particular. "Yes...what...that's impossible...when...no, he's with me now...we'll be there right away."

"What's going on?" Mayor Kamp asked.

"There's a situation," Jack said, acting more nervous than before. "Dr. Porter, Theodor, Jerry, I'm going to need you guys to come with me. I hope you have enough for the start of your interview, Nevaeh. We can show you more of the system later."

"Thank you," Nevaeh said. "What I have so far is great. Thanks."

The group started to follow Dr. Hall as Nevaeh started to turn for the exit. Jerry grabbed her by the arm and pulled her in close to him, "Want to see the real power of this system?"

"I'd love to."

"There's a party tomorrow night to celebrate this abomination. I have an invitation to attend with a plus one. Come with and I'll show you things that will get you massive hits on your newsfeed."

"Chairman Bosen...I've seen your name across the newsfeeds before. Dating actresses, singers, athletes. You've certainly had your fair share of women...so is this going to be a professional thing or a date?"

Jerry reached up to his glasses and adjusted the tint, turning his sunglasses transparent so he could look Nevaeh right in the eyes. Nevaeh's heart skipped a beat when his powerful, dark eyes looked through her eyes and into her soul.

"You won't know that until you get here," Jerry said, with a wink before changing the tint back on his glasses and releasing Nevaeh's arm.

"It's a date then," Nevaeh said, with a smile, as she turned and walked away.

Jerry nodded as he raced to catch up to the others who were heading toward a conference room. He noticed the fear in Dr. Hall's voice during the phone call and Jerry could only wonder if his destruction theory was already starting to come true.

Chapter #3

Inside a conference room, around a large wooden tabled surrounded by leather office chairs, Dr. Hall, Dr. Porter, Mayor Kamp, and Chairmen Bosen watched as two detectives paced in front of a drawing board. The name 'Danny Brown' was written on the top of the board as the two detectives were talking on their glasses as the rest of the group tried to figure out what was going on.

There was an unmistakable tension in the room. Something big had happened but no one would speak to what was going on. Both the detectives were ignoring the others in the room as they were speaking, almost yelling on their phones. Jack studied the detectives. He hadn't seen either of them before, didn't know what department they had come from. The male detective seemed to be the leader of the two. He looked to be in his mid-forties, fit, but his body starting to show its age. His brown hair was starting to gray and his goatee had turned completely gray. The detective wore a dark blue suit with brown shoes. He seemed to be the more frustrated of the two detectives.

The other detective caught Dr. Hall's eye. She was a tall woman in her late thirties. Pixie cut black hair sat atop a round, serious face. Her hazel eyes were bright but she was squinting, holding them to slits as she tried to talk on the phone and focus on her glasses screen showing her information. The woman wore black tights and an oversized black police shirt, held at the waist with a black belt.

Dr. Hall studied the woman, watching her every move. He had spent the last few years buried deep in the work of the system, having no time for socializing, even though he didn't socialize much before the project started.

As he was getting older the thought of finding someone and starting a family was becoming more prominent in his mind. Dr. Hall laughed at it though, knowing he wouldn't know how to approach this woman, wouldn't know what to say to her.

"What is going on here, Detective?" Mayor Kamp asked as both detectives ended their calls.

"I'm Detective Mike Russ and this is my partner, Amanda Drake," Detective Russ said, as he took his place standing at the head of the conference table.

"Are you a detective too, Amanda?" Dr. Porter asked.

"No," Amanda replied. "I was on the police force and am in the process of transitioning to detective."

"Please," Mayor Kamp insisted. "What is going on?"

"Danny Brown was found murdered this morning," Detective Russ said, sharply. "He was found in his apartment by his sister Sally. They were supposed to meet before work and he didn't show. She'd known him to drink a little heavy at times and miss the alarm, so when he didn't answer his phone, she drove over."

"Sally had a key to his apartment," Amanda added. "Went in and was horrified at what she saw."

"How did it happen?" Jerry asked.

"Knife," Amanda replied. "Stabbed multiple times."

As the implications set in, the door to the conference room opened and two men walked in. The first was a boy in his early twenties, fit and strapping with the vigor of youth about him. He wore red and silver baggy gym shorts with a blue athletic tee shirt, his computer glasses set to sunglass tint perched atop his wavy rusty hair. The other was a dapper and dull man in his thirties, gray slacks, red polo, shaved head, and cleanly shaven face. The older man looked overworked and overtired while the youth looked like he was ready to face any challenge that came his way.

"This is Gavin Rodgers," Mayor Kamp said, as the men sat at the table. "A software engineer here who worked with Danny. The other is Ben Hewitt, a graduate student who is interning with us over the summer. Gavin, Ben, this is Detective Mike Russ and Amanda Drake."

"Gentlemen," Amanda said, looking at the two who'd just sat down, noticing that Ben gave her a double take and a sly smile. "When was the last time you saw Danny Brown?"

"He was working here when I took off yesterday," Ben said, thinking back. "I had to get back to the university by three. He was still here."

"He left just before I did last night," Gavin said. "I would guess about seven or so. What's this about?"

"He was found dead this morning," Amanda said. "We are trying to piece together what happened. Did you have any contact with him at all last night?"

Everyone shook their heads.

"Did he say that he was going to be doing anything last night?"

Again, everyone shook their heads.

"This is a moot point, though, right?" Mayor Kamp asked. "I mean, this is a tragedy, but this gives us a chance to show the power of the system."

"I don't follow you," Amanda said. "How can your traffic system help us?"

"It's so much more than a traffic system," Mayor Kamp said. "But there are traffic cameras everywhere. He lived in an apartment that had a security system. This is part of the system. We have access to all cameras in the city. We'll simply see who entered and left the apartment and know exactly who did it. I said this system would end crime."

"Can you really do that?" Amanda asked.

"I'm working on it right now," Dr. Hall said, as he put his computer over his eyes. "I'm sending a request down to the control room right now. They'll analyze the information, watch the video feeds, and get back to me right away. We'll know who did it."

"What time did the event occur?" Jerry asked.

"Estimates are at about 1:30 in the morning," Detective Russ answered.

"And no one in the apartment building saw or heard anything out of the ordinary?"

"Nothing. Why?"

"It's just that Danny was a big guy," Jerry said. "I mean, he worked out four to five times a week. He lifted weights, ran marathons, and participated in a number of city sports leagues."

"Your point being?" Mike asked.

"He was a strong, fit guy," Jerry replied. "I'm wondering how he could have been overpowered and stabbed. I mean, was there any sign of him being drunk or otherwise subjugated?"

"Are you a detective?" Amanda asked.

"No ma'am," Jerry replied. "Mathematician. I've been trained to look deeper than the surface on issues."

Mike stared at Jerry, "What we can tell you is that there was no sign of forced entry. There were no signs of a struggle. There were no signs of drug or alcohol use. That's not to rule it out, it could have been cleaned up after the murder was committed. No murder weapon was found but there was a large cutting knife missing from his kitchen knife rack that would be consistent with the size of the cuts. There's no chance this was a suicide."

"WHAT?" Dr. Hall yelled into his phone. "How can that be...are you sure...okay...keep looking and let me know if anything changes."

"What's going on, Doctor?" Detective Russ asked.

Jack took his glasses off and set them on the table in front of him, "All cameras in a four-block radius were turned off at exactly 1:15 this morning. There's no street view of whoever drove to that apartment. The apartment cameras were turned off shortly thereafter. All the cameras come back on at exactly 2:00 am."

"Just enough time for someone to enter, kill him, and leave," Mike said. "And not leave a single trace."

"That's impossible," Mayor Kamp said. "There's no way that anyone could have turned the cameras off. Hell, how would they have even known that the cameras were already patched into the system?"

"Well, they did," Dr. Hall said. "That would imply that it was someone working here."

"How do you figure?" Amanda asked.

"No one else could have known about it," Dr. Hall said. "And anyone on the outside wouldn't have been able to breach the security measures we have in place."

"It could have been hacked," Mike said.

"Impossible," Mayor Kamp said. "There's no way to hack this system."

"This poses many questions," Mike said. "We will get to the bottom of this and make sure whoever did this faces our justice system. But you understand that this implicates all of you. For now, we request that you each come with us, individually, and go through a line of questioning. We want this solved as quickly as we can."

"Of course, of course," Mayor Kamp said. "And I hope that the details can be held off the newsfeeds until we have everything figured out. Don't want to scare people and cause a panic, you know. Ben will go first."

"Very well," Mike said. "Ben, follow us please."

Ben eyed Amanda as he stood and walked out of the room with the detectives. The others sat in shocked silence as a clock on the wall ticked the seconds away. Dr. Hall took his glasses off the table and put them on, activating a program. As he activated it, the drawing board on the wall morphed into a blank video screen, which was quickly filled by the outline of a man dressed all in black. The image of the man moving on the screen was far enough out of view that no one could get a clear look at his face.

"Seth," Dr. Hall said, addressing the man on the wall. "Can you explain what happened? How did those cameras get turned off?"

"There is only one possible explanation, Dr. Hall," a smooth, deep voice emulated from a speaker in the room as the man on the wall's mouth synchronized with the voice. "Someone accessed the system."

"There has to be a trace of the login," Jerry said. "Seth, who accessed the video files last night around 1:00 am?"

"All login information from that time has been deleted," Seth replied. "An information dump was activated on the system at 2:03:33 am to remove all information about that process from the system."

"Who authorized the information dump?" Dr. Porter asked.

"That information was also dumped," Seth replied.

"Who has authorization to do that?" Dr. Hall asked. "To remove that much information from the system."

"File not found, sir," Seth said.

"Couldn't you have given that thing a better sounding voice?" Mayor Kamp asked. "Why does it have to be *that* voice?"

"That's as close to the voice of my father as I could get it," Dr. Hall said. "The system is named after him, *Seth*, and I wanted to honor the man who always believed in me."

"Not to change the subject," Dr. Porter injected, "but Danny was a high-level engineer working on the system. We are shorthanded the way it is. We can't afford to lose someone right now and I don't have any contacts that are open."

"I don't either," Jack said. "All my connections are already working here. I suppose I could call Allen Day and see if he knows anyone available, but I doubt that. Gavin, do you know anyone open?"

"All of my connections are either under contracts or university appointments," Gavin replied. "The past few years have seen so many startup companies that there's a shortage of software engineers."

"I do have access to all employee files," Seth said. "I could search the network and discover a person to hire."

"Now we have computers doing our hiring?" Jerry said. "This is just great. They can run everything now."

"Would you shut up?" Mayor Kamp said.

"It would be a good idea," Jack said. "Seth, we need a computer engineer who is proficient in both hardware and software. They need to know the three major software languages and at least a couple of the minor ones. They need to have practical experience in large level networks and in debugging systems."

"I will search the system and find someone who is appropriate," Seth said. "Any other constraints on the hiring process?"

"Someone who has never been charged with hacking or corporate espionage," Jerry said. "Lots of people fit your requirements but you'd never want them working on this system."

"Good idea," Jack said. "Thanks, Jerry. Also, it should be someone who shows a great deal of ambition and drive. Someone who is motivated and wants to succeed."

"I will find the right person," Seth said.

The door to the room opened and Ben entered, standing one step past the threshold. "That was the easiest interrogation in my crime-filled life. Dr. Hall, they want to talk to you next."

"Very good," Dr. Hall said, standing as he took off his glasses. "Ben, as you were before I called you up here. See if you can make any headway on what happened."

"Sure thing, boss," Ben said, as he left the room.

Dr. Hall left the room as the image of Seth on the wall faded away and the area turned itself to match the texture and color of the wall around it, leaving no trace of the screen system integrated into the wall. The group remained silent, knowing that they would each be questioned by the police. They were all thinking of Danny, wondering the same thing, *'who would want to kill a harmless person like Danny Brown?'*

Chapter #4

Dr. Hall entered the small office room and quickly sat down. There was only a table with four chairs in the room, no windows or wall decorations, and two of the chairs were being occupied by Mike and Amanda. Mike stared at Dr. Hall like he was trying to see through him, trying to read his innermost thoughts. The look from the detective disturbed the doctor as he fidgeted in his seat, trying to make it look like he was getting comfortable. Dr. Hall didn't know what this was going to entail, but this was the first time in his life that he was sitting across from police to be questioned and Jack didn't like it.

"I'll start directly," Mike said. "Do you know who killed Danny Brown?"

"No, I don't," Jack said.

"Do you know of anybody who would want to hurt Danny Brown?"

"No," Jack said, as he adjusted himself in his seat, realizing he was starting to sweat.

"There's nothing to worry about, Dr. Hall," Amanda said. "We're just trying to solve this case. Tell me, what was your relationship with Danny? How did you know him?"

"It was a work relationship," Jack said, trying to relax. "When I got the contract for the system I knew I needed the best software engineers in the country. Danny came recommended from my alma mater. One of my classmates was now a professor at the Computer Engineering Department at Winter Falls University and she gave me Danny's contact information. He'd been doing freelance work out in California, attempting to start his own company. He wasn't getting the financing he was hoping for. I called him up and offered him a position here.

It was a contract position. He came here two years ago and had two years left on the contract. He was still planning on starting his own company once he left here."

"And you were okay with that?" Amanda asked.

"I would have offered to extend his contract," Jack replied, "but in this business people come and go. I think he enjoyed working here and the steady income was a great motivator for him. Danny had some major breakthroughs in the software that allowed us to move forward."

"Personally," Mike asked, "what was your relationship with Danny like?"

"It was strictly work," Jack said. "I don't socialize very much, not even with the people working here. I tended to bury myself in my work. I've always been that way. I don't know, I just have trouble finding people to connect with and I get so nervous around people, especially women. Anyway, Danny and I never really talked about anything outside of work. I know he dated a girl on and off, and I believe they were off as he'd been seeing someone else. And I know that Danny participated in city league sports and was exceptionally good at them."

"You ever get into an argument with him?" Mike asked.

"We had some disagreements on work things," Jack said. "Nothing major. The main ones I remember centered on how I wanted a project done compared to how he wanted it done and about overtime. He never wanted to work overtime since he had sports things to get to, but we had deadlines and were behind the ball on certain projects."

"You ever yell at him?" Amanda asked.

"I don't yell at people," Jack said. "Danny and I had a good working relationship and I was looking forward to seeing what he could do once the system got up and running. Danny has a very bright future in the software world."

"You ever hear of anyone wanting to harm him?" Amanda asked. "A sports competitor perhaps? Jealous teammate?"

"Not that I know of," Jack said. "As I said before, I don't pay much attention to what goes on outside my company and I simply don't have time to listen to idle chatter about other people's lives. That's one thing I really did like about Danny. When it was time to work he would stick to his task and get it done. You didn't need to keep a watch over him. He did his work and saved the talking for later."

"Okay," Amanda said. "I hate to do this, but we do have to ask you this question…where were you last night?"

"I was the same place I've been for the past four weeks," Jack replied. "Right here, living at city hall."

"You live here?" Amanda asked. "Why?"

"I have an apartment, Amanda," Jack said. "I just haven't been to it in a month. I have someone get my mail and check up on the place. I've been here getting the system ready to go. You can't believe all the final testing and checks, all the updates and rewriting that needed to be done. There has been so much to do that I'm amazed that we got everything done. Most of the time I'm working well into the night anyway.

"One of the things I did with the system was make it so I could talk to him, so he could tell me if there was a problem or how to fix it. I named the system after my father, Seth, since he always believed in me. Over the past few weeks. Seth has become my best and, at times, my only friend. He keeps me company as I work, he helps me with insights when I need them, and he's great at chess, checkers, backgammon, hearts, and cribbage. I take breaks to recharge myself and spend my time playing games, chatting with Seth."

"How intelligent is Seth?" Mike asked.

"Intelligence implies awareness, detective," Jack said. "Seth has no intelligence. He has no awareness. He can talk, he can perform a self-check and some light repair work. On some of the minor systems, Seth designed the code..."

"The computer designed itself?" Mike asked.

"We gave it parameters to fill in," Jack said. "Think of it more like a powerful calculator that can solve math formulas. We took it the next step so it could do a word problem, not just a straight numbers problem. The system is fully dependent on what we feed into it. There's no thinking or reasoning there. No chance of awareness. We have safeguards in place that will prevent all of that."

"The same safeguards that Mayor Kamp says will prevent hacking?" Amanda asked.

"Possibly," Jack replied.

"Give us some insight into it," Mike said. "I'm having a hard time believing that a system this large could be impossible to hack. That's my fear of this. I know the Neo-Luddites are fearful that the system will become aware of itself and destroy everything. I'm not so concerned about that, but hacking does bother me, especially when this system will be running bank security systems."

"Our main competitors, Wheaton Dumont Software Systems has been working on Artificial Intelligence for some time now. They've not even come close to a self-aware system, so the chances that we could create one by accident are remote. Our concern is with the new LBM system, light-based memory. It's so fast, so powerful, that it could create the bridge that allows Wheaton Dumont to crack the AI code. My worry was them, or others, hacking the system and using it for their research. LBM is so powerful that we could be running our systems and they could hack in and run their tests and it wouldn't drag the system down.

"Security was the main key. We needed something that would ensure our technology stayed safe, that Social Software Systems, 3S, and others, didn't use our system. And as you said, Detective, that things like banks and other valuables aren't hacked into. I came up with the idea myself. Mayor Kamp was against it at first, simply because of the cost, but in the end, he saw that it was needed. There was no other way we could guarantee the safety and security of the system."

"What did you do?" Amanda asked. "What security is out there that hasn't been hacked yet?"

"Humans," Dr. Hall said.

"What do you mean?" Amanda asked.

"We have two control rooms here at Winter Falls City Hall. One is called the Master Control Room, a room that's basically mission control, staffed at all times with about twenty people monitoring the system. If anything happens within the system, someone accesses a port, someone changes a function, that room will know instantly and be able to stop it if it isn't something we approved. The next room is called the Main Control Room. The Main Control Room will be staffed by one or two people at all times. These will be the highest-level people—the managers and engineers.

"When something happens, a change in the system, the Master Control Room will send it to the Main Control Room. A redundant system with many eyes watching. If any unauthorized computer accesses the system, or if something gets out of tolerance, we will know right away and be able to handle it. Complete control."

"Very interesting," Mike said. "Perhaps you could show us these rooms? Not now, of course, but later today or tomorrow."

"With pleasure."

"One other thing," Mike asked, "Is there anyone who can vouch for your whereabouts last night?"

"Dr. Porter can," Jack said. "She spent the night here last night."

"You two spent the night here together?" Amanda asked.

"Not like that," Jack said. "In the sub-basement, beneath the computer control level, there's a network of security structures, bomb shelters. They are designed to survive a bombing attack or natural disaster. They have beds, showers, everything a person needs to live. That's where I stay. No one ever goes down there, so I'm out of the way and no one is bothering me when I sleep. There are multiple rooms down there. I've claimed one for my room and Holly has a different one. Our relationship is strictly business."

"Interesting," Mike said. "Anyone other than Dr. Porter who can confirm you were here?"

"The cameras," Jack said. "I saw the janitor at about ten in the Master Control Room. I ordered food for delivery around midnight. The night watchman met the delivery vehicle outside and brought the food to me."

"Very good," Mike said. "We may have more questions later and we would both like to see the control rooms, but we need to keep this moving. We have no further questions for you at this time. If you would be so kind, please send Chairman Bosen in to see us. And Dr. Hall, we ask that if you leave town to let us know."

"Of course."

Jack got up and quickly scampered out of the room, feeling relieved to be away from the questioning. Mike watched Jack with skeptical eyes as the door shut behind him.

"What do you think?" Amanda asked.

"Hard to know what to make of that guy."

"A computer as his best friend? How sad and depressing is that?"

"You've got a point, Amanda. Maybe his mind snapped from no real or meaningful human contact."

"That's not what I meant," Amanda said. "I just see in him a brilliant mind and an amazing person who is letting their life slip away for others. He buries himself in work and only talks to a computer. That sounds like a tragic story."

"Tragic or not," Mike said. "If what he told us really is all he knows about the situation then we are no closer to solving this. That's your only concern on a case, Amanda. You are not here to play matchmaker, to solve others' problems, or to help them live their lives. You are here to solve crimes, remember that."

"I will."

"Good. Now, this Jerry Bosen is an interesting case indeed. He's strongly against the system and wants to stop it. He's spoken out against it and written books about it. He claims that he's not in league with the Neo-Luddites but he has connections to them."

"He's also a real heartbreaker," Amanda said, as she adjusted her hair. "I heard he's an amazing lover and has women lining up to date him."

"I've heard those rumors too," Mike said. "Let's just hope he knows something. We need a break in this case."

Mike watched as Amanda perfected her hair and adjusted her top in preparation for Jerry entering the room. The rumors of his exploits with women were legendary and he had intelligence and drive to boot. Mike was looking forward to the chance to finally question the renowned Jerry Bosen.

Chapter #5

"I have two alibies from last night," Jerry said, as he entered the room and sat down, leaning back in the chair. Draping his left leg across the top of the right as he crossed his arms in front of his chest, he said, "Jennifer and Heidi."

Mike couldn't help but smile. All the rumors about Jerry's bravura were proving to be true. Before Mike and Amanda had left the station that morning, another detective who'd questioned Jerry in the past described him as a man who had so much personality it flowed from every pore of his body. The detective had warned Amanda that Jerry could pull any woman that he wanted and there was yet a woman who had resisted his charm.

"You don't take this seriously?" Mike asked.

"I take it very seriously," Jerry said leaning forward. "Danny was a good kid. Smart and ambitious. I had many conversations with him and from what I'd seen of him I was ready to invest in him, even if I hadn't told him that yet."

"Invest in him?" Mike asked.

"Danny always had dreams of running his own company," Jerry said. "He'd tried to get a couple off the ground out on the west coast but he could never get the capital to do it. When his contract expired with Madison Software Labs he was going to try again. I was going to offer to be an investor in his work. He had some great ideas for software that could work on market analysis. Danny had a very bright future and I constantly told him not to work on this project."

"Why not work on this?" Mike asked.

"Because it will fail," Jerry said, plainly. "And when that day comes, when it fails, it will be such a horrific, spectacular failure that everyone working on it will be ruined."

"You know a thing or two about failure," Amanda said. "You've made a fortune off failure."

"You refer to my work in the stock market," Jerry said. "Look, I understand system stability. Everything we do is affected by system stability, down to the air we breathe and the rotation of the earth. I look at the numbers of the system and see how far out of balance things can go before the system collapses. My groundbreaking research in the stock market looked at what causes companies to fail. I applied my theory to hundreds of companies in the market and found ten that were past their threshold. No one believed my work, so I put my money where my big, fat, loud mouth was. I short-sold all ten of the stocks while not revealing publicly which stocks I had shorted.

"I made sure no one knew what stocks I was in. I couldn't have the public at large following my research or others trying to corrupt the research. It was an interesting test. Within two years, nine of the ten companies were bankrupt, exactly as I predicted they would be. These were big companies. Companies that had been around for long periods of time. One of them was a hundred and fifty years old. I turned a couple million dollars into over a billion dollars thanks to the leverage I used. Had I have been wrong, most of my amassed fortune would have been wiped out."

"You only batted nine out of ten though," Mike said.

"Right," Jerry replied smugly. "But I wasn't wrong though. The tenth company started to sink. They realized their problems before it was too late, and unlike the other companies, they did something about it. The board of directors fired most of the upper management and brought new people in. They slashed costs, sold divisions, and generally did the right, though not popular, thing to keep the company alive and the workers working. The price of the company did fall, and I made money. When I got out of the short sale I watched that company and when the time was right, according to my research, I invested in it. I've more than doubled my money since then."

"How much are you worth?" Mike asked. "Just a rough estimate."

"Is this for the investigation?"

"Just curious."

"Enough for this lifetime and many more."

Jerry just smiled at the detectives. He wasn't going to give up any personal information unless he had to. Jerry knew that the seriousness of this investigation would lead to more pressing matters with the system and who was running it. Danny had been a key player for the operations side of things.

"Getting back to your alibi for last night," Amanda said, after an uncomfortable silence, "Jennifer and Heidi…I thought you were still dating 'The Moroccan Princess Jasmine'?"

"The Moroccan Princess Jasmine?" Mike asked.

"That's her performing name," Jerry said. "Her real name is actually Jeanie Cruz. Wonderful girl, really."

"Wait," Mike said, "The Moroccan Princess Jasmine…you mean the pro wrestler?"

"They prefer the term grappling exhibitionist," Jerry said. "About thirty years ago, mixed martial arts was taking the sports world by storm. The fastest growing sport in terms of participation and fans. Huge money was being made but then the steroids and implants scandals."

"Medical breakthroughs allowed people to implant muscle," Amanda said. "New surgery techniques allowed for the procedures to be done in the morning and the person could be competing that evening."

"There was no such thing as a level playing field," Jerry said. "There were steroids that were completely undetectable. The heart and soul of sports had been destroyed. That's why all sports are scripted now. It's all exhibitions. Jeanie participates in grappling exhibitions. They don't do the theatrics that pro wrestling does. Their matches look real, but yes, the matches are scripted."

"I thought you were dating that singer-actress girl," Mike said. "I saw a story about that. She said she'd found true love with you."

"Ah," Jerry said, thinking back. "You refer to Sophia Summers. Fun girl but she's got some issues. That was my fault. She was only nineteen. I knew better than to get involved with a girl that young, but we met at a party and things happen. We only dated for about a month when she thought it was true love. I figured it best to break it off before it went too far. I didn't want her to get hurt."

"She spent a month in a mental hospital after suffering a nervous breakdown when you left her," Amanda protested.

"I have that effect on people," Jerry said. "Yes. Jeanie and I are on a break since she went back on the road. We still talk and if we happen to be in the same city or nearby, I'm sure we'll make it a point to meet...for coffee or something."

The detectives just looked at Jerry. So far, he wasn't disappointing them, but he wasn't giving them anything to go off. Mike knew he had to get Jerry back on point and discover if he knew anything that would move the investigation forward.

"Back to the system though," Mike said. "Jerry, why do you think that this system will fail?"

"It's too big not to," Jerry said.

There was silence as Mike waited for an explanation, but none was coming.

"Explain."

"Did you take a tour of this place before you started the questioning?" Jerry asked.

"A brief one, yes," Amanda said.

"You saw the CPU's and the memory banks?"

"Some of them, yes," Mike said. "I'm told there's room upon room of them. Large rooms that are nothing but processors. Other rooms that house the memory."

"The amount of information contained within this system is so vast that no human could read, let alone understand all of it in a single lifespan. It would take hundreds of years for one person to read all the code. There were thousands of people who programmed this system, not to mention that the computer programmed some of itself. With that many people and devices involved, it's statistically impossible for an error not to happen. The system is just too big. It's the one thing I've learned from studying system stability; the larger the system, the quicker it can fall into instability."

"That seems counter-intuitive," Amanda said. "A larger system should be inherently more stable than a small one."

"You'd think so," Jerry said. "But it's not true. The more factors there are in a system, the more that can go wrong. Bigger systems are harder to monitor. Small problems in an unwatched area can bring the entire system into chaos. It can happen in the blink of an eye and it will happen with this system."

"You know that it might be easier to take you seriously if you took your sunglasses off," Amanda said. "Or at least turn the tint down so we can see your eyes. We're indoors, you know."

"I'm well aware of my spatial location," Jerry said. "Or maybe you just want a look into my eyes? My eyes were damaged when I was younger. Not much younger, but younger. There was a boating accident and I'm now hyper-light sensitive."

"A quick surgery could take care of that," Mike said. "You wouldn't even have to stay overnight with the procedures they have now."

"I could do that, but I don't want to," Jerry replied. "Allowing myself to keep this defect makes my other senses work harder. It keeps me tough. So many people have gone so soft these days that it's a wonder that anything ever gets done. Any little problem and they are rushing to the hospital. Need stronger arms? Faster legs? Bigger breasts? Any of it can be done in a couple hours. They've started allowing people to get new faces. Surgery to completely reform a person's face. Soon we'll all look the same."

"I doubt that," Mike said.

"Why not? If everyone looked the same, then no one could whine about being discriminated against based on looks. We don't have to worry about taking care of ourselves. Go in once a year to have all the cholesterol removed. Smokers can get new lungs. Eat all the junk food you want. Pills and surgeries will keep you looking like a sports star. Notice something when you next walk around, fifty years ago there was an obesity epidemic sweeping this country. Now, you can't find an overweight person. Whether it's healthy or not, pills, surgery, and implants have made everyone fit and thin.

"But my question to you, and this goes back to this system and to all the computer systems that we are now using, what happens when they break down? What happens when the power goes out? Our brains are a muscle. The more we use them the more powerful they become. The less we use them the weaker they get. Image a sports star of old, when sports were real and legit. If a football player ended the season, then sat and watched the video feeds for the entire offseason, how would he do when the next season rolled around?"

"Not very well," Mike replied.

"Exactly," Jerry said. "But what we're doing here is the exact equivalent of that. No one is working their minds anymore. I, for one, am working very hard at keeping my mind sharp."

"You seem bitter about this," Mike said.

"I'm not bitter," Jerry replied. "I'm actually very happy right now."

"Happy that someone is dead?" Mike asked.

"You're putting words in my mouth," Jerry said, sternly. "Don't ever do that again, Detective. My research company is soaring, I've got a good position on the city council, and I can get great information for my next book and research project by watching this system first hand. Plus, my position allows me to meet a lot of ladies...and I met a very interesting lady already this morning."

"Did you kill Danny Brown?" Mike asked sharply.

"No."

"Do you know who did?"

"No."

"Do you know anyone who would want to hurt Danny?"

"No."

There was silence in the room again. Mike was certain he knew the answers to those questions before he asked them, but he had to ask them. Jerry was well connected and seemed to be in the know, but Mike was fairly certain that Jerry was being honest. Jerry wasn't involved, or he was a great actor.

"You've had some dealings with the Neo-Luddites," Amanda said.

"Dealings," Jerry laughed. "I like how you put it. I might have to copy that and use it myself. Dealings."

"I don't follow," Mike said.

"At different times in his life," Amanda said, "Jerry here dated Breeze *and* Rain Flynn."

"Breeze and Rain Flynn?" Mike asked. "Who in the world is that?"

"That would be Gary Flynn's daughters," Amanda replied.

"Gary Flynn, as in Gary Flynn, leader of the Neo-Luddites?"

"That would be the one."

"You've got an interesting taste in women."

"I like to sample the entire smorgasbord," Jerry said. "I was working on a computer system, studying its stability for Everyday Computers. I was working late one night when I heard someone trying to break into my office. I hid in the closet with a shotgun and waited."

"You keep a shotgun in your office?" Mike asked.

"Doesn't everyone?" Jerry replied. "I ported my security camera into my glasses and saw Breeze enter the room. She was looking for something. I made myself known and we got to talking. One thing led to another and we spent a few months together."

"That seems like a strange match," Mike said. "Considering you made a fortune with computers and she wants to see every computer destroyed."

"Love trumps all, Detective," Jerry said. "That's the key to my success. She was a smart girl. Very fun. It's too bad she was brainwashed by her nitwit father. Rain and I had a short fling long before she passed away from that accident."

"Do you think Gary and the Neo-Luddites could have been involved?" Mike asked.

"The thought did cross my mind, but I don't think so," Jerry said. "Danny wasn't high enough up. I don't think the Neo-Luddites would resort to murder. I could be wrong, but I don't see them going that far. They would try sabotage first. If they did resort to murder I would expect they would go after Dr. Hall or Dr. Porter."

"Anything else that you want to tell us?" Amanda asked. "Any other questions for us?"

"Nothing that I can think of," Jerry said.

"Thank you," Mike said. "Please call us if you think or hear of anything. And we hate to do this, but please let us know if you're going to leave town. If you would be so kind, could you send Mayor Kamp in here?"

"Certainly," Jerry said, as he stood up. "It's been a pleasure."

Jerry bowed to the pair before he turned and strolled out of the room. Mike and Amanda shared a confused glance in silence as they waited for the door to shut.

"What did you think?" Mike asked.

"A jerk for sure," Amanda said. "So full of himself. But again, he's got a quality that I couldn't define. I don't know. I think he's good."

"I think he's clean too," Mike said. "Strange though."

Amanda nodded as they waited for the mayor to arrive in the room.

Chapter #6

Both Detective Russ and Amanda had their computer glasses on—scanning files, folders, anything they had discovered about Danny Brown. Amanda was excited about this case. She'd been a street police officer for years, always wanting to make the rank of detective but always getting passed over for other people. She didn't know why she was always passed over. She was competent, well-liked, astute, and had a spotless record. Her only thinking is that she became a cop first, and the police commission didn't like turning cops, especially good cops, into detectives. Winter Falls was expanding. With more people came more crime and a need for more detectives. Mike's normal partner was given his own case and Mike was allowed to pick from a pool of candidates that wanted to make detectives. Mike picked Amanda and she still wasn't sure why.

Mike was intently lost in his computer glasses. Danny, it seemed, was almost the perfect person. No arrests, no jail time, no problems. From his file, Mike discovered that Danny broke his collarbone in eighth-grade football, tore his ACL in varsity basketball, and the only mark on his criminal record was an underaged drinking charge from college. Danny had never been involved, or at least arrested, from being violent or fighting. He never faced any drug charges. Danny didn't even have a hacking charge, even though he'd been working with computers his entire life.

"Great," Detective Russ said, as he took his glasses off and set them on the table. "I can't seem to find anyone that would want to hurt this guy."

"He's clean, yes," Amanda said. "Which makes me believe that this isn't about him."

"Trying your hand at detective reasoning already?" Mike asked with a laugh. "Great. What is your theory?"

"Danny was involved intently with this system," Amanda said. "Someone wants to harm the system. They went after Danny. My guess is that if we don't find out who did this right away, we're going to have more murders."

"It's a thought that's crossed my mind," Detective Russ said. "In a case like that, there would generally be a demand to shut the system down. Someone would—anonymously, mind you—inform us that there will be more murders unless the system is taken down. We haven't received anything like that yet. Granted, that isn't always the case, but it generally is."

"What do you think happened?"

"I keep looking for someone who invested in his companies out in California who got burned by him," Mike said. "Someone who had financial damage because of him and wanted revenge, but he paid everyone back."

"So, your thoughts?"

"There's a stunning lack of evidence," Mike said. "Lack of clues. It's just great. Hopefully, the mayor will know something."

"Hopefully."

There was a moment of silence between the two detectives. Neither knew what to say. Mike had worked on tough cases before, murder cases which seemed unsolvable at the beginning. He knew one thing about people, they're emotional creatures. And the emotion of killing someone couldn't be contained or bottled up. Sooner or later, like a balloon with too much air, the person would pop and let something slip.

The door to the room opened as Mayor Theodor Kamp entered. "I hope the investigation is going well. I'm confident in you and the Winter Falls Police Force to keep peace in my city."

Mayor Kamp sat down, glancing from one detective to the next.

"We have our process," Mike said. "How are you doing, Mayor Kamp?"

"Very good, very good," Theodor said. "But please, in a setting like this, call me Ted."

"Thank you, Ted," Amanda said. "We only have a few questions for you today. What did you know of Danny Brown? His work on the system? His relationships with the people who worked here?"

"I confess that I really didn't know him," Mayor Kamp said. "I mainly deal with Dr. Hall and Dr. Porter. Those are the two main contacts I had with the system. I'd met Danny in passing. I doubt I ever had a real conversation with the guy. I know that he had ambitions, and that along with studying Dr. Hall, he had studied a lot of the history of Allen Day and Everyday Computers."

"Now the world's largest company by market cap," Amanda said. "Didn't even exist fifteen years ago. Such a young company to put your faith into. Why did you choose Everyday Computers and Madison Software Labs?"

"If you ever meet Allen Day, you'll know why," Ted said. "He's got that charisma that could sell water to a drowning man. Beyond that, though, he has total conviction in his ideas. He's completely confident in whatever he does. It's a refreshing quality in this day and age. I don't know exactly how he and Dr. Hall were ever friends, being so different and all."

"How do you mean?" Amanda asked.

"Allen has the expressed goal of being the lead story on the newsfeeds at least once a month," Ted said. "He wants everyone to constantly hear about him and his company. He does charity work, not because he believes in the charity or the people they are helping, but for the press. Anything Allen does is to get eyeballs on him. Dr. Hall, on the other hand, does everything he can to avoid people paying attention to him. I've never met a loner quiet like him before."

"And they've been friends for a long time?" Amanda asked.

"Since grade school, I believe," Ted said. "They lived on the same block growing up. It was Dr. Hall's idea though, linking everything together, complete control. He was the one who had the idea of it all. He was the one who came up with the LBM system to store and access everything. Make no mistake about it, I'm confident in saying that when you talk to Dr. Hall, you're talking to the smartest man living today."

"Really?" Amanda asked.

"Really," Ted said.

"So, you contracted Dr. Hall to create the system?" Mike asked.

"I did," Ted said. "I was looking for something innovative to implement in my city. We haven't had a large-scale innovation since vertical hydroponic farming became commonplace. I knew Madison Software Labs had been working on projects, tests of something big, but no one had offered a proper testing grounds."

"Why were you so concerned about innovations?" Amanda asked.

Ted smiled with hesitation. He wasn't sure he wanted to answer but he knew that feeding little bits and pieces to people would help his cause. "Innovations are needed in this country. We need a leader who embraces innovation."

"You're talking about your rumored run for president," Mike said. "You plan to use this system to put your name on a national level."

"I cannot confirm or deny that," Ted said, with a smile. "But this system will be everywhere soon, and I can say that I was the one who saw the potential. I was the one who took the risk. People will take notice of that."

"Not if the Neo-Luddites keep gaining momentum," Amanda said. "They've been gaining in numbers in recent years and are become more powerful. There's talk in the next election that Breeze Flynn, the leader's daughter, might try and run for president."

"A fringe, lunatic group," Ted said.

"They seem to echo some of the talks of Jerry Bosen," Mike said.

"That son of a..." Ted trailed off. "Look, I love watching Jerry make an ass of himself as he stands there and spouts off his dribble. No one takes that nut seriously."

"He's sold a lot of books," Mike said. "His latest, 'The Shrinking Mind' topped every bestseller list. A lot of people listen to him."

"People love a good conspiracy," Ted said. "Just because they read it doesn't mean they take stock in it. I'm confident that most people read Jerry's books for a laugh. Now don't get me wrong, the man is brilliant. What he's done in the stock market and some of the work his company has done is amazing. I do give him credit for that. The problem is, the guy is so full of himself that you can't take him seriously. I think he does it just to egg people on, you know? Just to get a rise out of people. Like he doesn't believe it himself."

"I think he believes what he's saying, Mayor," Mike said. "I've read some of his earlier work, he believes what he's promoting."

"I'm not so sure," Ted said. "Maybe I just don't like the guy so I'm seeing something that's not there, but I just don't for a second understand how a smart individual could put any stock into those theories of his. Technology is causing us to lose intelligence. The human race is facing destruction because of it. It's interesting. Right after the dawn of man there was some nut predicting its downfall. There have always been people saying the end is near and we keep going."

"Do you think Jerry killed Danny or do you think Jerry would sabotage the system?" Mike asked.

"I'm confident that Jerry didn't kill anyone," Ted said. "Don't get me wrong, I would never leave Jerry alone with my daughter. I wouldn't let him near her. But to kill someone? No, Jerry wouldn't do that. I doubt he would try to sabotage the system either."

"You have a lot of bad things to say about him, yet you defend him," Amanda said.

"It's a double-edged sword," Ted said. "The man is smart. He's very brilliant. He can connect the dots on a lot of math formulas and he has done some amazing things. His theories, on the other hand, make him look like a fool. I don't know about Jerry some days but I'm sure he's not a killer."

"Do you know who killed Danny Brown?" Mike asked.

"No."

"Do you know anyone who would want to hurt him?" Mike asked.

"No."

"Do you know anyone who would want to hurt the system?"

"The Neo-Luddites," Ted said.

"Mayor?" Amanda asked.

"For all their talk of peace and harmony," Ted said, "I don't buy for one second that they aren't capable of sabotage. It's only a matter of time really. They are failing at every turn. No one takes them seriously, no one listens to them. Sooner or later, Gary Flynn needs to make some headway or people are going to leave."

"Their numbers are gaining though," Amanda said.

"According to whom?" Ted asked. "Them? You are going to trust his number? Please. I'm confident he's feeding the world lines of garbage. I would guess that the Neo-Luddites will go the way of the Flat Earth Society and black hole believers."

"Very well," Mike said. "Is there anything else Mayor Kamp? Anything else you would like to tell us or can think of that would help us with the investigation?"

"Nothing that I can think of," Mayor Kamp said. "If something does come up I'll let you know right away. Please, detectives, this has to be handled quickly and quietly. I don't want something like this dragging down the system."

"It won't," Mike said. "We don't have any other questions at this time. We don't need you to send anyone else in either. We're going to look around before heading back to the station."

"Very good, very good," Ted said. "If there's anything I can do to help, please let me know."

"Just make sure to let us know if you're going to be leaving town," Mike said. "Standard procedure and all."

"Very good," Ted said, as he stood up and walked out of the room.

As the door closed, Mike put his computer glasses on and started looking through files while Amanda sat for a moment, thinking. She thought back to cases she'd seen when she was a cop. It was normal, in this day and age of ultra-technology for a crime to seem unsolvable. The criminals of the world had embraced technology to a staggering degree. The latest criminal device was a magnetic-pulse-ion-blast, an MPIB.

The MPIB, a small device anyone could purchase off the 'net, or build themselves, with the right material. Commit a crime, leave the bomb at the crime scene, and have it detonated about ten minutes after you've left. Any hair, skin cells, or blood left at the scene will now be useless in DNA testing. The MPIB would corrupt any DNA within its radius, provided that DNA was isolated from the host's body, blood on the floor, a nail in the carpet, hair on the sofa. Grafting and surgery had rendered fingerprint technology useless twenty years ago and now DNA was out the window. Cameras and old fashion police work were what caught criminals now.

"Penny for your thoughts," Mike asked, looking to Amanda.

"There's no motive," Amanda said. "Why kill him?"

"Indeed."

"No record of a girlfriend," Amanda said. "Not a recent one anyway. Not in any financial or legal trouble. Who would want to kill this guy?"

"The mystery is deeper than you're willing at admit," Mike said. "I've done this for over ten years now, Amanda. I have a feeling about these things. You develop the ability to feel out these cases after you've done enough of them."

"What's your feeling on this case, Mike?"

"That we should have asked for a different case," Mike said. "I got a feeling this case is going to get much worse before it gets better...but it will get better. We will solve it."

"It's going to be a long case then?" Amanda asked.

Mike just smiled a knowing grin as he nodded. As Mike put his computer glasses back on his face, Amanda couldn't help but wonder what they'd gotten into. She wanted to be a detective and now she was sitting in on her first case, a case she couldn't afford to blow. Amanda knew that with Mike by her side they would crack this case. Amanda put her computer glasses on as she started to review Danny's work files again, looking for any clue that could give them a direction in this case.

Chapter #7

Dr. Jack Hall walked into the Master Control Room, stopping just inside the door. He slowly looked around the room before anyone noticed that he was there. The room was kept darker, with just enough light to see where you were going. The floors and desks were black. Light outlines on the floor showed the main walking paths. Starting from the back going forward, there were four rows of control panels, each with five stations in a row. The control panels were all facing the front wall that was covered with video monitors, each one showing a different part of the city.

Dr. Hall had modeled the control room after N.A.S.A.'s mission control room. Each workstation had hookups for glasses computers and a built-in desk computer. Any person could transfer what their station monitor or glasses were showing on the main screen for everyone to see or all the station or glasses computers could be set to see the same thing. It was all Madison Software Labs designs that were running the system. It was Dr. Hall's work that led to all of this, and he looked at this system like his child. The system was a living, breathing entity to Dr. Hall, and it needed to be treated as such. He impressed that point upon every person working there, including Danny Brown.

"Good afternoon, Dr. Hall," a female worker said, as she walked by.

"Um," Dr. Hall muttered softly. "Hello."

Jack blushed as he looked at the woman walking by. She was younger, in her mid-twenties, fresh out of university. She had a willowy frame, thin face, and too much makeup. Her braided black hair seemed to swing across her back like a clock pendulum as she walked. Dr. Hall tried to remember the woman's name. He'd hired her, but then, he hired a lot of the people here. Over two-thirds of the people working on the system were women, most of them in their twenties and thirties. Men just weren't getting computer engineering and software degrees anymore. It had become a female profession. In the past ten years, there'd been a resurgence of men who wanted to work outside. Sitting at a computer was no longer interesting to men.

Dr. Hall smiled at the women as he started walking slowly through the room, looking over everyone's station. He wanted to make sure they were clean. He despised messy workstations. All the workers acknowledged him and said pleasantries as he walked by. Dr. Hall did his best, smiling, nodding, and muttering something back to them. Of all the women working here, Dr. Hall could imagine himself with them, having a relationship, getting married, and starting a family. But, workplace ethics aside, he didn't even know how to talk to them outside of a workplace setting.

One thing Jack shook his head at were the uniforms the people wore in the control rooms. It was a place he needed to make a concession. Dr. Hall wanted everyone to be business formal, but Dr. Porter and Mayor Kamp didn't think dress code was as important as Jack did. There were other things more important to Jack, so he let Dr. Porter select the working uniform while he got to have final say on much of the design aesthetics of the system.

The men wore khaki pants or shorts with a black tee shirt bearing the Winter Falls name on the left breast and the city logo on the back. The women wore black tights or compression shorts, with either the same tee shirts the men wore or tank tops with the same city designs on them. The women's tops were all oversized and held in at the waist with a belt. Both the male and female uniforms were the standard fashion for the time—a commentary, Dr. Hall thought, about how sloppy the culture had become. Tights and a tank top had become the accepted business apparel of the women.

Jack left the Master Control Room and entered the Main Control Room. The main room was much smaller but similar to the larger master room. Everything was black, and the room was kept dark. There was just enough light to make out if anyone was in the room or where to walk. On the far wall was a massive video screen, currently set to a live feed of the City Center traffic flow. Pod-like cars zoomed to-and-fro around a massive shopping and entertainment district.

Jack sat down in the master chair, a large black leather chair that could move between two different stations on a powered track on the floor. The chair was currently in the middle of the room, set for watching the main screen. Two more workstations were behind the chair, inaccessible from the main chair, but open and ready for workers to man. Jack put on his computer glasses and adjusted them so his field of vision was unobstructed.

"Seth," Jack called out. "Set master screen to level functions please."

"As you wish, sir," Seth's disembodied voice rang out from the speaker system of the room.

The master screen changed to a matrix-like grid of code names and numbers. Everything was flashing quickly, reminiscent of a stock ticker screen. Number and names flashed quickly as Jack focused his eyes on the screen. He watched everything with interest, quickly making mental notes of what he was seeing.

"Give me a report, Seth," Jack said.

"All systems are operating within given tolerances," Seth said. "As you would say, 'all systems go.'"

"That's good news, Seth," Jack said. "You're working perfectly."

"Perfection is an impossible achievement, sir," Seth said. "Although we are within all tolerances there are sub-functions that are not at optimum levels, and..."

"It was an expression, Seth," Jack said. "I understand."

"Your stress levels are higher than normal, sir," Seth said. "Might I try something to bring your levels to a more acceptable position?"

"What do you have in mind?"

"It has been awhile since we've battled in chess," Seth said, as the main screen switched to a massive chess board. "You can take the first move, sir."

"I would love to, Seth. But I'm afraid I don't have the time for a game right now," Jack said. "Thank you though. I will have to find the time to play you soon. It's been too long."

"How about this," Seth said, as the screen switched to an athletic woman, tanned with long black hair, catching a perfect wave on a multicolored surfboard as water glistened off her seductively perfect skin and black bikini. "Your favorite scene, the extended solo surfing scene in the movie 'Waves of Summer,' and actress Paige Gianakos. Watching this relaxes you."

"Quickly back to City Center main cameras," Jack said, nervously looking around the room. The screen went back to streets. "That's not my favorite movie, Seth."

"You watch 'Waves of Summer' more than any other," Seth argued. "269% more viewings than your next highest, the dystopian war thriller, 'Wars of Time and

Farmers.' Granted, you don't watch all of 'Waves of Summer,' only parts of eight scenes."

"Seth, please," Jack said. "It's a human thing. I don't know, you wouldn't understand. I don't think you could understand."

"What don't I understand, sir?"

"About human companionship. Love, relationships, all that. You know, maybe eating something good would relax me. Seth, could you order me a meat lover's deep-dish pizza?"

"You haven't had any fruit or vegetables for three meals, sir. Your medical implant shows that you need to vary your diet. Might I suggest a large mixed green salad, with the vegetable and baked chicken option from 'Donny's Family Italian Eatery?' They are healthy, and you are currently located within their delivery radius."

"You're worse than my mother," Jack said. "Sure Seth, order me the salad and a large iced tea. Order yourself something to eat too. Whatever you want."

"I'm sorry, sir?"

"Nothing," Jack said, laughing at his joke. "Just a little human humor."

Before Seth could interject something, the door to the Main Control Room opened and Jerry walked in, sitting down in a comfortable large office chair at one of the stations, turning the chair toward Jack and taking his computer glasses off.

"I have to give you credit, Jack," Jerry said, as he made himself comfortable in the chair. "I like the dark of these rooms. I can take those glasses off."

"You could have the surgery to take care of your eyes you know."

"Now why would I want to do that?"

There was a pause. Jack didn't want to get into the debates with Jerry. Jack knew how Jerry loved to debate and argue with people and he didn't have time to deal with it today.

"How's the system running?" Jerry continued. "Everything working as it should be?"

"Everything is operating within tolerances," Jack said.

"That's not exactly what I asked," Jerry said, with a grin. "Is everything as it should be?"

"What brings you down here today, Jerry?" Jack asked, not wanting to take Jerry's bait. "Is there something I can do for you?"

"You know that reporter, Nevaeh, from this morning?"

"Um, yes."

"I've got a thing with her tomorrow. I want to give her a tour of the system."

"You're asking me if you can use a billion-dollar, tax-payer funded, government-operated computer system that's running an entire city to help you score with some reporter that you just met?"

Jerry grinned. "When you say it like that it doesn't sound as good. Trust me, Dr. Hall, I don't need your computer's help to move things along with Nevaeh, that race is an easy one to win. I want to show her what this system is really about, the human aspect of it, the people down in this cave running it."

"You get a lot of women, don't you?"

"An amazing amount."

"Do you think that it would be possible, I don't know, um, maybe, that you could find one for me, perhaps?"

"Hell yes, man. It's far easier than you think. You got a lot going for you. You look decent, you have a lot of money, I'm sure you've got other qualities."

"That's how you see me? A rich loner?"

"It was a joke, Jack," Jerry said, as he moved his chair closer to Jack. "That's rule number one, you have to loosen up a little. No woman wants to be with an uptight stiff. The best aphrodisiac in the world is laughter, Jack. That's the truth of it. Now I don't mean to sit there and rattle off a comedy routine but be playful, inject humor into your conversation."

"I don't understand."

"You ever notice how sarcastic I can be at times?"

"Yes."

"And also, how it's not directed at the person I'm talking to nor is it malic."

"Yes."

"That's what I'm talking about. Humor is the key. Get them laughing when they should be serious. Point number two, no woman wants a boring routine. I've noticed something about you, Jack. You have daily outfits. You have an outfit for Monday, one for Tuesday, and so on. You do that to save time, correct?"

"So I don't need to think about what I have to wear."

"That kind of routine is death to attraction. Women hate it."

"But you wear black and only black."

"True, but that's for other reasons. I'm very aware of what I do with women. Make sure to never settle into a rut. Sure, things are going to turn routine, but always have something in the wings ready to surprise her with something different."

"I don't know," Jack said. "You make it sound so easy, Jerry."

"It is easy, Jack," Jerry replied. "I've got a reputation. I've always had a velvet tongue when it came to chatting up the ladies. All the way back to middle school. I realized what got reactions and what didn't. I simply enhanced what worked and hid what didn't. It's the same thing I do in risk analysis. When I published my first book, I got some national attention. I used that to get into a party with some celebrities. That night, I made myself known to some of the most well-known women in the country. I started dating a starlet, then another, then another. I built a reputation.

"You only see the wins, Jack. You don't realize how many times I do get rejected. No one else knows about it though. Funny thing about my reputation, the women who have said publicly that they refused me, weren't believed. People thought they were making it up but there have been some. This is where I really shine. I don't let it bother me. Most of them cannot stand the fact that it doesn't bother me, that I don't start chasing them harder. Many have come around, if you get my drift."

"Stop," Jack said. "Just stop. I don't want that. I don't want to be like you, having multiple girlfriends, dating all sorts of people, getting shot at by a jealous ex-girlfriend..."

"That only happened twice."

"I just want someone to share my life with," Jack said. "I want a family. I want a wife. I have everything else that I could ask for. I've proven everything that I need to prove in the software world. It's time for the next chapter of my life and I want that to be as a husband and father."

"That's respectable, man," Jerry said. "Although it will be slightly more difficult. You can't just think the first lady you meet is going to fall into your arms. That's what dating is all about. I've got two kids that I love to death, so I know where you're coming from. Luckily, even though I'm not married to their mothers, we are close friends and do things together as a family. Hard as it is to believe, I've been thinking along the same lines as you, finding someone to settle down with. At the end of the day, you just want someone to be there for you. The drama of the game gets old after a bit."

"Funny how people kept saying the family unit wasn't going to last, yet it's what we crave the most."

"That it is," Jerry said. "I'm sure you haven't noticed but I've been avoiding the celebrity scene recently. The people in that world are not ready or in a position to settle down. Their lifestyle isn't made for families."

"Is that why you asked Nevaeh out?"

"I didn't ask her out," Jerry said. "I invited her to join me at something I was going to do anyway. I've spent so much time around women that I have a sixth sense about them. I'm not sure how to describe it, but I know that Nevaeh is a good person, a smart person. We'll see how it plays out. There is a spare bedroom around here, right?"

"Really?"

"When the time is right, man," Jerry said. "Bomb shelters are one level down, right?"

"Right," Jack said. "Listen, Jerry, umm, I don't know...when you take Nevaeh on your tour, since you always wear your glasses, could you record it and send it to me? Just so I can see how you talk to a woman?"

"That would be a violation of her trust," Jerry said. "Not something I would do. Tell you what, during the party, hang out with us. You can get a good idea of what I do there. Now tell me, so I can help you find someone, who is your dream girl? Would it be, Dr. Porter?"

"Absolutely not," Jack said, almost appalled. "Seth, show him."

Jerry looked at the screen as the girl on the surfboard reappeared. Jerry just started to laugh, "Paige Gianakos in 'Waves of Summer.' This movie is every teenaged boy's fantasy."

"But Paige is what I'm looking for," Jack said. "She's elegant and graceful. Carries herself with poise and refinement. She's amazingly intelligent, holds two Ph.D.'s, works with charities, and has held the 'Total Entertainment Zone' most beautiful person award five years, more than anyone else ever."

"She's a princess," Jerry said. "Her family is royalty. She was taught in finishing schools with private tutors. Her parents wanted nothing but the best for her."

"I don't want her, exactly," Jack said. "A woman like her."

"A tall order to be sure," Jerry said. "I'll tell you this though, get Paige worked up and her poise and refinement are out the window. She can get down and dirty with the best of them."

"You dated Paige?"

"Not exactly," Jerry said. "Four years ago, we were both on the coast of the Mediterranean Sea. She was filming 'Waves of Summer' and I was working on recreating the government crash. We met at a nightclub and one thing led to another. We met a few more times, always in secret, for obvious reasons…"

"The fact that she was betrothed to be married to a prince from another country?" Jack asked. "You would have been killed if anyone found out."

"She hated the prince and didn't want to marry him," Jerry said. "All women have desires, Jack. They just hide them much better than men do. When I got called for another project, I left and that was it. Never saw her again. We never exchanged numbers, had no delusions of creating a life together, it was simply for fun. She's a tall order to meet, Jack, but what I think you're asking for is an intelligent, refined woman who is past the party age and looking for something serious."

"Yes."

"That I can handle," Jerry said. "I've got to keep moving today but I'll see you at the party tomorrow night. I may even bring someone with to meet you. I'll keep you posted."

"Thanks, Jerry," Jack said, as Jerry left the room.

"Do I not provide you with good companionship?" Seth asked once Jerry had left the room.

"What?" Jack replied.

"Sir," Seth said. "We've spent so much time together. Am I not all the companionship that you need?"

"This is a different matter, Seth."

"Explain."

"Love is impossible to explain."

"Love is the chosen word for a set of chemical reactions humans experience within the body and brain when focused on a particular person who has peaked their interest. I see the chemical reactions in people, Jack. You have some of those reactions with me."

"There's a difference, Seth. I want someone to hold at night. Someone to hold hands with. I want to kiss someone. I want a woman who will hike with me to the top of a peak and watch the sunset. Love isn't just a set of chemical reactions, Seth. Love is cuddling with someone during a thunderstorm, not saying a word, and feeling like you've had the best conversation of your life. Love is caring deeply for someone and knowing that they will care deeply for you."

"That doesn't make logical sense," Seth said. "It doesn't follow any chain of reasoning that I can follow."

"There's no other way to describe it, Seth," Jack said. "Please, I don't want to talk about this anymore. On the main screen, power systems levels."

The main screen switched to a grid of numbers and symbols. Jack got comfortable in his chair as he looked at the numbers. Everything looked to be as it should, everything was working. Jack should have been ecstatic for the success of the system, but his mind was elsewhere, thinking about the kind of woman Jerry would introduce him to.

Chapter #8

Winter Falls City Hall sat atop a swell of land near the center of the city, adjacent to the massive river that flowed through the buzzing metropolis. The city hall had been designed to catch the rising sun and illuminate in the mornings. This fine morning was no exception. A marvel of design, the city hall, Mayor Theodor Kamp's idea, was shimmering in the first rays of light on the new day. There wasn't the crowd that had been outside city hall yesterday, but there were bikers, walkers, skateboarders, and people on rollerblades on the trails that ran along the river and around the parks of city hall grounds.

Inside, already hard at work, Dr. Hall was reviewing the system from the night before. Street lamp settings, cooling systems, water flows, traffic, and all the other functions of the system worked perfectly. Better than they could have hoped. Jack was on his way to bring the overnight report to Mayor Kamp. The mayor had insisted in the first few weeks of the system he see updates every day of what happened. The sheer excitement Theodor felt with the system was contagious, an infection that touched everyone he spoke to about it. Jack enjoyed talking to Ted about the system, but when he opened the door to the mayor's office, Jack's heart sank. Jerry was there. Jack liked Jerry, but Ted and Jerry bickered like an old married couple.

"Very good, very good," Ted said, as Jack peeked through the door. "Come in and sit down, Jack. Spare no delectable details, how did the first twenty-four hours go?"

Jack quickly moved to the nearest seat and sat down. Ted's office was huge. A mahogany oak desk sat opposite the door with a massive leather chair occupied by

Ted on the other side. Behind Ted, floor-to-ceiling glass gave a glimpse to the parks and gardens on the backside of city hall. Past the parks was Winter Fall's picturesque skyline, with its giant skyscrapers reaching into the sky. On the right side of the office was a grouping of sofas and easy chairs around a table, all focusing on a wall with a built-in computer screen. To the left was a full-wall bookcase, filled with paper books.

"All systems were within tolerances all night," Jack said, using his glasses to transfer a file to Ted's glasses. "You can see there were no warnings, no errors, and everything functioned as it should."

Ted put his glasses on and looked over the report. Jerry motioned that he wanted the report on his glasses too. Jack quickly transferred them. The three men looked into their glasses at the report. As Ted was beaming about how great the first twenty-four hours went, Jerry noticed something that didn't really make sense.

"What do you have to say now, you smug bastard?" Ted asked. "System worked perfectly. Guess you're not going to be able to run around in loin cloth like a caveman this summer. Society will still stand."

"Just because society stands doesn't mean I can't run around in loin cloth," Jerry said, looking over parts of the system that were peaking his interest. "Oh, Teddy, at the height of your confidence this system will jump out and bite you in the ass."

"You worry too much," Ted said. "And I've told you before, don't call me Teddy. You've never proven anything you've said. Your report on this system was pure propaganda to flame fear of the system, fear that you used to ride a wave of fame into a cushy position."

"Believe me, Teddy," Jerry said. "I can think of a few other positions I would rather be in right now...but you really believe that you can control all this? You really believe that this system will make our lives easier?"

"It will," Mayor Kamp said. "Just you watch. Allen Day is going to be here soon, and he'll be inspecting some of the new terminal stations we installed before entering meetings with myself and Governor Chad Jones. I believe that Allen's son Adam is going to be with him. Now that Adam has graduated, he's going to be taking a bigger role in the Madison Software Labs. Jack, you'll never guess what little rumor I heard this morning."

"What's that, Ted?"

"Adam is going to be proposing to my daughter Amber at the party tonight," Ted said, beaming with pride. "I can't wait for those two to get married."

"Money marrying money," Jerry said. "All cash and no brains."

"For some unknown reason," Ted continued ignoring Jerry's comments, "Allen insists that you are at the meetings today Jerry. I don't agree that you should be there, but you know how he is. I don't want any of your smart-mouthed comments."

"Yes, Dad."

"Damn it, Jerry," Ted roared. "I've about had it with you and your stupid ideas. Of all the disrespectful..."

"You're so busy patting yourself on the back," Jerry said, transferring a highlighted portion of the report to both Ted and Jack's glasses, "that you missed something pretty damn important."

Jack and Ted looked at the document on their glasses. Neither Ted nor Jack could understand what Jerry was getting at, why he showed them this. It was a traffic document, showing car movements and traffic lights from a northern quadrant of town; an upper-middle-class neighborhood known for its large families.

"What am I looking at?" Ted asked.

"Traffic light timing," Jerry said. "To keep all flows of traffic moving continuously, the system allowed an intersection to have green lights from all directions for over two minutes. Multiple cars went through the intersection. Now granted, the cars were controlled by the system, so there might not have been a need to worry, but what if there was a biker or walker? The system didn't allow a safe crossing of the street. Also, if someone would have been operating their car manually...well, no red lights."

"My God," Jack said. "He's right."

"One little glitch," Ted said. "It means nothing. A programming error that will be fixed in a minute, right?"

"Fixed already," Jack said, moving his hands as he worked on his glasses.

"What do you have to say now, smartass?" Ted said, grinning at Jerry.

"Just wait, Teddy," Jerry said. "I will be proven right."

"Are we really going to waste another morning arguing like kids again?" Jack asked, upset at the pair in the room with him.

Before anyone could answer, Mayor Kamp's glasses started to ring, indicating an incoming phone call.

"Answer," Mayor Kamp said, loudly, then softer, "Hello...who...I don't recall...very good, very good...send her in."

Mayor Kamp tapped his phone to end the call, "Apparently there's an Alyssa Babbage here to see me."

"Who is that?" Jack asked.

"Damned if I know," Ted said. "I looked at my schedule last night and didn't notice any meetings but it's there this morning. I have no idea what this is about."

Just then, the door to the office opened and a woman walked in. Jack's breath was taken away by the sight of her. She was tall and tone, a strong body wrapped in flawless, tanned skin. Thick, curly black hair flowed down to her lower back accented with subtle purple highlights. She had an elongated face with a high forehead, wide-set spider black eyes, button nose, narrow lips, and rounded chin. The woman projected an energy, powerful and sexual, that demanded to be noticed. Her movements were poised and precise, like she was consciously planning every move her body made, for the sole purpose of getting people to notice her.

She wore black tights with a purple top that was cut in a party style, exposing far too much skin than was appropriate in a business setting. Her makeup was caked on, slightly too heavy, purple eyeliner that formed a mask around her eyes and black-as-night lipstick. The woman was very gothic, right down to her stilettoed black boots. Despite her black and gothic look, she had an amazingly warm smile—a smile she gave to each of the men in the room.

"Can I help you?" Mayor Kamp asked as Jack's heart raced looking at the woman.

"I'm Alyssa Babbage," Alyssa said, in a deep, breathy voice as she extended her hand to shake the mayor's. "I was hired for the open computer engineer position."

"Very good, very good," Ted said, stunned at the powerful grip of the woman's handshake. "Hold on a minute, hired? Who hired you? For what computer position?"

"I'm a computer engineer who has worked on both hardware and software. I've run network systems, have practical experience in troubleshooting large, multilayered systems, I'm fluent in the three major computer languages and the six minor ones, and I have never been charged with hacking."

"Impressive," Jerry said, eyeing Alyssa up and down. "But you didn't answer the question as to who actually hired you."

"Seth hired me," Alyssa said.

"And it begins," Jerry almost yelled laughing. "Seth hired her."

"Seth told me that a position of utmost importance opened up due to the untimely departure of an employee."

"You can say that again," Jerry said.

"Seth told me I was far and away the best candidate he had seen. I just finished a university project and was looking for something new. This project is a perfect fit for me. He told me to come in today to negotiate salary and finalize all the paperwork. He said I could start today. He didn't tell me much about the project, but I do know about it from what I've read in the newsfeeds."

"How much do you know about the system?" Jack asked.

"Just that it's a massive computer network that compiles and aligns all the application systems needed to operate and maintain a city. Everything functions and runs out of city hall."

"That's the Sunday School version of it, yes," Jerry said.

"I'm the creator of the system, Dr. Jack Hall."

"I know who you are, Dr. Hall," Alyssa said. "Every computer person on the planet knows who you are."

"A part of the system that people don't know much about is Seth," Jack continued. "Seth is the interface of the system. We can talk to the system. Seth can reason and use logic to help us work on problems. He monitors the system for us. Yesterday we told Seth to look over all available candidates and find someone who would be a fit. One of our team members was murdered the night before. It's been in the news, although the story has been kept as quiet as we can. I told Seth to find us a replacement, with the implication being he brings us the file of the person, not go out and hire them without consulting us. But then again, Seth did exactly what we told him to do, find a replacement for Danny."

"Is there an opening here?" Alyssa asked.

"There is," Mayor Kamp said, "But we need to follow..."

"You're hired," Jack interrupted.

"But," Ted started.

"I trust the system," Jack said. "Don't you, Ted? Think about it, the system found the perfect employee. The system knows what it needs."

Ted sat silent for a moment, chewing on his lower lip as he looked Alyssa over. There was something about her, something that he couldn't put his finger on. He like the sound of her qualifications, if they were all true. And if the system found her, well, Ted could only think of the amount of time they would save not having to pour over resumes and files trying to find someone that matched their needs.

"You're hired," Ted said. "We can do six thousand a month with a standard benefits package."

"Um," Jack said. "That's kind of low, don't you think...for someone with her standards?"

"Standard review in six months," Ted said.

"That is fine for pay," Alyssa said. "I just want to work."

"You'll never last working for the government, honey," Jerry said, grinning. "Not with that attitude."

"You must be the redoubtable Jerry Bosen," Alyssa said, turning toward him and placing her hands on her hips.

"The one and only," Jerry said, standing, offering his hand to shake hers.

When Alyssa extended her hand to meet Jerry's, he took two paces forward, putting himself very close to Alyssa, so close their bodies were almost touching. Jerry still had his glasses tinted so Alyssa couldn't see his eyes, but Jerry could see into hers. He could see into her soul. Jerry just smiled. Alyssa never flinched, never showed one drop of fear or tension from him being so close to her.

"You have a very unique and interesting energy about you, Alyssa," Jerry said, as he slowly released her hand and descended back to his chair. "It will be interesting to see how far you go here. Dr. Hall, why don't you show Alyssa around the complex. Introduce her to the system."

"Um, sure," Jack said, standing too quickly. "This way, if you please, Alyssa."

"Thank you," Alyssa said, as she followed Jack out of the room.

"Why don't you go with them," Ted said. "She seems like your type, Jerry."

"That woman is trouble with a capital T," Jerry said.

"A woman that you're afraid of?" Ted asked. "Is this a first? I suggested you go with so that you were out of my office."

"I got that, Teddy," Jerry said. "But there was something about her. She's a troublemaker. I want to look at her file."

"I sensed something too," Ted said, as Jerry waved his hand, operating his glasses computer. "I've seen her before. I think I know her from somewhere."

"Okay," Jerry said. "I've got her file. Let's see here...no known convictions or charges...solid work history...nothing but good comments from employers...no major work incidents...in the top ninety-eighth percentile of her class...exceptional marks in math and science...solid high school extracurricular activities...president of the Future Programmers Club...drama...swimming...grappling...surfing...gymnastics...an avid rock climber...has surfed on six continents...and is a master yoga practitioner."

"Hell of a gal," Ted said. "Sounds like she's got some experience under her belt."

"That's for sure," Jerry said. "Amazing file really. Couldn't have asked for a better fit for the team."

"Why do I get the feeling that you're going to have a conspiracy theory about her?"

"Not a conspiracy, per se," Jerry said. "Something though. I'm not sure. Any rate, what's up for the rest of today?"

"How about you out of my office?"

"You're so much fun to bother though," Jerry said. "With your ideas of ruling the world with a computer and all."

"You are delusional, you know that? Now go."

"In a minute."

"I can't wait until you're voted out of office," Ted said. "Then I could have security remove you from here."

"Bet you a thousand dollars you get voted out of office before I do."

"If I take this bet will you leave?"

"Sure."

"Deal."

Ted and Jerry shook hands before Jerry stood up and left the room. Ted just shook his head. Jerry was always coming up with something, always working an angle of some kind. There was too much to deal with today to worry about Jerry and his theories. Ted put his computer glasses on and got ready to get down to business.

Chapter #9

Dr. Hall escorted Alyssa into the Main Control Room, holding the door for her as she entered. Dr. Porter and Ben were both in the room already, working at a fast pace on the system, Holly in the main chair in the center of the room, and Ben behind and to her left, working at a station. The master screen was showing a dam and channel water system that was above and beyond the city, near the edge of the town in a ritzy looking neighborhood. There were all kinds of trucks and repair vehicles on the screen, all bearing the Winter Falls logo on the doors.

Jack stared at the screen. He knew that the system was set to control all the water systems in and around the city, and with the simple error he saw with the traffic lights, he was worried that other little things might have been overlooked. A problem with the water flows of the city could quickly turn into a catastrophe if not handled properly. Jack watched as all the workers on the screen rushed to fix whatever they were working on. Big, industrial looking pieces of equipment and piping attached to pumps and engines were everywhere on the screen. Jack could only hope that something major didn't happen.

"What's going on here?" Jack asked.

Holly and Ben turned to look at Jack, both their faces glowing with excitement. Jack was stunned by their expressions; elation on both of their faces.

"It's wonderful, Jack," Holly said, cheerfully. "Early this morning, the system picked up a vibration that was out of tolerance on one of the motors that run the pumps on the upper water system. It started to reroute the water to take pressure off that pump while alerting power and water personnel to get there. The motor was off balanced. It was an old motor that was starting to wear out. It should have been replaced last year but was overlooked by a careless worker. If the system wouldn't have sensed that the pump was failing, the west half of town would be flooded right now. The system saved the day."

"That's wonderful," Jack said. "Truly amazing."

"We already got the story out to the newsfeeds," Ben said. "That reporter that was working with Jerry—Nevaeh, I think her name was—she's already out there and is going to do a follow-up story tonight at the party. The system saved lives today Jack. Who is that with you today?"

"This is Alyssa Babbage," Jack said, as both Holly and Ben got up to shake her hand. "Alyssa, this is Dr. Holly Porter, my chief software engineer, and Ben Hewitt, a grad student interning with us."

"Pleased to meet both of you," Alyssa said.

"Likewise," Holly replied.

"Alyssa was hired to fill Danny's position," Jack said.

"I'm sure you'll exceed here," Holly said. "This is a really nice environment to be working in."

"Such an amazing facility," Alyssa said. "I've never really seen anything quite like it."

"Dr. Hall has done an exceptional job in setting it up," Dr. Porter said. "He really is a visionary. This entire system, even down to the controls was his idea."

"Fascinating," Alyssa remarked.

"Where are you from, Alyssa?" Ben asked. "Where did you train?"

"I was born in Morocco, but was given up for adoption when I was one," Alyssa said. "My new parents were both American, and they couldn't have children on their own. They were good parents. When I was six, we moved to Winter Falls. I received my Ph.D. in computer engineering at the university here in town. I've worked remotely for a number of different companies while also working for the university."

"How many computer languages are you fluent in?" Dr. Porter asked.

"The three major and the six minor," Alyssa replied.

"You will do well here," Holly said. "If you need anything, don't hesitate to ask. It's a very warm and inviting culture here. We're all working together on a common project. That's the way Dr. Hall set it up."

"It's lovely," Alyssa said. "How did you conceive all this, Dr. Hall?"

"Please," Jack said, "Call me Jack. I started with control systems for traffic. I wanted to eliminate traffic jams forever. A dream, I know. But I thought, what if? Using work on load balancing systems, and some of Jerry's work on large system stability, I was able to implement a system that could logistically handle traffic and route it so there are no standstills. Once I saw that system working in theory, I looked to the water pumps in town. Then to medical.

"Before I knew it, we had a complete system that could handle everything. I was writing research papers about it, trying to find a sponsor to let us test the system on a small scale when I was contacted by Mayor Kamp. He wanted to innovate and could think of nothing better than a system like this. I was slightly hesitant to implement the system on a scale this large, but Ted insisted. He said he would take all responsibility for the system and wanted it installed as soon as possible."

"Mayor Kamp has grand ideas," Dr. Porter said. "He dreams bigger than anyone I know."

"Be glad he did," Jack said. "I don't know of anyone else who could have gotten us the funding to do this project."

"But aren't you and Allen Day both billionaires?" Alyssa asked. "Surely, you and Allen could have put this system together yourself."

"First rule of technology, Alyssa," Ben said. "Never risk your own money when there are taxpayers willing to foot the bill."

"Seth," Dr. Hall called out. "Main screen. I want to see the interior of the hardware room."

The screen switched from the bright and sunny day outside, with the hustle and fever pitch of maintenance workers, to the dim and dull scene of computer equipment as far as the eye could see. Switches, routers, panels, circuit breakers, computer boards, and long black tubes with miles upon miles of cable and wire attaching everything together.

"You're looking at the fastest supercomputers in the world," Jack said. "So fast that there's no reason to even attempt to build anything fast, in the conventional sense."

"What do you mean?" Alyssa asked.

"The computers are run off light, Alyssa," Ben said. "Light-based memory and the processors are using a light system. Theoretically, nothing can go faster than the speed of light, so there's no reason to try to invent a faster system. It can't be done...yet, anyway. Everyday Computers are now working on shrinking the size of the LBM so it can be used in glasses computers. Right now, it's too big and requires too much power to be in a wearable format. This is the fastest system we have right now."

"What could be faster?" Alyssa asked. "Is there another system being worked on?"

"Everyday Computers has two top-secret divisions that no one knows about," Jack said. "Except for the fact that Allen brags about them all the time. The first division is nanobots. Microscopic robots that can form or do anything. The implications of usable nanobots are staggering. They have been testing them to clean out sewage pipes and filter polluted water, but soon they could change everything we do in ways we can't even imagine. The second project is Quantum Computers. If they make a Quantum Computer, then our LBM speeds will look like a Model T compared to a super-charged nitro funny car."

"Quantum Computers?" Alyssa asked. "Do they really think it's possible?"

"Theoretically," Jack said. "And that's all Allen needs to try something."

"Lovely," Alyssa said. "You must be very proud of all your work, Jack. This system is truly amazing. I'm honored by the chance to get to work on it."

"I'm looking forward to seeing what you can do," Jack said.

Alyssa and Jack locked eyes for a moment. Jack couldn't believe how amazing Alyssa was. Her credentials, her abilities, and her life was perfect, exactly what he was looking for in someone to work on his system...and someone to be with him. He didn't know what the rules of love were, nor did he know the work rules, but he knew that he had to try something with Alyssa. There was a feeling inside of him about her. Even though they'd just met, he felt like he knew her, felt like there was a connection.

"Um, I don't know," Jack said, breaking the moment, "The system works because we created a dedicated wireless network around the city. This is the exact same as the network that your glasses run on for calls, texts, and Internet. Just set at a different frequency so there's no overlap. We were sending such vast amounts of data we needed to create our own network. We added new towers all over the city to make sure there were no blackout areas. That's how the medical implant system works."

"This will truly change the world," Alyssa said. "I can't even begin to comprehend the implications this has for bringing about changes in our lives."

"If we can keep all the damn bugs out of it," Ben said.

"Bugs?" Alyssa asked.

"There will always be problems with any system this large," Dr. Hall said. "I mean, just the sheer amount of code that had to be written by almost a thousand different people is cause enough for problems. When you factor in that the system wrote some of the code himself, there's a whole new realm of problems that could crop up that have never been seen before. There is room for error."

"Himself?" Alyssa asked. "The computer is male?"

"I named the system Seth, after my father," Jack said. "That's why we always refer to him in the masculine. Seth, you busy?"

"I'm never too busy to speak with you, sir," Seth's voice rang out.

"I gave Seth a voice for easy access," Jack said. "And so that I could have someone to talk to when I was spending long hours working on the system."

Alyssa smiled as she looked over the system. The screen changed from the equipment room to an outline of a man, shadowed by strange lighting. Although you couldn't see his face, his mouth synced up to Seth's words.

"All systems are operating within tolerance levels, sir," Seth said. "The faulty motor has been replaced and technicians are about to start the testing process to make sure the new unit will function properly. They should be out of the area within an hour, providing all systems function properly."

"How are our stocks doing today?"

"You are up an average of 5% today, sir," Seth said. "News of my detection of the faulty motor has reached the newsfeeds. Nevaeh Crick broke the lead story. Her site almost crashed from the traffic. The public at large thinks this is a very good sign for the stability and longevity of the system. There is heavy buying into both Madison Software Labs and Everyday Computers. Institutional buying is at the highest levels since the system was announced."

"Good news all around," Jack said.

"Sir," Seth continued. "You do have a meeting with Allen Day and Mayor Kamp coming up. It would be best if you made your final preparations and started making your way to the meeting now."

"Alyssa," Ben said, with a smile. "You can stay here, and we'll show you around some more. Teach you what you need to know about the system."

"Thank you," Alyssa said.

"Actually," Dr. Hall said. "Alyssa, why don't you come with me. I think you'll enjoy this meeting with Allen. There's more than enough time to show you around but I bet you'll find this meeting interesting."

"It sounds like fun," Alyssa said.

"As you were," Jack said, as he and Alyssa left the room.

"Man alive," Ben said, as he pulled Dr. Hall and Alyssa up on the screen, watching them with the security monitors. "She is something else. I've never seen a woman like that before."

"She's got a charm about her," Dr. Porter said. "She cute in that gothic kind of way."

"Looks like Dr. Hall is pretty interested in her."

Holly quickly shifted the screen back to the water pump work site. There was still a fleet of equipment working around the area, people rushing back and forth working on the water systems.

"We have work to do," Holly said. "Keep your mind on the system, Ben. I know you're in college and have your sights set on other things right now, but we have a job to do."

Ben just smiled as he put his computer glasses on and went back to work. He had a nagging feeling he'd seen Alyssa before. They couldn't be too far off in age, so maybe he saw her at a college party or something. He didn't let the thought get to him. He had his date for the party tonight and was getting ready for a fun time.

Chapter #10

The Winter Falls Police Station was a dedicated historical landmark, a building over one hundred years old, whose exterior had been restored many times to resemble the iconic stone block wheat mill the building used to be. Set next to the lower falls of the mighty river moving through the town, the gray granite building was a tall island in a sea of single-story commercial buildings, separated only by the waves of trees and shrubbery that Winter Falls is famous for.

One of the first buildings built in Winter Falls, the former mill had been the main police station for over twenty years, a sore point of contention with the citizens considering they'd spent twice as much money fixing and retrofitting the mill than it would have cost to build an ultra-modern new building. The former owners had planned to convert the mill into condominiums but ran out of money very early on in the process. The building was seized by the city to cover their back taxes. Auction after auction and the city couldn't find a buyer. No one wanted to take the risk of ownership since the historical society had ordered the building couldn't be torn down and the exterior had to be restored. With no other options, the city took the building over and converted it into the new police station.

Inside the building, the faint smell of grain dust never did go away. And no matter how much they tried, they could never rid the building of its former residence; mice. Always a beehive of activity, buzzing with a coffee-induced fervor of excitement, the station was the command center for the peace and security of Winter Falls, a city which often made it onto the top-ten lists for safest cities to live in the country. The safety of the town was from the dedication and hard work of the men and women of the force and their constant efforts to educate and assist the citizens. A murder on their record was a tremendous black mark against the force and no one was going to rest until the perpetrator was behind bars.

Inside a small office on the third floor, a bare and lonely office, Detective Mike Russ and Amanda Drake sat around an old wooden desk looking at documents on their computer glasses. Steaming cups of coffee sat in front of them on the empty desk as the pair scanned document after document. The office was small, barely large enough for the desk, the three chairs, and the pair of file cabinets in the corner. A small window looked out over a city street and past to a strip-mall that sat upon the rising swell of land on the west side of the city.

"This is so frustrating," Mike said, as he took his glasses off and rubbed his eyes. "This is the first case I've ever had where there isn't a single clue to use as a starting point."

"That could be a clue in itself," Amanda said. "Correct?"

"Don't grasp at straws, Drake," Mike said. "I wanted to comment on your actions in questioning this morning. You asked far too many questions that were off point and allowed the witness to ramble about things not important to the investigation. You want to be a detective? Keep on point at all times. There's no need to discover these people's life stories."

"Sorry," Amanda said. "I thought it would be best to get to understand these people. Maybe there would be information there that could shed some light on this."

"Stick to the main points first," Mike said. "Then move to the lesser items. Very rarely does a case present itself where a clear motive and suspect isn't standing right in front of you. It's been a long time since I've seen something like this and I've never seen anything at this level."

"Danny Brown had no enemies, no problems, and there are no clues."

"That is something I need to double check. We must go back further. Maybe this has nothing to do with anything recent, but could be related to something long ago. Revenge can fester, cause a person to do strange things. Maybe he hurt someone years ago that we are missing. We need to check for past lovers, past business partners, and see if there were any sudden changes in his behavior."

"I think we should check his apartment again. I mean, how could there be no sign of any struggle, no break in, no fingerprints, and no DNA? There were no signs that a DNA clearing device was used that night."

"Someone out there killed him," Mike said, as he put his glasses on his face again. "That's what we focus on. A human did this, and humans tend to make mistakes. Humans have hard times keeping secrets. We need to force whoever did this to slip. We need to force them into making a mistake in our favor. The key to this is that there were no cameras on the crime scene. Video footage has made solving crimes so much easier. Get an image of the criminal, run facial recognition against all cameras, and great, we know exactly where they are. Without video, this becomes much harder."

"Maybe that Jerry guy was right," Amanda said. "Maybe we are getting softer, our minds shrinking. We rely too heavily on technology and now that a criminal has figured a way around that technology, we are racing to catch up."

"I don't buy his talk, Drake," Mike said. "Not for a minute. He's a pompous ass who likes to promote himself to sell more books and get more business contracts for his company."

"You think he did it to stop the system from coming online?"

"No," Mike said, quickly. "Jerry isn't a killer. I've interviewed killers before. Before I came to Winter Falls, I was in a pretty bad town. I've interviewed monsters like you wouldn't believe. There's something about their personalities that gives them away. A tick, if you will. I can't qualify it, but I know it when I see it. Jerry might be arrogant and a womanizer, but he's no killer."

"He could have hired someone to do it."

"Why do you think it's Jerry?"

"He's so against the system," Amanda said. "Did everything to try and stop it, but the system is now online. Kind of makes him look bad. Maybe he wants to destroy it."

Mike laughed for a moment. "Now you're really grasping at straws. If Jerry wanted to stop the system he would use sabotage, not murder."

"Then who do you think is behind this?"

Mike removed his glasses again and took a sip of his coffee. He turned to look out his small window, looking at the bright, sunny day, and the beautiful city and Winter Falls. He took another sip of his coffee as he felt Amanda's stare on him, burning into him, waiting for an answer. Mike could only guess at this point, and none of his guesses seemed very good. He knew Amanda wanted an answer, but he didn't want to say what his gut told him.

"I asked Mike, who you think is behind this?"

"It's not going to stop at Danny's murder," Mike said. "There will be more. A lot more, I'm afraid. When this is over, we'll find that it was a much deeper mystery than we could have imagined."

Amanda had a confused look on her face, almost scared.

"You asked me and that's what my gut says," Mike said. "From years and years of doing this. You wanted to be a detective, well, welcome to detective work, Amanda. I'm afraid to say this, but if I were you I wouldn't get too comfortable in this position."

"Why?"

"I've seen things like this before. You'll be back on the street before this is over. I'm amazed that they haven't given me a more senior partner yet. That's nothing against you, Amanda, you'll make detective one day, but a case this pressing needs to be solved. Mayor Kamp needs this city on the safest cities list..."

Mike was cut off by the door opening. Walking in was a tall and hefty black man with horseshoe black and gray hair surrounding a shiny bald spot. He wore a dull blue suit that fit him well. He carried himself as a force to be reckoned with. His round face was pulled into a worried look as his gray smoky eyes darted back and forth between Mike and Amanda.

"Chief Rhoads," Mike said, as both he and Amanda stood up to greet Police Chief Marley Rhoads. "What brings you to the third floor today?"

"This murder you're working on," Marley said, as he motioned everyone to sit down. "I've been in contact with Mayor Kamp. He called me earlier."

"I figured that," Mike said. "You two are friends going way back, correct?"

"We are," Marley said. "He's in a fervor over this murder. So far, the only thing the newsfeeds have is that there was a murder. They know where Danny worked but no one has yet to suggest this has anything to do with the system. But that is because of inherent pressure that the mayor's office is putting on the newsfeeds to keep that out of the press."

"Theodor doesn't want his system called into question," Mike said. "Although, at this time there's no reason to suggest that it actually has anything to do with the system."

"That's what I wanted to talk to you about," Marley said. "I sent you a file...a contact actually. Her name is Nevaeh Crick. Delightful young lady, really. A real charmer who works for the Winter Falls Minor. She's been granted the rights to some interviews about the system. I guess they are letting her see the behind the scenes of the system for her newsfeed."

"Chief?" Mike asked, shifting in his chair.

"I want you to draft a press release about the murder," Marley said. "Basic, simple. Have our editors go through it before you send it to Nevaeh."

"What's this release going to say, Chief Rhoads?"

"It's going to suggest that this murder had something to do with Danny's personal life," Marley said. "You are going to say that there are two persons of interest that are involved. One is already in custody being questioned and the other is being tracked down. You should conclude this is an isolated incident, reflecting on Danny's personal life, and that there is no danger for the greater public at large."

"Are you ordering me to do that, Chief?" Mike asked.

"Mayor Kamp strongly suggested it," Marley replied. "I'm sorry, Mike. You know how the political games get played."

"This is someone's life we're talking about," Amanda interrupted. "A man is dead, and he's worried about how it affects his political career?"

"Theodor wanted me to remind you of one thing before you continued," Marley said.

"What's that?" Mike asked.

"That your paychecks come from city hall and that the mayor has the right to dictate police usage," Marley said. "Just draft something quick and send it to Nevaeh, Mike. I'm sorry."

Police Chief Rhoads didn't wait for a response, he just quickly stood up and rushed out of the room, slamming the door behind him. Mike and Amanda sat in a dazed confusion for a moment.

"What did he mean by *police usage*?" Amanda asked.

"That Mayor Kamp can come in and assign officers as he sees fit," Mike said. "That if we don't draft that press release, we'll both be street cops in the lower district of the city."

"Would he really do that?" Amanda asked.

"You've heard the rumors that he's going to run for president, right?"

"I've heard them, yes."

"They are true. Everything he's done for the past ten years has been to gear up for a run at the White House. I know a little of the promises that he's made to people. Chief Rhoads has been promised a high-level security position, provided Ted can campaign on the fact that his city was one of the safest in the country. An unsolved murder doesn't bode well for that campaign."

"Who else is going to be involved?"

"Governor Jones will be his running mate. Since he hasn't remarried since his wife passed away, I believe his daughter Amber will act as First Lady, then as vice president when Governor Jones runs, then a run at the presidency herself."

"That's an awfully long timeline," Amanda said.

"People in power tend to crave more power," Mike replied.

"So, what do we do?"

"We write a press release and send it to Nevaeh."

Amanda stared at Mike. She couldn't believe what she'd just heard. He was caving to the pressure and was suggesting they lie to the press and the population of the city. She wasn't going to let him do it without a fight. "You can't be serious."

"I am," Mike said, sharply. "This is the politics of police work, Amanda. We got our orders and we're going to do them. In the end, I'm sure he's right. This must be something personal. I'm going to draft the release while you look at every business contact Danny had in California. Find out everything you can. After that, we are going to go back to the apartment and questioning everyone in the building again. Someone knows something, and we have to find out what that is."

Amanda nodded as she worked her computer glasses, looking over lists of names that had business dealings with Danny Brown. She instructed the computer to cross-reference every name to any police trouble or criminal record they'd ever received. Amanda didn't like the fact that Mike was writing the press release, but she was glad that her name wasn't going to be on it. If it did turn out to have something to do with the system, Mike would have a false report released to the public in his name.

And that's when it hit her, even if it did have something to do with the system, Mike now had to make it look like it was personal. He had a report out, a report that could be used to destroy him if it proved to be false. The chief and mayor could hold it over his head and take his badge. They set him up for the outcome they wanted. Amanda swallowed in a dry throat as she continued looking into the names on her list.

Chapter #11

A trio of people walked through the Master Control Room in city hall, inspecting every little detail about the system. There was an air of reverence from all the workers, a hushed silence as the trio walked through the room. Everyone knew why. Two of the members of the trio were some of the richest people in the world. Their companies controlled so much, stretched far, and so important to the careers of everyone in the room that no one dared utter so much as a whisper, least of all to hurt their chances of moving up in the company. The two men were aware and accepting of the situation but for the female with them, this was her first exposure to this kind of behavior.

Dr. Jack Hall and Alyssa led Allen Day, founder and CEO of Everyday Computers, through the Master Control Room. Allen was a man unto himself. Towering over everyone else, standing six feet, five inches tall, with a hefty, well-nourished frame, Allen looked almost comical in his Hawaiian shirt and khaki shorts. His shovel-like feet exposed in a pair of cheap flip-flops and his shaved head shining in the dim light. Allen's beard was his trademark though. A black-as-night bushy goatee that formed a point four inches below his chin.

"The Master Control Room turned out better than we'd hoped," Dr. Hall said.

"Magnificent, laddybuck," Allen said, in his jovial voice through his heavy Eastern European accent as he stroked his thick beard. Allen's parents had immigrated to the United States during the third world war when Allen was still young. Although Allen retained the accent and appearance of his former country, he had spent years carefully crafting a public persona that had defined who he was. The image he crafted became his personality. "Saving the world and all. Such a wonderful idea, Jack-old-boy."

"The system has been functioning perfectly," Jack said. "The initial reviews of the system have all been positive and there was an incident this morning, something that could have killed people and destroyed a lot of property that was detected by the system. The system has already saved lives."

"I heard about that," Allen said, with a hearty laugh. "Damn water pumps not getting replaced. Why this town built itself in the path of a yearly flood is damn beyond me. Guess the old boys had a soft spot for the hills. Magnificent though they are, initial reports of the matter suggest that had the pump failed and flooded the town the clean-up costs and damage to property would have been in the hundreds of millions of dollars. Think about that, champ. The first day and this ugly bastard recovered almost half its costs."

"The implications are staggering, Allen," Jack said, calmly.

"The implications are staggering, Allen?" Allen almost yelled as his arms flailed wildly about him. "Laddybuck, look at the big picture here. The biggest sticking point the damn voters have with this system, the cost, has just been neutralized. I've got my top scientists looking into what happened and how everything went down. Reports will be filed. The world will know, champ. No one can piss and moan about the damn costs again."

"That issue has been simplified."

"There's just no getting you excited about this system, is there?" Allen asked.

"Come on, Allen," Jack said, walking toward the Main Control Room, "you have to see what we did in here."

Allen laughed as he shook his head and followed Jack and Alyssa into the Main Control Room. The main room was empty. The large screen on the wall was set to a video feed of a busy park. Dozens of people were rollerblading, skateboarding, and jogging on the paths and trails in the popular park. Jack sat in the large chair in the middle of the room while Allen and Alyssa sat in the chairs flanking him.

"You haven't introduced me to Elvira yet," Allen said, looking at Alyssa. "She looks like a real pistol, Jack. What's her role in this game of ours?"

"Where are my manners?" Jack asked himself. "I got so caught up in showing you the newest setups I completely forgot to introduce you two. Allen, this is Alyssa Babbage, a computer engineer replacing Danny. Alyssa, this is Allen Day, CEO of Everyday Computers."

"A pleasure to meet you," Alyssa said, standing and extending her hand to shake Allen's.

"A pleasure indeed," Allen said, as he stood and hugged Alyssa. He pulled back as Alyssa had a very confused look on her face. "A hug is more personal my dear. Can't know a man or woman from a damn handshake. Now a hug, on the other hand, that tells you something."

"What did it tell you about me?" Alyssa asked as they returned to their seats.

"That you know what you want and damned be the fool who tries to stand in your way,"

"Lovely," Alyssa said, with a smile.

"You've got an energy about you, dear. Very captivating," Allen said, before turning his attention back to Jack. "Now see here, champ, we need to spread the word far and wide about what this system did. Everyone needs to know about our success. Think about it, Jack, soon the world will run on Everyday Computers and be powered by Madison Labs Software."

"Um," Jack stuttered. "The system will be popular."

"Can you believe this guy?" Allen asked Alyssa. "Think about it, dearest. Cities around the world are going to be lining up to have us install systems for them. They will be tripping over themselves to be the next city to have the system. Mass migration will happen. Cities without the system will become ghost towns, dying relics of a forgotten past. We will need regional command centers to control it all. A master control center that will house the largest computers ever imagined. Thousands of workers. Think of the money involved Jack. You have no idea the money we are talking about."

"I'm just here for the science of it all, Allen," Jack said. "I've always been here for the science. To improve mankind."

"I'm talking multi-billion-dollar a year contracts for software and hardware," Allen said, rubbing his hands together. "For at least fifty years into the future. Then add to that the repairs, upgrades, and monitoring services. Hell, we'll have enough money to get the damn anti-trust lawyers off our backs, if this plan with Mayor Kamp here doesn't fully pan out."

"What plan with Mayor Kamp?" Alyssa asked.

"Laddybuck here made a wise decision even if he won't admit it," Allen said. "Mayor Kamp is going to run for president on the platform of being a technical innovator. That's why he needs this system to work. Once he's president, do you really think he's going to persecute the company that got him there? He'll make sure we don't get singled out by the damned government again."

"That's not why I picked Winter Falls," Jack said. "This location..."

"Say what he wants," Allen said. "I know the truth of it even if he won't admit it."

Before Jack could protest, the door opened and a young man around twenty-five entered the room. Although he didn't have the considerable height of Allen, it was obvious from the face they were father and son. The man was tall though, over six feet, and had a powerful body that projected his muscle even through his custom-made, three-piece, black suit. A sinister looking face, with obsidian black eyes and a perfectly trimmed black goatee. His hair was black and slicked back. He wore gold rings on his fingers and a custom gold watch on his left wrist.

"Ah," Allen said, jumping up and walking over to the man, "here's a laddybuck who knows the value of power." Allen put his son in a headlock and ruffed up his hair as the boy tried to push his father off. "Just look at that face, Jack. This ace will be running the show before we know it. He and the First Lady there."

"Allen," the man said, sharply.

"Don't be shy, ace," Allen said, releasing his hold on the man as the man quickly fixed his hair with a pocket comb. "At your age, I was the same way. Find the richest, cutest little thing you can and sow your wild oats while you can."

"Alyssa," Jack said, before the man could respond to his father. "This is Adam Day, Allen's son. He's romantically involved with Amber Kamp, the mayor's daughter."

"Romantically involved!" Allen shouted, his arms flailing. "They're knocking boots like a pair of champs." Adam's face turned a shade of deep red. "Don't be embarrassed about it, boy. She's a stunning catch and a looker to boot. They went on a 'business trip' together about a month ago. Yeah, ace, I've been on a few 'business trips' before in my day. Hey, Jack, remember when we got our first major contract over in Europe and we were at that brothel in Austria?"

"It wasn't a brothel," Jack said, quickly. "It was the campus of an all-girls university."

"Same thing," Allen smiled. "I tell you what, I loved business trips after that...until I met your mother of course. Only woman who could tame me. Jack here was like normal, all business."

"We had work to do," Jack said. "We have so much work to do."

"No man on his deathbed reflected on his life and thought that he should have been at work more, champ," Allen said. "This isn't healthy for you Jack, in all seriousness. You need to loosen up a little and have some fun. You're working yourself into an early grave instead of living a magnificent life like mine."

"You're the one who is looking at controlling the world with these systems," Jack said. "You know the number of hours of work we are going to have to put in to accomplish what you are asking for?"

"I have it under control," Allen said. "I delegate. I have other people handle stuff. I only handle the running of the company, I'm not designing computers every day anymore. You've got ace here running some of your company now, Jack. When he's not shacking up with Amber."

"Allen," Adam snapped. "I was looking for you. There's a conference call that you and I need to take together. Investor relations and all. You told them you would speak to them today and they are getting impatient."

"Here's another one that's too serious when it comes to life," Allen said, standing. "Might be why the will was changed...very well. If we have to take the call let's move to one of the conference rooms upstairs so we aren't bothering anyone. Alyssa, it was nice meeting you. Jack, you should bring Alyssa to the party tonight. You two would make a magnificent couple."

Allen gave a big wave goodbye and left the room with Adam a pace behind him. Both Jack and Alyssa were blushing from the comment Allen had made. Jack couldn't keep his eyes off Alyssa and she had been eyeing him up and down a few times as well.

"He seems nice," Alyssa said. "Has he always been like that?"

"Always," Jack said. "You put him in a room full of strangers and within five minutes he will be controlling the room. It's his nature. Very outgoing and outspoken."

"He doesn't seem to filter what he says," Alyssa said.

"That he doesn't. His mouth has gotten him into trouble more than once, but he never learns. What do you think of our facilities so far, Alyssa?"

"Lovely. I really like what I am seeing here. The people are so nice as well."

"Allen's been my friend for a long time Alyssa but all he can see is the money. I'm not in this for the money. I dread his new projects. The software that we need to create for the nanobots alone are taking more time than I ever thought we would need and if they ever crack the code on his Quantum Computers, then look out, every piece of software ever written would be instantly obsolete."

"Nanobots?"

"Tiny little robots that can perform a specific function," Jack said. "They can be made to make a perfect replica of a hand or a leg, can replace a weak heart or destroyed liver. Nanobots can be used to create almost anything, in theory, that is. They haven't done a lot of experimenting with them yet, government oversight and all. Allen thinks that when Mayor Kamp is president he will allow them to do all the research that they want."

"You don't sound like you agree with it."

"I don't want to live forever," Jack said. "I just want to enjoy my life."

"What do you do for enjoyment?"

"Lately? Nothing. I've been so busy that I simply don't have time for anything. I guess playing chess with Seth is fun. Having conversations with him. But there needs to be more to life than chess with a computer."

"You could play chess with me sometime?" Alyssa asked sheepishly.

Jack turned his chair to look at Alyssa. "What do you mean?"

"I do have a confession to make to you, Dr. Hall. But you must promise me something first."

"What's that?"

"Promise you won't get mad at what I'm about to tell you."

"Okay," Jack said, confused. "I promise."

"I know who you are," Alyssa said. "Well, I know you as well as I can through every book that you wrote or has been written about you. I've watched all the documentary's that have been made about you. I've watched every interview you've ever given."

"What? Why?"

"It started as a love of computers and science," Alyssa said. "Ever since I first became aware of myself and my surroundings I've had a deep interest in the computer fields and there is no one bigger in that field than you are. I've dreamed of meeting you, working with you. I did all my thesis work on your ideas. I've followed your career for a long time.

"When I received notification that there was a position open and that I was being considered to work for you, I could hardly contain myself. You have no idea how nervous I was in that meeting room this morning. All my life had been building up to meet you, work with you, and here I finally am. I realize that I sound a bit obsessive, but my passion is computers, and you are computers. I've followed your career so much that I feel like I know you. Please, Dr. Hall, Allen said you should escort me to the party tonight. I would be ever so happy if you did. We would have a lovely time together."

Dr. Hall sat stunned at what he'd just heard. In front of him was the woman that he'd dreamed about. Smart, fun, knowledgeable about the world, and beautiful to boot. He couldn't have designed someone better. And here she was, offering herself to him. Jack didn't know how to play it. This seemed to go against all the advice anyone had ever given him about dating and women. Jack was about to respond when a thought crossed his mind. Although it hadn't happened in a long time, they always had to keep a watch out for competitors sneaking a worker into their ranks. Someone might have known and used his taste in women and faked documents to get Alyssa in. Even with the thought of that, Jack knew he couldn't take being alone much longer.

"I don't know if I'm even going to the party," Jack said. "I told Dr. Porter she'd be giving a speech on my behalf, she's better with the politicians anyway. And I'm sure Jerry and Ted will be at each other's throats the entire night like they always are. It just isn't something that I want to attend."

"We could have supper together then," Alyssa said. "Alone."

"That could work," Jack said. "I have some frozen pizza in my bunker. I could cook that up and we could chat."

"You don't entertain women often, do you?"

"I'm afraid not."

"Tell you what," Alyssa said. "I'll pick a lovely place for us to go tonight. We'll both get dressed up and have a great meal with even better conversation."

"I like that."

Jack smiled as he turned the chair back toward the main screen. He could hardly believe that Alyssa was interested in him, let alone enough to set up the first date. Jack swallowed though, realizing that it had been almost ten years since his last first date, and that one didn't go well at all. Alyssa told him to dress up, he didn't know what she meant by that. He hoped he could hold her interest in conversation. Jack realized that there was more pressure with this date than there was in monitoring the system. With thoughts of his date flooding his mind, Jack tried to focus on his work but knew that it was going to be a long day.

Chapter #12

As the sun began to dip past the hills to the west of Winter Falls, the brilliance of the downtown skyline began to light up. The sun on the hills cast yellows, oranges, blues, and pinks as the yellow and white lights that illuminated the skyline began to cast their glow over the city. One building, to the east of the skyline, on a massive and sprawling campus adjacent to the river, seemed to have more twinkling lights and flashing signs than all the other buildings combined. The campus seemed to have more people about than anywhere else also. It was the Winter Casino and Entertainment Gallery.

Gaming buildings, hotels, theaters, stages, and arenas were linked together with skyways that crisscrossed around massive parking garages. Lines of cars from all directions were making their way to the casino as boats passed up and down the river. There were people everywhere on the campus, no matter where you looked, this place was the happening spot to be on an evening in Winter Falls. Loud, ruckus people were preparing to spend hard earned money on the chance of winning big.

Inside the main gaming room was controlled chaos. The noise of the machines and their incessant flashing of lights made people feel like they were part of something big. Cheering and crying could be heard all around the circular gaming floor. Toward the north end of the building, the scene was quieter but intense none the less as table after table of games spread out on the floor. Blackjack, poker, craps, roulette, and other assortments of gaming tables were beginning to be packed with people.

At one table, a single man sat playing blackjack. He had been rude and uncouth, practically chasing the other players away so he could have the table by himself. The dealer, a stout man in his fifties allowed the actions only because the man was known to be a very good tipper. As the dealer got ready to deal the next hand, Gavin Rodgers placed his $1,000 bet.

"Give me some good cards this time," Gavin said, as the dealer finished his shuffle.

"Can I get you anything?" a bubbly waitress asked, placing her hand on Gavin's shoulder.

"Whiskey cola and a dealer who knows how to shuffle," Gavin said, as the card was dealt. "Come on, damn it."

Gavin looks at his cards. He has two eights while the dealer has a six facing up and one card facing down.

"Split."

Gavin pushed his eights apart as he pushed up another $1,000 dollars. The dealer nodded and dealt two more cards, a two and a three.

"Jesus. You just can't make this easy, can you?"

"Ten and eleven, Gavin," the dealer said. "What do you want to do with them?"

"Get a damn win would be nice," Gavin said.

"Here's your drink, sir," the waitress said handing Gavin a glass.

"Keep this for yourself, doll," Gavin said, tossing her a $10 chip.

"Any thoughts on the hand, Gavin?" the dealer asked.

"Don't push me, buddy," Gavin shot back. "I can take my sweet time at this. You've been pushing me all night and it's screwing up my rhythm."

Gavin took a big swig from his drink, "God, I hate weak whiskey. Figures that bimbo used the cheap shit."

"What do you want to do with your cards, Gavin?"

"Don't rush me," Gavin almost yelled. "I need to think."

Gavin looked at his cards for a solid minute, forcing the dealer to stand in silence while he debated what he was going to do. A ten and eleven versus a six. Gavin had already lost a lot of money on cards tonight, hadn't even had any kind of winning streak, and was starting to feel the effects of the four whiskeys he'd already drank.

"Screw it," Gavin said, pushing up more money. "Double down on both hands."

The dealer's eyes got wide as Gavin stacked his chips on the table. He now had four thousand dollars riding on the flip of his next two cards. The dealer swallowed in a dry throat as he turned over the next two cards; a two and a five. Gavin threw his hands in the air.

"Son-of-a-bitch," Gavin said. "Are you Goddamn kidding me? Bust, damn you. I want your hand to be a bust bigger than your easy sister's."

The dealer glared at Gavin as he flipped over his face down card; a five. The dealer took another card from the pile, flipping over a jack. Gavin screamed out.

"Twenty-one," the dealer said. "Dealer wins."

The dealer started to take Gavin's money as Gavin slammed the table with his fist causing chips to scatter across the table.

"Just calm down, sir," the dealer said.

"Don't tell me to call down," Gavin shouted. "I've dropped twenty grand on this table tonight and haven't seen a winning hand anywhere. You must be cheating me. You are a crook just like this crooked casino. I want my money back, you thief."

"SECURITY!" the dealer called out as he activated a call button on the table. "I need security here."

"There's no reason for that," Gavin said, putting his hands up in an apologetic manner. "No reason to get them involved."

Before the dealer could respond, two security guards approached the table. Both were big and muscular, wearing black pants and black tee shirts that had 'SECURITY' written across the chest in yellow letters. Both men were bald with goatees and wore mirrored sunglasses. Gavin swallowed as he looked at them towering over him.

"Fellas," Gavin said. "I was just joking around. Ya know, all part of the excitement of the game. How 'bout you boys go over and make sure there are no minors in that cute bachelorette party."

"How 'bout you come with us, sir," one of the guards demanded.

"Piss off," Gavin said, as he waved the men off.

The guards wasted no time. Each one grabbed one of Gavin's arms and dragged him out of his chair, knocking the chair over as they pulled him away. Gavin started kicking his leg, screaming to be let go but one of the guards dropped him hard on the floor, twisting his arm into a painful lock, lifting him by the locked arm as the other guard grabbed his legs and stopped him from kicking.

"You're hurting me!" Gavin screamed out. "He's gonna break my arm! Someone, please help me!"

No one went to help Gavin. The crowd looked up from their games just long enough to see what the yelling was about before they returned to their drinks and games as Gavin was pulled into the back of the casino.

Through the back hallways of the casino, Gavin tried to struggle with the security guards. The hallways and carpets in the back area were a plush, deep crimson color with dim lighting. There were no decorations on the walls, just lights above them. Gavin struggled with the guards even though one of them could have easily held him down.

The guards turned a corner, passing doorways before they came to a door that was partially open. They walked through it as the rear guard kicked the door shut with his foot. The pair dropped Gavin onto the floor. Gavin stood up and adjusted his suit as he tried to massage his arm that had been twisted by the guard. Gavin watched as the guards smiled before leaving the room.

"Where do you think you're going?" Gavin asked.

"I've been waiting for this for a long time," a deep, female voice said, from behind Gavin.

Gavin spun around on a heel, taking in the room in a quick glance. The room was ten by ten, with nothing in it except the woman who'd spoken to him. Gavin knew her instantly, Cassie North, the Winter Casino head of security. Cassie was a rough and tough no-nonsense lady in her mid-forties. She was from Southeast Asia originally, coming to America for the position at the casino after working in casinos all over the world.

Gavin stared at Cassie. He knew that he was in trouble, but he wasn't sure how bad it would be. He'd been in this room before, but he always had the money to buy his way out of trouble. Tonight, he wasn't sure though. He was supposed to be at the party at the city hall but figured that a few hands of blackjack couldn't hurt. That had been three hours ago. The party was surely well underway, and his work associates would be wondering where he was.

Gavin couldn't help but notice that Cassie was wearing bulky black gloves with her black security uniform. He swallowed, knowing they were weighted gloves.

Weighted to increase the pain from a hit but padded on both sides as to not damage the skin. Gavin knew what those gloves were for.

"Cassie," Gavin said, starting to stand. "I'm sorry about..."

Cassie cut him off by quickly cutting the distance between them and drilling Gavin with a right hook that connected squarely with his jaw. Gavin screamed in pain as he hit the ground. Gavin rubbed his jaw as Cassie smiled, moving a step back and away from him. Gavin quickly scrambled to his feet and acted like he was going to rush Cassie, but he stopped dead in his tracks when she pulled the night-stick she had clipped to the back of her tights. Cassie cocked her arm back ready to blast Gavin.

"Don't make me do it, Gavin," Cassie said. "I'll scramble your brains this time. We are done with you. When Mr. Timm gets here you are in serious trouble this time, pal. You knew what the rules were, and you still flaunt them in our faces...after we were so nice to you and all."

"Oh, please," Gavin begged getting onto his knees. "Don't bring Mr. Timm here. You and I can work this out, Cassie. I'm sure you can come up with something for me. Mr. Timm doesn't need to know about this incident."

"He's on his way, Gavin," Cassie said, lowering her arm. "And he's not happy. We were watching you since you walked into the casino tonight. You have a lot of explaining to do."

Gavin inched toward Cassie on his knees. "I'll do anything for you."

Before Cassie could respond the door swung open and a short, wiry man walked in. A wide smile across a rat-like face underneath a mop of slicked, greasy black hair filled Gavin's field of vision as the man bent down to stick his face right in Gavin's. Cassie closed the door and stood in front of it, making sure no one could enter. The man just stared at Gavin, making Gavin more uncomfortable.

"Please, forgive me," Gavin shouted when the tension of the room became unbearable.

The rat-faced man swung and clobbered Gavin on the side of the head, causing Gavin to fall into a pile on the floor, crying.

"Mr. Gavin," the man said. "What did I tell you about coming in here?"

"Please, Mr. Timm," Gavin begged through his tears. "I have your money, sir. I promise."

"I told you no more gambling until your debts were paid," Mr. Timm said, as he kicked Gavin on the floor. "I said don't come into my casino until you have one hundred thousand dollars to pay your debts. But now my floor manager tells me you lost twenty thousand dollars on blackjack? Gavin, this is unacceptable. Cassie, search him."

"With pleasure." Cassie clipped the night-stick to her tights and dropped down on the floor, starting to run her hands over Gavin. Gavin started to fight her, started to resist, causing Cassie to quickly tag him in the head with the weighted glove before getting on top of him. Gavin was seeing stars as Cassie finished the search, discovering the other $30,000 dollars in cash Gavin had in his suit coat. Cassie handed the money to Mr. Timm.

"You walk into my casino with $50,000?" Mr. Timm yelled, "Not coming directly to me to pay your debt? You start gambling with this money? Cassie, stick him."

Cassie wasted no time grabbing the night-stick and whacking Gavin a few times in the stomach and back. Gavin howled in pain, trying to cover up. Pain shot through Gavin's body with every blow. He tried to stand, but Mr.

Timm would kick him to the ground, allowing Cassie to get more shots in.

"That's enough," Mr. Timm said.

"Please," Gavin begged. "Mr. Timm, hear me out. Let's play a game. Me and you, one on one. You can pick. If I win, my debt is wiped out. If you win, I owe you double. You can't lose."

"Unless I lose," Mr. Timm snapped. "What do you take me for Gavin? A pathetic rube like you? You see, Gavin, you are my favorite type of customer. You have access to a lot of money and you spend that money here. Even when you win, you can't stop playing. You always give it all back to the house. I have to maintain a balancing act though. Once you run out of money, I have to front you just enough to make my books look amazing while not floating you more than you can afford. I know you can get my money, Gavin. You walked in here with fifty thousand dollars. You can get my hundred grand." Mr. Timm pulled a couple thousand dollars out of the stacks Cassie took from Gavin's coat and handed the money to Cassie. "For your trouble in this, Cassie."

"Thank you, sir," Cassie said, as she stuffed the hundred-dollar bills between her breasts. "Want me to get the others and take Gavin out back?"

"Oh, please God, no," Gavin begged. "Not out back with them. Please, no."

"No," Mr. Timm said. "I'm giving you one final option to get my money, Gavin. You have forty-eight hours to come up with $125,000. Consider that interest and penalties. I'm keeping the rest of this, I'll just say I found it floating around. Forty-eight hours or we come after you, Gavin."

"Then kill me now," Gavin said.

"You didn't let me finish," Mr. Timm said. "Once we've taken care of you, I'm sure you'll want us to look after your dear old mother."

"You wouldn't," Gavin shouted.

"But I would," Mr. Timm said. "It's only business, Gavin. When you gamble you have to be prepared to lose. It's the nature of the game. I just wonder where all this money you keep getting comes from. I know your salary, have seen your credit score. Where does it come from, Gavin?"

"We could work something out, Mr. Timm," Gavin said. "I have access to the city's new computer system. There are competitors who are willing to pay millions for that information. Think about it."

"Get me my money, then we'll talk," Mr. Timm said. "If I don't have my money in forty-eight hours then there's nothing to talk about. Always remember, Gavin, never trust a gambling addict. You never know who they'll sell out to get what they want. Cassie, give him one for the road."

"Gladly," Cassie said, with a smile.

Cassie used her weighted gloves to pepper Gavin with shots to the head and body. He screamed in pain as Mr. Timm sadistically looked on. When the pair stopped, Gavin's body was throbbing with pain. Shooting pain running over every inch of his body. Mr. Timm and Cassie left the room as Gavin stayed on the floor, crying, trying to figure out how he could come up with that amount of money.

Chapter #13

The front of Winter Falls City Hall was lit for a party. Massive searchlights were projected into the air, moving about, signaling the event. Twinkling lights hung from the eaves of the building, flowing down in a brilliance of silvers, reds, blues, and golds. Outside the steps of the hall, polished stretch limousines waited their turn to drop off the very important people they were carrying. Around the entrance to the hall, paparazzi stood, taking hundreds of pictures of all the people going in to the party. Newsfeed reporters were trying to get interviews as the people entering the hall gently waved while walking up the stairs.

At the top of the stairs and to the left, Jerry Bosen stood in a loose and relaxed position, his sunglasses on, taking in all the hubbub of the event. He was in his black shirt and pants, like he always wore, just waiting for Nevaeh to arrive. Nevaeh instantly caught Jerry's eye when she walked between to limos, flashing her invitation to the guards, and walking up the stairs. She looked beyond stunning in a tight black strapless dress, six-inch heels, and her hair styled so part of it was stack up, the other part framing her alluring, feminine face, in a design that looked to have taken at least an hour to complete.

Nevaeh noticed Jerry on the top of the platform and slowly, seductively, walked over to him. Jerry just smiled as she made her way to him. When she got to him, Jerry reached his hand out, took hers, and gave her a slight twirl, so he could see her entire outfit, front and back. Jerry pulled her close and gave Nevaeh a kiss on the cheek.

"So, it is a date," Nevaeh said.

"I never said that," Jerry replied.

"You look nice tonight," Nevaeh said, looking over Jerry's outfit.

"I always look nice...come on, let's get inside."

Jerry put his arm around Nevaeh's waist and led her into the building, both of them showing their invitations to the security at the entrance doors to the building. Inside, they were directed to the master gallery, a large meeting hall that looked more like a museum with all the paintings, bust reliefs, and statues lining the walls. The room was domed, with intricate carvings in the mock stone ceiling. Over two hundred people were mingling about, all in tuxedos and ball gowns, as a twelve-piece string band played on the stage at the head of the room.

To the left were tables lined with foods of all kinds. Workers were busy making sure all the food bins were full to the top, no matter how many people were taking the stuffed shrimp, beef medallions, caviar, and other assortments of fine, rich food. At the other wall was a massive bar setup with any kind of drink a person could imagine. Servers were walking around with trays full of champagne, one stopping to offer glasses to Jerry and Nevaeh.

"I'd love one," Nevaeh said, as Jerry took one and handed it to her.

"Not for me," Jerry said.

"Don't drink?" Nevaeh asked as the server walked away.

"Not champagne. I'll get something real in a moment."

"Can I bring you a drink, sir?" a waitress asked, overhearing the conversation.

"We'll each take a shot of your highest shelf vodka then I'll need a Tom Collins please."

"Very good selection, sir," the waitress said. "Anything else for you, ma'am?"

"This is good for now," Nevaeh said, sipping her champagne.

"Decent turnout to this shindig," Jerry said. "All of Winter Falls' political scene is here, not to mention a lot of the top dogs from Everyday Computers and Madison Software Labs."

"And I'm the only reporter on the inside," Nevaeh said, with a grin. "Thank you so much for inviting me."

"Think nothing of it, Vaeh," Jerry said.

"Vaeh?" Nevaeh asked. "No one has called me that before."

"So, I'm your first?" Jerry asked with a sly grin.

Before Nevaeh could answer, the waitress came back with the drinks. Jerry and Nevaeh toasted their shot glasses before downing the vodka in a single gulp. Nevaeh winced heavily at the strong drink, but Jerry didn't even flinch. He just took a sip of his drink as he put his arm back around Nevaeh's waist after tipping the waitress.

"You have a taste for the finer drinks," Nevaeh said. "You've got some experience with it."

"When you work on math formulas all day you have to," Jerry replied. "You don't seem to have much experience with it though."

"As much as you get drinking cheap beer and wine coolers in college," Nevaeh said.

"There's the rest of our group," Jerry said. "Come on."

Jerry and Nevaeh walked up to the group in deep conversation. In the group was Mayor Kamp, Dr. Porter, and Allen Day. Ted was in a fine tuxedo and Holly in a stunning, sparkly blue ball gown, while Allen was in his same outfit from the morning; the Hawaiian shirt and the khaki shorts. They all smiled when Jerry and Nevaeh approached, all except the mayor.

"Jerry, you came," Ted said. "How disappointing."

"Wonderful party you're throwing Teddy," Jerry smiled, toasting his glass to the mayor. "You remember Nevaeh from yesterday, correct?"

"Of course," Ted said. "Enjoying the party, Nevaeh?"

"It's totally wonderful, sir," Nevaeh said, before noticing who was in the group. "My gosh, you're Allen Day."

"That's what my underwear says," Allen said, with a hearty laugh.

"I'm sorry," Nevaeh said. "I've done a number of stories on your company for the newsfeed. It's an honor to meet you."

"Honor's all mine, dearest," Allen said, as he took Nevaeh's hand and kissed the back of it. "So long as they were good stories."

"They were about your work into nanobots," Nevaeh said. "Too bad I couldn't get much information from anyone. You've kept those projects tightlipped."

"For good reason," Allen said, before addressing Jerry. "Laddy, you didn't tell me you were bringing such an intelligent partner to the party. Tell you what, dearest. I've got Jerry's number and I'm sure he has yours. When I'm ready to get a story out I'll get into contact with you and give you the exclusive."

"Oh my God," Nevaeh exclaimed. "Thank you so much, sir."

"Sir," Allen said, laughing. "She called me sir. Hear that, Mayor? I told you Bosen here has good taste in women."

"Charming," Ted said, as he noticed someone was approaching the group.

Ted looked to see his daughter Amber walking toward them, in her stunning red party dress, being escorted by Adam Day. Amber was a lean girl, with a face of stone seriousness. One look at her told you she was all business. The back of her short golden-brown hair was held in a tight braid while the front bangs were stacked and styled. Her tight, low cut dress showed off her prodigious body. She approached the group, began to address her father only, but he spoke before she got the chance.

"Everybody," Ted said. "You remember my daughter, Amber. She's got a contract position at Everyday Computers now and when she's finished with that she's got a contract with Madison Software Labs...Jerry, eyes on me please."

"Hey, Teddy, I got a date tonight," Jerry said.

"So, this is a date," Nevaeh smiled as she gave Jerry a nudge.

"I never said that," Jerry said. "You're misquoting me. Slander, I call slander."

Jerry and Allen laughed heartily at his joke while Nevaeh blushed.

"Work demands my attention, Father," Amber said, ignoring the rest of them. "I'm sorry, but I must leave the party for a moment. Something came up that I must handle."

"Something for work, doll?" Allen said. "Let someone else handle it. You're young. You and ace over there should be enjoying this party. Getting her enough liquor, son?"

"You really should stick around here, Amber," Ted said, trying not to glare at Allen. "There are going to be some very important people showing up later who I want you and Adam to meet."

"I understand, Father," Amber said. "I will attempt to return as swiftly as I can. This is a delicate situation and I need to prove myself adept at these types of circumstances. I want to do this. I just wanted to let you know that I would be leaving for a moment."

"Ace going with you?" Allen laughed. "Yeah, yeah. I'm sure something *very important* came up, if ya get my drift. She's going to handle it all right. Good for you, laddybuck."

"Allen!" Ted snapped. "That's my daughter you're talking about."

"Lighten up, champ," Allen laughed. "It's a party. They're young, drunk, and in love."

"Allen," Adam said, in a harsh voice. "This is serious. Everything is a joke to you, isn't it? The whole world's just one big Goddamn joke. You're the richest fool in the room so you can say whatever you want, and everyone has to laugh along with your jokes. And my name is Adam. Not sport, champ, ace, laddybuck, or any other stupid designation you can come up with."

There was a moment of tension. No one knew what to say. Jerry had heard before that there was some trouble between Allen and Adam, but he didn't know whether to believe it or not. Allen's jovial nature often crossed the line, but most let it slide, knowing that he was only playing around.

"Perhaps it's been a long day and the stresses of more drudgery have us all on edge," Amber said, ever the diplomat. "Allen, I assure you that Adam and I have real obligations to meet. Father, please don't take Allen's jokes personally, I'm an adult woman and can enter into relationships of my choosing."

"No harm, no foul," Ted said. "I guess I still view you as my little girl."

"I did want to alert you, Father," Amber continued, "Governor Jones has arrived. He's expecting a private meeting with you to discuss some matters before enjoying the party at large."

"Of course," Ted said. "Thank you, dear. Everyone, if you'll excuse me, I need to meet with Chad."

Mayor Kamp took off in one direction while Amber and Adam walked toward the exits. Allen watched his son walk away with a tinge of sadness in his eye, like a child who'd been scolded and had their favorite toy taken away. When Allen was sure Ted was out of earshot, he said, "If I were Adam, I'd be proud of how she planned to handle the situation. He keeps wondering why he was written out of my will and removed from the company...we just don't get along. I don't understand it. Jack took him in and gave him a good job, so hopefully, he sees the error of how he acted toward me."

"So, he's really going to run for president," Nevaeh asked, quickly changing the subject.

"I hope to hell so," Allen said. "He's got my support. Both vocally and with my wallet."

"That's going to be one heck of a war chest to compete against," Jerry said. "His opponents don't stand a chance. Too bad he doesn't have a good idea left in his head."

"You really don't like him, do you?" Allen asked.

"What gave that away?" Jerry asked. "It's not that I don't like him. On a personal level, I think he's a good man. At least he believes in something and believes in what he says. He had a rough hand dealt to him. His wife passed when Amber was thirteen years old and he had to raise her on his own. She appears to have done well for herself. What I don't like about him is that he gets bad information and does nothing to verify the information he's using."

"Again, with the criticism of our system," Holly said.

"I'll always criticize the system, Holly," Jerry said. "Someone needs to. Here's the big issue...the overriding one anyway. People don't need to think anymore. No one has to use logic or reason to maintain their daily lives. The brain is like a muscle, you stop working it and it weakens, gets soft. Studies have proven that without constant exercise of the brain, mind function decreases and it's almost impossible to get it going again."

"You'd have us in the Stone-Age then?" Allen asked.

"Think about it," Jerry said, with a smile. "You'd like the Stone-Age Allen. People spent about ten hours a week cleaning and maintaining their dwelling and hunting and preparing food. That's it. Ten hours a week. They spent the other hundred and fifty-eight hours playing, learning, exploring, and having wild caveman sex. None of this nine-to-five, rat-race bullshit. But in all seriousness, computers are wonderful tools. But that's all they should be; tools. They should supplement and compliment, not control and dominate."

"You've carved out quite a niche writing books and creating websites speaking out against it, Jerry," Allen said.

"Someone has to provide a counterpoint," Jerry said. "If there was a counterpoint we could have avoided the third world war and all the horror that went with it."

"So, you think this system is going to fail?" Nevaeh asked. "Why?"

"There are many ways this system could fail," Jerry said. "The short-term answer is that it will fail because it's simply too large for any group of humans to control. Look at it in terms of government. When we were all small bands of nomads, or maybe cave dwellers, there were only a couple hundred in a tribe. It was easy to govern because, for the most part, everyone is in the same position and wants the same things. As we moved into cities it became slightly harder because of the diversity of the group. Group a few cities into a county and there are more problems. By the time you get to state and federal levels it turns into a nightmare where only certain people are getting the advantages meant for the entire group.

"This system is the same thing. There are far too many variables for the system to maintain stability. In my report, I documented the four main ways the system could fail. First, is communication breakdowns between systems. System A needs power for item A and system B needs power for item B. The system has no good way of deciding which is truly needed, so it splits the power and both systems fail due to lack of power.

"The second fail point is hardware. This is not a dig at Allen and his company, but the fact that there's so much hardware involved in the system. A failure at a critical point could tip the system into instability. Like, say in the water supply or power. Think what would happen if the power grid failed because of a faulty router. The entire grid would go down and the system, controlling everything, would be gone.

"The third way is software and programming. The computer wrote some of its own programs and I guarantee there will be problems because of it. It's impossible for the amount of coding and software to not have bugs, bugs that could manifest days or years down the road.

"The fourth possible failure is the one I'm predicting will happen though. It's the most accurate prediction I'll ever make in my life. This system will fail due to sabotage. There are other methods of failure but those are the main ways."

"Sabotage," Allen scoffed. "Laddy, why would anyone want to sabotage this system?"

"That's the way of it," Jerry said. "I'll bet you a thousand dollars right now that someone is trying to gather intelligence on this system."

"It can't be done," Allen said. "I'll take your bet."

"Do you realize that there are three waitresses here tonight who are members of the Neo-Luddites?" Jerry asked. "Breeze Flynn is right over there."

The group looked to where Jerry was pointing, and they instantly noticed her in a waitress costume. Her normally bald head was covered with a black wig, and she wore an abundance of makeup, but Allen and Holly could tell who it was.

"I'll be damned," Allen said. "Laddybuck, you've got a sharp eye on you. I still wish I could hire you to help me run my company. You don't know the money I'd be willing to pay you. I guess I have to pay you a grand now, sport."

"He's offered you a job and you turned him down?" Nevaeh asked.

"Many times," Jerry said. "I've got my own work to do."

"Please," Holly said. "Let's not argue all night. Let's get some drinks."

"I like the sound of that, lass," Allen said. "But what about the Neo-Luddites?"

"They are just gathering information," Jerry said. "We'll alert security and I'll take a scan around and see if I find any more of them hanging about."

"Eyes up, laddybuck," Allen said. "Use caution with those people."

"I'm always cautious with women," Jerry nodded as he and Nevaeh walked away.

"I don't like how close he's getting to that reporter," Allen said. "If something did happen, which I doubt, she could have it on the newsfeed before we have control of the situation."

"Allen," Holly said, with a grin, "Jerry's only looking to get another notch on his bedpost."

Allen looked back at her with a grin, "Honey, his bed post was notched down to a toothpick before he was out of university."

"Get you drinks?" a waitress walked up and asked them; Breeze Flynn, staring at Allen.

"Glass of Merlot please," Holly said.

"Double shot of your finest Caribbean rum and a bottle of your darkest German beer."

"Very good," Breeze said, taking off.

"Interesting combination," Holly said.

"If this is a party," Allen said, with a smile, "then let's have a party."

Allen watched Breeze walk away. He couldn't believe that with all the security of the party, she was able to get inside. He couldn't help but notice the nametag on her uniform said her name was 'Whisper,' a code name she'd been known to use before. Allen was confident that Jerry would do the right thing tonight, even if he was ticked that Jerry made the bet with him. As Breeze returned with the drinks, Allen decided that he was determined to enjoy himself tonight, no matter who was at the party with him.

Chapter #14

The Waterfront Promenade was always magical on summer nights in Winter Falls. A network of bars, clubs, and restaurants lining the waterfront that lit up in the night with the help of neon and trick lighting. The entire front had been restored and remodeled to look like the original, historic waterfront that had been used for early commerce on the river. There were no wheat mills or lumber yards, no livestock gates, or fires of industry, just the finest dining and entertainment in the upper Midwest. The crown jewel of the Waterfront Promenade was the newly opened Seasons Steak House.

Opened by one of the top beef chefs in the world, with meat sourced locally, from the grassy plains to the west of Winter Falls, Seasons Steakhouse was built on the main floor of one of the oldest buildings on the waterfront. Inside, the restaurant was kept in a dim glow from lights mounted on the wall. The interior was modeled to resemble a steakhouse or saloon in the old west with knotty pine on the walls and floors, the distinct smell of beef cooking over an open fire, and a player piano wailing in one of the corners.

In a back corner of the serving floor, away from the prying eyes of most of the patrons enjoying their massive steaks and baked potatoes, a couple on their first date were just finishing their meal.

"Can I take those plates from you, love?" a waitress asked Alyssa.

"Yes please," Alyssa replied as the waitress cleared the table. "The food was lovely."

"Did we save room for dessert?"

"I think we'll split a piece of the chocolate ice cake," Jack said. "Everything was so good here tonight. Thank you."

"Excellent choice, sir," the waitress said. "Need a refill on those drinks?"

"I'll take another glass of wine," Alyssa said.

"I could go for another cola," Jack replied.

"Back in a minute, sugar," the waitress said, as she took off.

Jack looked around the restaurant, taking all the décor and trinkets that were mounted on the walls and ceiling. It was an interesting look. Something that felt true to what was trying to be accomplished. Jack glanced across the table and realized that Alyssa was staring at him, gazing at him dreamily with a smile on her face. Alyssa blushed and looked away when Jack caught her staring.

"So, what are your future plans?" Alyssa asked. "Once this system is up and running, then what are you going to do?"

"Pardon me?" Jack asked. "What do you mean?"

"I mean, once the system is up and running, once all the checks and tests have been pasted, what do you plan to do?"

"I really don't know," Jack said, finishing the glass of cola in front of him. "I haven't really given it much thought. I'm sure there'll be new towns to set up systems in. More work. And with Allen pushing his nanobots and Quantum Computers, I think my life will always be very busy."

"Will you always allow your work to consume your time?"

"Is there something you're not telling me, Alyssa?"

"Like what?"

"I don't know," Jack said. "I get this strange feeling around you…like I've known you before. I don't know. Did we meet at a summer camp years ago or something?"

"I've never been to a summer camp," Alyssa said. "The feeling you get around me, what do you think it is? Love?"

"Um, um, um," Jack said, trying to think. "I don't know. I think it's far too early to say if I love you or not, Alyssa. Why do you ask something like that?"

"This is really hard, Doctor," Alyssa said. "I mean, normally it's the guy that's chasing the girl and I really don't have a lot of experience in the romance department."

"I'm sure you've had plenty of boyfriends," Jack said. "I'm sure you've had your share of romantic flings."

"You would think," Alyssa said. "But sadly, there were no boys at my school. My parents kept me very sheltered."

"Your file indicated that you did a lot of things," Jack said.

"With girls," Alyssa replied. "It was an all-girls school. After school and activities, I always was forced to come right home. I didn't get to socialize with other kids."

"That's too bad," Jack said. "I'm sure you would have had lots of friends."

"I don't worry too much about it anymore Dr. Hall," Alyssa said. "The thing of it is, I don't know how this is supposed to work. I've dreamed of meeting you for so long. I followed all your work. I'm sure you must get lots of girls like me who've done that."

"There have been a few," Dr. Hall said. "I limit myself now and am very careful as to who I let in. Most of them were just after a job or money. It really doesn't look like you needed me for either."

"I didn't," Alyssa said. "I just wanted to meet you, Jack. And you're everything that I hoped you would be and more."

Jack shifted in his chair. He couldn't believe what he was hearing. For so long he'd been longing for a woman just like Alyssa and now here she was, practically throwing herself toward him. Jack felt that it was almost too good to be true, she must have been working for Social Software Solutions. He didn't know how he should play it. He had such a longing for romance but if it turned out to be false, would it be worth it?

"I've never really dated before," Jack said.

"Have you ever dated?" Alyssa asked. "Has there ever been anyone in your life?"

"In high school, there was a girl," Jack said. "A sweet girl named Sarah. She was in my math class. We did homework together and watched the video feeds. We used to stay up all hours of the night playing Dungeon Raiders against each other. We would sit in the back of our first-period history class and sleep the next day."

"Sounds like a wonderful relationship," Alyssa said. "For kids."

"It was," Jack said. "We dated through high school but ended up going to different universities. We agreed to go our separate ways and not try a long-distance relationship. It was for the best. That night though, before we both left for college, was greatest night of my life."

"Your first time?"

"Yes."

"What other ladies have you dated?" Alyssa asked. "There has to be more in there somewhere."

"I dated a couple in college. Nothing ever got too serious. I was so busy with schoolwork and software development that I didn't visit the social scene very much.

Nothing ever lasted more than a month or so. After college, I founded Madison Software Labs and there were a few lean years in there where I didn't have the time or money to date, and by the time the money part was taken care of I was so busy with the company that there was no time for romance. There were a couple women though, who sought me out, wanted to have a relationship with me, but I later found out they were just using me to get either a job or a look at classified software for a competitor."

"That's horrible," Alyssa said. "What kind of person would do something like that?"

"That's a good question," Jack said. "Alyssa, I have to tell you this, you seem too good to be true. You showed up into my life, and on paper, you're the perfect woman for me. Exactly the right kind of personality, background, and even looks that I want. I mean, if I could create a perfect woman, you'd be it. Heck, you even dress the way I like."

Alyssa looked at her clothing for the evening. She'd said they would dress up and for her, that meant designer black tights and a matching sleeveless blouse.

"I just don't know," Jack continued. "There's something about this that seems all too good. You're perfect and you're coming at me without a challenge or asking for anything. I guess the thing I'm saying is that I'm worried you might be working for 3S, Social Software Solutions."

Alyssa was silent for a moment, a look of pain spreading across her face. Jack realized that either she's a great actress or he just hurt her feelings.

"I swear to you, right now," Alyssa said, looking Jack deep in the eyes. "I swear to you I am here because I care about you. I've studied you and I made a promise to myself that I would get a chance to work with you. Now that I'm here, I want you, Doctor Jack Hall. That's all I have to say. I want you. I don't work for anyone but you. I promise you I'm not here to steal software or gain some kind of advantage. I am here because I love you, Jack and this is to prove it."

Alyssa leaned over the table and grabbed Jack by the shirt. She pulled him in, surprising him. Alyssa planted her lips upon his and gave him a deeply passionate kiss. As the pair was kissing, the waitress arrived with their drinks and cake. She paused a moment before clearing her throat. Jack pulled away from Alyssa as she sank back into her seat.

"Sorry," Jack said, as the waitress set the drinks and cake down.

"No worries," the waitress said, with a grin. "Enjoy your deserts."

The waitress smiled and left the table as Jack's eyes got huge. He'd heard Allen talking about Seasons Steak House and how great the ice cake was. Jack wasn't sure what it was, but now, looking at the eight-inch tall piece of cake, layered with ice cream, pudding, frosting, and fudge, all chocolate and drizzled in chocolate syrup, Jack wondered how the pair would finish the massive dessert.

"Seth isn't going to like me eating this," Jack said, as he forked a chunk of the cake and brought it to his mouth. "He's always trying to get me to eat healthier."

"This is lovely," Alyssa said, as she tasted her first bite. "I'm going to have to stay in the gym an extra twenty minutes tomorrow just to work this cake off. I'll need an hour for that steak."

"The food here is amazing," Jack said. "When this place opened a few months ago I desperately wanted to come but just didn't have the time...or anyone to go with."

"I'm glad I could bring you here then," Alyssa said.

"Um," Jack said. "I told you about my first relationship...now you tell me about yours."

"You don't want to hear about that," Alyssa said. "It's not that good of a story."

"Oh, I want to hear about it," Jack said. "You need to tell me."

"Lovely," Alyssa said. "Just remember though, you asked to hear this. When I was thirteen years old, just finished the eighth grade, I spent the summer with some friends of my parents who lived on the beach. They had an amazing house that was just a couple hundred feet from an amazing surfing beach. I met a group of kids who were into surfing and they invited me to join them. I was already into surfing because of my parents, so I loved this group of kids. One of the guys, Brad, was a year older than I was. He was a cool guy. He loved to surf, was handsome as could be and was super built; muscles everywhere with six-pack abs."

"Sounds like an interesting guy," Jack said. "What was he like?"

"He was into surfing and not much else," Alyssa said. "He surfed as often as he could, participated in surfing tournaments, and in school, was a champion on the swim team. He helped me to take my surfing to the next level. We would spend entire days in the water together. I knew that he was always looking at me, checking me out, and at the time, I loved it. At night, we would always have bonfires on the beach. He and I would always share a log together, sitting with his arm around me, staring into the flames. It was a magical time."

"What happened to him?"

"Summer comes and goes," Alyssa shrugged. "Brad and I knew that once summer was over, I was going home.

There was nothing that could change that. I wasn't ready for what we did but I knew that if I didn't I would regret it forever. Our last night together we stayed on the beach long after all the other kids had left. My first time was in the moonlight upon the sand, the waves rolling in around us. It was magical. The next week I started at an all-girls school and my parents found out about what happened. Someone saw us, and word got back to them."

"That must have been embarrassing," Jack said.

"You have no idea. That's why I was under such strict rules from my parents. They wouldn't even let a guy talk to me let alone go out on a date with me. It was hell, but I understand why they did it."

"That must have been very hard for you," Jack said. "Did you ever see Brad again?"

"I did, actually," Alyssa said. "It was many years later. He'd found someone else, of course, and was a champion surfer. They lived by the ocean and had three future surfing champions running around their house. He was very happy. At times, when I was younger, I thought about him a lot, wishing we could still be together. I never felt as good as I did sitting on those logs on the beach, looking into that fire. Well, until now, sitting here with you, Jack."

"That's amazing," Jack said. "I've never surfed before. Never even really swam before."

"What about that story that Allen was talking about?" Alyssa asked. "You the two of you were in Europe?"

"That's his version of a joke," Jack said, as he offered the last bite of cake to Alyssa. "Allen was pretty wild with the ladies before he met his wife. I really don't know how she got him to settle down but once they were together he was completely faithful. Considering how wild he was before that, I didn't think it would last."

"So, you didn't go to wild parties with him when you guys were getting started in your businesses?"

"I went to some but didn't enjoy them like Allen did," Jack said. "I'm not much of a partier. I'd rather be doing something constructive."

"Now that dinner's finished, what do you think we should do?" Alyssa asked. "We could go out for drinks and dancing or we could go somewhere quiet to talk."

"I'd like that...going somewhere quiet."

"Where do you want to go?"

"We could go to my place," Jack said. "I've got some nice coffee and we could play some chess."

"That would be lovely."

Jack motioned for the tab as the pair got ready to leave. Jack was excited, he had a bag of imported coffee that he'd been wanting to try but didn't want to open just for himself. He was already debating how he should play chess with Alyssa, go for a fast kill to prove superiority, or let the game go long, maybe letting her win. Alyssa was also excited for what was to come, but her ideas of what they would do at the apartment were far different than what Jack was thinking.

Chapter #15

To the north end of the mighty river, cutting its way through Winter Falls, stands the old district of town. Buildings that were built when the community was settled still stood, renovated to modern standards but outwardly looking like the turn of the 20th century. Former wheat silos and manufacturing plants had been converted into condominiums and apartments. Lumber mills and barge loading facilities were now mini-malls. The entire area was a delicate balance between the old world of the first peoples in the area, the non-computer age, and the new world where everything was controlled by a computer.

Nestled in a glen next to a bend in the river, a former wheat storage and shipping facility, the largest ever built at the time, had been converted into upscale apartments named the River Drive Apartments. From the upper floors facing east, the residents had the most wonderful view of the river and the outlying metropolis past that. One of the highest rent apartments in the city, rivaled only in price and luxury by some of the top-end apartments in the downtown area, River Drive Apartments had a three-year waitlist to get in.

The interior lobby of the apartment showed a different tone than the exterior. The exterior was the dull gray cement color of wheat silos whereas the interior lobby was a lavish and magnificent area. Deep red plush carpets lined the floors. The walls were splashed with the richest chocolates and browns. Lining the hallways were portraits of all kinds of people and scenes, each piece being museum quality. Through the main doors and to the left were a set of sofas and chairs, each overstuffed Italian black leather, polished daily to present that special shine that showed how little they were actually used.

Sitting in the chairs tonight, in the dimly lit lobby, was a broken and beaten man. He'd tried to get to an apartment, but the guards wouldn't allow him past the front desk without proper authorization. They had called the tenant who told them she'd be there presently. The man was softly sobbing, his head buried in his hands. As the man sobbed, wondering how his life had gone so wrong, he heard someone clearing their throat. Gavin Rodgers looked up to see Amber Kamp standing near the entrance to the lobby. She softly motioned with her head for him to follow her.

Silently, the pair passed the guards at the front desk. Amber gave the pair of men a smile and a wink as she passed, and the guards followed her with their eyes until they could no longer see her. Through the elevator, as decorative and extravagant as the hallways, with its artwork and gold-plated buttons, and to the top penthouse levels, Amber and Gavin didn't say a word. There was a tension between them as Gavin was trying to stifle his sobbing but couldn't. He was a man who knew he'd screwed up and didn't know how in the world he would ever get out of the trouble he was in.

At the top floor, Amber led Gavin to the southeast corner of the building, to apartment 1001. Amber opened the door and allowed Gavin to enter in front of her. Gavin never got used to the sight of the interior of Amber's apartment. A 1,200-square foot paradise of modern style. Not warm and inviting like the lobby, but almost a cold, sterile feeling, with its stainless-steel accents, polished bronze, and almost industrial like feel. The floors were cement, covered with a patchwork of rugs and runners. The outer walls, also cement, had been adorned with tapestries and art, all pre-war cityscapes. The furniture was all imported, dark and haunting.

As Gavin looked over the apartment, Amber slowly moved closer to him, pulling his body to hers, and planting a soft, gentle kiss on his lips. "Did they hurt you?"

"More than you could ever know, Amber," Gavin replied.

"Take a seat," Amber said, motioning to a leather sofa. "Want something to drink? I'm going to have some wine. I've got some beers or gin."

"Beer would be fine," Gavin said, sitting down. "Thanks."

Gavin sank into the sofa, wondering how he was going to explain himself. He knew that Amber was upset with him, had warned him about gambling, but he was addicted. No matter how many times he tried to stop the lure of victory was too great.

"Here you go," Amber said, handing Gavin an imported beer. "Bottoms up."

Amber clinked her wineglass against Gavin's been and took a sip. Gavin took a swallow of the dark, heavy beer. He looked at the label, but it was written in German, not something he could decipher.

"Are you kidding me?" Amber asked softly.

"What?"

"I said," Amber almost screamed as she stood up. "Are you goddamned kidding me? What have I told you about gambling?"

"How did you know I was gambling?"

"You sent me a message that I have to meet you here right away, that you're in trouble. I get here and see you've been beaten up. Let me guess. Just let me guess for one second, you lost the hundred grand that I gave you."

"I went to pay them back, Amber. Honestly. I was going to give the money to Mr. Timm and leave. I thought it wouldn't hurt to play a couple hands of blackjack before the party, but one thing led to another and I was down a little. The dealer was cheating, and I called him out on it. They took me to a back room and kicked my ass. Mr. Timm and Cassie. Now they say that I owe them a hundred and twenty-five thousand and I only have forty-eight hours to pay them back."

"I know," Amber said, flatly, sitting back down on a chair.

"What?"

"I called Mr. Timm."

"Why?"

"When I got your message at that party, which you were supposed to be at, I knew who you were in trouble with. Who else would you be in trouble with, Gavin? You're so predictable."

"So, can I have the money?"

Amber smiled at Gavin. A sinister, seductive smile. She slowly stood up and moved to Gavin. She started kissing him. Amber planted her lips on Gavin's and pulled him in tight. Gavin stood. He started to unzip the back of Amber's dress. When the zipper was to the bottom, Amber pushed Gavin back into his seat, working her body out of the tight dress to reveal a matching lacy black bra and panties set. Amber leaned in again and kissed Gavin.

"You know I love you, right?" Amber asked.

"What?"

Amber kissed Gavin again before pulling back and cracking him across the skull with an open-handed slap. The sickening thud echoed through the large apartment.

"How damn stupid can you be?" Amber shouted. "Are you kidding me?"

Amber cracked Gavin across the head again, putting all the force her small body could muster into the hit.

"For crying out loud," Gavin yelled, trying to cover his head. "Knock it off. What's the matter with you?"

Amber hit Gavin a few more times. Gavin was trying to cover up, trying to protect the blows, but wasn't fighting back. When Amber realized Gavin was too protected for her to get another good shot in, she took a step back and just stared at him. His face was black and blue from getting hit at the casino. There was swelling around his right eye. Amber could tell he was favoring his left side, like he'd taken some heavy shots there as well. She noted where it looked like he hurt the worst, letting him sweat it out in the silence between them.

"You simple, stupid, son-of-a-bitch," Amber said, standing directly in front of Gavin. "I hired you to do a simple job for me. Very simple. I thought you'd be the perfect candidate to get the job done. You are smart, capable, and have a degenerative gambling problem, which means you can be bought."

"That's why you hired me," Gavin said. "I was the only one high enough that could be bought. You know that I can deliver the results that you want. I'm the only one who can."

"I hired you for a very specific mission, Gavin," Amber said. "I only want one thing from you. It's very easy to do. I want chaos."

"I have everything set, Amber. Trust me. Tonight, before the party is over, the system will begin to show cracks. There will be a problem they won't be able to keep quiet. This will cause everything about the system to be called into question, just like you wanted."

"But this gambling. You were supposed to get help."

"What do you care about me?"

"I don't give a rat's ass about you, Gavin," Amber said, pacing in front of him. "I think you're a pathetic weakling who can't even control himself. But here's the thing, Gavin, I can't have someone at that casino buying you off."

"Maybe I should start a bidding war for my information."

Amber rushed over and hit Gavin in the head before he was prepared for it. She got on the sofa and started throwing punches aimed directly at his head. Gavin covered up and was able to protect himself, but the first surprise shot left its mark. Gavin was feeling the pain of Amber's hit. Finally, Amber stepped away from the sofa and resumed her pacing.

"God, you pack a hell of a punch for your size," Gavin said. "Stop that, Amber. I swear, you hit me one more time and I'm going to hit back. I don't care who you or your father are."

"Look here, you simple ass," Amber said, venom dripping from every word she spoke. "I spent those first few weeks with you letting you do whatever you wanted with me so I could own you. I needed someone with credentials, someone who could get inside. Look here, Gavin, I'm willing to do anything for you. Sex, drugs, money. Hell, I'll even bring in other women if that's what it takes. Whatever you need. But we can't have you in that casino getting bought by someone else. That's very important. You can't put yourself in that position."

"I could go to the newsfeeds," Gavin said. "Expose this little plan of yours."

Amber didn't hesitate. She grabbed the bottle of beer from Gavin's hand and smashed it against his head. The bottle shattered, sending dark beer everywhere as Gavin fell out of the sofa and rolled to the floor, a trickle of blood coming from his left temple. Amber jumped on top of Gavin and began to throw wild punches directed at his head.

"Don't even begin to joke with me," Amber yelled.

"That's it," Gavin shouted.

Gavin used his size advantage to push Amber off him. Amber rolled onto the floor and tried to scramble to her feet, but Gavin was on top of her. Gavin grabbed Amber's head in his hands, lifted it, and slammed it into the cement floor. Amber screamed out in pain, tears welling in her eyes as a dull throbbing surrounded her head.

"Son-of-a-bitch," Amber moaned.

"You can only push me so far," Gavin said, as he pinned her to the ground. "As long as we're down here and you're in such a frisky mood..."

Gavin started to kiss Amber as he held her down. Amber struggled with everything she had but Gavin was too powerful for her. She could barely move beneath him. Amber tried everything to get free. As Gavin was kissing her, Amber got his lower lip between her teeth and bit down hard. Gavin, startled, moved away, allowing Amber to use her foot to kick him in the groin. Gavin rolled off the top of her, doubled over in pain. He attempted to stand, but Amber had already reached her small purse, pulled out a derringer pistol, aiming it right between his eyes.

"Don't move," Amber said, as she rubbed the back of her head. "I should kill you where you are for that. Don't ever think that you can do something like that to me again."

"Go to hell," Gavin said, sitting back down on the sofa.

"I already paid Mr. Timm," Amber said, taking a step back from Gavin. "I did that before I came over here. I paid him the entire $125,000. I also gave him strict instructions that you were being cut off. I am not bailing you out again. If he floats you money on the blackjack table, it's his risk, not mine."

"Why?" Gavin asked. "Why did you pay it off?"

"Here's the thing, Gavin. I gave you a hundred grand earlier today to pay off that gambling debt. You lost twenty on the table and Mr. Timm took thirty. That leaves fifty thousand. Where did that fifty go, Gavin? Please tell me."

"Piss off."

"I'm not in the mood, Gavin," Amber said, taking a step closer. "I'm really not in the mood tonight. Where did that money go?"

"I owed a couple girls at the Summer Lodge. I used it to pay my tab there."

"The Summer Lodge? My God, Gavin. That place is a dump and the women there are no better than standard hookers you'd pick up on a corner. I could have got you a much higher caliber of woman, you know that."

"I don't deserve better," Gavin said.

"No arguments here," Amber said.

"Please let me spend the night with you, Amber," Gavin said. "That's what I really want. I promise, tomorrow I'll go to a meeting. I'll find a gambler's anonymous meeting and get help. The program works. I'll take it seriously this time."

"My bosses told me to find someone to destroy the system," Amber said. "That's my goal. This computer system my dad is putting in his town has to be destroyed. That's the only way. I'm into you for a couple of months and now, over half a million dollars and I've yet to see one result. That makes me very upset, Gavin."

"The first time," Gavin said. "Our first time, when there was such innocent flirting and you were so soft and gentle with me, I thought that this was real. I thought that you actually liked me. I knew you were involved with Adam, so I knew I was just someone on the side for you. But I thought that maybe, just maybe, you actually liked me and that we could get married someday. You didn't offer me money or tell me about the system until I told you that I loved you, Amber. You don't know how bad that hurt, to find out that you were only using me for your own ends."

"And you were so easy to use, Gavin. You really think you could compare to a man like Adam? What do you have to offer me that he doesn't?"

"Why are you doing this? Why destroy your father's system and ruin his chances of becoming president? He has good ideas."

"My father would be so proud of how ruthless and cunning I'm being. You can't even begin to imagine the web of lies and deceit that I've spun around this. Not only will I come out of this rich and famous, but I'll be able to do whatever I want. I'll be at the top without spending years paying dues to get there. It will be amazing. So, here's my question, are you on board or not?"

"Tonight, maybe even as we speak, an error will occur in the system. The newsfeeds will know by the morning and everyone will be questioning the system."

"Good," Amber said, as she put her gun back in her purse. "There's one more thing, Gavin. This is something that you really must understand. You tell anyone what I'm doing, and they won't believe you. No one will. If you try and push the issue, remember you have a family. Your brother's business is really taking off. You'd hate for some vindictive bitch to destroy it for him."

"You wouldn't."

"If I don't get the results I want, I will," Amber said. "This is bigger than you could ever imagine. You have no clue who is signing my checks. You have no clue who is paying for all of this, Gavin. You don't know where the money to pay your gambling debt came from. Create chaos. Give me headlines that question the integrity and stability of the system and tomorrow I'll give you a choice."

"Between what?"

"I'll let you choose. Me for the night, or an open tab at the casino. You can play cards all night long on my dime. Either one."

"I'll take the casino," Gavin said. "I'll always take the casino."

"I figured that," Amber said. "Money is no object for us. Now get out."

Gavin stood, hanging his head in shame as he slinked out of the apartment. Amber watched him before going to her kitchen and filling her glass with more wine. Amber pulled her glasses out of her purse, put them on, and dialed a number as she sat in her chair.

"It's me...I talked to him...gambling again...it's under control...he said tonight...I have faith that he can deliver...I dangled something very tasty in front of him...I have to get back to the party...I love you."

Amber took her glasses off and set them on the table. She took another sip of wine before standing and putting her dress back on. She quickly looked at herself in a mirror, fixed her hair, grabbed her purse, and left her apartment.

Chapter #16

Outside the River Drive Apartments, a car sat hidden in the dark shadows. Gavin didn't notice the car as he hailed a taxicab from the main entrance of the building. As Gavin gingerly got into the cab and pulled away, the car just sat, not moving. The cars tinted windows matched the black exterior of the car. Inside the car, two people sat in stunned silence at what they'd just seen. Detective Mike Russ and Amanda Drake had been tailing Gavin all night and couldn't have imagined where they would end up, but sitting outside of Amber's apartment is the last place they expected to be.

"He looked more beat up than when he left the casino," Amanda said.

"But Amber?" Mike asked. "No way could she do that to him. She's half his size and doesn't look to be the physically aggressive type."

"Maybe they do some freaky stuff in the bedroom," Amanda said. "Even a small woman, when pushed or threatened, can get aggressive."

"But why?" Mike asked. "Why are they together? It makes no sense. A common worker at the system and the daughter of the mayor. She's dating Adam Day. What could someone like Gavin offer her?"

"She's into him deep enough, moneywise," Amanda said. "We should question Mr. Timm and Cassie. See what they know about the relationship between the two."

"That's a bad idea," Mike said. "Mr. Timm is a lowlife to be sure. The thing of it is, he's on our side. When we need information about *other* people and activities, he's the best. I don't want to risk that relationship...not yet. We need to figure out why these two are together.

We've proved a relationship between them. Is Amber simply cheating on Adam? Is this just sex? Or could there be something more we're not seeing."

"What do you think is going on?" Amanda asked.

"We know Amber had contact with Danny Brown before he died," Mike said. "Amber had been seeing Danny, meeting at strange times and locations. I think we can safely assume, based off witness testimony, that they were in a sexual relationship, the same as Amber and Gavin. Now Danny turns up dead."

"Are you implying that either Adam or Gavin knew about the other men?" Amanda asked. "They killed Danny and will kill the other to make sure that Amber is all theirs?"

"Possibly," Mike replied. "Look, our plant at that party confirmed that Adam left the party with Amber after telling the group that something for work came up and she was going to handle it. Where's Adam? Why is Amber paying off massive gambling debts? These are questions that must have answers."

Before Amanda could answer him, a phone ringing was heard.

"Answer," Mike said, before, "Hello?"

"Mike," Police Chief Marley Rhoads' voice rang out through the car's stereo system as his face appeared on the screen on the front dash. "We've tracked Adam's car as you requested."

"Where'd the guy go?" Mike asked.

"He went to the joint Everyday Computers Madison Software Labs technology campus here in town. The one they built when the system was announced. He entered alone and has been working in a locked office. Security confirmed it."

"Damn it," Mike said. "That makes no sense. Have they been able to tell what he was working on? Where he's logged into?"

"He's on a secure server," Marley said. "There's no way to tell. He's accessing a large amount of data though. Doing something that requires a lot of computing power...what do you think? What's your feeling on this?"

"What we just witnessed here leads me to believe that the pair of them are up to something no good."

"I have to agree," Amanda said. "Has the analysis come back on the pump that failed this morning?"

"It did," Marley said. "I sent the file to your glasses, but the shorthand version is what you suspected, someone had changed that pump after the new one had been installed. The motor removed from there this morning had been tampered with."

"That could have killed hundreds of people and done untold damage to property," Amanda said. "The costs would have bankrupt the town."

"Would have given new meaning to backyard swimming pools," Mike said. "That's for sure. I'm confident that there was no danger to the town or the people in it."

"What are you thinking?" Marley asked. "This smell like an inside job?"

"Think about it, Chief," Mike said. "They spend over a billion dollars to install this system, not to mention the billion dollars that Madison Software Labs and Everyday Computers spend researching and developing this system. Now, if the system doesn't take off you can assume that both companies are going to be hurting. Don't you think that a little good press would go a long way? Who would ever know or question it?"

"Even if we did question what happened it wouldn't make a difference," Amanda said. "The system functioned perfectly. We expose this, and they say it was a test of the system. The reporter, Nevaeh Crick, she was the one who broke the story."

"What's her deal?" Marley asked. "A no-name gets a big story like this? Something doesn't add up there."

"Jerry Bosen has his eye on her," Mike said. "She's his date to the party tonight."

"Not really his type," Marley said. "Doesn't he usually go for the famous party-girl type?"

"That's who he's seen in the newsfeeds with," Amanda said. "But recently he's been talking about wanting to settle down. He says the lifestyle doesn't interest him anymore and he wants to relax."

"I don't understand..."

"We don't have time to take about Jerry Bosen's dating habits," Mike said, cutting Marley off. "Why is Adam working at the technology campus while Amber is here with Gavin? Could Amber be playing the three off each other?"

"Could be she just really like sex," Amanda said. "One guy isn't enough for her."

"I don't believe for a second," Mike said, coldly, "that Amber does anything without it being well thought out and there being a solid, firm reason behind it."

"I agree," Marley said. "She's cold and calculating, just like her father."

"Wait a minute," Amanda said. "Here she comes now."

Mike and Amanda looked out the window of their unmarked police car as Amber exited the apartments and waited for her luxury sports car to be pulled up. The valet got out of the car as Amber slipped him some money. He held the door open for her as she got in, closing the door when she was in her seat. Amber gave the man a wave as she revved the motor and tore out of the parking lot.

"We could get her for reckless driving, accelerating too fast, and speeding," Amanda said. "Strange that if she drives like that she doesn't have any marks on her record."

"She should have quite a few," Marley said. "Her father is the mayor, Amanda. She's been written up a number of times, but it's always thrown out. Perks of being the mayor's daughter. I wonder what other perks there are? Perks that we don't know about?"

"We'll find that out, sir," Mike said. "I don't know about this case. Something tells me there's something else out there, elusive. We're missing a key point and I can't seem to figure out what that is."

"What are you thinking, Mike?" Marley asked.

"I don't know," Mike said. "I've done this long enough to know what things don't add up, it means you're missing part of the equation. The pump goes bad and the system finds it. Everyday Computers' and Madison Software Labs' stock goes up limit today. There are towns lining up to buy the system. The government says there has to be a test period of two years, but with this, who knows? Maybe they are setting it up so the system can start being installed elsewhere this year. Think of the money they stand to make off this."

"And if Mayor Kamp runs for president," Marley speculated, "holding all that stock in the two companies that he does, and with Allen Day's backing, he doesn't even need another donor. He'll have enough money to buy the election like an honest politician normally does."

"Then as president," Mike continued, "he sets the entire country up to run off the system. Every city in the country will be ordered to have it, paid for with tax dollars."

"If that's true," Amanda said. "We're talking about more money than I could even imagine. I mean, these guys would be the first men to have a net worth over a trillion dollars."

"If the third world war didn't happen, other families would have hit that mark," Mike said. "But they were destroyed in the war. I don't know though, maybe Amber was using Gavin and Danny to facilitate this plan. They were the ones setting things up."

"Why kill him?" Amanda asked.

"He switched out the motor," Mike said. "Or at least ordered it done. There's no way to trace it back to them now. The only real witness is dead."

"But what is Adam working on now?" Marley asked. "That's the stumper. There has to be a reason for him to be on that computer right now, while his girlfriend is off paying another man's gambling tab, most likely sleeping with him."

"There's so much more here than we're seeing Marley," Mike said. "I'm thinking that we need to get to that party tonight."

"That's another thing I need to talk to you about," Marley said. "The real reason I contacted you. Breeze Flynn and two other Neo-Luddites are working the party as waitresses. Something fishy about that too."

"That actually makes perfect sense," Mike said. "They are gathering information. Hoping to overhear conversations and find information and events they can use to blackmail people with. That's the Neo-Luddite way. The only question is, who hired them?"

"As far as we can tell," Marley said, with a laugh, "they weren't hired here. They just showed up dressed as servers and started helping. There are so many workers there tonight, they slipped through the cracks."

"You have got to be kidding me," Amanda said. "With as tight as security is there?"

"They arrived with the catering company and walked in with a group of servers. The others didn't know the difference. They're all making just above minimum wage, you think they are going to question an extra set of hands? The cooks? They only know the food. The coordinators? They have enough else to worry about. We can't say for sure if they are going to try something, but we have enough people there watching."

"Great," Mike said. "This just keeps getting better."

"I want you to get to that party and try to get Breeze alone," Marley said. "We don't have grounds for a warrant or an official questioning, but she can be in trouble for being at that event without an invitation. Remind her of that. Also remind her that two years ago she received a ban from setting foot in the city hall for her little graffiti stunt. Remind her that she is violating that ban."

"You want her questioned?" Amanda asked.

"Gently," Marley said. "Don't push. Don't let her know the truth about the pump. See what she knows. See what the Neo-Luddites have planned. See if there's any connection between her and Amber."

"We'll get right on it," Mike said.

"Report just came in," Marley said. "Amber has returned to the party. No sign of Adam though."

"We'll figure this out, Chief," Mike said. "I promise you that."

Mike ended the call and turned the car on. Flipping on the lights, Mike looked around to see that no one was watching him. Mike put the car in drive and took off, speeding away from the apartments and toward the city hall, wondering what they were going to find at this party.

Chapter #17

Jerry Bosen walked confidently through the Master Computer Room with Nevaeh's hand in his. The pair had no business being there at the current time, but he was allowed access and figured that if anyone questioned him he would tell them that he was giving Nevaeh a behind the scenes tour of the facility for her newsfeed, which was true, in a certain sense. Nevaeh's eyes were wide with amazement as they walked through the massive computer room. None of the workers looked up from their stations to see who was moving through the room, all hard at work monitoring the system.

Jerry opened a door and ushered Nevaeh into the Main Computer Room. The room was dimly lit. All the monitors were off. The pair walked in and Jerry closed the door behind them as Nevaeh looked over the room. It wasn't what she had imagined it would be, but it was amazing none the less. Jerry sat in the main chair and motioned for Nevaeh to come over to him. He grabbed her hand and pulled her into his lap, kissing her for a moment before looking into his eyes.

"This is the main computer lab," Jerry said. "The Main Computer Room they call it. Everything about the system filters through this room."

"Couldn't we get in trouble for being in here?" Nevaeh asked. "I mean, are we supposed to be here right now?"

"I like a little risk," Jerry said. "Keeps me on my toes."

"Does it now?"

"It does," Jerry said, as he kissed her. "Watch this."

Jerry pressed some controls on the chair and the monitors in the room came to life. On the main screen was an image of the Winter Falls skyline, a live video feed showing the brilliance of the city at night.

"A high-class girl such as yourself Nevaeh," Jerry said, with a sly grin. "I know just the type of program you like to watch."

"What's that?"

The screen switched from the skyline to an arena filled with screaming fans as two monster trucks raced each other over piles of crushed cars.

"World Monster Showdown!" Jerry shouted. "The biggest trucks on television today!"

Nevaeh busted up laughing, "Not quite my show."

"Okay," Jerry said.

Jerry pressed some more control buttons. The screen split into four equal boxes. The upper left displayed the cityscape they'd seen before. The upper right showed a live camera feed of the party taking place upstairs. The bottom left was the feed from the camera over the door outside the room, watching if anyone was coming in. The bottom right screen was an arena filled with fans watching two men compete in a grappling competition.

Nevaeh looked the screens over, focusing in on the bottom right screen. "You do know that's fake, right?"

"Looks real to me," Jerry said, with a smile.

"Wait a minute...Jasmine has a title match tonight, doesn't she? We're going to watch your ex-girlfriend on our first date?"

"Not our first date, remember?" Jerry said, with a smile as he kissed her. "Her match is already over. She lost."

"It is fake, right?" Nevaeh said. "I know the other companies are but this one used to be real. Is it still?"

"They are all scripted now. Ever since they started surgically enhancing muscle. Once it was realized that it was no longer a contest between two gladiators and who was the most exquisitely trained but instead who had the best surgeons, there was no way it could continue. It's considered an exhibition. They demonstrate the moves and forms that would have been used in a real match of old. New medicine and surgery destroyed professional sports. Strange the way this world works."

"What do you mean?"

"How something can be so stable but then a little push in one direction and the system collapses. Look at fashion for example. Starting in the later part of the twentieth century people started to wear denim jeans for casual events. It wasn't long before jeans and jean shorts were the most common form of pants worn. Everybody wore jeans. Now, nobody does."

"What happened," Nevaeh asked. "Why was there a shift?"

"Starting in the first part of the twenty-first century, girls started wearing tights, or yoga pants, as they referred to them back then. It started with high school girls and quickly spread to all women. The tights were far more comfortable and stylish than jeans. Once people started using technology to end obesity through pills and surgery, the last block was gone. You can eat all you want now and not gain a pound. So, with a thin, fit body, you can wear whatever you want. Tights became the common outfit for women.

"There are changes that have happened since that first started, as there are things that have stayed the same. Cotton farming was destroyed by weevils, so all tights are made of synthetic spandex. For a time, everyone was wearing brightly colored tights with funky patterns and neon colors but now it's solids. Primarily black, some red or blue. Even shorts, which used to be denim, are now just short versions of the tights.

"Look at the way this changed the market for women's blouses and tops though. At first, when this trend took off, the style of the day was athletic. Almost every woman walking down the street looked like she was going to the gym. It matched the tights. Then, slowly, a vintage trend started. Women were trying to get authentic tops from the 1960's and 1970's. Thank God that didn't last long. Now, women primarily wear tops that are designed more for formal occasions. Business formal is the trend of the day."

"But what does that have to do with anything?" Nevaeh asked. "Why do you even know about the fashion trend for women's pants?"

"If there's anything I'm into," Jerry said, with a grin, "It's women's pants. In all seriousness though, jeans were the standard fashion for many years. It's interesting how slight the events were that caused a massive shift. The reason I know so much about it is we did consulting work for a fashion designer. They wanted to know what happened. They were the top maker of denim and were on the verge of bankruptcy. I showed them what went wrong and how to fix it."

"Did they make a comeback?"

"They did. They owned massive cotton farms that were useless. Cotton, like many other crops that used to be standard, didn't grow anymore. They couldn't keep the bugs under control. It's why the vertical farms took over for food production. There wasn't enough plant space available for food, fiber, and fuel, so food won out. They were still trying to grow cotton, getting pathetic crops, and doing more damage to the land. After my report, they sold the land to cattle ranchers, used the money to invest in new lines of tights and matching tops, and now are back on top. You were wearing their brand yesterday actually. Looked very good in it."

"That's the story then?" Nevaeh asked. "Seemingly unrelated events cause a massive shift in the stability of the system?"

"Quoted from my books," Jerry said.

"I brushed up on some of your work today," Nevaeh smiled.

The pair kissed for a moment. Kisses that were lasting longer than they should have, considering where they were sitting.

"So, what about you?" Nevaeh asked. "Some men wear tights. Others, like you, wear synthetic pants. But you always wear all black. Most men don't wear black pants anymore."

"Most don't, but it's still considered acceptable dress wherever I'm at. I don't have time to think about what I'm going to wear. My time is precious and valuable to me. I wear all black because it's appropriate for any occasion and it's quick and easy to get. I simply don't have time to think about what I'm going to wear."

"I spent almost an hour trying on outfits for tonight," Nevaeh said, sheepishly.

"You wanted to look stunning."

"Did I now?"

"You did. And it worked."

The pair kissed some more, their hands freely roving over the other's body. They were kissing intently for almost a full minute before Nevaeh stopped.

"Tell me something else about you," Nevaeh asked. "I've seen you on the newsfeeds. Jerry Bosen, playboy to the stars. Tell me a fantasy you have."

"That's a spicy idea," Jerry said. "I really don't have fantasies anymore. Believe me, I've done it all already."

"There must be something though," Nevaeh said. "What's your favorite movie scene that you would love to act out with someone?"

"'Waves of Summer'," Jerry said laughing. "The scene where Anna Holms's character comes out of the closet in her bikini."

"The office scene?" Nevaeh asked. "Where Anna tries to seduce Paige's husband?"

"Yes," Jerry said. "Just the way she comes out of that closet and surprises him is amazing. It'd be fun to have that happen sometime."

"Really?" Nevaeh asked as they kissed some more. "Seriously though...could we get in trouble here?"

"For what?"

"Why do you have access to this place? I thought it was for the computer workers only."

"I'm a member of the city council. I'm the chairman of the council actually. That's a very important position."

"Important position?"

"You wouldn't believe how important I am, Vaeh. All the amazing things I get to do...all the difficult decisions I have to make."

"Important."

"I can tell you where all the bodies are buried."

Nevaeh laughs for a moment before the pair starts kissing again. Again, the kisses last much longer than they should, and Nevaeh starts to unbutton some of the buttons on Jerry's shirt. His hands are all over her dress.

"I've never done anything like this before, Jerry," Nevaeh said, pulling back and looking in Jerry's eyes.

"Neither have I."

"Yeah, right. I'm sure you've got a notch for every intern and secretary in city hall."

"Don't forget reporters."

"We can't forget them."

The pair kissed again.

"Seriously though," Nevaeh said. "Why me? I'm a reporter you know. It's not like the newsfeeds are like the papers of old. Most of the information we put out is fluff that has no bearing on anyone. I've seen the different women you've dated. Jasmine, Paige Gianakos, Anna Holms, Sarah Summers. They are all so famous...and attractive."

"And nuts," Jerry said. "Look, yes, I've dated a lot of women. I love women. There was a time in my life that the only concerns on my mind were system stability, gin, and finding the next woman. As I get older though, I grow tired of that scene. The thought of going to one of those celebrity parties doesn't get me the way it used to. I'm more of a stay-in kind of guy now. Spend the day with people I really enjoy, people I can have normal conversations with. People who have something to say. I still love women, so I'm looking for someone I can spend time with."

"You actually mean to settle down?" Nevaeh asked.

"I've got two kids," Jerry said. "They are seven and four. I want to be a father to them more than anything. I want them to have a stable mother. A nanny doesn't count as a mother figure."

"That still doesn't answer the question of why you picked me."

"I've been around women long enough to have a sixth sense about them," Jerry said. "Like I can see an aura around them. I can tell just by looking at a woman what her personality is like. Her intelligence level, her sexual level."

"What did you sense from me?"

"That you are very intelligent and driven but are being held back at work. Your work isn't a challenge for you."

"Nailed that one," Nevaeh said. "It's so hard to get into a legit newsfeed that actually has news and not just fluff. I was so lucky to get this system story. I want to be a respected journalist and maybe even anchor the news someday. More than that though, I want to write books that will forever be remembered as documenting the events that shaped our world. Look at you, how many bestselling books do you have out now?"

"Seven," Jerry said. "I think. Books are not my main passion. System stability is."

"So, you picked me because I was smart?"

"Because you're driven," Jerry said. "Because you see a prize and don't stop until you've won it. That and you have a very healthy view of relationships."

"That's not what my dad called it growing up," Nevaeh said, with a chuckle.

"I want you to know something though," Jerry said. "I saw something about you yesterday and I invited you to join me here tonight. I don't think that you're my soulmate or anything like that. I'm trying something new and seeing where it leads."

"Do you believe in soulmates?"

"No," Jerry said, flatly. "I don't believe that there's one person I'm destined to be with forever. If there's one thing I know about relationships, they take a hell of a lot of work. I'm willing to work with someone, but it needs to be a very special someone. I'm looking for that person that

I'm willing to work with and who's willing to work with me."

"Fair enough," Nevaeh said.

The pair kissed some more.

"So, what else can this system do?" Nevaeh asked.

"It can destroy mankind," Jerry said.

"Again, with that," Nevaeh said. "Do you always resort to that? Will it really get that bad?"

"There was an old saying that only the strong survive," Jerry said. "The third world war proved that to be false. Since the beginning of time, it wasn't the strongest who stuck around, it was the smartest. While the strong man was chasing down a Wooley Mammoth, the smart man was planting crops and trapping small animals. While the strong man was fighting for control of the tribe the smart man was ruling from the sidelines. While the strong man was marching in formations, the smart man was building bombs."

"What does that have to do with the third world war?"

"A new form of government had started to take shape. It wasn't anything new, but it was a very perverse form of dictatorship and subjugation. Under the guise of protecting and helping the poor and meek, rulers commanded vast armies of the unemployed and starving. They promised them work when the war was over, promised them housing and a good life. They couldn't deliver though, they were just saying whatever they could to gain more power, absolute power.

"They had training cadres which were the toughest around. The men and women who went through those trainings were absolutely devastating on the battlefield. The Allied nations couldn't resist the onslaught of the sheer force. The United Forces looked to be overwhelming the Allies by strength. Until a new president was elected to lead the Allies. She was a different sort, promising an end to the war.

"Had people known what she was going to do, I wonder if they would have voted for her. A snowstorm had kept the United Forces at bay for three days. They were trapped, and it looked like they would be there for a full week. On that third night, a woman slipped into the barracks of the frontline soldiers. She claimed she was hired by a general to give the men a rest from all the hard work they'd been doing, a break from all the fighting. Little did they know what they were doing.

"I felt sorry for that woman, what she must have gone through that night. One by one, every man in the barracks had their turn with her. By the next morning, they were all dead. The plague ravaged through the military complex and by the time the storm lifted, the entire frontline force was dead, and the virus, engineered to last only twenty-four hours, was harmless now. There was nothing stopping the Allies from getting right to the generals of the military forces. There was a mass desertion of United Forces troops, top lieutenants were defecting by the day, and when it was all said and done, even though the war lasted a year after that, the United Forces never had a victory again."

"Brains over brute strength," Nevaeh said. "But that doesn't tell me why this system is bad."

"Because it allows people to stop thinking," Jerry said. "A person's brain starts to shut down when they stop using it. It's almost impossible to get that brain going again. We are living in a society where people aren't trained to do anything, just to use computers to do things for them. This system is a stepping stone to something grander though, or scarier, depending on your viewpoint."

"What?"

"Allen Day is testing creating robots from nanobots," Jerry said. "Humanlike robots that can do even more, so the human race can do even less."

"A humanlike robot?"

"He thinks it's about five years off," Jerry said. "That's really going to destroy everything that we have."

"Let's not talk about this anymore tonight, Jerry," Nevaeh said, kissing him. "Let's talk about something fun."

"Sounds good to me," Jerry said, kissing her back. "What are you passionate about?"

"My career."

"That's good. What else?"

"I'm very passionate about keeping good company."

"Now we're getting somewhere," Jerry said, kissing her. "You passionate about this?"

"Oh, yes."

They kiss for a few more moments before Jerry pulled back and motioned for Nevaeh to stand up. "Come on," Jerry said, standing. "There's other parts of the system I need to show you."

"Where?" Nevaeh asked.

"Downstairs," Jerry said. "There are some amazing things in the bomb shelters in the sub-basement."

"I can't wait to see them," Nevaeh said.

Jerry kissed Nevaeh passionately as the pair made their way toward the door. Nevaeh's heart was fluttering with excitement while her stomach was in knots. She was really starting to like Jerry but the thought that she couldn't shake, with all the other women he'd been with, would she be able to compare to any of them?

Chapter #18

In the southeast corner of Winter Falls, a quiet neighborhood of split-level homes and modest apartment buildings nestled themselves among the trees and shrubs that dotted the banks of the river. The area, not nearly as grand as other parts of Winter Falls, was a nice little annex to the city, a simple place to call home. Set back a few blocks from the river was the Rolling Hills Apartment complex, a network of five separate apartment buildings that shared some common areas. Throughout the parking lots and parks, kids biked, rollerbladed, and skateboarded on this warm and pleasant night.

Inside one apartment, on the second floor of the third building, apartment 3215, a couple had just finished with their ultimate expression of passion for each other. On simple blue bedsheets in a bedroom that was bland and bare, Dr. Jack Hall and Alyssa Babbage finished their love-making and sat up in the bed, still in each other's arms, pleased at the way the evening was going. The pair stayed silent in their embrace, not wanting to spoil the moment. Jack asked if Alyssa wanted anything to drink. The pair threw on robes and headed into the living room.

Alyssa sat on a powered blue sofa that was next to a green easy chair. There was nothing on the walls, no pictures, no artwork, nothing of any design. The entire apartment had a musty smell to it like it hadn't been used in years. Sounds lingered in through the thin walls. The conversations and activities of the people in the building could easily be heard. Jack returned, a can of cola for both himself and Alyssa.

"Sorry," Jack said, sitting down next to her. "I thought I had a wine cooler or beer left in there, but I don't. All I've got in my fridge are a few cans of cola."

"That's fine," Alyssa said, taking a small sip while Jack took a giant guzzle from his. "So...how was it?"

"The soda?" Jack asked. "Good as any, I suppose. I guess I shouldn't drink so much of this, but I love the taste. I try to limit myself but when you're working sometimes there aren't many options."

"No, Jack," Alyssa said, with a smile. "What we just did. Was it good for you?"

"Um," Jack said, taken off guard. "It was amazing. The best ever. You?"

"Lovely," Alyssa said. "Couldn't imagine it being better."

"Yeah right," Jack said. "You know how long it's been for me? I shudder to think about it. I'm just glad we could share it together."

"I love you, Jack," Alyssa said, looking deep into Jack's eyes. "I know, I know, we just met and all, but I felt like I've known you for so long. Reading your books, reading about your works, and now that I've met you, you're everything I ever thought you would be. I have to say it...I love you."

"Um," Jack said. "Um, um..."

"Don't you love me?" Alyssa asked.

"It's not that," Jack said. "I really like you. I don't know if enough time has passed to say that I love you."

"That's what you need for love?" Alyssa asked. "More time?"

"I don't know," Jack said. "I don't think I've ever really been in love before. There was Sarah in high school, yes. But we were so young, I don't know if those feelings were love or not."

"I think love is a state of mind where you'll do anything for someone," Alyssa said. "It's knowing that there's someone out there who cares deeply for you. It's the ability to lay together, not saying a word and feeling like you had the greatest conversation ever…know what I mean?"

"I do," Jack said. "That all sounds wonderful. Alyssa, I want to spend time with you. I want to be with you. We just need to take it slow and see how things develop."

Jack took another gulp from his cola. He couldn't get over the nagging thought in the back of his mind that he'd seen Alyssa before. There was something about her that seemed so familiar. Maybe it was the story she told about her first boyfriend. It seemed very similar to a story he'd heard before. Jack was certain he'd met Alyssa at least once before in his life, but after the session they'd just had in the bedroom, he wasn't going to do anything to jeopardize the chance of seeing her again. Jack wrote the feelings off to being tired from working on the system and being paranoid about someone trying to access the system through him.

"Where do you see yourself in ten years, Alyssa?" Jack asked, breaking the silence.

"That's a difficult question," Alyssa said. "Before, I would have said simply working on a large computer system somewhere. Living my life as it came. Now, I think I want to be here, working on your system, spending time with you. Where do you see yourself?"

"I meant it more as…well, whatever," Jack said, finishing his cola. "I've been thinking more about that lately. When I moved to Winter Falls to start work on the system I didn't think I would like the area very much, but it has definitely grown on me. There's a lake not too far north. Very picturesque. Has some of the best fishing in the state, yet it's a private lake that doesn't have very many cabins around it. I purchased three plots of land, three spots big enough for cabins."

"Why three?" Alyssa interrupted.

"So I can build my dream cabin," Jack said. "And have a lot on each side filled with trees so my cabin is private."

"What's your dream cabin?"

"A little log cabin. On the lake so I can walk from my front door to my fishing boat. A small pontoon perhaps. Something just big enough for a couple of people, maybe a dog as well. The cabin would have a master bedroom, an open kitchen, dining, living room area, perhaps a game room with pool table, and a room for each of the kids if I ever have any. It would be the main level with a loft above for the kids' rooms. It would be nothing fancy, just what we need."

"I don't think I could ever live in a situation like that," Alyssa said, seriously.

"What?" Jack asked. "So simplistic and perfect."

"There would have to be a cat, Jack," Alyssa said, with a grin. "Not a dog."

"I don't think the cat would like to go for rides on the boat though," Jack said. "But we could have a cat at the cabin."

"I think that's a wonderful dream, Jack. I've never fished before, but I've spent time in the water. I've loved being in the water. Swimming, surfing, and the like. We could teach our kids to waterski. I doubt there's surfing waves around here."

"Probably not. What's your dream house, Alyssa? Seriously. If you could live anywhere in the world, in any kind of house, what would you want to have?"

"A little cottage like you mentioned," Alyssa said.

"Seriously?" Jack asked. "You just heard me say that. What do you really want?"

"I've always dreamed of a place on the water," Alyssa said. "A little bungalow that overlooks the ocean. Something where the salty air can blow through the windows, waking me up in the morning. Where I can spend my days on the water and not have to worry about the everyday hassles; work, bills, taxes, and all the other stuff that distracts us from what's really important, living life."

"That sounds wonderful," Jack said.

"And the cabin you describe sounds a lot like what I would like," Alyssa said. "Something peaceful and tranquil. Something away from all the messes of society."

"It's funny when you think about it," Jack said. "I developed the most advanced computer software in the world. Built a company around it that made me a multi-millionaire, maybe even a billionaire, depending on the winds of the stock market, and all I want is a little cabin on the lake where I can go fishing. I bought the two side lots so that I would be secluded from others, not have people encroaching on my land. I also bought it so there would be room for a garden. I always thought it would be nice to have a garden. Maybe grown enough and fish enough that I could sell my produce to a restaurant or something."

"That sounds like a wonderful dream," Alyssa said. "But I have to ask you something though. I mean, you are a billionaire, why do you live in an apartment like this?"

Jack chuckled as he thought about the story of it. "When we got the contract here in Winter Falls, both Allen and I knew we'd be moving here, building the technology campus here. Allen went to the best realtor in town and asked for the best house on the market. He got the old Rolling Wheat Farms house. It's a six-thousand-square-foot turn of the century house built on the top of the hills on the west edge of town. The house is set on ten acres, has a number of barns and granaries, a guest house, and some of the best landscaping in town. He didn't even look at anything else. That was the most expensive place on the market.

"Even though I knew we'd be here for a long time, I was slightly more pragmatic about my decision. I rented this apartment with the thought that I would get to know the town, where I would be working, and my requirements for living space before I bought something. I looked at the pre-war houses on the east bank, the smaller single-family homes that looked so nice, but when my mind was made up to buy one I was so busy with work and there was no time to move. I've lived at the technology campus and city hall more than I've lived here."

"Lovely," Alyssa said. "I couldn't help but notice that this place doesn't reflect your true station in life. Not that I'm saying just because you have money you should be living in a mansion, but this is almost the opposite end of the spectrum."

"I guess," Jack said, looking around his place. "But I like it here. Truth be told, this money doesn't really mean anything to me. I only wanted to develop software, not rule the world, like Allan and Mayor Kamp. They love the video interviews and journalists hanging around them. Allen secretly loves when the paparazzi snaps pictures of him, no matter what he's doing. Life is just one big game to them. I just want to live and let live, you know?"

"I think I understand," Alyssa said. "You are more about creating life events, not so much worried about what those events are worth to people on the outside."

"That's a good way of looking at it," Jack said. "Yes. So, in this fantasy of ours, the cabin by the lake, how many kids do we have running around?"

"Two girls and two boys," Alyssa said.

"What makes you say that?"

"I've always wanted two of each," Alyssa said. "I don't know why, I just think that it would be a good number. And on a lake like that, with trees around, they could have so much fun, you could build a fort with them, it would be a lovely time, Jack."

"I think you're right," Jack said, as he leaned over and kissed Alyssa. "I think that would be more than lovely."

"Perfect."

"Well," Jack said. "Maybe someday that dream will come true. We need to make sure this system works first."

"I promise you I'll do everything in my power to make sure the system stays running properly."

Jack was about to reply when the harsh beeping of an incoming message came from his glasses. Jack looked around and noticed his glasses on the table. "Sorry, that's the ring of the control room. They only call in case of an emergency."

Jack put his glasses on and pressed the read button. He was silent for a few moments.

"What's going on?" Alyssa asked.

"This doesn't make sense," Jack said. "This isn't good. We need to get to city hall right away. Quickly, we need to get dressed."

Jack rushed to his bedroom, dropping his robe, and running around gathering his clothes. Alyssa strolled into the room and slowly got dressed, trying to project her calm demeanor onto Jack, but it didn't work. He was rushed, in a panic over something. Alyssa hoped it wouldn't spoil their evening, but she feared that when they got to city hall, things would be in a state of panic.

Chapter #19

The Master Control Room was a beehive of activity. People were rushing around in all directions, shouting orders, and passing files around like candy. No one seemed to have any idea as to what was going on, they just knew that there was a problem. Jack and Alyssa stood in the entryway, soaking it all in. Jack was mystified as to what could have happened. The message he'd received was from Ben Hewitt, simply stating there was a problem with the system and that Jack needed to get to the control room right away. Jack couldn't see Ben in the Master Control room, so he and Alyssa moved to the Main Control Room.

Inside the Main Control Room, the mood was somber. Everyone there seemed to be walking on eggshells as Jack and Alyssa pushed their way to the front of the room. The room was full. Ben and Dr. Porter were sitting in the chairs flanking the main chair, while Amber and Adam were at the back terminal. Mayor Kamp, with a drink in his hand, was near the front of the room, next to Allen Day and Governor Chad Jones. Jerry Bosen and Nevaeh were to the opposite side of the room, watching everything that was happening. Jack sat in the main chair and looked over the screen, which was showing a video feed of water pumps to the west of town.

"What's going on?" Jack asked, turning to Ben.

"I discovered the issue when I was making my rounds," Ben said.

"There's a problem with the damn system," Mayor Kamp shouted in a slurred voice. "Oh, I knew I should have found another team."

"You weren't supposed to do rounds for another hour," Jack said, ignoring the drunk mayor. "What was going on?"

"I was catching a nap in the bunker," Ben said. "When two people came in and…let's just say *caused a disturbance*."

"Guilty as charged," Jerry said, smiling.

"Damn you to hell, Bosen," Ted shouted. "I should have you impeached for sabotage. I knew you would try something like this."

"You can threaten all you want, Teddy," Jerry said. "But you know damn well I didn't sabotage your system."

"Who are you and why are you here?" Governor Jones asked.

Jerry looked at the governor. Chad was a tall and slender man in his mid-fifties. Perfectly cut gray hair sat atop an effeminate face with delicate features. A custom suit and pounds of gold jewelry said the governor had been financially successful throughout his life. Jerry, never one to miss an opportunity, already had a strategy in mind.

"I'm the chairman of the City Council," Jerry said. "Jerry Bosen, system stability analyzer. And you are?"

"I'm Governor Chad Jones," Chad said, offended to even be asked that question. "I've been governor of this state for six years now."

"Never heard of you," Jerry said.

"Enough!" Ted shouted. "Fix the damn system."

"Please," Jack said. "Ben, what's the issue here? What are we looking at?"

"Water pumps in quadrants four through eight were only running at half capacity when they should have been running full. Then they started to shut down."

"Why?" Dr. Hall asked.

172

"I don't know," Ben said. "It is so odd though. It's like the system doesn't even realize that there is a problem. Funny thing about it, we are facing problems like we did this morning when the bad pump was discovered. But here we are, and the system says that all systems are running normally."

"Damn you, Jack," Mayor Kamp yelled, taking a shaky step forward, spilling his drink. "You'd better fix this."

"Come on, Dad," Amber said, standing up from the computer terminal. "You need to get upstairs and to bed. You've had a long day."

"I can't go to bed until this problem is fixed," Ted said, glaring at his daughter. "And don't treat me like a kid. I'm not drunk. I'm pissed off that this system isn't working the way he promised me it would."

Before anything else could be said, Gavin walked into the room. Everyone gasped at how mangled his face was. He had swelling over both eyes and black and blue marks everywhere. He looked to have been through a lot tonight.

"What happened to you, Gavin?" Dr. Porter asked.

"Nothing much, Holly," Gavin said. "I went to the casino tonight. They had a mixed-martial-arts tournament there. I compete in them from time to time. Needless to say, I didn't win."

"I didn't know you were into that," Jerry said. "And I didn't know they were having a tournament there tonight."

"It was a small one, Jerry," Gavin said, looking away. "What's going on here?"

"We are having water pump problems," Dr. Hall said. "Water pumps in quadrants four through eight are shutting down."

Gavin nodded as Jack brought up a service screen on his main computer. There were designations for all the different water pumps and the percentages that they were running at. He noticed that everything between four and eight were at 0% while the rest were between 80% and 100%. Jack tried to run a number of programs, but nothing would work.

"This is so odd," Jack said. "It's like the pumps aren't even there."

"What the hell does that mean?" Ted shouted.

"It looks like the pumps have been pulled offline."

"Let me see," Gavin said, looking at the numbers. Gavin put on a pair of computer glasses and attempted to try some things. A number of other pumps' percentages changed on the big screen, but none of the ones in quadrants four through eight.

"I tried to get them myself," Ben said. "But I couldn't figure out the system. It's like there's a command code overriding all operations and not letting us have access to anything else in those quadrants."

"But how could there be a command code if we didn't implement one, or program a backdoor around it?" Dr. Hall asked.

"Would that have been a system that the computer designed on its own?" Jerry asked.

"Um," Jack said. "Yes. Why?"

"There's your problem," Jerry said. "You're trying to fix something you didn't program yourself, something you don't even understand. The system designed and implemented this command code, and now you're trying to figure out what it did and why. You have no idea the language it used for those codes or how it divided them among processes. There's little chance that we can figure out what happened."

"That's fancy talk for how he sabotaged the system," Ted yelled. "Get security down here and arrest him."

"Ted," Chad snapped. "Knock it off. He's not going anywhere. We've come this far. Don't throw it away on a drunk evening. Come on, Ted, we still have some supporters we have to meet with. Think you're up for it? Let the technicians deal with the problems."

"Fine," Mayor Kamp said. "Let's get this over with. Jack, you'd better get this system running right away. We can't take any problems like this. One word of bad press and the voters will pull the plug on this system. Your career will be over."

Mayor Kamp and Governor Jones walked out of the room. Although everyone was still on edge over the system not working, the tension of the room seemed to let up. There was breathing room now and they didn't need to be as careful over what they said.

"Seems the champ there can't handle his booze as well as he thinks he can," Allen laughed. "Bit of a lightweight, don't ya think?"

"I don't know what we can do," Jack said, ignoring Allen. "The computer doesn't seem to think there is a problem with the pumps. Seth, why are water pumps in quadrants four through eight not working properly?"

"The pumps are operating within tolerances, sir," Seth's voice boomed from the speaker systems in the room.

"What do you mean?" Jack asked as he turned the volume on the speakers down.

"I mean that all pumps in quadrants four through eight are functioning perfectly, sir," Seth said. "All of the pumps listed in those quadrants are within given tolerances."

"This is not good," Jack said.

"What do you mean, Laddy?" Allen asked.

"The system thinks that everything is running perfectly," Jack said. "It doesn't realize there is a problem."

"You gotta think like a computer, Jack," Jerry said, taking a step forward. "Seth, why are water pumps in quadrants four through eight turned off now?"

"Pumps in the forth to the eighth quadrant have been shuttered for the evening," Seth said. "Energy saver mode has been activated."

"What?" Jack said. "This is serious."

"What's the deal with those pumps?" Nevaeh asked. "Why are they so important?"

"They remove the snowpack melt off from the forests and hills," Jerry said. "This is really a horrible place for a town. The area was settled during a dry spell. There wasn't a lot of snowpack in the hills and forests to the west. When the winters got worse the spring flooding almost wiped out the town. They dredged the river, built dikes and canals, and devised a system of pumps to hold the water back and slowly release it throughout the year.

"There's an upper holding pond and a lower. A delicate balance has to be maintained, keeping the water flowing without causing floods or upland damage. If those pumps don't run, the water will back up and flood over the dam. That water is a very destructive force of nature. If it starts to go over the dam, there's a good chance the force of it will cause the dam to burst, allowing all the water of the lower pond to flood the town."

"How bad would it be?" Nevaeh asked.

"The destruction of the west side of Winter Falls in about five minutes," Jerry said. "There would be a wall of water that couldn't be stopped that would wipe every building and person in its way off the face of the earth. As I said, this was a very poor place to build a town, but you know politicians, they think they can control anything."

"May I take a look at the system, Jack?" Alyssa asked.

"Go ahead," Jack said, offering his place to Alyssa.

Alyssa sat in the main chair and started working on the system. She was intent and was working quickly. Jerry watched closely as Alyssa smoothly worked over the system.

"So, Jerry," Alyssa said. "You're telling me that the pumps in question should be aligned with all the other pumps that are marked for water stoppage and removal?"

"That wouldn't be perfect, but it would avert a disaster," Jerry said. "Those pumps should have their own programming. In fact, I demanded those quadrants have a special set of programs which I'm going to demand we bring back. Those are the master pumps for the system. If they shut down, or if this wasn't discovered, I would say we have about twenty-four hours before the water would be going over the dam."

"I think I fixed it," Alyssa said, as the percentages changed on the main screen.

Everyone was silent, staring at the screen before Dr. Hall spoke, "What did you do, Alyssa?"

"In an effort to run systems more smoothly," Alyssa said, beaming with pride. "The system divided water pumps among routers. The ones that had been shut down were running like energy conservers, not water pumps. The system didn't understand the difference between water and power, when it came to humans that is."

"Very interesting," Jerry said.

"I don't like this," Dr. Porter said. "Dr. Hall, this is a serious problem."

"Come now, lass," Allen said, from the back of the room. "A little confusion is all. I'm sure Jack and his fine people can hash this out over a cup of java. Be fixed by the morning and all."

"That's not what she means, Allen," Jerry said.

"Jerry's right," Jack said. "If the system didn't understand this set of differences, what other differences could it have missed? We are going to have to go through all of the code that the system programmed for itself."

"That's going to be a lot of work, Dr. Hall," Dr. Porter said. "We don't have the manpower to do something like that."

"If this wasn't caught in time it could have cost thousands of lives," Dr. Hall said. "It would have been catastrophic."

"Is there any way this could have been sabotage?" Allen asked. "I mean, those Neo-Luddites are here tonight. Could they have hacked the system somehow?"

"No," Jack said. "Any changes in the system would have come through this room. The people outside, in the Master Control Room, would have also noticed the changes as they would have been trying to make them. There's no way it could have been them."

"Dr. Hall," Jerry said. "It is my strong opinion that you pull this system offline until a thorough and complete systems check has been performed. We cannot risk a catastrophic systems failure this early in the game. The system would never recover."

"And that's what you'd want, isn't it?" Adam asked from the back of the room. "You've been predicting the downfall of this from the start. If they take this system offline as you're suggesting, the voters and government would never be allowed back online."

"Boy," Jerry said, with irritation in his voice. "If this system fails within the first week it will never be used again anyway, stable or not. This is their one chance to preserve the system before any real damage is done."

"You saw what it did this morning," Adam said. "It saved lives."

"And tonight, it almost killed all it has saved and more," Jerry said. "Dr. Hall, you know I'm correct. All we have to do is say that there was some command overrides due to power influxes."

"What does that mean?" Jack asked.

"Nothing," Jerry said. "That's the point. Tell them something simple that they can't understand. Say we just want to make sure the stability of the system isn't compromised since it's so new."

"A power surge?" Adam said. "You want to tell the people we are pulling the system offline because of a power surge?"

"Or you can tell them it's being pulled offline because it almost killed half the town tonight," Jerry said. "The choice is yours, Adam."

"We're not pulling the system offline," Allen said. "The boy is right, they'd never let us bring it back. Jack, what do you need? We can spare all people on this matter."

"It's going to take more than all our people," Jack said. "We are going to need hundreds of computer programmers. We can get them from the university, get them credit for it or something. This room will have to be staffed round the clock, the system will have to be monitored at all times. That will be our defense. We should be able to spot anything before it happens."

Jack heard the words he was speaking but he didn't believe them. He thought, like Jerry, they should shut the system down while they did these checks. Go back to the old way of things until they were certain the system was ready. Jack didn't know if the system would ever truly be ready though. He didn't know what else could go wrong. As he was worrying about everything with the system, Jack didn't notice two people slipping into the room, Detective Russ and Amanda Drake, ready to ask the people in the room a few questions about that evening.

Chapter #20

Detective Mike Russ watched the commotion in the Main Control Room as the group of people worked frantically to control the problem. He was interested in seeing the reactions of people and wanted to speak but knew that in their current state, no one would be of any good use to him. He need to let the crisis resolve. It appeared that Alyssa had figured out. Mike noticed that both Allen and Adam Day were in the room. He knew he would have to separate Amber from the pair to get any real truth out of her. If there was some relationship going on with Gavin, exposing it in front of her boyfriend and his father wouldn't help to procure more information for the case.

Amanda too noticed the panic in the room. Whatever they were talking about was above her head, more technical than she could figure out. Amanda couldn't help but wonder why they met Mayor Kamp and Governor Jones in the hallway. Why those two men hadn't stayed in this room. Surely, Amanda thought, they had to have been coming from here. The governor looked upset and Ted looked drunk. There were so many unknowns about this murder case and all signs seemed to be pointing back to his place of work, although there weren't very many signs.

"Is everything on the system functioning properly?" Mike asked, alerting the room to his presence.

"Lovely," Alyssa said. "There was a small error that has been taken care of."

"Very interesting," Mike said. "I don't believe we've met yet. I'm Detective Mike Russ and this is my partner, Amanda Drake. You are?"

"Alyssa Babbage," Alyssa said. "Computer engineer. This is my first day working here."

"She was hired to replace Danny," Jack said. "Detective, has there been a break in the case? A new development perhaps?"

"There are a number of questions that need answers," Mike said. "A very curious number actually. I want to pose a question to everyone in the room right now though; is it possible that an outside group attempted to use Danny to harm, hijack, or steal the system?"

"It's very possible," Jack said. "I mean, with the technology we are using with this system the lives of millions of people are at stake. That presents a very tempting target for competitors."

"Do you have any proof that anything like that has happened?" Mike asked.

"None," Jack said. "That's the problem. There's no evidence anything like that has happened. Unless they are waiting to use what they got from Danny until the investigation is over."

"I'm going to request that Amber and Gavin come with us to a private room for questioning," Mike said. "Adam, I'd like you nearby so we can ask you some things."

"What's this about?" Allen asked. "I want to know what's going on here."

"I'm sorry, Mr. Day," Mike said. "This is an ongoing murder investigation. We really can't divulge details right now."

"It will be fine, sir," Amber said. "Gavin, detectives, follow me to the main floor conference rooms. We won't be disturbed there."

Amber, Gavin, Adam, Detective Russ, and Amanda left the room. Jack and Alyssa were intently looking over the system, making sure there were no more errors. Jerry and Nevaeh had moved against the back wall, next to

Allen, while Ben and Dr. Porter were at the other computers in the room. There was a silence in the room until it was broken by Allen, in his normal, jovial voice, "At least the system is up and running champ. We can be thankful for that."

"I'm not too thankful yet," Jack said. "This shouldn't have happened. I don't know what could have caused an error like that. If the system didn't know the difference between water and power, who knows what else it doesn't know the difference between."

"Come on, Jack," Allen said. "Let's get back to the party upstairs. The bar is still open for an hour or so. You should mingle with the people up there."

"I have to work on this," Jack said. "Ben, if you want to go up and visit the party, go ahead. I'll relieve you for tonight. I'm nervous about the system. I want to do some checks."

"I'll stay with you," Alyssa said. "But I'm going to change out of my formal clothes first. If you'll excuse me, I'll be back in a moment."

"Holly," Jack said. "You can go back to the party too. I'll need your help in the morning though."

"Come on, Ben," Holly said. "Let's see what's left at the bar."

"That's what I like to hear, lass," Allen said.

"Nevaeh," Jerry said. "Why don't you follow them up? I'll be up in a moment."

"Okay," Neveah said, following the group out of the room.

Jack and Jerry were the only two left in the room. Jack was working so intently on the system that he didn't even notice that Jerry had sat down in the chair next to him and was staring at him. Jerry glanced at the monitor on the wall, numbers and functions were streaming past,

Jack trying to comprehend all of them, making sure that all systems were functioning properly.

"What are you doing, Jack?" Jerry asked.

"Monitoring the system," Jack said.

"With Alyssa, I mean."

Jack stopped the scrolling of the system and turned to look at Jerry, "I don't believe that's any of your business, Jerry. Alyssa and I went out for supper tonight."

"You don't find it strange at all?"

"Find what strange?"

"Danny dies and all of a sudden, Alyssa just happens to show up, dying to work with you?"

"What are you implying, Jerry?"

"I'm not implying anything, Jack. I'm merely posing a question. The stability of the system is my only concern, Jack. You know that. I don't want to see this system fail. I don't want people getting hurt or losing their jobs. I certainly don't want any more murders to happen. I just find it odd that Danny dies and the computer hires her right away."

"Are you suggesting Alyssa hacked the system without our knowledge, set it up so that she would be hired, before killing Danny? Are you suggesting Alyssa killed Danny? Because if you are, then you are as crazy as Ted says you are. Alyssa is a sweet flower, she's so soft and innocent. A little girl inside who could never hurt anyone."

"I want you to stop for a second and think about the overall structure of what you just said," Jerry said. "You, a man who has been with, what, two, maybe three women before Alyssa is going to tell me, Jerry Bosen, about the inherent nature of women? Believe me, Jack, women are deadly. There isn't a woman alive that when pushed to it, wouldn't rip out your heart in a second.

Women appear all sugar and spice and everything nice but if you betray one or hurt one, and I refer to emotional hurt more than physical, then woe to you, my friend. I don't care how nice and sweet she appears on the outside, it's what's on the inside that counts."

"Do you really believe she could do something like that?"

"I believe that every woman carries inside of her the ability to do whatever it takes to achieve her goals."

"When you first met Alyssa, Jerry," Jack said, shifting in his chair. "Um, there was a, um, moment. You got close to her, very close. You looked deep into her eyes. What did you see there? Why did you do that?"

"I have a few systems I use to evaluate a woman very quickly when I first meet them," Jerry said. "I've been around women enough to know a few things about them. One thing that I always do is look into their eyes. It allows you to see past what's on the outside, to see inside them. I got a strange feeling about Alyssa. Now, I don't remember ever face that I've ever been with. Sadly, I don't remember every name I've been with, but I remember the eyes. I can know a woman and remember her by her eyes. When I first set eyes on Alyssa, I got a very powerful feeling that I'd know her before…"

"Have you slept with her?" Jack interrupted. "Is that what you're trying to tell me? You had her once before? Because you didn't, Jerry. She told me her story. She told me about her first time and how many she's been with since. You weren't a part of it."

"On first glance I thought she was someone I had known before," Jerry said. "But then I looked in her eyes and knew that she wasn't. I also knew something else about her the instant that I looked in her eyes."

"What's that?"

"I'm not going to say just yet," Jerry said. "I need to gather a little more information about Alyssa before I make my final judgment about her."

"But your line of questioning gives you away," Jack said. "You wouldn't ask about these things if you didn't think Alyssa was the killer. Please, Jerry, there's something you're not telling me. There has to be. Because if what you've said is all you've got then there's nowhere near enough to assume that Alyssa could hurt anyone. What else do you have?"

"Just a knowledge of human behavior," Jerry said. "Remember I got my start modeling stability in human systems. Most people tend to think that humans, in a group, behave in strange and erratic ways, but I found that there are some very predictable patterns that they follow. This can be filtered down to individual people too. It was a very interesting study, how I got into system stability."

"How?"

"When I was sixteen years old there was a girl in my math class who I was dying to ask out," Jerry said. "Trisha. Now here's the funny part, I had no idea how to do it. I had no idea how to talk to her, how to get her to like me. We were partners on a project. We had to spend time together during and after school working on this project. I was nervous around her, didn't know what to say."

"Really?" Jack said. "I thought you were always smooth with the ladies."

"Not even close," Jerry said. "We got an 'A' on the project. Of course, I did all the work while she messaged with her friends. She wasn't the brightest in math. After we got our grade, I said that we should go out and celebrate. She agreed. I was ecstatic. After school that day we went to an ice cream shop and had our treat. We talked, awkwardly, and when she was about to go I asked her out again. She laughed at me and said no."

"I never knew that," Jack said. "You got shot down hard?"

"Yes," Jerry said. "And it pissed me off, Jack. I was so mad. I knew what to do though. My parents trained me well. When you get an outcome you don't like, study what went wrong. Study those who do it right. I approached two members of the high school wrestling team who were amazing with the ladies. I offered to help them with their sport. I knew the mathematics behind the sport. I knew how to model the sport to figure out who would win and how. I helped them get much better. All I asked in return is to hang out with them, ya know, to hang out with the cool group. They were fine with it. They didn't know I was watching what they did with women, how they got all the girls.

"I learned a lot from those two guys. A lot of things that didn't make sense. But then, I started to do more research on the subject. My passion for women led me to design a system to make any person, man or woman, instantly like me and want to be around me. I did a lot of testing with the girls in my school."

"You ever get your date with Trisha?" Jack asked.

"Yes," Jerry replied. "She was about the longest girlfriend I've ever had actually. We started dating as seniors in high school and dated in college as well. We went our separate ways but still keep in contact with each other. Now my system isn't foolproof. It doesn't work 100% of the time, and trying to get everyone to like you is far too challenging. I focus on keeping the best company possible."

"And being with the most attractive, famous women in our society."

"Not so much anymore," Jerry said. "There comes a point where all the parties just blur together. Where all the women seem the same. It gets to the point where you just want to find someone you are comfortable with. I'm getting to that point. The overall lesson I've learned is that nothing is out of the realm of possibilities. I've looked into the eyes and souls of hundreds of women, thousands maybe. I saw something in Alyssa that I've never seen before. Something that I don't really understand. She doesn't act like a woman normally acts. There's a strange motivation there. It could be, as I heard, that she fell in love with you through reading your work and studying you. That's possible, but something doesn't feel right about her. All I'm telling you is to be careful. I know how the game of love works and she's violating some of the cardinal rules for women."

Jack was stunned silent. He wasn't sure how he was supposed to respond to Jerry. Alyssa was exactly what he was looking for and Jerry was telling him to use caution. Jack knew he shouldn't tell Jerry about the time he spent with Alyssa before they came to city hall tonight, knew that Jerry wouldn't approve of it. Jack felt a pang in his heart every time he thought of Alyssa and wasn't going to let her slip away because of Jerry's concerns.

"Just speak plainly, Jerry," Jack said. "Tell me outright what your theory is."

"I see two possibilities," Jerry said. "One, Alyssa is a member of the Neo-Luddites. There were members working as servers tonight. Breeze Flynn was one of them. I spent some time with Breeze and know she is controlled by her father to a sickening degree. Alyssa could be a member of Gary's brainwashed cult. The other possibility is that Alyssa has fallen in love with you and will do anything to be with you, even murder, to get a position here. I checked some files earlier today. Alyssa has never applied to work here before, but another woman has, Alyson Bertram. A little surgery, some hair extensions and dye, and Alyson becomes Alyssa."

"I don't believe you," Dr. Hall said. "I don't believe either scenario for one second."

"I could be wrong," Jerry said. "But I could be right. Dr. Hall, all I'm asking you is that until the killer is caught, be careful."

"I will."

The door to the room opened and Alyssa walked back in. Jerry eyed her up and down, smiling slightly. Alyssa had changed from her tights and formal blouse to black shorts with a black tee shirt that bore the city logo on the left breast. The shirt was a size too large for Alyssa and she had it tied at the midriff. Alyssa was all smiles as she entered the room and sat at the computer on the other side of Jack.

"I hope I didn't miss anything interesting," Alyssa said.

"Just guys talking guy stuff," Jerry said.

"We were discussing the system and what this challenge represents," Jack said.

"I'm confident that we can prevent something like that from happening again," Alyssa said. "Just so long as the newsfeeds don't get word about what happened."

"I'll talk to Nevaeh now," Jerry said, standing up. "I need to be getting her home anyway. She won't put any of this in the newsfeed. Goodnight, you two." Jerry walked to the door and paused, turning back, "And kids, you behave yourselves down here."

Jack's face turned a shade of deep red as Jerry closed the door behind him. Alyssa didn't seem to understand the joke. Jack quickly returned to his work as Alyssa stood and stretched.

"It's rather warm down here," Alyssa said. "Don't you think?"

"I could adjust the air-conditioning if you'd like," Jack said, not taking his eyes off the screen.

"I think this is better," Alyssa said, as she took her shirt off, revealing a black bikini top underneath. Jack didn't look up from his work. "Jack, look at me."

"Um," Jack said, stunned at what he saw.

"This won't distract you from your work, will it?" Alyssa asked.

"Not at all," Jack said, as he nodded his head. "Are you planning on going swimming or something?"

"There is a hot tub in the workout area," Alyssa said. "Maybe we could have a break there later tonight."

"Um," Jack said. "Sounds great."

Jack tried to go back to his work as Alyssa sat down and started working on her computer. Jack couldn't help but think of what Jerry had said, how Alyssa didn't act like a normal woman. She was stunning in her outfit, but he'd never seen a woman be that open and outward with a guy. Jack tried to focus on his work. No matter what, he decided he had to keep the system running and he would simply enjoy the ride with Alyssa.

Chapter #21

Amber Kamp escorted Detective Mike Russ, Amanda Drake, and Gavin Rodgers into a small conference room on the second floor of city hall. They were off a bank of offices for city administrators and in a small meeting room. The room had no windows, no markings on the walls. The walls were carpeted with the same dull gray that was on the floor. The magnificence of the building seemed to stop right where the average civilian wouldn't go. The room held a roundtable, made from oak and stained a dark red color. Six leather office chairs ringed the desk and there was the subtle depression of screens in the walls, showing that the part of the gray color was a video screen perfectly mimicking the wall.

"This office should do just fine," Amber said, as they all took a seat. "No one will bother us here."

"Great," Mike said. "We have just a few questions that we wanted to ask you two. Amber, you are in a relationship with Adam. The pair of you have been dating for a number of years now…"

"Four," Amber interrupted. "To be honest, we are engaged but we've kept that our little secret. We are planning a wedding over New Year's in the Caribbean."

"Congratulations," Mike said. "Why keep it quiet?"

"Our lives have been very public," Amber said. "Thanks to our fathers. The newsfeeds don't seem to care about real news, about what's going on in the world, they'd rather report what party I was seen at. What kind of suit Adam was wearing. What drinks we were having."

"I've noticed that the newsfeeds tend to follow superfluous items," Mike said.

"We want our wedding to be a private affair," Amber said. "Family and close friends only. We even have a system worked out. We've purchased plane tickets to a different destination, Las Vegas. Everyone will think we are flying there to get married. When we land in Vegas, Allen has chartered a private plane to take us the rest of the way. A long way out of the way, I know, but this way we can be sure no reporters will be there. The wedding will happen the instant we land before anyone knows that we've arrived."

"It should be amazing," Amanda said. "So, if you are marrying Adam and are in love with him, why are you paying off Gavin's gambling debts?"

"Why does there appear to be a relationship between you and Gavin?" Mike asked. "A relationship that also seemed to exist between you and Danny, before he met his untimely end."

"Are you implying that I'm a murder suspect?" Amber asked. "Because if that's what you dare imply, Detective, then..."

"I don't need to *dare* anything, Amber," Detective Russ said. "Don't get your tights in a twist, dear. Answer the question."

"I don't like the tone of all this," Amber said. "I think it best if we get my father in here. I'm sure he'd love to see how his police are acting."

"Amber," Amanda said, with a smile. "We are trying to solve a murder case. We are asking you simple questions. You realize how bad it looks on your part when you threaten us with your mayor father?"

"I'm sorry," Amber said. "I've had a bit too much to drink tonight. Forgive me. I'll certainly cooperate with any investigation. Now, what was the question?"

"Please speak to the relationship between yourself and Gavin."

"The thing of that is..." Gavin started.

"Boy," Mike shouted, cutting Gavin off. "I didn't ask you a thing. I told you to sit there quietly until I was ready for you. Amber, you were saying?"

"Gavin here is an old friend of mine," Amber said. "There was a time that we could have been a couple, could have married, but when Adam showed up with his father and I saw him for the first time, I knew he was the man I wanted to marry. I felt bad for Gavin, so I still help him to this day. That's all there is to it, Detective."

"And the late-night rendezvous with each other?" Amanda asked. "Just sitting together, watching movies and eating ice cream like a slumber party?"

"What we do behind closed doors is no one's business but our own," Amber said.

"Do you admit to having sexual encounters with both Gavin and Danny even though you are engaged to Adam?" Mike asked.

"No," Amber said. "We never did anything inappropriate."

"We're just supposed to believe that you and these men met late at night and talked for twenty minutes then left?" Mike asked. "That's the way of it then?"

"Yes," Amber said. "I don't like having my character called into question, Detective. I didn't do anything with these men."

"And the gambling debt?" Amanda asked. "Such large sums of money. And Gavin here seemed to have such large sums of money to gamble with in the first place. Care to speak on that?"

"I was helping a friend."

"The help you should have given him was an intervention," Mike said. "Not enable him to go so far into debt that he would never be able to pay it off."

193

"It's a tough position to be in," Amber said. "I didn't want to hurt Gavin, but I wanted to make sure he didn't destroy himself. I was trying to be a good friend."

"And Danny?" Amanda asked. "You paid him large sums of money as well. Danny had a sister he cares for very deeply. She wanted to go to college but there was no money. All of a sudden, there's a scholarship coming from the mayor's office. A full ride for four years, initiated by you to Danny's sister. No one else got to apply for the scholarship."

"My father does a lot of charity work," Amber said. "He has provided a college education to many children. This was simply an extension of that. I was working to take the program over. Danny's sister will be working here once her college is completed."

"So, Amber," Amanda asked. "I have one more question for you on this line, if we were to pull Adam in here and ask him the same questions, would we get the same answers?"

"Of course."

"Would he be surprised to hear about the late-night meetings?"

"Not in the least."

Mike was gawking at Gavin, looking at the extent of the bruising to his face, "What happened to you, boy? What did the other guy look like?"

"It wasn't good," Gavin said, looking down. "I was in a mixed-martial-arts fight tonight. I didn't win. Didn't last a round."

"Now, of course, we all know that's bullshit," Mike said. "You weren't in any MMA fight tonight. You were at the casino then at Amber's apartment. So, why don't you tell me what really happened?"

"Mr. Timm and Cassie," Gavin said. "She had weighted gloves on. You know, Detective, for how high and mighty you are acting, you really should get out to the casino. They took me into a back room, a room with no cameras mind you, and pounded the stuffing out of me. How come you're not out there arresting them?"

"If there's no camera," Amanda said, "And both Mr. Timm and Cassie were in the room, it would be their word against yours. There wouldn't be enough evidence to suggest that anything happened. We did see the security footage of you being taken from your seat at the blackjack table. Were they excessive? Yes, but well within their rights. The damage we see could have been caused by that. So, what really happened? Why did you come out of Amber's apartment looking worse than you went in?"

"Delayed bruising and swelling," Gavin replied.

"That's what you are going with?" Amanda asked. "The fact that some of Amber's neighbors heard yelling and glass breaking? Thought they heard the sounds of a fight? Did little Amber beat you up that badly?"

"If she did," Gavin said. "Just know that I would never hit a woman. If she did swing at me, I would only cover up, never fight back."

"Such an interesting comment to make right now," Mike said. "Amber, you have anything you wish to add to this?"

"I hope you catch Danny's killer soon," Amber said. "It looks bad for the town, and for your record detective, to have an unsolved murder on the books."

"Gavin," Amanda said, placing her hand on top of his, "If there's anything you want to tell us, or want to ask us for, protection of any kind perhaps, just let us know."

"Am I in trouble?" Gavin asked.

"Are you?" Mike retorted.

195

"Come on, Gavin," Amber said. "They don't have any more questions for us."

"Please send Adam in on your way out, Amber," Mike said. "We have some questions for him too."

Amber glared at Mike, but she managed a polite smile and nod as she rushed Gavin out of the room. Mike and Amanda remained silent as they waited for Adam to enter the room. Mike knew Adam was just outside the door. He should have been in the room in less than thirty seconds, but Mike was certain Amber was coaching Adam.

"What's this about?" Adam asked as he walked in and sat down. "Why are we getting questioned?"

"Why do you think we are questioning you?" Mike asked.

"I have no idea, Detective," Adam said. "I can't figure it out. I had nothing to do with Danny's death."

"Who said this has anything to do with Danny's death?" Amanda asked. "We simply said we had a few questions for you."

"If it's not about Danny," Adam said, quickly, "Then what is this about?"

"We noticed some strange behavior out of your girlfriend," Mike said. "Very strange, actually. Care to enlighten us as to why she was paying off Gavin's gambling debts?"

"They have a long history together," Adam said. "If we hadn't met, she would have most likely married him."

"We heard that story, yes," Amanda said. "But as far as we can tell, she's into Gavin for almost half a million dollars. That's a lot for an old friend."

"I don't know the specifics," Adam replied.

"And what about the late-night meetings that Amber has with Gavin?" Mike asked. "Sure, seems like, oh, what the devil do you kids call it these days, a midnight hookup?"

"If you think that Amber is cheating on me behind my back you are sorely mistaken," Adam almost shouted. "She is faithful to me and only me. Amber and I are bound together by our common love. An endless love that will last the ages."

Mike tipped his head back in a deep, hearty laughter. "Still wet behind the ears and he thinks he has it all figured out. Wow. I would have thought you'd know better by now."

"You know nothing about me," Adam snapped. "You pathetic fop, think you know me? Have me figured out, eh? I didn't do anything. Amber is faithful to me. We had nothing to do with Danny Brown. Detective, I suggest you double your efforts to find the real killer."

Adam stood up and marched out of the room in disgust. His glare could have burned a hole through the door as he exited the room. Mike didn't say a word, just smiled as he looked at his notes on his glasses computer.

"What do you think?" Amanda asked.

"There are very few reasons why a witness would be that hostile to detectives," Mike said. "Very few. Either he killed Danny, which I doubt, or he is a spoiled brat who has never been disciplined once in his life. From the stories I've heard, Allen let him do whatever he wanted as a child. He was spoiled rotten from the day he was born."

"And that is why he is so dangerous," Jerry Bosen said, as he walked into the room.

"Chairman Bosen," Amanda said, perking up in her seat. "What brings you here?"

"Think about it, Detective," Jerry said. "Adam has been spoiled his entire life and now he's out on his own."

"You have a theory?"

"I have thousands of theories," Jerry said. "But unlike my theory on the financial causes of the third world war or the real reasons for the last two emergency N.A.S.A. trips to space, this theory is much more localized and pressing to our cause."

"What have you got for me, Jerry?" Mike asked.

"Earlier tonight, Allen Day made an offhand reference to the fact his will had been changed," Jerry said. "Allen and Adam had just had a tiff."

"Something that's happening a lot lately," Amanda said. "If the newsfeeds are to be believed."

"Father and son quarreling all the time," Jerry said. "I did a quick check to figure out what Allen meant by his comment. Guess what happens to Everyday Computers when Allen Day checks out?"

"What?" Mike asked.

"The company is transferred to the employees," Jerry said. "The company is given to every worker there. Guess who isn't a worker at his father's company? The terms of the will clearly dictate that only full-time employees get to benefit in this."

"Adam is working for Madison Software Labs," Mike said.

"So, when Allen dies," Jerry said. "The entire fortune of Everyday Computers goes to the employees, not to Adam. Adam gets a trust fund of one million dollars that he cannot touch until he's sixty. That's all Allen is leaving to his son."

"Why?" Amanda asked. "Why would he do that?"

"They don't get along," Jerry said. "And Adam has made some questionable decisions in his day. Allen doesn't trust him with the company. Adam would be out completely. He wouldn't even have a guaranteed job. He'd be all on his own."

"But he'll be married to the acting First Lady," Amanda said. "If all goes according to their plans. Adam and Amber are set for life, even without Allen's money."

"But what happens if Teddy doesn't win the presidency?" Jerry asked. "They believe that Ted will win with Chad as his vice. Amber will be acting First Lady since Ted is a widow. Once his eight years are up, Chad will run with Amber as his vice. After those eight years, Amber is marked for the big house."

"You mean the White House," Amanda said.

"Big house, White House," Jerry said, with a smile. "They both hold criminals. If Teddy wins, then Chad wins, then Amber wins, yes, Amber and Adam are set for life. But what if Teddy loses? Where does that put them?"

"This is all very interesting, Jerry," Mike said. "But your hatred of Mayor Kamp is coming out strong."

"I don't hate the man," Jerry said. "I simply don't agree with him. We have differences of opinion on certain matters. Look, Mike, I study system stabilities for a living. I'm damn good at what I do, and I've made a lot of money off it. I've learned one thing when dealing with the motivations of humans."

"What's that?" Amanda asked, gazing at Jerry.

"Money trumps all."

"Money?" Mike asked.

"Money," Jerry said. "99 times out of 100, you follow the money and you find the answer."

"You know something?" Mike said. "Something else?"

"No," Jerry said. "I'm simply saying this should be on your radar. And to watch Alyssa Babbage. Something about her doesn't add up."

Jerry stood and quickly left the room. Mike and Amanda were stunned with the conversation they'd just had. Neither of them had put those clues together yet. Adam wasn't a suspect before, but he was now. Mike was impressed that Jerry had seen the connections. Mike tried to contemplate how this scenario could play out, what Adam and Amber could gain from it. Mike motioned to Amanda to leave. It was time to go back to the station and look over all the evidence again in a new light, a light of a money trail that led back to Amber and Adam.

Chapter #22

As the sun started to rise on another day in Winter Falls, the remnants of lasts night's party could still be seen inside the building. Security stations were still set up. Decorations and supplies lined the hallways toward the ballroom. Workers were in the process of removing all the tables and cleaning the floors as Detective Mike Russ and Amanda Drake walked in. The pair stopped at the entrance to the ballroom, looked over the workers. Mike was feeling his age this morning, having been out late last night questioning people at the party, people he was going to have to question again today.

Amanda was incessantly fixing her hair, wishing there was a mirror to catch a glimpse of herself. She'd thought she'd noticed Jerry eyeing her the day before, even if he had been with that reporter. All the stories that Amanda had heard about Jerry, she knew she didn't stand out against the women he was usually with, but she thought that maybe if she presented a good image, she'd stand a chance. She'd worn her lowest cut police tank top this morning, hoping that it might be enough to catch his eye. Amanda realized Mike had already started walking toward the computer room, so she ran to catch up with him.

Through the maze of offices and computer labs, Mike looked for anyone that he needed to talk to. He had bad news to deliver and had never quite mastered the art of subtly and softness when bad news was being given. He was a blunt speaker and that's how he always spoke. Other workers indicated that the people they needed to find were all in a conference room, going over the day's events. Mike quickly walked into the conference room, not bothering to knock, but bursting right in.

Around a metal, circular table, sitting in large leather chairs, were Dr. Hall, Dr. Porter, Alyssa, Ben, Jerry, Amber, and Adam. They all looked surprised to see the detectives walking into the room.

"Detective Russ?" Jack asked. "What is the meaning of this?"

"Has anyone seen or spoken to Gavin Rodgers this morning?" Mike asked.

Everyone shook their heads no.

"Did he say anything last night?" Amanda asked. "Talk about what was going on? If he was meeting anyone?"

"No," Jack said. "Last I saw him was when he left the computer lab. What is this about?"

"He was found dead in his apartment this morning," Mike said. "Beaten to death."

There was a gasp followed by a silence in the room. No one wanted to speak.

"It was pretty bad," Amanda said.

"Could it have been from injuries from his MMA fight last night?" Ben asked.

"He didn't have a fight last night," Mike said. "Not an MMA one anyway. Those bruises you saw were from a real fight, not a sports competition. The question is, who and why? No, he did not die from injuries from that fight. There were new injuries to him when he was found."

"Who found him, Detective?" Jerry asked.

"His sister, Kim," Detective Russ said. "Gavin left a very cryptic message on her phone last night. She was worried about him. When she couldn't get ahold of him this morning, she went to his place. She had a spare key to get in."

"Here's the kicker," Amanda said. "The message he left her was a prelude to the suicide note that was written on his table. Handwriting analysis has confirmed that Gavin wrote it. It appeared that Gavin had three methods of suicide he was choosing from. He had a bottle of pills, a knife, and a noose on the table. He was in the process of deciding how he was going to kill himself when someone came over."

"This is horrible," Dr. Porter said, looking sick. "I can't believe it."

"Detective," Jerry continued. "What did the note say? Why was he going to kill himself?"

"The note talked about his gambling problem," Mike said. "Gavin had been struggling with it for a long time. He'd been to rehab, he'd been to counseling, but nothing seemed to work for him. Gavin was ashamed that he'd slipped again, gambling away his entire saving and retirement. He'd blown every dime he had and still couldn't stop. Gavin said he didn't want to face the shame of letting everyone know he'd failed again."

"And the injuries from the fight?" Jerry asked. "They were bad?"

"Every rib was broken," Amanda said. "Jaw shattered. Bruises everywhere."

"Whoever did this, knew what they were doing," Mike said. "It looks like they hurt him then gave one solid punch to the heart that was strong enough to stop it. Whoever did this was very strong. This is the second person working on this system to turn up dead. I'm going to ask a question, Dr. Hall, but I suspect I already know the answer."

"Anything," Dr. Hall said.

"Please look up the cameras around Gavin's apartment starting at about three this morning."

Dr. Hall put on his computer glasses and started racing through programs and video feeds. He knew that

Gavin lived on a busy street with lots of activity and cameras, so there should be no trouble bringing up the video feed. To Jack's surprise, the cameras went dead around 3:05 in the morning. Every traffic cam and video surveillance in the apartment hallways was blank.

"There's nothing," Jack said. "All the cameras were turned off."

"Just like Danny," Amanda said.

"Seth," Dr. Hall called out. "Who was accessing the traffic cameras around three this morning?"

"No one was accessing the traffic cameras, sir," Seth's voice floated through the room as the video screen switched to an image of a man whose mouth movements synced with Seth's voice. "The cameras were not accessed this morning."

"That's impossible, Seth," Dr. Hall said. "We are looking at cameras right now. They were turned off last night at 3:05. Someone had to turn them off. I want to know who turned them off."

"No one, sir," Seth said. "The cameras were turned off as part of an energy saving program. They remain off at certain times to conserve energy and to avoid extra wear and tear on equipment."

"No, they aren't, Seth," Dr. Hall protested. "The cameras were clearly labeled as high-priority systems that were supposed to be on at all times. Why were they switching off?"

"After the startup of the system, that file was changed, sir," Seth said.

"Changed?" Jerry asked. "By whom?"

"I cannot access that information," Seth said. "It was changed by someone using an administration password. Anyone who has that password could have done it."

"Detective," Dr. Porter asked. "Do you suspect that the same person who murdered Danny also murdered Gavin?"

"It is our belief," Mike said. "Yes. Although they were not killed in the same way, Danny stabbed while Gavin was beaten, there are some subtle clues that indicate this was the same person. No usable DNA found at the scene, cameras shut off, and in both cases, there were personal effects and money left at the scene. Gavin had about five thousand dollars sitting on his table that was untouched. He also had this."

Mike reached into his briefcase and tossed a red binder on the table. Everyone around the table went silent, their eyes enlarging to the size of dinner plates. The binder on the table changed everything. There was no question now, they knew this had to be related to the system. There was only one thing written on the cover of the binder, 'Madison Software Labs –Operations X22B --- Confidential.'

"That's the operations manual for the system," Jack said.

"Kind of small for such a large system," Amanda replied. "Isn't it?"

"The full operations manual for the system is over five thousand pages long," Jack said. "It's stored on the computer and transferred by external memory. We printed some small parts out to have to look at when we were working on the system. When we had steps to follow and didn't want to be switching back and forth between screens. Passwords and command codes were also written down and stored in binders like that."

"I've looked through this binder Dr. Hall," Mike said. "Lots of important information in there. How to change higher level functions of the system."

"Those instructions were never supposed to be printed," Dr. Hall said.

"Say a competitor got ahold of this book," Amanda said. "Or a hacker…how much trouble could be done?"

"Untold damage," Dr. Hall said. "This system controls so much that who knows what could happen."

"If a terrorist got ahold of it, for example," Dr. Porter said. "And wanted to create an attack, they could reroute wastewater into the drinking water system. They could shut down heating systems in the winter. They could stop the water flows and flood the town. There's no telling how far they could really go if the system got broken into."

"So, having this manual would lead you to believe that Gavin was working for someone else?" Mike said.

"It would be just like Social Software Solutions to try something like that," Dr. Porter said. "There's no other reason for him to have that manual at home."

"In our contracts," Dr. Hall said. "It states that discovery of the removal of a manual or protected information from city hall would be grounds for instant termination."

"Are there any other indications as to who did this?" Jerry asked. "Or is there any indication that Gavin reproduced this manual and distributed it to someone else?"

"Excuse me?" Mike asked.

"If other people have that information then the system is compromised," Jerry said. "It could lead to massive problems. We need to know if other people have that information or if Gavin was using it for himself."

"We don't know that, yet, Jerry," Amanda said. "But good thinking. You're so quick to pick things up."

"We need to alert Mayor Kamp," Dr. Hall said.

"I'll tell him," Jerry said.

"No, you won't," Dr. Porter said. "You'll use this as an excuse..."

"We all know Teddy's temperament," Jerry said. "He tends to fly off the handle and say things in the heat of the moment that he doesn't mean. He will never apologize for it either. Doctors, let me take the storm for you. There's nothing Teddy could say that would insult or hurt me. I'll take his anger. You don't want his wrath coming down on you. Now, remember, in my report, what was the first thing I said was going to happen to this system?"

"Hackers and tampering," Dr. Hall said.

"Right as rain."

"Jerry," Dr. Hall said. "Just tell him, don't gloat or rub it in."

"No promises," Jerry said. "Detective, I trust that you have the whereabouts of both Gary and Breeze Flynn from last night?"

"Their statements have already been taken," Mike said. "We are going to be questioning all of you throughout the day. We have some other things to follow up on right now, so we will be back later. I'm sorry for your loss. I know Gavin was a good worker here and well-liked. If you think of anything, please call. Be on the lookout as well. Dr. Hall, I would suggest that you double the security around the system and it wouldn't hurt to double check the files of all the employees who have access to the system."

"Of course," Jack said. "Thank you, Detective."

Mike and Amanda started to walk out of the room. Amanda gave a slight wave to Jerry which he responded to with a head nod. The room was silent for a moment as everyone contemplated what just happened.

"Jerry," Dr. Hall said, softly. "You cannot let Nevaeh know a word of this. This cannot get into the newsfeeds."

"I'm not evil, Dr. Hall," Jerry replied. "If word of this got out, it would destroy your company and quite possibly the town."

"What do you mean?" Dr. Porter asked.

"This system is predicated upon trust," Jerry said. "The people of Winter Falls trust that you built them a system that will remain stable and operate within given tolerances. What happens when they find out that that trust has been violated? What happens when they find out that the grand system designed to save time and money is responsible for deaths? They will turn against this system and everyone working on it. Riots are a likely possibility. None of you will be able to find jobs anywhere in this country again.

"Nevaeh can be your greatest strength right now. When the timing is right, when we have to tell the public what is going on, she can draft the stories and get them into the newsfeed. We will have to be very careful about what is said and how it is said. We must make sure the public keeps their trust in the system. Above all else, we must keep the public's trust."

"You sound like you're defending us," Dr. Porter said.

"I am defending you," Jerry said. "You are good people, bright people, who deserve better than what Mayor Kamp is giving you with this system. I know I talk a lot about the harm this system will do, but I don't want to see any of you hurt with it."

"Thank you, Jerry," Dr. Hall said. "But we find ourselves in a precarious position. Again, we are short-staffed, and Gavin was essential to operations. We need someone to fill in for him."

"I can do it," Jerry said.

"You don't have the experience or the abilities to run the system," Jack said.

"I've studied this system enough, Jack," Jerry said. "I've seen you working on it and I know I can handle the day to day portions of it. I can fill in until a proper replacement is found. I suggest not hiring anyone new until we know exactly what is going on with these murders."

"Mayor Kamp will never allow you," Holly said. "He'll think it's a case of the fox guarding the chickens."

"Let me deal with him," Jerry said. "I know how to sell this to him so he'll accept it."

"That's all well and good," Dr. Hall said. "But we need to get back to work. This system needs to stay running."

Dr. Hall watched as the others got up from the table and shuffled out. He knew their backs were against the wall. With a second murder and proof that it had something to do with the system, Jack wanted to implement a new level of security, but he wasn't sure what he could do. Jack knew that from this point on, he needed to suspect everyone. He didn't know who he could trust, but for some reason, he knew that he could trust Alyssa above all the others. Jack just hoped his instinct on this was right.

Chapter #23

Amber Kamp walked slowly around the computer stations in the Master Control Room. Every person she passed seemed to shudder like a winter chill was tickling their spine as Amber walked by. With eagle eyes, Amber made sure to glance at every screen, every workstation, to see what the people were working on. Amber wanted to be sure that every person in the room was doing what they were supposed to be doing and that no one was slacking off on company time. Even though her current role within Everyday Computers didn't give her any authority here, everyone knew that she was a woman who grasped power in her hand.

As Amber finished making the rounds through the Master Control Room, she glanced into the main room to see that Ben was sitting in the main chair, looking at various traffic cameras throughout the city. Amber scoffed at the way Ben always dressed for work; baggy gym shorts and tee shirts. Amber looked at her ensemble in the reflection of a mirror; black tights, a formal blouse, topped with a designer blazer. Amber was dressed for a professional boardroom meeting, not a street basketball game, like Ben. Amber watched him for a moment before she felt her glasses vibrate, indicating that a phone call was coming in. Amber quickly rushed to a side room, somewhere out of the way, so she could speak on the phone without fear of anyone hearing her.

"Answer," Amber called out as she shut the door to a large conference room. "Hello...they questioned me all morning...where the hell were you?"

Amber moved around the long, rectangular table and pulled out a chair at the head so she would be facing the door. Amber sat down. "The bastard was going to kill himself anyway...these deaths are attracting far too much attention to the system...I just wish I knew what exactly was going on...I understand...I had nothing to do with it...you know where I was last night...we can argue about this all day and get nowhere...we need to move forward with plans...I would do it myself but I don't have the access to the command codes nor the master system plans."

Amber took a deep breath as a shadow passed by the glass window next to the door. She didn't think anyone saw her come in and certainly didn't want anyone listening. Amber paused a moment longer to make sure she was alone. "We will need a master engineer to do this...I don't think it will cost a lot...I will have to do a certain job or two...I have no problem doing that again...both Danny and Gavin were in love with me, there's no reason this person won't either...I know...Nevaeh was there with Jerry yet she didn't put the story on the newsfeed...the public must get word of this soon...how are things going with Breeze...is she on board with the plan...good...no one must ever be able to trace it back to us...no one will believe her as long as our story stays the same...I know who I'm going to get but I'm going to need a change of clothing first...I know...love you too."

Amber stood up from the chair and looked around the room. Even before Gavin died she anticipated that she was going to have to bring another player into the game today and she was ready for it. Amber quickly removed her blazer jacket and blouse, leaving just a tight black tank top with the city logo across the chest. Amber kicked her shoes off, watching out the window to make sure no one was looking in. She took her tights off, exposing the black shorts she wore underneath. Amber folded her formal clothing up and left it on the table, adjusting her tank top so it exposed her navel.

Amber gave a quick glance of the room, hoping she'd picked the right room when she hid for her call. A box along the wall made her smile. Amber rushed to the box and found the supplies that she'd asked her contact to stash here earlier in the week. Amber wasn't certain the exact date she'd need to execute this plan, so she was prepared. Amber pulled her hair into a ponytail and took the baseball cap with a university logo on it and put it on, pulling her hair through the back hole of the cap. She slipped on a pair of sneakers before spraying herself with a cheap perfume. Amber looked in the glass by the door. She could just barely make out her reflection. Where a businesswoman stood a moment before, was a college party girl. Amber put her formal clothing in the box and stuffed it in the back corner.

Amber quickly made her way out of the room, glad that the Master Control Room's light was held at a very low level. She thought with the hat that most people wouldn't be able to see her face, but she also put her glasses on to further hide who she was. Amber didn't care what these people thought of her, but the last thing she wanted was pictures of her in that outfit surfacing on the Internet newsfeeds. She had a reputation to protect and would do anything to make sure it stayed intact.

Amber made it to the Main Control Room without anyone spotting her. She quietly closed the door and studied Ben for a moment. Ben was intently looking at data from the system on a vast majority of the screen. What Amber hadn't noticed before was that in the lower righthand corner of the screen, obscured from view from anyone not sitting in the main chair, a movie was playing. Amber recognized it instantly, 'Waves of Summer' right at the part where Paige Gianakos was surfing by herself, her skin shimmering with sparkling water in the bright day sun.

Amber smiled an evil grin before moving two steps behind Ben and loudly clearing her throat. "Mr. Hewitt, I don't recall your contract having a movie-watching clause in it."

Ben scrambled to close the screen with the movie and replaced it with data from the system. "I'm sorry, ma'am." Ben stood and turned around, stunned at the condition he saw Amber in.

"What?" Amber asked, spinning on a heel so he could see all of her. "You don't' think I like to be comfortable when I work?"

"No," Ben said. "I've never seen you dressed down before. You always look like you're ready to enter the boardroom or something."

"What do you think of it?"

"Not bad."

"You're a hard man to please," Amber said, as she pushed Ben back into his seat. Amber moved to the computer console and leaned against it, in a seductive pose. "Anyone else here right now, Ben?"

"Not that I know of," Ben said, eyeing Amber up and down. "The doctors are working on some stuff upstairs, Allen and Adam are back at the technology campus, Dr. Porter is at home, she's taking the night shift, and Jerry and your dad are probably fighting right now."

"Why do you say they are fighting?"

"What else do they do? They had a meeting with each other."

"Work can be so stressful at times, can't it, Ben?"

"Oh, yeah," Ben said, with a smile.

"Sometimes you just want to cut loose," Amber said, dancing a little in the room before moving back to her leaning position against the console. "I mean, I've got all these expectations on how I'm supposed to behave when all I really want to do is dance. You ever get that feeling, where you just want to dance?"

"I don't know," Ben said, confused. "I'm not sure."

Amber smiled and winked. "Tell me, Ben. I know that we haven't really socialized with each other before, but tell me, you have anyone special in your life?"

"There's always someone special," Ben said. "But *how* special is the key. No one super special right now."

"That's a shame. A powerful, cute guy like you should have women all over him."

"Oh, there's always a couple but I'm being careful not to get too attached right now. Never know when something better will pop up."

"So, you're a player then?"

"From time to time," Ben said. "I've had my fair share of home runs."

"You batting at Jerry's level?"

"No one bats at Jerry's level, Amber," Ben laughed. "They had to invent an entirely new game to chart those numbers."

"So, he's your role model then?"

"Hardly," Ben said. "An interesting case study. Besides, he's going after that reporter now. His blog feeds talk about wanting to settle down."

"Are you ready to settle down?"

"I really don't want to," Ben said. "But if it was the right time with the right woman I'm sure something could be worked out."

"I know you've been checking me out recently, Ben," Amber said, posing a little more for him. "I see you catching a glance then looking away. You don't have to be shy, Ben. That's okay...I have just one question for you though."

"Ask away."

"Why haven't you made a move on me?" Amber asked. "What? Am I not attractive enough to you? You don't have the guts to talk to me? I know you like me, why haven't you acted on it?"

"It's not a question of guts," Ben said. "Look at who your dad is...and the fact that you are dating Adam."

"I think it is guts, Ben," Amber said. "I think you're scared of me. Think about that, you, a rough and tough guy scared of little old me."

"I'm not scared of you."

"Prove it."

Ben stared at Amber as he swallowed in a dry throat. He had lusted after her since he first saw her but had never acted on it, or thought of acting on it, due to her personality, who she was, and what she stood for. Ben rarely saw Amber without Adam around and Ben knew that getting involved with the mayor's daughter when he was interning on this project, hoping to get a job there when he graduated, would not bode well for his career.

As Ben was thinking about it, Amber was tired of waiting. Amber slowly took off her tank top, revealed her black bra, and tossed the top, letting it land on Ben's lap.

"Prove it," Amber said, again, this time firmer.

Ben stood up and almost ripped his tee shirt off, exposing his well-muscled chest and arms, his broad shoulders, and his washboard abs. Before he moved, Ben touched a pair of buttons on the computer console, one to turn the cameras in the room off, the other to lock the door to the room. He then rushed forward, grabbing Amber in his arms, and planting a kiss on her lips. In one fluid motion, Ben lifted Amber and gently placed her on the floor, on her back, getting on top of her and kissing her, his hands running everywhere along her body.

"How's this for proving it?" Ben asked.

"It's a start," Amber said. "I still don't believe you aren't afraid. Anybody can kiss a girl. I want you to really show me."

Ben swallowed again, hardly able to believe what he just heard. He started kissing her again, running his hands everywhere. He was using all his effort to maintain control, to keep this safe. He wanted nothing more than to rip every stitch of clothing off her that second, but something in the back of his mind was screaming caution. Ben knew women never moved this fast. He'd never seen a woman this open to him before. Ben knew that something had to be wrong. Even though he wanted more than anything to go through with it, he paused, looking deep into Amber's eyes.

"What about Adam?" Ben asked.

"What about Adam?" Amber said.

"You two are dating," Ben replied. "It's rumored you are getting married soon. Some people say you are already married."

"Let me tell you something about Adam," Amber said. "He isn't the man you think he is."

"You mean, he's gay?" Ben asked.

"Not at all," Amber said. "I don't know what the term is. He doesn't like sex."

"I think that's considered dead," Ben said. "What kind of man doesn't like sex?"

"He doesn't," Amber said. "I've never had sex with him. He wants to be with me but not in that way. I get to have partners, for sex only, on the side."

"Bullshit," Ben said. "I don't believe it."

"Ben," Amber said, firmly, "You're seconds away from blowing this deal. I'm on the floor, half-naked, ready for you. Now's not the time to be thinking about someone else. Now let's get back to where we were before I decide

216

that it would be more fun to look at spreadsheets than to spreadsheets with you."

In that instant, Ben saw Amber, truly saw her physical form and his powerful lust overpowered him. All thoughts of why he shouldn't be doing this and how there was no positive outcome were pushed out of his mind and with one fluid motion, Ben had Amber's bra off and flung it across the room. Amber giggled as she tossed her cap off her head and started kissing Ben, the pair giving themselves over to their lust.

Chapter #24

Jerry sat in a chair opposite Mayor Kamp's desk. Ted and Jerry had been discussing the events of the past twenty-four hours with Jerry giving the mayor all the gritty details of what had happened. Like Jerry predicted, Mayor Kamp had flown off the handle, used a copious amount of curse words, and made plenty of idol threats toward Jerry. Jerry, to his credit, smiled and sat silently through all the abuse, not letting any of it get to him. Jerry was glad he was the one who offered to deliver the news, anyone else would have been fired.

As Jerry and Ted were getting ready to go another round of arguing with each other, Dr. Hall and Alyssa entered the room. Jack was carrying a packet of papers and had a long look on his face. Jack and Alyssa took seats opposite the mayor before they were offered. The look on their faces told the entire story, they had discovered something in their investigation that didn't bode well for Winter Falls and the system Dr. Hall had created.

"You'd better have some good news for me, Jack," Ted said, leaning back in his chair. "I've been getting horrible news from Jerry all morning here."

"I'm afraid it's about to get worse, sir," Jack said. "Mayor Kamp, Alyssa and I have spent the morning analyzing the system. We've checked every possible outcome and double checked it. Everything points to one thing…sabotage."

"Impossible," Mayor Kamp said.

"I've run a regression analysis on the pump system five times," Alyssa said. "Each time we come up with the same parameters. The only way that is possible is sabotage."

218

"The order of operations was changed," Dr. Hall said. "The order of operations at the root base caused a series of overdrives on the nominal function of the..."

"English, please," Ted interrupted.

"Someone changed the system," Alyssa said. "They changed it at the base function. The primary operating code that the entire system runs off of."

"Damn you, Jerry," Mayor Kamp said. "I'll see you hanged for this."

"It couldn't have been Jerry," Jack said.

"Thank you, Dr. Hall," Jerry said. "I shouldn't even have to defend myself. I would never resort to sabotage. My theories will always be proven right by time. I told everyone that this would happen."

"Why couldn't it be Jerry?" Ted asked.

"He doesn't have the access codes required to do this," Alyssa said. "The only people with those codes would have been Dr. Hall, Dr. Porter, Danny Brown, Gavin Rodgers, Ben Hewitt, and now myself."

"What about that book found at Gavin's place?" Ted asked. "If someone had found that book or if Gavin had shown it to someone, could they have figured this out?"

"Not in the timeframe they had," Jack said. "Just using that book and public knowledge about the system it would take even the best hacker's months to get in. And even then, we'd know about it instantly. That's the kicker, Mayor, we are supposed to know the moment there is a change in the system, that's how we learned about the faulty water pump yesterday morning. The fact that the system didn't register the change is very frightening to me."

"How do we protect ourselves, you fool?" Ted asked. "Damn it all to hell in a handcart. When I ordered this system, you promised me garbage like this couldn't happen. I can't have this happening to me right now. We need this system to be perfect."

"Perfection is an impossible goal, Mayor," Jerry said. "I'm not trying to rile you up here, but you need to have realistic expectations about this."

"Don't talk to me that way, Jerry," Ted said. "I'm sure you're laughing inside about this. Now listen here, you simple ass, get this system running properly. I should hardly have to tell you that your job and career is on the line with this. If this doesn't work, you know what would happen to Madison Software Labs?"

"That's hardly fair," Alyssa said.

"Quiet child," Ted snapped. "Adults are talking."

"Mayor Kamp," Jerry said. "That's no way to address her."

"Don't you start lecturing me," Ted said. "I told that bozo to have this system up and running a year before the election cycle started. We cannot have little problems like this cropping up if we are going to sweep an election. It is my destiny to become president. I have planned this since I was a little boy, watching my first State of the Union address. Damn it, Jack, don't mess with me on this one. Get this under control."

"You can't talk to us like that," Alyssa said.

"I wasn't talking to you," Ted said. "I was talking to Jack here. I want this system to be perfect. Now get it right before I get someone else. You have the entire resources of the city behind you on this. Anything you need is at your disposal. Now get the system working."

"We need to figure out who is causing this though," Jerry said. "Yelling at him to get this figured out won't help if people are destroying the system. We have two murdered workers and I think it's pretty safe to say they died because of this system. Ted, what's the human cost of this system going to be? Three lives? Ten?"

"What are you getting at?" Ted said. "And if you say stability I'm going to scream."

"The population of this town is at equilibrium," Jerry said. "They are content. Happy. This system is supposed to raise that happiness to a higher level. If it doesn't, expect chaos. System instability. Sooner or later, someone is going to link these deaths to the system, Teddy. I've got Nevaeh's word that she won't issue anything without your permission but there are other reporters out there, hungry for the chance of a big story."

"So, what are you suggesting?" Ted said.

"Pull the system," Jerry replied. "Just until these murders are figured out."

"You would love that, wouldn't you?" Ted said. "Then how many millions of books would you sell talking about the downfall of this? That's your endgame, isn't it? Another bestseller for your collection."

"Please," Jack said. "Both of you knock it off. We can't go bouncing off the walls for ten minutes only to end up right where we are. There's been a security failure. I suggest we bring in another security expert to look at the system. They could add a layer of security and maybe help us figure out what went wrong."

"Very good, very good," Ted said. "That would be an all right solution."

Jack shifted in his seat, pleased that Theodor was starting to calm down. Jack had dreaded telling him what had happened, especially since he knew Jerry was still in the room, but so far this had gone far better than he imagined. Before Jack could say anything else, the door to the office swung open and Allen Day bounded into the room, slamming the door behind him. Allen's usual jovial demeanor was gone, replaced with an expression of anger and rage. His face and bald head were red. Sweat was covering his face. In his hands, he clenched a report so tightly his fingers were turning white. Allen stared at Jack, rage burning a hole through the doctor.

"Laddybuck," Allen said, with venom dripping from his voice. "You'd damn well better have a good explanation for what I'm holding in my hands. I tolerate a lot, but this is something I will not stand for. I don't care if it was you, Jack, we've been friends for a long time. But I want whoever was behind this fired immediately."

"We don't know who sabotaged the system in regard to the pumps, Allen," Jack said. "We were discussing the possibilities of who it could have been."

"I'm not talking about the sabotage of the damn pumps, champ," Allen said, slowly, every word being controlled with precision. "I'm talking about the son-of-a-bitch who switched a new motor out for an old one."

Jack shook his head. He wasn't even sure what he thought he heard was actually what he heard. The system, on its first day, had detected a faulty motor that saved lives. Allen was implying that someone fabricated the story to promote the system.

"I don't understand," Jack said. "Are you saying that the system didn't detect the motor on its own?"

"I'm saying I hold a private report in my hand," Allen said. "A report compiled by Everyday Computer engineers. They conclude that the pump motor had been changed as scheduled but the night before the system came online someone was out there and switched the motor out with a faulty one. The system was scheduled to detect it. I want the son-of-a-bitch who did that fired."

"You shouldn't talk about yourself like that," Ted said. "Allen, it was Adam's idea. He ran it past me first and I thought it was great."

"That had better be a sick joke, Laddy," Allen said. "Adam couldn't have come up with that idea on his own. He's not the sharpest crayon in the box."

"He's smarter than you give him credit for," Ted said. "Ever since you took him out of the will and out of the company he's been trying to find a place to fit in. Think about it, Allen. The boy was raised his whole life for one purpose; to follow in his father's footsteps. He makes one little mistake and you cut him off and cut him out. What is he supposed to do? Wither away and die? You've left some damn big shoes to fill and he's expressed interest in running this city when I go to the White House. He'd be good at it and we'd have someone who knows the system, knows what it takes to keep it running."

"You're telling me you approved that, Ted?" Allen asked.

"Yes," Ted said.

"I don't approve of this at all," Allen said. "Listen here, Adam had many chances to make things right and he didn't. Now he's taking shortcuts with this system. What good could come from doing things like that?"

"Look at all the press we got because of it," Ted said. "Every newsfeed in the country was running it as their top story. No one is ever going to find out."

"I had two entry-level computer engineers figure it out," Allen said. "And they weren't even looking for it. They happened to stumble across some carelessness in how it was executed. What would happen if it was a reporter who figured it out?"

"We have a reporter on our payroll now," Ted said. "Nevaeh…"

"Vaeh is her own woman and her own reporter," Jerry said. "Don't ever make the mistake of thinking that she will put out a false story for you. One story proved false and she's banned from the newsfeeds. It won't happen, Teddy."

"You threw your son out, Allen," Ted said, almost shouting. "I gave him a place and a job. I'm giving him a future. I'm confident in our plan. Everyone needs to trust me, and this will all work out. The world running on Everyday Computers and Madison Software Labs. I'll be the president. You two will have more money than you could ever imagine. It will all work out."

"We have two murders," Allen said. "A case of sabotage and a fake crisis to promote the system. We're off to a bang-up first few days, Laddy. This all needs to be taken under control before it gets out of hand. I don't want to see people getting hurt over this. If we don't stop this foolishness, then there's no telling where it will stop."

"Okay," Ted said. "The next time we are going to do something slightly underhanded with this system, I'll let you know about it, okay?"

"You'd better," Allen said. "So I can make sure it stops."

"Listen to me," Ted said. "I'm going to make this clear as can be. I don't care what you want, what you think, or who you are. This system will launch me and my career. I'll burn and bury every single one of you if need be."

"Isn't it a little early in the game to be making those kinds of threats?" Allen asked.

"The system fails now, you and Jack are taken down with it," Ted said. "That's a fact you cannot escape."

"There's no need for this," Jack said. "We can work this out."

"He's right though, champ," Allen said. "The system fails here and there goes all our nanobots research and Quantum Computers. We won't have any funding left. But we need to work together on this, Ted. Keep everyone in the loop."

"So, you're on board?"

"Yes," Allen said, a smile coming to his face for the first time in the office. "Just make sure Jerry here is with us."

"I'm just sitting back and enjoying the show," Jerry said. "You guys just went from digging your own graves with a trowel to digging them with a backhoe."

"Good," Ted said. "Jack is with us, so that means we agree. Let's get this system under control and working right. Let the detectives solve the murders."

Ted stood to usher everyone out of his office. Alyssa looked at Jack. He was looking at the ground, like a child who'd been scolded. They didn't even let him get a word in edgewise toward the end of the meeting. Alyssa wished Jack would have stood up to them. She wished he wouldn't let them push him around. Alyssa knew that Jack had it in him to fight for himself, what he thought was right, she just needed to figure out how to get it out of him.

Chapter #25

Ben couldn't believe the fun he'd just had. Not his first time by any means, but definitely the best. He'd always viewed Amber as an uptight, business-minded prude. Ben never thought for a moment that Amber could get wild and crazy like the college girls he was used to. The pair sat in the Main Control Room. Ben in the main chair, Amber draped across him. They'd both put most of their clothes back on, but had left just enough off to warrant the outer door still being locked, although Ben's shirt and Amber's tank top were near the chair they sat in.

Ben had the system running, monitoring all the levels of the pumps running on the west edge of the city. It was boring work but with Amber there, he found the time to be much more enjoyable. The thought still nagged him, that Amber seemed to move things way too fast, and that she made it far too easy for him. But with the experience they just had, Ben wasn't about to question it. He didn't know the real terms of her relationship with Adam, but Ben had gotten himself into fistfights over women before and came out okay. Ben was certain he could handle Adam.

"What are you thinking about?" Amber asked as she watched Ben.

Ben smiled down at her, "That's classified, like everything in this room, Amber. I could tell you but then I'd have to kill you."

"Playing a tease? Two can play that game, Ben," Amber said, as she kissed him.

"You are a question wrapped in a question," Ben said. "You know what, Amber? I just don't get you."

"What do you mean?"

"You come off as all professional and businesslike. I mean, you're stunning, but I always kinda thought you were a prudish bitch, no offense."

"None taken."

"You just seemed to be all business and work and everything and it didn't look like you knew how to have fun at all. Turns out I was wrong on that point. Way wrong."

"Never judge a book by its cover, Ben," Amber said. "The amazing thing isn't how many different faces a person can wear; the amazing thing is how we are so surprised every time we see a new face."

"I'm glad we did this …but seriously, what about Adam? Be honest."

"You really want honesty?"

"Yes, I do."

"Adam and I enjoy great sex like you and I just experienced. Even better than what you and I did. Adam and I have plans…well, I have plans and he has ideas. The point is, sometimes to get where you need to go, certain things need to be handled in certain ways. What would you say, Ben, if I told you that any time you wanted, you and I could have amazing sex like we just did? What if I told you I would do anything you asked? Any fantasy that you wanted? What would you say then?"

"I'd do anything for you," Ben replied.

"That's exactly what I wanted to hear," Amber smiled. "Ben, tell me, what do you think about the system?"

"The system?"

"Yes, the system. Please tell me your thoughts on this system that Adam's dad helped create and that my dad is using to get to the presidency."

"I mean, without this internship and the scholarships that I've received from your father and Dr. Hall I wouldn't be able to afford to get my Ph.D. My other scholarships ran out after my undergraduate and if I wouldn't have found this work, I'd be selling computer glasses to teenagers and helping grandparents send e-mails. This system has given me everything I have plus I have a good job lined up after I graduate. This system is everything to me."

"What if I could give you more? Money, power, women...would you take it to come and work for me?"

"Work for you?" Ben asked, motioning for Amber to get up. Ben stood up and started pacing the room. "I didn't know that you had a company that was hiring."

"I do, and I don't," Amber said, leaning against the console. "So to speak, I have goals to achieve. A vision for my future that I want to carry out. I need good workers to help me. Can't do everything myself, you know. I think you would fit in nicely with my team, Ben. I really want you to join us."

"And I get what we just did whenever I want?"

"To start with," Amber said. "When you get bored with me we can call in some other people I know. You'll never be alone or wanting for someone, I promise you that. You'll have money and be in a position of power. It's a good deal, Ben. You'd be foolish not to take it."

Ben remained silent, staring at Amber. He was curious what kind of job she had to offer but all his instincts told him to walk away right now. He knew that to offer what she was offering couldn't lead to anything on the level. Ben felt a sinister motive behind Amber and her offer. Ben's mind said that he should walk away right now, call the detective that had questioned him, and wash his hands of this, but as he looked at Amber, leaning against the console, partially clothed, other parts of him caved in and he knew that he would do whatever she wanted.

"What do you need me to do?" Ben asked. "What does this job entail?"

"I just need a little chaos," Amber said.

Ben's eyes got huge. The problems they were having with the system, he never imagined that Amber was the one behind it. He couldn't believe what he'd heard.

"Chaos?" Ben asked. "You mean sabotage the system?"

"That's what I mean, Ben. You have to understand, this is the only way."

"The only way to what?"

"The end game is for me and Adam to know. That is one thing I cannot allow you to know. No one has even glimpsed what we've seen yet. When this is over there will be more money and power than you can ever believe, Ben."

"What you're asking me to do could get me banned from ever touching a computer again, Amber. I've spent six years already in university. All that would be thrown down the drain. I would be banned from ever touching a computer. No company would hire me because there is hardly a job left that doesn't use computers. There would be nothing that I could do."

"But you won't get caught," Amber said. "That I can guarantee."

"How?"

"When the end game is written," Amber said, with a sadistic smile, "We have a scapegoat all nice and trussed up for the slaughter. She will be the perfect sacrifice for this game."

"Who?"

"Breeze Flynn," Amber said. "As I have spent time with you, Breeze has been spending time with Adam. She sought him out, trying to get information for the Neo-Luddites. Adam played along with it. Breeze thinks that she controls him. Pathetic. She is nothing compared to me. Breeze and that entire band of misfits will learn what true power and manipulation are about."

"So, Breeze takes the fall? Who is going to believe that, Amber? Breeze's very religion bans her from touching a computer. They say computers are the devil on earth. To do what you're talking she would have to use one."

"Her father uses one all the time, Ben," Amber said. "All the time. They are just as hypocritical as any other protest group. The followers actually believe they stand for something while the leaders of the group use and profit off that which they hate."

"Profit from it?"

"Gary Flynn set up a trust account many years ago," Amber said. "It's difficult to trace, and if Breeze hadn't told Adam about it we wouldn't know. Gary owns massive amounts of stock in Everyday Computers, Madison Software Labs, Social Software Solutions, and Pacific Creek Computers and Hardware."

"He owns stock in the biggest computer companies," Ben said.

"The dividends alone have been funding the Neo-Luddites the past few years. None of them know about it. If that information got out it would be the end of Gary and his little movement."

"Why does he own stock in them when he says they are bringing the end of the world?"

"That is a question for him," Amber said. "What do you say though? A little chaos here and there? Can you deliver for me?"

"I wouldn't be able to touch a computer again," Ben said.

"And I have connections," Amber replied. "Even if you got caught, which you won't, but let's say you did somehow. My father owns all the judges in town. This system is giving the university more money than they thought possible, and the president of the university is a friend of my father. Even if you did get caught, I could get you out of any charge they could bring."

Ben thought about it for a moment. He knew his judgment was being clouded by lust. He wished in that instant that Amber was wearing her normal business clothing, or at least covered up so he wouldn't be so tempted by her. He realized, of course, that was her goal. She'd shown him a great time and now he was hooked. A thought kept nagging him though, something he couldn't put his finger on. When the thought finally formed in his mind, he was horrified at what it meant, thought about running, but knew that he couldn't.

"You killed Danny and Gavin," Ben said, softly, "Didn't you?"

"I assure you I didn't kill either of them," Amber said. "I have witnesses to my whereabouts on both nights. Adam didn't kill them either. I have no idea who was behind those killings."

"Did Gavin sabotage the water pumps?"

"Yes," Amber said. "He was doing a good job before he got himself killed. Look, Ben, I didn't kill them. I don't know who did or why they were killed, but I need you. I promise you nothing bad will come from this."

"Amber," Ben said, slowly, thinking about the situation, "No matter what happens, if I get caught or not, my name will still be tainted with this. I don't foresee how we can get through this without getting caught."

"As I said," Amber replied. "It will all be traceable back to Breeze. She's such a naïve girl. Her father kept her sheltered for so long that she doesn't have the ability to function in the real world. It's sad really, but sometimes for great purposes, people need to be sacrificed. That's what separates a great person from an ordinary person, Ben. Great people are willing to make sacrifices where others aren't."

"Theoretically, if I were to do this, what would you want me to do? Do you have a plan for how I am to create chaos?"

"We are getting close to the end of the workday. I want a traffic jam the likes of which this town has never seen."

"Okay," Ben moved to the computer and brought of video feeds of the main traffic centers of the city. All the cars were moving along orderly and quickly on the streets. Ben started to pace again. "Since the traffic system is controlled through here, I can set the system to create a gridlock. The load-balancing unit that controls the streets could be set to malfunction, maybe to believe that there's been a disaster, so it reroutes all traffic. That would be good, no way to trace it here, except that I would have to create the disaster and it would be very easy to prove that someone did that. I would see it right away on my systems and would have to report and fix it."

"You are smarter than I thought," Amber said. "I didn't know how the traffic jam would happen but a disaster? I like that."

"Why are you doing this?"

"I need this system to fail. I did have Gavin sabotage the water pumps in the hopes that everyone would find out and with a new disaster that we had I was certain the voters would demand the shutdown of the system. I realize now that it must appear natural. If it's sabotage they can keep adding security systems. It must appear the system is failing on its own or that it's too big to work right."

"There's something," Ben said, perking up. "I could make it look like the system thought there was still a problem with the pumps. The pumps failed, and the system thought all the roads to the west of town were flooded and impassable. It would look like we forgot to reset systems after the first problem so not only would we get a traffic jam of epic proportions, everyone would know about the pump problem and that your father covered it up."

"That's incredible," Amber said, as she rushed up and kissed Ben. "I knew you were the right man for the job."

"But there's still the problem of knowing I changed the system," Ben said. "It will be obvious that I did something."

"Gavin gave me a very special command code, Ben. He gave me the code to wipe out any changes to the systems recorder files. You can change it, making sure we have at least ten minutes before the traffic starts backing up, then erase everything you did."

"I didn't know it was possible to erase files from the recorded portion of the system," Ben said. "I thought the light-based memory system prevented that."

"It's amazing what they didn't tell everyone about this system."

"There's only one more thing that I want, Amber," Ben said, sitting down in the chair. "There's one thing that you have to tell me before I start doing this."

"Anything you want."

"Why?"

"What?"

"Why are you destroying your father's chances at the presidency and destroying Allen and Dr. Hall's system? I mean, your father will be thrown out of office, Allen's company will be bankrupt, and there will be nothing left for either you or Adam. I don't get it."

"One day you will understand what is going on," Amber said. "But that is something I cannot divulge right now. My reasons are my own. Just know that you will profit greatly from it."

"Okay," Ben said. "Have the codes ready to wipe the memory systems."

Ben sat up in the main chair and got to work, his arms waving wildly in front of him as he shifted screens and reprocessed the code. Amber stood back and watched, smiling, knowing that she'd found the right person for the job.

Chapter #26

The air was filled with the angry sound of car horns blasting. Up and down the streets, cars sat at a standstill, the drivers laying on their horns, yelling out their windows, trying to figure out why no one was moving. The intense heat of the evening sun didn't help tempers or moods as the traffic had been stuck for well over a half hour with no signs of breaking up. Along the city streets, no one could figure out why the traffic was worse now than it had ever been before the system.

People, getting desperate to get home, were starting to drive their cars into the grassy median between opposing lanes, parking their cars and starting to walk. Others were pulling into the parking lots of stores and restaurants, spending time hoping that when they were done the traffic would be gone. To make matters worse, all the computer-controlled cars had noticed their air-conditioning units turned off. The system told them energy conservation was key, and the load was too great, on the electric grid. With all the cars receiving their power from the grid, only having an internal motor and no battery system, the people were at the mercy of the system.

In the middle of all the gridlock, laying on his horn and sweating in his brown suit, Detective Mike Russ pounded the steering wheel in frustration. He looked to his partner, Amanda Drake, who was tugging on her police shirt, trying to fan herself. Both individuals looked beyond miserable in the car, with the outside temperature still hovering around ninety degrees. The windows rolled down didn't seem to help as there was no breeze or air movement of any kind. There was nothing to do but sit and wait it out. Amanda put on her computer glasses and looked over traffic reports, but the news wasn't good.

"Son-of-a-bitch," Amanda said, looking in her glasses. "It's like this everywhere. Traffic stopped up worse than we've ever seen before."

"What is causing it?" Mike asked.

"Seems like last night the system had a problem and was shutting down water pumps on the west side of town. No one reported the problem because they got it fixed right away. Now the system seems to think that the pumps from yesterday were never fixed. The system believes that most of the roads on the west side of town are flooded and impassable. It's rerouting traffic accordingly."

"That's strange," Mike said. "I wonder why Dr. Hall's people can't override the system and get it to rebalance the traffic load?"

"The problem was already at critical mass when they discovered it. By the time they knew there was a problem, the roads were already backed up. The only way out of this is to let the roads clear themselves."

"What about the air-conditioning?"

"The system detected massive amounts of energy drawn on the grid from areas around roads and cut the power. It needed to keep the cars moving so the air-conditioning was the first system cut. The system is functioning perfectly. That's the problem."

"Can they get the air back on?"

"Not until they clear some of these cars out of here," Amanda said. "They figure it will be a solid hour before traffic is moving regularly again. Look around, Mike. People are abandoning their cars and walking. This does not bode well for the system."

"It doesn't bode well for this case, Amanda," Mike said. "We've got two murders that appear connected, but we have nothing concrete. There are no witnesses and only speculative motives at best. If we don't get something to break soon I shudder to think what is going to happen. Sorry about that. I know you want to be a detective, but if we don't get a break soon, I think we'll both be scrubbing floors by the time this is done."

"Why did you pick me, Mike?" Amanda asked, turning in her seat to face him.

"What?"

"You got to pick anyone you wanted to be your partner," Amanda said. "I was most likely the least qualified out of the bunch. I've been a cop with the dream of making detective, but I'm years away from it. You chose me out of all the others. Why?"

"There's something about you, kid," Mike said. "I don't know, it's a talent I have for reading people. You've got some spunky characteristics I like to see. You're sharp and determined. I don't know how many cases I've seen go unsolved because the detective didn't have the guts to push on in the face of danger. It's a strange world we live in, kid, and you gotta be strange to survive it."

"Put on the spot," Amanda said. "Answer without thinking, who's behind all of this?"

"The murders are unrelated to the system and the system is simply breaking down on itself," Mike said. "But I know that's not right. That's what this appears to be, but I don't think so. There's something else going on here. Something I can't put my finger on."

"Maybe the system became aware of itself and is killing the people running it?" Amanda asked with a laugh.

"That was my biggest fear when I heard about this," Mike said. "But I was assured by Dr. Hall and Allen Day that that could never happen…and they had a safeguard in place if it did."

"How and what?"

"To have a neural network capable of consciousness, which is required to become aware of yourself, there has to be a multi-faceted synapse connect system. The system is linear."

"English, Detective."

"You have trillions of cells in your brain, Amanda," Mike said. "Any one cell can talk to another cell. Think of the phone network. What they did on this system was build it linear, straight line, so it has to go in order. Think of it this way, you want to go to the store to buy an apple. You grab your keys and money, lock the door, and go. In a linear system you would decide to get an apple, then get your keys. Then you would decide to get an apple, get your keys, and get your money. Then you would decide to get an apple, get your keys, get your money, and put your shoes on."

"So, if it did become aware, it would be so slow it couldn't do anything?"

"Exactly," Mike said. "They can get around this by using multiple systems at a time. Each light-based memory tube can perform one function. If it developed awareness, it could only use one tube at a time."

"Interesting," Amanda said. "You said there was also a way to stop it if it did become aware of itself."

"That was in case a competitor tried to bring it to consciousness or if it discovered it on its own. The entire system is wired with a massive electromagnetic pulse blast. The bombs are wired directly into city hall. If it even begins to show any intelligence or consciousness, one button will fry the entire system."

"But then it would take years to rebuild," Amanda said.

"That's the beauty of it," Mike replied. "They have a backup system in place at the technology campus. It's off right now. It would be instantly turned on the second the blast happened, making sure the consciousness couldn't transfer to the other system. There is another back up ready to go in a bunker at the old city building too. They have all the components to rebuild the city hall system within a few weeks."

"So, this was a real concern?"

"It was," Mike said. "But they have done everything they can to prevent it from happening. I'm not going to lose any sleep over it, Amanda, and I suggest you don't either. So, tell me, you've looked at all the aspects of this case, who do you think is behind it?"

"I would say Breeze Flynn," Amanda said. "But she's being manipulated by Jerry Bosen. That's what I think this looks like, but that's why I think it's someone else. They are setting Breeze and Jerry up."

"What makes you say that?"

"Jerry doesn't need to prove himself right," Amanda said. "He has said and done things before that were wrong and it didn't bother him. He just doesn't seem like the kind of guy that would go to this extreme. Perhaps Breeze is behind it and she's trying to set Jerry up. They did date for a while, long ago."

"I don't think dating is the word I would use to describe it, Amanda," Mike said. "They were romantically linked, *linked* being the operative word."

"Whatever it was. I don't think Jerry would resort to that."

"I agree with you there," Mike said. "So, give me your overall theory right now."

"I think this has to do with someone wanting to prevent Mayor Kamp from running for president," Amanda said. "We have two major political parties. He's definitely on the left side of the aisle, pushing technology without restraint and open social programs, but maybe the left has seen that technology is racing too fast. Some are starting to question the benefits it has brought us."

"Interesting," Mike said. "Go on."

"But the right could see him as a major threat," Amanda said. "People want the newest and shiniest technologies and they want it right now. Mayor Kamp has proven he'll take the risk to get people what they want. The right has been in power for ten years now and it always seems like a party has power for around ten to twelve years before the pendulum swings back the other way. There is no other major candidate who's being floated for the left. If Mayor Kamp is destroyed here, then there isn't another good candidate to pull up. It could allow the right to stay in power longer."

"I like your way of thinking, but I can assure you this isn't presidential," Mike said. "Well, it might be but it's much closer to home than you are thinking."

"What makes you say that?"

"A hunch," Mike said. "That's why computers will never replace us. They can't have hunches. They process the data and give you an answer, that's it. Good information in, good information out. Garbage in, garbage out. It really is that simple."

"So, who do we focus on from here?"

Mike was about to answer when his glasses started to ring. Mike shifted the call so it went through the speakers of the car, "Hello?"

"Mike, it's Chief Rhoads," Police Chief Rhoads said, as his face came on the screen on the console of the car. "What's your twenty?"

"Century Street," Mike said. "Just past the Winter Mall."

"How's the traffic there?"

"Stuck."

"It's bad," Marley said. "It's like this everywhere. The system really bit the bullet on this one. By the look of it, you don't have air-conditioning in your car either."

"None," Amanda said.

"The air-conditioning is being shut off in houses near stopped up areas," Marley said. "The grid can't handle it, or so the system thinks. Are you any closer to solving these murders, Mike? I need to hear something good."

"There's a lot of pieces to put together on this one," Mike said. "I don't know. We don't have a motive yet. That's the key, we need to figure out the motive. What was there to be gained by the deaths of these men?"

"Word is starting to get out," Marley said. "A damn reporter added everything up and there's an article on the newsfeed linking the two deaths to the system and now we've got gridlock. There's panic out there, Mike. We need to get something moving on this. I've added detectives to this. Nothing against your work but we need to get this done quicker. You'd ordered some analysis done. I've got more men working on it."

"You can put the entire force on it and it won't get done any quicker, Chief," Mike said. "Detective work is painstaking and time-consuming. You solve crimes by sifting clues, not processing data. There's a difference."

"We need something, Mike," Chief Rhoads said. "We need someone brought in for questioning at least. Formal questioning."

"I'm just supposed to pick someone?"

"Bring in Gary and Breeze Flynn," Marley said. "Bring them both in. Amanda, you question Breeze, Mike you take Gary. Get them to talk. Compare their testimony. I want both of them questioned about where they were when the murders took place and to see if they know where the other was. Pit them against each other."

"I don't know if we have enough to bring them in," Amanda said. "We can talk to them, but bring them in?"

"Find something," Marley said. "But bring those two in. I've got to go. Bye."

The screen went blank as Amanda looked on in shock. She couldn't believe what she'd just been asked to do. To formally bring someone in that they weren't certain about could lead to problems down the road in pressing formal charges. Everything had to be by the book. She could understand Marley wanting something to show the press, but this wasn't right.

"I wonder where they are at right now," Mike said.

"Most likely the Neo-Luddite house," Amanda said.

"Safe bet," Mike said. "We need to be sure though. We walk in there asking for them, word could get out and they could run."

"Then we'd know who was behind it," Amanda said.

"They don't have the best relationship with the cops," Mike said. "A while back, when the system was first proposed they staged a protest. They demanded police protection and all sorts of other things. When someone threw paint at them they sued the police and the city. We haven't really been on speaking terms with them since then."

"I remember that," Amanda said. "I was there."

"Well," Mike said, sighing, "we go to their house and pick them up. Let's hope the chief is right on this."

Amanda nodded as Mike turned on the lights and siren on the unmarked car. The lights, hidden in the grill of the car, flashed blue and red, while the siren wailed over the sounds of the horns honking. Although it was a law that cars had to move for emergency vehicles, no one was moving, there was nowhere for them to move to. Mike pounded the steering wheel in frustration as he tried to inch his way out of the traffic mess while Amanda looked on in silence, wondering how this system could go so wrong, and also felt odd about the conversation she had with Mike. Something bothered her, something about why he had selected her as a partner. Amanda figured it was just nerves about the case as the car slowly started to inch its way forward.

Chapter #27

As the group gathered around the conference table, Dr. Hall couldn't help but wonder what this emergency meeting was going to be about. Mayor Kamp had told him that he had to be there, seven o'clock sharp that morning, and here it was, five after, and the mayor was nowhere to be seen. Alyssa hadn't been invited to the meeting, but she was sitting next to Jack anyway, the pair holding hands beneath the table. Jack had been over the data all night from the traffic jam and he couldn't understand how a mistake like that had happened. He knew the mayor was going to be upset when he told him what happened but there was no avoiding it. Jack was glad there were so many people in the room, it might keep the mayor calmed down and keep him restrained in what he said.

Next to Jack, on his left, were Jerry and Nevaeh, intent on their own conversation. Amber and Adam were sitting next to Allen, while Doctor Porter and Ben were looking over the same documents on their glasses computers, trying to figure out the mystery of the traffic jam. The only person other than Alyssa who Jack had spoken to that morning, was Allen, and he didn't know any more than Jack did. Simply that a meeting had been called and they were all to attend.

"I want you to remember something, Jack," Alyssa said, softly, as they waited. "Don't let the mayor walk on you this time. Stand up for yourself. He can't be mean to you."

"There are so many people here," Jack said. "He won't be mean."

"The worst damn traffic jam in five years," Mayor Kamp shouted as he walked into the room being trailed by

244

Governor Jones. "Traffic was backed up for hours. People were abandoning their cars in the median. Anyone care to explain to me just what the hell happened to my system?"

"The system functioned perfectly," Jack said. "So it would seem. After the pumps went out we forgot to reset the system to indicate the problem had been taken care of. Manual resets were something you insisted upon, to prevent hacking or awareness. The system thought the roads to the west of town were flooded, and it perfectly redirected traffic to compensate for that. The system even told people that their commute was going to take much longer than normal. The average commute time yesterday was three hours when it's normally around twenty-five minutes."

"I don't mean to say that I told you so," Jerry said, calmly, "But I told you so."

"What are you blabbering about today, Bosen?" Mayor Kamp asked.

"The people could have looked to the right or to the left," Jerry said. "And saw that streets were open. My commute was actually shorter than normal because there were no other cars in my way. Granted, I drive manually, something most people don't know how to do anymore, but simply by verifying the information that the magical box in the car told me, I avoided the traffic jam. They sat for hours instead of thinking for themselves. Their minds aren't thinking like they should anymore."

"Would you shut the hell up?" Ted shouted. "No one is interested in your Goddamn end of the world, humanity is in the dumps, theories. We have real problems that need real solutions."

"All I'm saying is..."

"Enough!" Governor Jones shouted, interrupting Jerry. "This is a meeting to determine the stability of the system. There have been two major errors that have taken place since this system came online. I want to know why."

No one spoke, all looking to Jack to answer. Jack didn't want to, but he spoke softly, "As I said before, the system actually designed part of itself. We're working round the clock now to check overall functions that the system designed. We didn't have time to check everything before due to the rushed schedule Mayor Kamp wanted this installed on. We should have all the system looked over by the end of the week. At that point we'll have a much better idea of what is going on and if there are any more problems that need to be addressed."

"We got lucky," Governor Jones said. "There were no accidents or deaths because of this screw-up. If there were, you can bet every lawyer in the state will be lining up to get on that lawsuit bandwagon. It would destroy everything we've worked so hard to build here."

"The only sure way to prevent something like that from happening again is to turn the system off," Jerry said. "Turn it off and let people think again."

"The only sure way to not get a woman pregnant is to not sleep with her," Ted snapped back. "Are you going to stop doing that too? Maybe you're the one who was sabotaging the system."

"Jerry was with me yesterday," Nevaeh said, grinning, "And I can assure you..."

"It's so very important you don't make a joke right now, kid," Ted said. "The only reason you're here, Nevaeh, is we need your newsfeed. It has been established you are an insider into the city government now. People believe that you have access that no one else does. You are going to run a story that says these issues we had were the result of Dr. Hall's lack of oversight. He will apologize to the people of Winter Falls and he will guarantee that these problems will be handled swiftly and efficiently."

"That's not fair," Alyssa said. "You can't blame this on Dr. Hall."

"It is his fault," Governor Jones said. "He's the one who created the system and he is the one that is going to take the fall for it. There are people out there right now calling for the system to be turned off. It isn't just the damn Neo-Luddites either. The average citizen is furious over this. We need control and we need it now."

"You don't have control of it," Alyssa said. "I was the one who found the root problems last night. I fixed the system so traffic would get routed properly. In my honest opinion, someone had changed the system."

"Sabotage?" Mayor Kamp asked.

At the word sabotage, Ben's eyes got huge. He fidgeted in his seat and looked at Amber who was cool and calm. Ben tried to get her attention, but she ignored him, giving him a clue that he needed to remain calm and not raise suspicions.

"I was told this was an error based on the pump problem," Allen said. "Lass, what are you trying to tell us here?"

"That's what it was meant to look like," Alyssa said. "But the real issue is that someone changed the system at the basic code level. They changed the code so it would look like a continuation of the problem from the pumps but it wasn't. The system was changed."

"How could the system be changed without the Master Control Room knowing?" Allen asked. "That is supposed to be impossible."

"Whoever did it, also has a series of command codes," Alyssa said. "They were found written down in the papers Gavin had at his house. The codes allow someone to change the system and then erase the trace of it being changed."

"How did you discover this?" Mayor Kamp asked. "How did you figure that out?"

"I would prefer not to say," Alyssa said.

"Why not?" Governor Jones asked.

Alyssa took a deep breath, "Because the level of sophistication needed for that process, and the working knowledge they would need to have of the system, indicates that there is a strong possibility that it was someone sitting at this table. I don't want to reveal how I figured it out, in case someone here is causing the problems or in league with someone who is."

A nervous silence fell over the room. No one knew what to say or how to act. Everyone was trying to make themselves not look guilty, thereby making themselves look guilty in the process. The mayor paced around the room, looking at everyone. His entire future was hanging in the balance. Jerry knew that when a man was being threatened the way the mayor was, that he was liable to do anything to save himself.

"We all just need to step back from this and think about it," Jerry said. "Ask the question, what is to be gained by causing these problems?"

"If I find out you did it to sell more of your damn books, Jerry," Ted said. "I swear that I will have you behind bars for the rest of your life."

"I don't need your system to fail for me to write books," Jerry said. "This is what I told you would happen, Teddy, but you didn't listen to me. In the report I prepared about this system, I clearly stated that once the breakdowns started to happen, whether natural or manmade, the stress of it would turn workers against each other. A cutthroat environment would develop where everyone was trying to prove their loyalty, lest they be the next ones blamed and fired over the problems."

"What happens next?" Governor Jones asked. "In your report. What do you predict will happen next?"

"Two outcomes," Jerry said. "Either the person who is causing the problem slips up and is caught or infighting causes the system to break down further. The person who is causing these problems now has the newsfeeds alerted to the downfalls of the system so there is no reason to continue with pushing the system. Everyone is turning against it and the rumor mill will take care of all the fears. By the end of the day, there will be people calling for Mayor Kamp to resign and for Jack and Allen to face a federal investigation."

"Will it get that bad, laddybuck?" Allen asked. "Will the people really start demanding our heads?"

"They will unless you show them you are serious about fixing the system," Jerry said. "You need to start right now, this instant. If you are unwilling to shut the system down until more tests can be run, then the public must be placated. We'll issue a statement through Nevaeh that Madison Software Labs and Everyday Computers have brought all their top-rated engineers and designers in to look at the stability of the system. I will have my team prepare a report on the major points of what they need to look at. During this time, we tell the people that certain systems may go offline for a bit. There will be some inconveniences, but it will be necessary for the stability of the system."

"And in this press release, I want Jack to take full responsibility for what is going on," Ted said. "I don't care what else. Jack, you are putting your neck on the line for this."

"You can't do that," Alyssa said. "Jack, tell him he can't do that."

Ted walked over and put his hand on Jack's should, "Jack, I trusted you to build me a system that would take me to the White House. One way or another, this system has to work, and someone has to take the fall for it. It's not going to be me, nor Chad. Allen doesn't have enough access to the system, he just designed the hardware. You are the only one. This all rides on your shoulders so you need to take responsibility for it."

"I told you we needed to wait," Jack said. "I said it many times. The system will work, the system will change lives, but it can't be rushed. You are the one who forced us to go before the election cycle."

"I don't want to hear another word about this," Ted said. "Get this figured out. Everybody out but Adam and Amber. I need to talk to them."

Everyone started leaving the room while Adam, Amber, and Allen remained in their seats. Jack slunk out of the room like a kid who'd just been suspended from school while Alyssa's glares toward Ted could have cut glass. When the door was closed, Ted looked at Allen who hadn't moved a muscle.

"I didn't tell you to stay, Allen," Ted said. "This doesn't concern you."

"I think it does, laddybuck," Allen said. "And I need to talk to these two as well. Something that concerns you."

"Of course, Father," Amber said. "We understand that we've been associating ourselves quite closely with the system. I understand your concern that if it fails our futures will be at stake, but I want to assure you that we have complete faith in you and the system."

"Adam," Ted said. "Is there something you want to tell my daughter? My daughter, who you are going to be marrying in less than six months?"

"Not that I know of, sir," Adam said.

"Ace," Allen said, turning toward his son, "What is this about?"

"I don't answer to you anymore, Allen," Adam said. "You made sure of that yourself."

"I received pictures of you with Breeze Flynn!" Ted screamed. "You are having sex with another woman while engaged to my daughter. This will not stand."

"Father, please," Amber said. "Don't work yourself up."

"You knew about it?" Ted said. "Otherwise you'd be furious right now. What the hell is going on? I want answers from you two now."

"A good spy must commit to the role completely," Adam said. "Breeze sought me out after the public display between Allen and myself. She thought that since I was now on the outs with technology, I might be willing to join the Neo-Luddites, the ultimate hostile witness for their cause. Amber and I discussed what it would entail and we both agreed, I should go for it. Breeze knows about my engagement to Amber. She knows we are going to get married. However, I tell her I truly love her and would do anything for her. I'm in close with the Neo-Luddites. They will confide anything to me now."

"So, it's a game?" Allen asked. "What do you hope to get out of it?"

"We have jobs now," Adam said. "I need this system to keep running otherwise I'm out of a job. We have as much at stake in this system as you do. It fails, you realize how many out-of-work computer technicians there will be?"

"So, you are sleeping with her to gain access to information?" Ted asked.

"Yes," Adam replied.

"And you are okay with it?" Ted asked Amber.

"I suggested it," Amber said. "With this plan, we know everything the enemy is doing. We are prepared to battle with them."

"I don't like this," Ted said. "I don't like this one bit. Get out of here, both of you. This scam of yours sickens me. To think, my precious little daughter, sharing her future husband with that troll of a Luddite. Out! Now!"

Amber and Adam rushed out of the room. Allen studied the mayor as he paced around the room. Allen was impressed at the pair's drive and cunning in the situation and he thought maybe he underestimated his son.

"I'm going to put both of them under surveillance," Ted said. "I don't like this plan one bit. It's too aggressive for them."

"I don't see the harm in it," Allen said.

"That's because your son is involved," Ted said. "If it was your daughter you'd have a much different view of the situation."

"Fair enough, laddy," Allen said.

"I've also ordered Jerry and Nevaeh to be monitored at all times."

"With all the rumors I heard about Jerry," Allen said. "That's a video I would love to see."

"This is serious, Allen," Ted said. "Someone is trying to destroy us. I'm not going to let that happen. Consider this a warning. Someone is trying to get our attention and they got it. We need to fight back with all we got. This is war, Allen, and I intend to win. Come on, we need to plan our next move."

Ted rushed out of the room while Allen simply watched, shaking his head. He knew that Ted was determined to move on to greater things, but now he was simply going too far. Allen didn't think monitoring people would help, especially the people Ted had suggested. Allen shrugged his shoulders though and got up, ready to see what Ted had in store next.

Chapter #28

Jack sat in the main chair in the Main Control Room. He felt horrible over everything that had happened over the past couple of days. Being yelled at by the mayor, being forced to take the blame for the errors, and not having enough sleep was really starting to wear on him. Jack was miserable in every sense of the word. The only thing that was feeling good to him right now were the amazing backrubs and massages Alyssa was giving him. It's like her hands knew exactly where to go and how much pressure to apply. It was a great feeling, a shimmer of light in a dark pit.

"Does that feel good, Jack?" Alyssa asked.

"Um," Jack said. "Amazing. You have amazing hands."

"Thank you," Alyssa said.

"Sir," Seth's voice intruded into the room. "Even with the techniques that Alyssa has applied, your stress levels are still off the charts. You are very worried about something. You need to get yourself in the right frame of mind so that you can properly focus on your work."

"What do you suggest, Seth?" Jack asked.

"You need a major distraction with a large release of endorphins," Seth said. "Might I suggest copulating with Alyssa?"

"I don't think you're using that term correctly, Seth," Jack said, with a laugh. "And there's far too much work to be done."

"He's right though," Alyssa said. "You always seem to feel better after we do that. The door can be locked, and the camera shut off. We could do it right here."

"I don't think now is the wisest time to be fooling around," Jack said. "Believe me, Alyssa, I want to, but if there's another error in the system then I could be looking for a new job."

"You can't let the mayor push you around like that," Alyssa said. "You have to stand up to him."

"I can't."

"Why not?" Alyssa said. "You just need to put him in his place. One time, that's all it will take and then he'll never push you around again."

"I doubt that," Jack said. "He will continue to push me and others around as long as he is in power."

"You have to stand up for yourself, Jack," Alyssa said, moving in front of him. "You don't need to be a doormat to anyone. The next time he tries to walk over you, you tell him that you're going to take your fancy computer system and go to another town. Take it to a mayor that will appreciate the work you do. He pushes you around you tell him that you're going to tell his political opponents and all the voting public how he acts."

"Seth used to say the same thing to me," Jack said. "I can't do it."

"Alyssa is right, sir," Seth said. "You deserve better than what you are getting here in Winter Falls. Mayor Kamp is only looking out for his own interests and will sell out anyone who gets in his way."

"I don't understand why he's so determined to be president anyway," Alyssa said. "Doesn't seem to make sense to me."

"I think it's an ego thing," Jack said.

"Ego?" Alyssa asked.

"To show the world how big of a man he is," Jack replied. "He has a need to be the best at everything he does and becoming president would prove to the world that he's the best. I really don't know if he cares about anyone other than himself and what his plans are. I don't know, there might be more to it than that, but that's the feeling that I get with it."

"You have to stand up for yourself," Alyssa said. "You cannot allow him to get away with what he's done. You need to march into his office and tell him where he can stick it, making you take the blame and all."

"I don't stand up for myself," Jack said. "I never have before, and I doubt I will start anytime soon."

"It's the Barry Josh situation all over again," Seth said.

"Barry Josh?" Alyssa asked. "Who is Barry Josh?"

"He's nobody," Jack said. "Nobody worth remembering."

"Dr. Hall told me about him before," Seth said. "One night when we were playing chess. Barry was in Dr. Hall's class in high school. He picked on him all the time."

"What did he do?" Alyssa asked.

"He tripped me in the halls," Jack said. "Forced me to pay for his lunches. Took my homework and passed it off as his own. He would constantly embarrass me in front of my friends, and family. He even tried to steal my girlfriend from me, but she brushed off his advances."

"That is so horrible," Alyssa said. "You should have stood up for yourself."

"He just would have picked on me worse if I did anything," Jack said. "He never stopped and wouldn't have stopped no matter what I did. You just don't understand it."

"Why do you even think about him anymore?" Alyssa asked. "If he was so mean to you. Just forget him completely."

"I had forgotten him for a long time," Jack said. "But when I moved here to Winter Falls, I discovered that Barry was here too. He works on the river, loading barges.

He's just a grunt worker but I saw him here. I guess he hangs out at some bar every night, The Blizzard Bar, I think it's called."

"So, he's just a drunk loser?" Alyssa asked.

"Right," Jack replied. "While I founded one of the biggest companies on the planet. Seth and I actually figured it out, I make more money per second than Barry does in a year. That's why I never stood up to him, why risk the fight when I know that I'm a better person? Not because of the money. Look how many jobs I've created. Look how much easier and smoother business goes because of the software I invented. What does he do? Sit in a bar and drink. He's gotten his punishment."

"But if you would just stand up for yourself…"

"Knock it off, Alyssa," Jack interrupted. "I don't stand up for myself, okay. I've always let people walk on me. I hate confrontation and I'm not about to risk myself or my position to get some smug satisfaction. I don't want to talk about this anymore."

Jack returned to his work as Alyssa curiously stared at him. She couldn't understand why he wouldn't want to stand up for himself and fight for a better life. Alyssa could see the tension and pain that was on Jack's face. She realized how some of her words had upset him. Alyssa smiled. She knew of one way for certain that she could cheer Jack up, and even if he'd already said no, she thought she knew how to push him in the right direction.

"Hey, Jack," Alyssa said, as she moved between Jack and the monitor, starting to sway her body side to side before slowing taking her shirt off, revealing her black bikini top underneath. "I really think we should have some fun right now."

Before Jack could say a word, Alyssa moved forward to Jack's chair. She positioned herself in front of

Jack and placed her hands on his shoulders. Alyssa smiled, and Jack looked her up and down. Alyssa winked at Jack and moved her head in, kissing him. The pair started kissing, Jack started moving his hands all over Alyssa's upper body, complete disregard for the work that he should be doing.

"I hope I'm not interrupting anything," Jerry's voice rang out.

Jack pushed Alyssa off him and stood up. "Jerry...what are you doing here?"

"Just in the neighborhood, you know," Jerry said. "Wanted to see how you were doing."

Even though Jerry had his sunglasses on, Jack could feel the weight of Jerry's stares. Jack's face was a shade of deep red, embarrassment running through his body. To make matters worse, Alyssa hadn't even attempted to cover up. Her top was still on the floor and she was standing next to Jack, her upper body covered only by a black bikini top.

"Jerry," Jack said. "This isn't what it looks like."

"Jack," Jerry said. "This is me you're talking to. If I had a dollar for every time someone walked in on me and a lady, at work mind you, trust me, I'd be slightly richer than I already am. I'll one-up you, buddy. I was hired to model a regional business and got caught by the CEO, with his daughter."

"You keep the account?" Jack asked.

"You know I did," Jerry said. "Don't be ashamed of it. Hell, I'm proud of you man. Alyssa is an amazing woman; smart, funny, polite, and knows how to have a good time...you know, it finally hit me."

"What's that?" Jack asked.

"Where I know Alyssa from," Jerry said.

"I'm quite sure you don't know me," Alyssa said.

Jack swallowed in a dry throat, "Jerry, if you and Alyssa knew each other before, I don't want to know about it."

"No," Jerry said. "It's not that. I was positive that I've seen you before, Alyssa. Now I know. Seeing you in a black bikini top...you look exactly like Paige Gianakos from 'Waves of Summer'. Although, I was always more partial to Anna Holms from that movie."

"Never seen it," Jack said, nervously.

"The top you're wearing," Jerry said. "That's what gave it away. That's identical to the one she wore during her iconic surfing scenes. Seriously, even your hair is like hers."

"I styled it after hers from that movie," Alyssa said. "That's when Paige was voted the most beautiful person in the world by that online site. Dr. Hall and I were going to relax in the hot tub at the workout facility on the first floor later on today. You know how we girls are sometimes though, have to wear what the celebrities are wearing. I bought this bathing suit after the movie came out."

"I have a daughter, Alyssa," Jerry said. "Believe me, I know how celebrities influence your apparel habits."

"Do you have a reason for being here, Jerry?" Jack asked.

"I was hoping to talk to you," Jerry said. "What do you make of all of this? Who do you think is behind what is going on here?"

"I don't know, Jerry," Jack said. "Let the detectives do their work."

"I've got a feeling that someone is hindering the detectives, Jack," Jerry said. "I think that someone within this organization is feeding them lies."

"I don't get you," Alyssa said. "You preach that this system will fail, yet you are defending it and trying to stop it from failing. I can't understand your logic or motivations."

"Just because I demonstrate that something will fail," Jerry said, "Doesn't mean I want it to fail. If this system goes down it will destroy a lot of lives. I don't want to see that happen. I wrote my report to prevent this system from failing. We need to take steps, so it doesn't. That's my goal. The world can operate computers and still think on its own. That's what I am trying to achieve."

"So, you are on our side?" Alyssa said.

"Yes, I am," Jerry replied.

"Okay, Jerry," Jack said. "Who do you think is behind it?"

"That's a good question," Jerry said. "I'm not entirely convinced that Gavin was the key in all of this. I think he was being used by someone else here. I want you to do something for me, Jack. I want some information from the system."

"What's that?"

"I want to know every user that was logged in for an hour leading up to the two events."

"You think that you can figure it out that way?" Jack asked.

"I also want to know what they were doing," Jerry said. "I want to what systems their computers were using and how long they had been using them for."

"The detectives already looked at that information," Jack said.

"They don't know the system like we do, Jack," Jerry said. "There has to be something that will give us a clue. We can figure this out and make sure no one else dies and there are no more problems with the system."

"Okay," Jack said. "I'll get you the information and send it to your messages."

"Thanks, man," Jerry said. "You two kids have fun in here now. And Jack, be sure and lock the door next time."

Jerry left the room as Jack and Alyssa watched him. Alyssa went to a computer terminal and quickly made sure that the door was locked from the inside so they couldn't be bothered again. Jack was sitting in his chair, thinking.

"What is it?" Alyssa asked, moving in to kiss him, but he didn't even notice her.

"There's something about this that doesn't make sense," Jack said. "I wonder if Jerry is trying to get that information to set someone up."

"I doubt it," Alyssa said. "He seems like a good man."

"I don't know," Jack said. "We are going to have to keep an eye on everyone right now."

"Jack...honey...the door is locked...let's just have a lovely time with each other."

Before Jack could protest, Alyssa sat down on top of him. She threw her arms around his neck and planted a kiss on his lips. Although Jack tried to stop her at first, tried to get back to his work, his passions took over and he gave himself to Alyssa there in the Main Control Room.

Chapter #29

Jerry Bosen paused for a moment in the Master Control Room, looking over all the workers who were busy monitoring the system. All the people were so intent on their work that they didn't even notice Jerry walking through. The thought of the destruction of the system and all the layoffs it would cause was a concern for Jerry. Winter Falls was home for him and he wanted to see his city thrive and succeed. If the system went down, every person in this room would be out of a job, and all the people who'd migrated to Winter Falls for careers at the technology campus would be out of work.

Jerry pushed those thoughts out of his head as he moved toward the exit. He had work to do and was going to try everything he could to stop the sabotage of the system. Jerry knew he had a lot of legwork to do on this, had a lot of files and documents to pour over to figure out what was going on. Jerry wanted to meet with the detectives to see if he could get any information out of them, but so far, they'd been pretty tightlipped about the investigation. Jerry moved swiftly through the halls of city hall, past all the offices and meeting rooms, to the third floor, where his chairman's office was located.

Jerry stopped short of his office, moved back to the break room, and purchased a bottle of cola from the vending machine. It had been a long day already and Jerry wanted a slight boost for the afternoon. He nodded to the secretaries in the breakroom who were busy discussing the latest fashions, like what Paige Gianakos had been spotted wearing the night before at some ritzy nightclub in New York. He made his way back to his office.

Jerry's office was large, with a metal desk and brown leather office chair set with his back to a beautiful floor-to-ceiling window, overlooking the park outside city hall. The opposite side of the desk had three overstuffed brown leather chairs. To the left side of the room was an open area with brown leather sofa and three matching chairs circling a glass coffee table, the wall lined with a bookcase and to the right of the desk was basic closet space, the façade of the closet doors covered in a mosaic colored mirror pattern.

Jerry sat in his chair and looked out over the park. He took two big swigs from his bottle of cola before reaching into his desk drawer and pulling out a bottle of rum. Jerry put a strong shot of rum in his cola bottle, closed the lid, and turned the bottle upside down and right-side up a couple times before letting it sit on his desk as he returned the rum to his bottom drawer. Jerry paused for a moment before taking a swing of his mixed drink, leaning back in his chair, and looking out over the park, trying to sort out the clues of this case.

As Jerry was looking out the window, he didn't notice one of the mirrored panels to his closet slowly start to open. It opened just enough to see that the door to his office was still open. A hand and arm shot out and grabbed the door, ever so gently closing it so it didn't make a sound. The hand reached out, stretching to silently latch the lock on the door so no one could get in from the outside. The door to the closet opened further, and a figure emerged, stepping out of the closet and in front of the desk.

"You told me you loved me once," Jerry heard a woman say behind him. "Now I'm here to collect on that."

Jerry just smiled as he turned his chair back toward his room. His smile went from ear to ear as he saw Nevaeh standing in front of his desk with a smile on her face, clad in only a yellow and red bikini. Jerry just started laughing as Nevaeh walked up to him and kissed him.

"I didn't think you'd have the guts to do something like that," Jerry said. "Fifty points to Nevaeh for effort and creativity. One hundred points for looks."

"Exactly as Anna Holms did to Brad in 'Waves of Summer'," Nevaeh said, as she moved back to the closet and grabbed a bag. She pulled out a t-shirt and some tights and quickly covered up. "Do I look as good as Anna did from the movie?"

"That's like asking which child is my favorite," Jerry said, as he offered Nevaeh a pull from his drink.

Nevaeh took a small sip, which turned into large swig when she realized what was in the bottle. "Rum before four o'clock?"

"Drinking rum at work doesn't make you an alcoholic," Jerry said, taking a swig. "It makes you a pirate. Arr matey."

Nevaeh busted up laughing as the pair moved to the sofa on the opposite side of Jerry's office. They sat down together, Nevaeh leaning into Jerry, his arms around hers, as they looked out over the park on the gorgeous summer day.

"You know it's the damnedest thing," Jerry said. "That was not my first bikini experience from 'Waves of Summer' today."

"What do you mean?"

"I just came from the Main Control Room. Jack and Alyssa were there, and I think I interrupted something."

"No way," Nevaeh said, looking at Jerry. "Seriously? Jack, actually with a woman?"

"Yeah," Jerry said. "Alyssa was in her tights and a bikini top...the exact same top that Paige Gianakos wore in that movie. That's when it dawned on me where I knew Alyssa from. She looks identical to Paige."

"God," Nevaeh said, thinking about it. "You're right. Now that I think about it, she looks very similar to Paige."

"I did some checking before," Jerry said. "There's still something about that woman I can't put my finger on. Something in her eyes. Her story doesn't check out. Not fully. I can find records of where she worked and what she did, but no one really remembers her. It's like she was invisible or something."

"People are going to remember her," Nevaeh said.

"That's what I thought," Jerry said. "So, I dug a little deeper. There was a woman, Alyson Bertram, who'd applied to work here a number of times. She never made it past the first round of applications. I thought maybe she did something underhanded to get here, but I found Alyson and talked to her. She's out in Seattle now."

"So, now what are you thinking?"

"I don't know...there's something about her and I want to know what."

"I've got something for you," Nevaeh said. "I had some people do some digging for me. I found out Amber Kamp had dealings and liaisons with both Danny and Gavin before they died. From accounts, neighbors are certain that Amber had been sleeping with both Danny and Gavin. Amber has flimsy alibis on the nights that they were killed, and she disappeared for long periods of time both nights."

"Very good work," Jerry said. "What do you think would be her motive?"

"I don't know," Nevaeh said. "I don't get it. This system is her ticket to the White House. I mean, they have it planned out how she's going to become president for crying out loud."

"Always remember," Jerry said, "There's the right reason and the real reason."

"Fighting with her father?" Nevaeh said. "Wants to give him the finger by making sure he doesn't become president?"

"I had my system stability team run this through our computer," Jerry said. "Then I looked at the most likely outcomes. Which outcomes the computer said were most likely? There are some interesting points that it makes."

"Such as?"

"Well, I had to figure out what motivated each person the most. That's where things fall apart with Amber and Adam. I don't know them well enough to know what motivates them. Allen is all about money. All he can see is money. He will look past everything else to get money. Teddy is about power. This whole presidency thing is about him grabbing power and holding onto it, which is why he wants his daughter in the White House and why he is so keen on her marrying Adam. His father is one of the richest men in the world and Ted believes that once Adam marries Amber, Adam will be back in the will. Teddy could be setting up a dynasty here.

"Amber is a different question. I'm certain her motives are not simple, like safety and security, or the need to be loved. If she proves to be the one behind it, I don't know if her motive was money, power, domination, or revenge against her father. Adam is a different story. He wants revenge against his father for what Allen did to him in the will."

"What happened?"

"Allen doesn't think Adam is capable of running the company or deserving of its profits. When Allen dies, Adam will receive the sum of one million dollars in a trust that he can't touch until Adam is sixty. The company will be given to the employees and all his money and assets will be donated to charities. His wife's expenses plus an expense account will be paid by the company until she dies."

"So, essentially, Adam gets nothing."

"Yes," Jerry said. "But here's the kicker, Adam is aggressive and wants to have a massive bank account like his father, but I don't believe that he has the mental fortitude to do this. I don't think he could plan it. Amber, on the other hand, could. Together they could mastermind this whole thing."

"But if this system fails, think of all the people who would be out of a job."

"Damn, Vaeh," Jerry said, standing up and starting to pace. He took a big swig of his drink. "Quickly, write this down."

Neveah grabbed a pad and paper, excited to see Jerry in his analytical prime.

"What if this is misdirection? What if this is the prelude to something grander. Any crime can be solved by the proper application of understanding motives and human behavior. When the system fails, which it is being led to do, what will happen? The stock prices will plummet. We know someone switched the pump motor and caused the system to find the error. What happened then? Madison Software Labs and Everyday Computers both went up limit that day.

"What if that was a sign? What if the pump motor was the signal for someone in a position of certain power, let's say, a money manager who has complete control of an account. The pump is discovered and the stock's shoot up. Hell, it pulled the entire market up with it. Now the system starts to fail. The money manager, using that signal of the pump, short-sold, applied options, and used other leveraged financial instruments to bet the price would fall. He could later go back and show some kind of technical analysis he could claim was why he shorted the stock. With all the different forms of analysis, there has to be something that would show the stock price would go down.

"Those bets that the stock would fall, would be worth billions once the cracks start to show. The size of the two companies would pull the entire market down with it, possibly causing a short-term bear market. All the computer technicians and engineers working for Everyday Computers and Madison Software Labs would be out of a job...ripe for the picking for someone who just happened to have a billion or so dollars lying around and the knowledge of computer systems.

"All those people could be hired on the cheap. They could be hired for a lot less than they are working for now since there wouldn't be any other jobs available. This could cause a new company to rise from the ashes of what was once the two largest companies in the world. This company could handle both hardware and software under one umbrella. All the assets of Everyday Computers and Madison Software Labs would be for sale. It could lead to the greatest transfer of wealth of our generation, putting the company his dad denied for him into his hands while at the same time embarrassing and destroying his father."

Jack took another massive swig of his drink and collapsed onto the sofa. Nevaeh kissed him while he thought about what he said.

"That's an amazing theory," Nevaeh said. "Your mind is so incredible."

"I know," Jerry said. "It could work. That would give Amber a position in the new company that her husband Adam was running. It screws over both their fathers while at the same time, they come off free and clear because they didn't actually short the stock, a money manager did. As I said, he could find a reason, after the fact, to have been shorting it."

"Do you think the detectives will be able to put this together?"

"There's something about the detectives I don't like either," Jerry said. "They don't seem to be pushing very hard. I've been questioned by detectives all my life, for various reasons, and Mike Russ has to be one of the easiest interrogations I've ever had."

"Could he be on the payroll?"

"Either him or Amanda," Jerry said. "No, I don't think so. They wouldn't need to own the cops in this scenario. If they are killing whoever did the deeds, there is no fear of having the police come after them. There would be nothing to tie it to them anyway."

"And that still doesn't explain how Alyssa fits into all of this," Nevaeh said.

"If she fits in at all," Jerry said. "Maybe she just happens to look like Paige. Maybe she just happened to fall in love with Jack following his work. I mean, stranger things have happened, right?"

"I guess...so, where does that leave us?"

"That's the million-dollar question," Jerry said. "I think no matter what the outcome, you and I will be safe. We're not main players in this game, but we do need to be on the lookout. If we do crack this case and they find out about it, well, they've proven that they will kill. We have to be damn sure before we go public with anything."

"Okay," Nevaeh said. "I've got to get back to the newsfeed office though. I have a deadline to meet. Can I see you tonight?"

"Only if you keep that bikini on and meet me at the hot tub downstairs," Jerry said. "I'll bring the drinks."

"Sounds like fun," Nevaeh said, as she kissed him. "Can't wait until then."

Jerry watched Nevaeh grab her bag and leave the room. Once she was gone, he looked at the notes she'd taken when he was talking. He was trying to see a connection, trying to see how it all fit together. Jerry knew they needed to move soon before the killers made another move.

Chapter #30

On the Italian Leather sofa of a highly decorated office, Amber Kamp and Ben Hewitt held each other in an embrace. Ben had been working on the system when Amber found him. They'd flirted for a moment before she invited him to an office upstairs. Ben knew he should stay with his work. He knew what he was doing was wrong on a number of levels, and if he got caught, he would be in big trouble. But he didn't care. He was following his lust, which Amber was manipulating perfectly to her needs. Ben smiled as he looked at Amber on the sofa.

"This is amazing," Ben said. "You are amazing."

"You're pretty good yourself," Amber said. "I'm amazed you haven't been snatched up by some bouncy coed yet. I would have thought you would be tearing through that campus."

"I did my time," Ben said. "This is good now. I'm enjoying this, Amber. You are not at all the person I thought you were."

"That's good," Amber said. "And it's a good thing you like me. Did you like that money that I put into your account?"

"A hundred grand?" Ben asked. "Yeah, that was good. What was it for? I thought we were settling our accounts on more intimate terms."

"Oh, we are," Amber said. "And that money was sent to you under the guise of you doing consulting work, which is allowed per the terms of your internship. Some internships don't allow you to have outside projects. Yours didn't until I made a couple phone calls."

"Thank you," Ben said. "I still wish I knew what this was all about. Why are you doing this to your father and everyone else involved? I mean, look at the stock prices of

Everyday Computers and Madison Software Labs since that last attack happened. They are way down."

"I know this can seem strange, Ben," Amber said. "But you have to understand something. My father raised me to go after whatever I wanted and not care who got stepped on or hurt in the process. I see the prize I want and the people I'm working for will stop at nothing to get what they want. The easiest way for me to get to where I want to be is to help them get to where they want to be."

"So, who are *they*?" Ben asked. "Who are you working with...or *for*, whatever it is?"

"I can't let you know that, Ben," Amber said. "But now, that money is to cover the expenses of what you're going to do next. I have something big planned that will really get the ball rolling in the right direction."

"What are you thinking?" Ben asked. "What kind of mayhem will we cause today?"

"There's a little caveat with this one, Ben," Amber said. "But I trust you're man enough to do it. Only a strong man will be able to handle this one."

"I can handle anything you throw at me, Amber," Ben said.

"We need something to grab major headlines," Amber said. "World headlines. We need the full stability of the system to be called into question and we need someone to step in and shut this system down. With what I'm thinking, the president himself will have to come in and shut this system down."

Ben stared at Amber. He couldn't believe what he was hearing. There was nothing he could think of that would create that kind of panic, although it did occur to him that Amber was thinking much grander than he was. Ben didn't know how far he was willing to go, but one look at Amber, and all the money she'd put into his account, and he knew he would have no choice but to follow her.

"So," Ben said. "Are you thinking about having me create a car accident somewhere?"

"Think bigger."

"A car pile-up?"

"Bigger yet, Ben."

"What do you want then?"

"I want deaths," Amber said, coldly.

Ben recoiled in horror. "You did kill Gavin and Danny then. You had it done."

"I assure you that I didn't do it," Amber said. "I would have in a heartbeat if it would have served my purposes, but no, sadly, they were both still useful to me when they met their untimely ends. I don't know who or what killed them, but it wasn't me."

"Amber," Ben said. "I can't kill anyone. Do you realize what you are asking me to do? This isn't simple computer hacking we are talking about here. Life in prison is what murder leads to. I don't care how many judges you own or who your father is, Amber. I can't commit murder for you."

"I think you'll find it's easier than you think," Amber said. "Just think about how grand your life will be. Think about how easy you'll have it. You can have a position anywhere you want. I'll make sure you get it. If you want a position in my company when this is over, maybe a position at a home office on the beach, it's yours. I can even make sure to send some friends of mine over to help, if you know what I mean. Ben, you can have the life you want, the life you dream of, and all I ask in return is a little chaos."

"Murder isn't a little chaos," Ben almost yelled.

"Keep your voice down," Amber said. "You don't want anyone to hear this. Ben, believe me, if there was any other way, I would do it. The system has to come crashing down. By tomorrow, we need people clamoring for its shutdown. We need the federal government getting involved."

"There is nothing you can say or do to make me do this, Amber," Ben said. "You can have your money back. I'll never touch or look at you again. Please, I can't do this."

"Yes, you can, Ben," Amber said. "I've got you on video hacking the system. Sure, say you were working for me, like anyone would believe it. I've got enough stroke to get out of that one. You'll be charged with a high degree of hacking and won't be allowed to touch a computer again after you serve your ten years in jail. Once you're out, you'll spend all your time trying to find a job but no one will be able to hire you. You'll also be spending time at your little sister's grave."

"You wouldn't," Ben said, turning toward Amber, his blood running cold. "You wouldn't dare harm Stacy."

"Such an incredible story," Amber said, "that little Stacy has. She was very sick as a baby. Almost didn't make it out of the hospital. They said she would never walk but she fought and clawed and fought again to becoming a state champion runner on the track team. You must be very proud of her. She runs every morning along the riverside trail, correct? Be a damn shame if some drunk driver mowed her down one morning."

"You wouldn't," Ben said. "You wouldn't dare. I should kill you here and now for even suggesting such a perverted thing."

"There are the instincts I'm looking for," Amber said, sitting up on the sofa. Amber grabbed a bag off the floor and started to rummage through it. "You can do it,

Ben. Think about it, I'll make sure that Stacy gets any job she wants as well. Both of you will be set for life. All I need you to do is cause one little problem."

"Screw you, Amber," Ben said, turning for the door. "I'm leaving right now."

Ben took two quick paces for the door but froze in place when he heard the unmistakable sound of a pistol being cocked. Ben looked in a mirror on the wall of the office to see Amber holding a shiny silver pistol, which looked to be the size of a 9mm, right at his head. Ben swallowed in a dry throat, realized for the first time how serious Amber really was.

"I don't want to have to do this to you, Ben," Amber said. "Once you've finished the deed I will deposit another nine hundred thousand in your account. You'll make a cool million off this job and be set for life. Any job you want, anywhere you want. Both you and Stacy. You haven't even heard the job yet. It's not as bad as you would think."

"There's no level when it comes to murder," Ben said. "Murder is murder. I cannot be a part of it. What are you going to do, Amber? Shoot me here in your office? How will that play out? How will you hide that?"

"I have another gun in this office," Amber said. "Plus, the cameras are off. I shoot you, put the other gun in your hand, and claim self-defense. Who would question it?"

"I don't believe you."

"And once I'm through with the police questioning here, your little sister Stacy will be joining you in the morgue."

"Amber, please," Ben said, turning and dropping to his knees. "Please don't make me do this. There has to be another way. I'll make the system land a plane on the highway, cause it to steal people's money, and shut off everyone's power...think about that. Let's have the system kill the power to the city, thereby shutting itself down. It could look like a paradox loop that would cause the system to shut down every few days. Oh, think of how the people would be upset then. If that were the case, no one would want the system. No one has to die, Amber. Please, I beg you. Don't make me kill people."

"You disgust me," Amber sneered. "Look at you, groveling on the floor like some common peasant. I thought you were this big strong man, here I find you're nothing but a little baby. Come on, baby, cry some more for me."

"What are you talking about?" Ben said. "Amber, you are asking me to take lives. You are asking me to murder. If you're such a tough bitch with all the answers, why don't you do it yourself? You know how to keep me clean from it, why have a middleman? Do it yourself you chicken-shit coward."

"You think you're going to goat me into doing it myself?" Amber asked. "Not going to happen. No matter how many layers of protection are added, I cannot do the deed. They were very specific about that. They know all about you, Ben. They know everything about you. Something happens to me and they will come after you. All you need to do is this one little thing for me."

Ben's mind raced as he was on his knees. He thought about waiting until Amber was distracted, then rushing her, taking her gun, and pinning her down, but nothing would come of that. He could physically best her in the room, but she would destroy him in court, most likely say he tried to take advantage of her. Plus, if the gun went off in the tussle, either one of them could easily die.

Ben tried and tried to think of an alternative. There was nothing coming to his mind. The only thought he had was to appear that he was working with her. Somehow, he could convince her that the system was doing what she wanted it to while he sent a message to his sister to get to a safe place, the police station, and wait for him.

"Okay," Ben said, standing up. "Put the gun away. I'll do it as long as you promise me my sister will be safe."

"That's more like it," Amber said, lowering the gun but keeping it in her hand. "Here's what you're going to do. The system controls the ventilation system for all the industrial exhaust and the exhaust from the power plants. You will reroute the raw exhaust to feed into the fresh air systems of a building."

"Wait a moment," Ben said. "The second that the air quality sensors picked up the exhaust coming into the building they would go off, like a fire alarm, causing everyone to exit the building."

"The sensors will have to be shut down," Amber said. "Well, not exactly shut down, but recalibrated. They need to sense the toxins coming in, but their threshold levels won't be triggered. It will look like a dual error; the exhaust dumps into the fresh air, and the sensors to prevent this didn't work. Route the exhaust through a recycling program. The system was trying to conserve, so it took old air and recycled it to new air."

"You do understand that hundreds of people are going to die?" Ben asked.

"That's the plan," Amber said. "Just be glad that the building that's been selected is the River Grove Retirement Community. Think what this would be like if we picked an elementary school."

"Everyone there is close to death anyway, so it won't be the worst thing in the world," Ben said.

"That's the spirit," Amber said. "Now get to it. Use the spare pair of computer glasses on my desk. All the codes you need are on that sheet of paper next to them."

Ben quickly moved to the desk and sat down. He worked the system while at the same time compiling a note to his sister. Ben hoped she would get it in time. Ben's mind was racing for how he could make it look like he was actually doing what Amber ordered, while at the same time avoiding any deaths. There was only one way to do it, but Ben didn't know whose glasses he was wearing, who he was logged into the computer as. Ben just hoped Dr. Hall was in the Main Control Room watching what was going on.

Chapter #31

     The main screen in the Main Control Room was a giant chess board. Pieces were spread out everywhere, an intense battle of wills and knowledge being decided by the game of intellects. Jack was studying the board. He considered himself a chess expert and had played thousands of games over the years against his various computer programs. It was rare for him to play against a human, someone he could see and read the facial expressions of. Alyssa was a formidable player who'd obviously known the game quite well and was giving Dr. Hall a great challenge on the game.

     "It is your move, Jack," Alyssa smiled. "Or do you just want to concede the game to me?"

     "Not likely," Jack said. "You've developed a very strong defense on your left side, but your right is very weak...except, that's what you want me to think. You're trying to force me to bring the attack to the right side. Here's the problem, I've built a robust defense around my strongest three-pieces, the king, the queen, and my king's rook. I can beat anyone with just those three pieces. You will lose all your pieces trying to attack, and I can come back with those three and take you."

     "What you're saying is I control the board," Alyssa said. "While you are trapped against the edge. I control the game and can force you to do what I want."

     "You actually control nothing, Alyssa," Jack said. "You have a strong defense, but you've developed no offense...and now, this is about to happen. Computer, move queen's knight, D4...check."

     Alyssa looked at the board. She was stunned. She knew it was a possibility his knight could put her in check, but it left an opening for her queen to threaten his defenses around his king. She then realized the only way she could remove the threat to her king, was by killing his knight with her queen, a move that would allow his bishop to kill her queen. Alyssa was impressed by Jack's style. He'd set her up and now he was losing a knight, a piece he didn't seem to use very much, to get her queen, a piece that she'd been relying heavily on.

The pair executed more moves on the chess board, calling out where they wanted the pieces to move to, until, three moves later, Jack called a checkmate. Alyssa's king had been forced to remain against the back of the board and was trapped by some of her own pieces on the left. Alyssa studied the board, trying to figure out how she'd lost the game, where she went wrong.

"That was a good move," Alyssa said. "You are an amazing player."

"Thanks," Jack said. "I've had a lot of time to practice with Seth. You are a good player too. That was a close game, Alyssa. That game could have gone either way until I got your queen. That was the fast turning point."

"What do you think I need to do to become a better player?"

"Don't rely on your queen so much," Jack said. "You had your knights in good positions, but you never attacked with them. You could have forced me to make some bad moves, but you got pieces into positions and didn't follow through with them. You have to remember though, I've played thousands of games of chess against hundreds of different computers."

"You ever play against humans?"

"Not really," Jack said. "I guess I could have found people to play against on the Internet, but I would rather play with Seth. That way if I got called away, I could save the game and not have to worry about it."

"Have you ever done ultimate chess?"

"Four-player chess with the extended board?" Jack asked. "No. I'm more of a traditional guy, Alyssa. I like my chess to be straight one on one. I've never studied the art of four-person chess."

"What other games do you like to play on here?" Alyssa said. "What other games are you good at?"

"I dabble in checkers," Jack said. "Backgammon too. I mainly play chess though. I know some of the other people play games on here. Ben seemed to be hooked on that fantasy game, Knights and Wizards, while Gavin played a lot of Mercenaries of the Third World War."

"That's the first-person shooter game that got so much press for how accurate and educational it actually was," Alyssa said. "And for how bloody and violent it was, right?"

"Yes," Jack said. "Dr. Porter actually plays that life-simulation game, where you have a character and you bring it into an online world to live. I've never understood that game, why don't they just live a real life instead of one online?"

"Does Jerry ever play any games?" Alyssa asked.

"Not very often," Jack said. "He's mentioned playing some empire building game and a zombie shoot-em-up game. He's never played a game when he's on the system here."

"I think you can tell a lot about a person by the games they play," Alyssa said.

"What do the games we play here say about us?"

"You are a thinker," Alyssa said. "And a loner. Chess allows you to challenge your brain and push yourself. Ben and Gavin want a release from reality. They want to escape. Ben into a fairytale and Gavin into a fighting scenario he knows he wouldn't survive in real life.

Holly doesn't have time for a real life, so she creates one on the system. Jerry is all about strategy and stability."

"What kind of games do you like to play?" Jack asked, "other than chess?"

"Chess is the big one for me," Alyssa said. "But I also like card games. Pyramid solitaire, blackjack, and poker."

"You're a gambler?"

"Only online with play money," Alyssa said. "I'd never go to a casino and gamble with real money. I'm too afraid to lose everything."

"I didn't think you were afraid of anything, Alyssa."

"There are some things," Alyssa said.

"Tell me some of your fears," Jack said. "Tell me what frightens you the most."

"I don't know," Alyssa said. "I don't think I should tell you that."

"Why not?"

"It's embarrassing," Alyssa said.

"Come on," Jack said. "You tell me yours and I will tell you mine. Come on, what frightens you the most?"

"Okay," Alyssa said, as she took a deep breath. "You have to promise me you won't make fun of me."

"I promise."

"Okay...I'm deathly afraid of power outages."

Jack was silent for a moment, looking at Alyssa.

"Power outages?"

"You asked."

"Why?"

"I'm not sure," Alyssa said. "I think it's like the thought that maybe, since we are so dependent on power in this world, that once the power goes off it might not come back on. Every time the power goes out, I wonder if this is the big one, the one that will set humanity back to a world before power. It's silly, I know, but every time the power goes out I get nervous."

"Very interesting."

"Now you have to tell me yours," Alyssa said. "Come on, Jack, what is your biggest fear?"

"I would have to say my biggest fear is that I'll be alone for the rest of my life," Jack said. "Putting work so far ahead of myself that I don't have anyone to spend my time with."

"I love you, Jack," Alyssa said, moving to him and kiss Jack. "You know that I love you. I've already told you that. I want to be with you. I can think of no one else that I would rather be with."

"Alyssa," Jack sighed. "I like you...I really do. Um...um...I love you too, Alyssa. I think that I really do love you."

The pair kissed. They kissed a deep, passionate kiss.

"We need to celebrate this, Jack," Alyssa said. "I heard that there is a street fair going on by the riverfront. We should go this week. It would be a lovely time."

"I've never been to the street fair," Jack said. "But it sounds like a great idea. We'll go there together."

"I do have a question for you, Jack," Alyssa said. "I know this is going to be hard to answer since there's a lot of unknowns in it, but the system seems to be having problems. What if Jerry is right and it gets shut down? What will that do for you?"

"My stock holdings in the company could be completely wiped out and I would still be okay, Alyssa," Jack said. "I had a money manager work with me. I've got all kinds of investments. I'm not worried about it though. Even if this system was shut down, Madison Software Labs has plenty of other projects."

"Where did the name come from?" Alyssa asked. "Madison Software Labs?"

"Madison was my mother," Jack said. "She always joked that I was down working in my lab when I was on the computer. I guess I wanted to honor her. Madison Software Labs sounded like a good name too, a nice name for a nice company."

"It is," Alyssa said. "You're not like Allen at all, are you? He names his company after himself, you name yours after your mother. How did you two become friends anyway?"

"When we were younger," Jack said, "I guess computers and software brought us together..."

Jack was cut off by a strange beeping on the system. They looked at the main screen which had an error warning flashing in the bottom right corner. Jack and Alyssa quickly moved to their computer seats and attempted to figure out what was going on.

"I don't get this," Jack said. "What is the system trying to do?"

"The error message says that there's an overflow of exhaust in one sector," Alyssa said. "It appears that the City Center exhaust system is being overloaded."

"That doesn't make any sense. They have a system of exhaust vents and ports that can handle more than the volume that they could produce. Is there a problem with one of the vents?"

"Found it," Alyssa said. "The system seems to think that some of the vents are plugged up, so they are routing exhaust through the dump system. I would guess that sensors went bad in the exhaust ports...but there's a bigger problem, Jack."

"What?"

"What the hell is it doing this for?"

"What is it, Alyssa?"

"The exhaust is being routed to a fresh air system," Alyssa said. "Dear Lord, the industrial exhaust is going to enter a building."

"What?" Jack almost shouted. "What building. Activate every alarm the building has! Wait a moment, every building has air quality monitors. It will set them off."

"The building it is heading to is the River Grove Retirement Community," Alyssa said. "There are two hundred residents there and approximately fifty workers."

"We need to get them out of there before that exhaust gets there," Jack said. "It will take time to move everyone out."

"There is another problem, Jack."

"What?"

"I'm looking at the air sensors for the retirement community," Alyssa said. "They are set to go off if CO_2 levels reach ninety percent. They are also set to go off only when oxygen is at one percent."

"Those levels would mean everyone would be dead before the alarms registered a problem," Jack said. "They were supposed to alert if oxygen got below eighteen percent."

"The levels for all other particulate matters in the air are also set at ranges that would kill a human before the alarm would go off."

"How the hell did that happen?" Jack asked. "This should not be happening. Alyssa, can you adjust the sensors to go off in the right range?"

"I do not have the command codes to access them," Alyssa said. "You should have them though."

Jack started to work frantically on the computer. He went through all the command systems that he could find but nothing was allowing him to change the levels of the system. No matter where in the system he went, something blocked him from working on the system.

"I'm blocked," Jack said. "We have to do something. How long until the exhaust hits the building?"

"About five minutes."

"That's not much time," Jack said. "Seth, main screen, River Grove Retirement Community."

The screen switched to a building that was set against a nice grove of maple and walnut trees. The building looked peaceful and serene. Jack was staring at the building, wondering what he could do to help the people inside.

"I've got something," Alyssa said. "I just took two fire sensors and turned them down. They are setting off the fire alarm in the building right now. The fire alarms automatically call the fire departments and the police. I also faked a message from the retirement community that they see flames and smell smoke, so the fire department will respond as if it's real, not a faulty sensor."

"Thank God," Jack said. "Look, people are already starting to exit the building."

The screen showed the first people making their way out of the building. Most of them were still able to walk on their own but they had canes, crutches, and walkers helping them. Some were in wheelchairs and the workers were trying to make sure everyone stayed in the right area. Police cars were already starting to arrive on the scene.

"We have to prevent the exhaust from getting to that building," Jack said. "Once they realize it was a sensor error, everyone will be taken back inside."

"There's not really a good way to do it," Alyssa said. "But there is an external smokestack we could use for a dump valve between the exhaust and the building. It will be very visible to the residents of the city that we are venting smog and not cleaning it."

"That's better than killing people," Jack said. "Vent the exhaust."

"Got it," Alyssa said. "None of the exhaust should be able to reach the retirement community."

"Good," Jack said. "Now we need to figure out how to stop the exhaust from coming this way, how to get the sensors back to normal range, and just why the hell this happened in the first place."

Jack and Alyssa went to work on the computers, working at a feverous pace trying to discover how the error had happened. Jack knew he'd be called into the mayor's off soon and would have to give a detailed report on this incident. He knew this could very well be the final straw that would see his employment with the system come to an end. Mayor Kamp was upset before, but Jack was sure he would now be furious about the system. As Jack looked for answers, he contemplated what a different life, perhaps a life on the lake, would look like.

Chapter #32

The air around the conference table was ripe with tension, so thick it could be cut with a knife. No one dared speak. Mayor Kamp had just spent the last five minutes on a venom-filled, curse-word-laden tirade about what had happened to the system. Ted had blamed everyone around the table for what had happened. No one was spared, not even his daughter who was wiping tears from her eyes, from the wrath that Ted brought down upon them. Allen had tried to get Ted to calm down, but his efforts were ignored and met with terrible indictments.

Ted paced in the front of the room, finally pausing from his verbal storm to catch his breath. He realized that he took it too far. Dr. Porter and his daughter Amber were in tears. Ben and Jack looked visibly shaken. Alyssa and Allen's faces were locking in pure disgust. Nevaeh was white as a ghost, shaking, afraid to move or say anything. Only Jerry, with his sunglasses on, was leaning back in his chair, a smug grin spread across his face with his arms crossed in front of him.

"I ought to have the police come and arrest you right now," Ted said, pointing to Jerry. "I bet you were behind this. What could make you want to kill those people, Jerry? What?"

"Teddy," Jerry said, choosing his words very carefully. "You know I wasn't behind this. You know that no one in this room was behind this. You know who was behind this, yet you won't admit to yourself that the system isn't perfect."

"What are you talking about?" Ted asked.

"The system was behind this," Jerry said. "Sensors and exhaust routes. The system doesn't understand human needs or conditions. The system can't reason, it can't think. All the system can do is what we tell it. This is like asking a toddler who has just learned to construct sentences to recite complex poetry. It's like asking a toddler, who has just learned to walk, to run a marathon. You are putting impossible expectations on this system, and even worse, on the people trying to run it. Everyone in this room is on your side, Teddy, even myself."

Ted stopped pacing and looked at Jerry. Although Ted didn't want to admit it, he needed Jerry and all the rest in the room much more than they needed him. The presidency hung in the balance. If this system worked, there would be nothing stopping him from reaching the White House. If it didn't work, then he might still be able to make a run, but his chances of winning would be greatly reduced. Ted knew that above all else, they needed to get control of a situation that was wildly spinning out of control.

"I want to know exactly what happened," Ted said. "Dr. Hall, tell me every detail."

"The system thought the exhaust ports were plugged at the City Center complex," Jack said. "To prevent damage to the exhaust systems, it rerouted the exhaust. For some reason, it decided to dump it into the fresh air systems that fed River Grove Retirement Community. All the air monitors in River Grove were set at levels that wouldn't have registered a problem until everyone inside would have been dead. We were able to set off the fire alarms in the building to get everyone outside."

"You'll be happy to know, Teddy," Jerry said, "that I had Nevaeh release a newsfeed report stating the incident at River Grove was due to slight heating in the wiring system and a pair of oversensitive heat sensors. Everyone thinks the system responded perfectly, albeit too cautiously, to a fire. The system is again being herald as a hero since the bad wiring was discovered in the building and is now being replaced."

"You added that entire story to make the system look like a hero?" Ted said. "You could have let this destroy us."

"I don't want you destroyed, Teddy," Jerry said. "I've never wanted that. If the true story would have gotten out today, there would be riots in the streets of Winter Falls. They would be asking for your head, Teddy. And the fall in stock price of both Madison Software Labs and Everyday Computers would pull the entire stock market down. People are warning we are getting close to a crash, all it takes is one catalyst to trip the entire system into instability."

"So, what do you recommend in all of this then?" Ted asked.

"Shut the system down," Jerry said. "Pull it offline while we run some stability tests. We have the perfect cover story right now; we have caught sensors that are out of calibration. We need to recalibrate all the sensors, which is true. The people will buy this story and the damage done will be minimal."

"We are not shutting the system down," Ted said. "I don't care how many people you hire, I don't care what you do...just get this system running the way it should."

"People almost died today," Jerry said. "That's the last straw of this system, Mayor. I've been talking with other members of the city council, they agree that we might have to vote over your head to take this system offline until more tests can be performed."

"You take this system down and it will never be turned on again," Ted said. "I can promise you that. This entire project of yours will be done. Jack and Allen will both lose control of their companies, be forced out, and face massive lawsuits from the city. The council will not vote over my head on this. The system stays running until I say otherwise."

"And if there is a death?" Allen said. "Think about that sport. If there is a death, it's on your head. You are the one telling us to keep the system running. Everything is on your head now. Are you willing to take that responsibility?

"It's Jack's responsibility," Ted said. "It's his software and his system. Any death will be on his head, and the blood of it will be on his hands. I told him to make me a system and he didn't do a good job."

"It's hardly fair to blame Jack in all of this, Mayor," Alyssa said. "Jack, say something."

There was a moment of silence while Ted waited for Jack to say something, but Jack just kept his eyes down, glued to the table and he remained silent.

"That's right, Alyssa," Ted said. "Jack isn't going to say a word. He knows what they mean and what the problems are. I've had talks with Governor Jones about this. We are in agreement that it might be time to remove Dr. Hall and Dr. Porter from the system and bring new computer engineers in."

There was a gasp around the table. Eyes were shifting around looking at each other. Dr. Porter lost all the color in her skin, turning white as a ghost. Her hands were starting to tremble. Jack, however, remained with his head down, not looking at anyone. He could feel the eyes of everyone in the room upon him, but he didn't want to say anything, Jack didn't even want to look at anyone.

"Just think what would have happened if this wouldn't have been discovered?" Ted said. "Just think of the lawsuits the city would face. Think of the lawsuits that both Madison Software Labs and Everyday Computers would face. There could have been up to two hundred and fifty people killed in this incident. What would that have done to your companies? What would have happened if this wasn't discovered? Who discovered it anyway?"

"I did," Alyssa said. "Jack and I were in the Main Control Room when an alarm went off. I pieced everything together and was the one who set off the fire alarms."

"Interesting," Jerry said.

"What?" Alyssa asked.

"Just that you've been the one to discover and fix all the problems, yet you are the newest one here and the least experienced with the system."

"What are you implying, Jerry?" Ted asked.

"The system hires her without consulting us, there are no real problems until she gets here, and each time she saves the day. If the newsfeeds had the full story of what happened today, she would be considered a hero."

"I don't know where you are going with this, but you, sir, are way off," Alyssa said. "I know computers inside and out. I've trained my entire life for something such as this. I have a fast mind and can reason out any problem."

"I don't care how you figured it out," Ted interrupted. "Alyssa, I want you in that room all the time. You need to be keeping an eye on the system."

"I'll transfer the main screen and the warning systems to my glasses," Alyssa said putting her glasses on. "That way if there's a problem I can see it right away."

"Good," Ted said. "But onto the point, Allen, do you know anyone that could replace Jack and Holly?"

"Laddy," Allen said, staring right at Ted. "I don't think replacing them is the answer. These two know every bit and piece of this system. They've worked on it since the beginning. You aren't going to do yourself any favors by replacing them."

"A new team couldn't do worse," Ted said.

Amber cleared her throat as she wiped the final tear away from her eye. "Father, Jack and Holly are good people. They are only doing what you asked them. If you replace them now, who knows what kind of errors we'll miss. Now is not the time to let emotion cause you to make a bad situation worse."

"Action needs to be taken," Ted said. "We need to have a clear idea of why these problems are happening and what we are going to do to make sure they don't happen again."

"The system of checks installed seems to be working perfectly," Jerry said.

"What do you mean?" Ted asked.

"That was the one thing I insisted on. In the original design, there wasn't going to be people monitoring at all times. There'd be one or two people who would adjust the system as it went along, someone on standby if the system needed service. I said we needed humans watching it at all times. Each one of these problems would have been a disaster if humans weren't watching the computer. I think that's the direction we need to go. I think we should create more control rooms and staff them with people to monitor the system. Although I hate arguing for increasing the size of government or adding people to the government payroll, if this system is going to stay online, we need to have every aspect of it monitored at all times."

"The budget isn't unlimited," Ted said.

"When you ordered this thing built, you said money was no object," Jerry said. "But of course, money is always the object. You've now been over budget on just about every part of this system, which is normal for government work, and now we are going to need more budget for it. It's the only way, Teddy. If you refuse to do the right thing and pull this system offline, then we need to make sure that the people who voted you into office are protected."

"I don't understand why you can't just do the job right, Jack," Ted said. "I will not be pulled down by this. Chad and I are going to have another meeting about finding a new management team to run the system. This appears to be a management problem so that's how we'll fix it. Action needs to be taken and I will take the action necessary to get the job done. Everyone is dismissed."

The group got up and started leaving the room. Jerry nodded to Nevaeh, signaling her to leave while he hung back. Jerry motioned to Amber to stay in the room. Once everyone left, Jerry closed the door and looked toward Amber.

"I have a lot of work to do, Chairman Bosen," Amber said. "I don't have time to play games with you like my father does."

"It's not games that we play," Jerry said. "I don't play dice with the universe either. You must understand, Amber, my only interest is keeping the people of this city safe. I also want all the people working here to be safe and successful. I really like Jack. He's a brilliant man and who has a lot to offer the world. I'm so glad that he and Alyssa hit it off. That isolation he had himself in, wasn't healthy."

"So, we're here to talk about Jack's health?"

"No. I've got my ears to the ground on a lot of things, Amber. You would be amazed at how plugged in I am. I happen to know that the Neo-Luddites are not involved with this. They have been protesting it, are strongly against it, but they are not the ones causing the problems."

294

"Why are you telling me this?"

"Because Adam has been hanging around Breeze Flynn recently," Jerry said. "That's how she and some of the other Neo-Luddites got to work catering at the party here. Through Adam...and you."

"What are you implying?"

"Those people are not to be messed with," Jerry said. "They carry far more power than you could imagine. Remember, Amber, no matter how many connections you have, no matter how high your station, money holds the real power in any society. Money buys people. Money buys votes. Money can change everything in the blink of an eye."

"Why are you telling me all of this?"

"It doesn't take a genius to figure it out."

"Say it," Amber said. "Say out loud that you think I'm behind this. Say that you think I sabotaged the system and murdered two workers of that system. Say it out loud, Jerry. You got the guts to do that?"

"I don't have to say anything," Jerry said. "Do I think that you are behind this? Whoever is behind this is a very smart, ambitious, well connected, well-funded individual. Above all of that though, they are tactical and intelligent. No, I don't think you're behind it."

"You insult me," Amber said.

"If you interpret my comments that way," Jerry said. "Yes. But that depends on how easily insulted you are."

"I should have you destroyed for that," Amber said. "How dare you say such things about me? You really believe that I am behind this."

Amber stood from her seat and marched up to Jerry, slapping him across the face with a resounding crack. Jerry just smiled.

"Amber," Jerry said. "I need to tell you just one more thing…no woman, in the history of women, was able to sleep her way to the top. Oh, you can go high, but you'll never reach the top, not that way. And once you stop, you lose all the power you had. I hope you know what you are doing."

Jerry removed the tint from his glasses and winked at Amber before he walked out of the room. Amber stood there in a stunned silence as she fumbled for her glasses and placed a phone call.

"It's me…Jerry Bosen knows…I don't know…I couldn't tell…he speaks in riddles with no meaning…I don't think he knows who you are…he knows we plan to blame Breeze and her freaks…he needs to go…I don't care how…just kill Jerry."

Amber took her glasses off and looked around the room. She caught her reflection in a window to the hallway. Amber glanced at herself, looked at herself in her black business suit. She loved how powerful she looked in that suit. She knew that her plans were just about to come to fruition and that she would get everything she wanted while those in her way would be destroyed. 'It's just business,' Amber said, aloud, as she walked out of the room.

Chapter #33

The Winter Falls State University campus was set to the northwest of the downtown area. The campus was made up of brick and metal buildings in an area about the size of five city blocks. Throughout the campus, trees and flowers dotted the landscaping, as the perfectly manicured green grass was being used for a number of leisurely sports. Coeds were rushing about in the warm evening air, taking a break from their summer studies to enjoy the perfect weather. It was evening, so no professors were about, and the coeds were outside in their shorts and tank tops. One person stuck out, however, in a powerful black business suit.

Amber looked around, glancing in her glasses for the proper directions. She'd never gone to the state college, but the private university that was downtown and very exclusive. Amber never went to parties or fraternized with anyone at the state school. She preferred to be with the people in her private school. Those, like her, whose parents had either money or power...or both. Amber located the building she was looking for, a residence hall that was made up of efficiency apartments that housed only grad students.

Amber walked through doors and directly to the elevator. She pressed the button to call the elevator as two girls walked past, giving Amber strange looks. The college girls looked ready for the beach, while Amber was ready for the boardroom. The elevator doors opened, and Amber slipped inside, almost needing to hold her nose at the assault of odors in the elevator. It smelled like a party spun out of control and people who didn't know how to drink were using the elevator as a ride. She pushed the button for the third floor and hoped that the elevator was quick.

At the third floor, Amber got off and rushed to a room in the middle of the building, breathing deeply as she'd held her breath on the elevator. The hallway smelled better, but not by much. Amber found the door she was looking for; 326. She knocked on the door and didn't wait for a response before she entered the room.

The small room was a mess with empty pizza boxes, beer cans, and dirty clothes littered everywhere. The small sink was stacked full of dirty dishes as posters of half-naked women and sports stars covered the plain white walls. Amber moved further into the apartment to see Ben, sitting in a chair, crying. He looked like he'd been crying, and drinking, for some time now. Six empty beer cans were next to his chair and he was opening another can, guzzling the can as Amber watched in disgust. Amber took off her suit jacket and set it on a chair, carefully positioning it so a pocket was easily accessible. Amber had an uneasy feeling about what this was going to be about.

"What's going on, Ben?" Amber said. "I know our arrangement says I will come over here anytime you want for sex, but really, you can't clean up the place a little before a girl comes over?"

Ben just remained silent, drinking his beer.

"Cut the melodrama bullshit," Amber said. "You called me over here, what's going on, Ben? What do you want?"

Ben tossed Amber a pill bottle. Amber looked at the bottle with confusion.

"It's a bottle of prescription sleeping pills," Amber said. "So what?"

"I took the whole bottle before you got here," Ben said. "And drank six beers in the last twenty minutes on top of it."

"I'll call the hospital," Amber said, reaching for her glasses.

"Don't," Ben said.

"Ben," Amber said, trying to sound sympathetic. "It's not worth dying over. You have a lot to look forward to in your life. You're going to be a very rich man."

"It's not worth dying over?" Ben asked as he stood up. "Not worth dying over? Tell that to the people I almost killed for you. Tell that to the people of River Grove Retirement Community."

"Ben," Amber said. "They were so close to death anyway. What difference does it make? Now, if I had ordered you to send the exhaust to Snowflake Elementary School, then yes, you would have the right to be mad. Two residents died at River Grove today anyway. It wouldn't have made a difference to them."

"How am I supposed to live with myself?" Ben asked. "You ordered me to kill people, Amber."

"It's easy to live with yourself," Amber said, "when you are rich and powerful. You'll have anything you want, Ben."

"Money won't clear my conscious," Ben said. "Money won't console those families."

"What are you crying about?" Ben asked. "Man-up and act like an adult about it. This is a terrible world with terrible people. Look at the third world war. If that wouldn't have happened, we'd be light years ahead of where we are. Look at the technology destroyed. The brilliant minds that were destroyed. We were fighting for our lives and now we need to move forward, but there are so many people who remember the war who don't want to move forward. This is an important moment in the human race, you can make a decision that will affect the entire world, every human on it."

"I don't get it," Ben said. "Tell me this, Amber, what are you doing this for? What are you trying to get out of it?"

Amber studied Ben. She'd never pegged him for someone who would get this upset over what she was trying to do. She thought her power of lust over him would allow her to bend him to her will without question. This entire encounter seemed strange to Amber and she realized Ben might be smarter than she thought.

Amber started to step forward and removed her blouse. "Ben, are we going to be lovers or fighters tonight?"

Amber approached Ben and started to kiss him. She began running her hands over his chest and back. Ben quickly pushed her away.

"You trying to pat me down?" Ben asked as he tore off his t-shirt and spun around. "See, no wire. No recording device." Ben grabbed his crotch, "Want to pat this down while you're at it?"

"If you want me, too," Amber said. "I have no problem with it. That's what I thought I was coming over here to do until I found you crying like a little baby. Ben, let me call the hospital and get them here. You don't have much time."

"You call the hospital and I tell them everything you did," Ben said. "I will give them the entire story and there will be no way for you to get out of it."

"As I've explained to you before, Ben," Amber said. "Even if you told them, there would be no way for them to pin me with anything. I have enough power to get out of anything. They wouldn't have enough evidence to do anything anyway. Now you, on the other hand, you'd be admitting to committing the crime. You'd have to admit to accepting money and hacking a system. No, if you called the police you'd be in far more trouble than I would."

"Joke's on you," Ben said. "When I routed the system, I made absolutely sure someone in the Main Control Room would figure it out and stop it before the exhaust got to the building."

"You double-crossed me?" Amber said. "Ben, I want to know one thing, why did you call me here if not to save you?"

"Two reasons," Ben said. "One, please, just leave Stacy alone. She's had a hard-enough life the way it is, overcoming all the obstacles that were put in her way. There's no reason to punish her. I'm punishing myself here."

"What's the other reason?" Amber asked.

"I want to know what this is all about," Ben said. "I mean, do you hate your father? Want revenge on him? What about Adam? I mean, this is destroying your future father-in-law as well. You are going to hurt the entire country with the fall of those two companies. I just don't understand your reasons for all of this."

"Who says there are reasons?" Amber said. "Maybe I'm just insane and want to bring destruction to the world, you ever think of that?"

"You're not insane, Amber," Ben said. "What are you doing this for?"

"I don't think you deserve an explanation," Amber said. "If you do the next event I have in mind then I will tell you. I'll let you know the real reasons for all of this."

"What's the next event?" Ben asked.

"You are dead anyway," Amber said. "I have no reason to tell you. There wouldn't be enough time for you to do it."

"Just tell me why?"

Amber took a step closer to Ben, so the pair were almost touching, and looked him right in the eyes, "You're dead anyway. What do you care why I do this?"

"Just tell me."

"Just die already."

"Bitch," Ben said, as he pushed Amber.

Amber was forced back two paces, up against a desk. She scowled toward Ben, and rage overtook her. Amber rushed Ben, not exactly sure what she was going to do. The force caused she and Ben to fall into the chair together, Amber on top and Ben underneath. Amber tried to swing at Ben, but he was able to quickly wrestle her to the ground.

"Tell me why you are doing this!" Ben shouted as he painfully pinned Amber down.

"Go to hell!" Amber shouted as she struggled underneath him.

Amber realized Ben was far too strong for her to mount any kind of offense, so out of desperation, she stopped struggling and let her body go limp. Ben eased up on her, allowing her the opportunity to take her foot and jam it as hard as she could into his groin. Ben let out a scream and rolled off Amber. Amber struggled to scramble to her feet but Ben grabbed her and took her to the ground again. Ben was behind her and locked her into a chokehold.

"Tell me why you are doing this!" Ben shouted as Amber struggled and gasped for air. "Tell me why you are killing people."

"I didn't kill anybody," Amber gasped as her breathing got harder and harder. "I didn't, Ben. Please, you're hurting me."

"Tell me why!"

Amber coughed and gasped. Her face was turning red and her mind was going fuzzy. Ben's shouting seemed to be in the distance. Her body was going limp when she felt something hit it. It was a hard, dull smack that seemed distant, yet she could feel pain rushing through her body. She could hear coughing and gasps that weren't coming from her. Amber realized the pain was because Ben, in his anger, had lifted her up to apply more pressure in the chokehold, and he had released her. The pain was from her body hitting the floor.

As Amber began to get her mind and her vision back, she turned to see Ben on his hands and knees, crying harder than ever. He was gagging, coughing, and having trouble standing. Ben dropped to the floor as Amber wearily stood up. She let a smile come across her face as she put her blouse and suit jacket back on, pulling a silver pistol out of the pocket she's made sure was accessible when she took the jacket off.

"You are getting what you deserve," Amber said. "Goodbye, Ben. I thought so much higher of you before I came here."

"Please," Ben gasped, struggling to speak. "Please don't hurt Stacy."

"You'll see her soon enough," Amber said, as she turned and walked out of the apartment.

Ben coughed and struggled on the floor for a moment more before collapsing into a pile on the floor. He lay there motionless, barely breathing. He remained like that for almost half a minute before he reached out and grabbed his can of beer, sitting up and taking a drink. The door to the bathroom opened and Amanda Drake exited into the apartment.

"She saw through it," Ben said, putting his shirt on. "She knew I was trying to get information."

"She believed the suicide though," Amanda said. "Otherwise she would have shot you and left the gun. Made sure you were dead."

"But that gun could be traceable."

"We know that she stole some guns from the police station," Amanda said. "Well, we think she did. Cameras turned off at just the right time."

"But you can arrest her now," Ben asked. "Right?"

"I'm sorry, but I can't," Amanda said.

"Why the hell not?" Ben asked.

"She really didn't confess to anything," Amanda said. "You admitted to what you did and implicated her, but she never confirmed or denied anything. I don't think we would have enough for a conviction. It would be your word against hers. I told you we needed her clearly talking about it. She didn't even give enough information about ordering the sabotage and she didn't even talk about the two murders."

"I'm scared, Amanda," Ben said. "I really am. I'm afraid Amber is going to kill my sister, Stacy."

"We have Stacy in police custody now," Amanda said. "We are taking her to a safehouse until this is over. Do you have your bag packed?"

"I do," Ben said.

"When Amber finds out you aren't dead, we might see things moving faster," Amanda said. "She might look to come after you. I'll make sure she gets certain details and we'll keep an eye on her."

"What are you going to do now?"

"I'm going to put a watch on Amber full time," Amanda said. "I'm going to make sure that Mike and I focus the investigation on her. She won't get away, Ben. She will answer for what she's done. I promise she won't hurt you, or your sister either."

"Thank you, Amanda."

"You didn't need to choke her out though," Amanda said.

"I guess that was me taking some of my rage and hatred for what she'd done out on her," Ben said. "I stopped before I hurt her."

"Wasn't the right thing to do," Amanda said. "Come on, grab your bag and let's get out of here."

Ben grabbed a gym bag out of the corner of the room and followed Amanda. He paused at the door, shutting off the light to his residence hall. He looked around the darkened room hoping one day, he'd be able to come back and finish his doctorate. As of now, he had just confessed to hacking in front of a cop, but he was trying to get a murderer to confess, so maybe they would go easy on him...he hoped.

Chapter #34

Lighthearted music and the joyous sounds of children laughing filled the air. The smell of popcorn, deep fried foods, and candy wafted through the nostrils. The area was filled with blinking and twinkling lights as the Winter Falls Waterfront Carnival was in full swing. Booths and vendors were everywhere. Rides lined the grassy area along the riverbank. Games and food vendors were packed with people racing to experience three days' worth of games and food into one night. The carnival was packed, and everyone was having a wonderful time, even Dr. Jack Hall and Alyssa Babbage.

Jack and Alyssa were enjoying the sights and sounds of the carnival. Having ridden some rides, watched some jugglers and firewalkers, and sampled much of the greasy, fried food, Jack was attempting to win a prize for Alyssa at one of the many games. Jack had tried a few different games with no luck, but he'd promised Alyssa he would win her something. That's when Jack spotted the game he knew he could win; darts. He wasn't much for knocking over milk bottles, or skeet shooting, or ring tosses, but he did know how to play darts.

"Simple enough, my fine man," the carnival worker said, as Jack got close to him. "Easy to win the little lady a prize. White balloons are one point, red balloons are ten points, and if you get the blue balloon, you instantly win a big, hundred-point prize."

Jack looked at the board of balloons. It was full of white balloons. There were a few red balloons scattered about, and only one blue balloon, which to Jack, looked like it was slightly deflated compared to the other balloons, making it harder to pop. Jack handed the man a ten-dollar bill and the man handed him five darts.

"Five for ten," the carny said. "Let's see what you can do."

Jack threw his first dart and it popped a white balloon just below the blue balloon.

"One point," the carny barked. "Nice shot. Although, I hope you weren't aiming for the blue one."

Jack smiled and aimed again. This time he popped a white balloon just above the blue balloon. The carny laughed.

"Come on, Jack," Alyssa said. "I believe in you. You can do it."

Jack smiled and aimed for his next shot. What Alyssa, or the carny, for that matter, didn't know, was that in college, Allen and Jack would take study breaks and shoot darts in their dorm room. Jack had gotten quite good at the game and could land a dart pretty much where ever he wanted. He'd popped the two white balloons to get a feel for the darts and for how much force he would need to pop them. Jack took aim and released the dart with laser-like precision, popping the blue balloon.

The carny's jaw dropped as Alyssa clapped and kissed Jack on the cheek. Jack simple set the other two darts on the table as he smiled at the worker. "We'll take the giant white rabbit please."

Silently, the carny took a four-foot-tall stuffed rabbit off the shelf and handed it to Jack. Jack turned and handed the rabbit to Alyssa, who hugged it before kissing Jack on the cheek.

"It's the best present I've ever gotten," Alyssa said. "Thank you so much, Jack."

"You're welcome," Jack said, as the pair started walking. "You were right, though. I definitely needed to get away. This is exactly what I needed to clear my head and think."

"This is a lot of fun," Alyssa said. "Although I don't understand the concept of eating greasy, heavy food and then getting on a device that spins and twists and twirls you in all kinds of directions. I just don't understand that."

"I'm not much for rides myself," Jack said. "Slower ones like the Ferris wheel and the carousel are good. That's about as fast as I want to go."

"I'm glad you are having fun," Alyssa said. "And now we've got Ricky here to watch after us."

"Ricky?" Jack asked.

"Ricky the Rabbit," Alyssa said. "That's what I just named him now. Girls do those kinds of things, Jack."

"Okay," Jack said, laughing. "This has been a great evening. Anything else you want to do here?"

"Not really," Alyssa said. "I'm up for anything. Even just walking around and watching the people is fine with me. I just want to see you happy, Jack. That's all I really want. I also wish you would have stood up to Theodor today, Jack. You cannot take the blame for this system. He pushed everything too fast and didn't give you the time needed."

"Can we not talk about that?" Jack asked. "I don't want to think about that tonight."

"You need to stand up to him," Alyssa said. "You can't let him do that."

"Alyssa, come with me."

Jack led Alyssa to a bench and the pair sat down. Jack kissed Alyssa and looked her deeply in the eyes. Alyssa was confused, wondering what Jack was going to say. She hated seeing him get pushed over by the mayor and the others in the room.

"I think I've come to a decision, Alyssa," Jack said. "I know when you first started here I thought you might be working for someone else. I never apologized for not fully trusting you."

"It was a strange situation," Alyssa said. "You weren't used to it. I accept your apology."

"I haven't apologized yet, Alyssa," Jack said. "I will though, I will after all the dust has settled. I've come to a decision and your reaction to this decision will determine what happens between us next."

"What are you going to do?"

"Tomorrow morning, I'm going to give Allen what he's always wanted," Jack said. "I'm going to sell him my ownership stake in Madison Software Labs. By tomorrow evening I will have no interest in it at all. It will all be gone."

"You'll be one of the richest men in the world," Alyssa said. "What are you going to do with that money? What are you going to do with your life?"

"I'm going to donate most of the money," Jack said. "Maybe even all of it. I don't know who I'll donate it too or for what, but I'm going to get rid of most of it. I don't need it. After I work out a deal with Allen, I'm going to find a contractor to build a log cabin on my lake lot and go shopping for a pontoon. I think I'll volunteer my time to the Winter Falls Historical Society and be a volunteer assistant at the science and computer museum.

"Alyssa, I wanted to change the world, I wanted my software to better humanity. I realize now that that was a naïve goal. The world is run by dominant men and women who push the limits to get themselves ahead, not to better others. I'm a throwback and am tired of all of this. I'm going to keep just enough assets so that I don't need to work again. I'm going to donate myself and my time to help others. Do you think you could be happy in a situation like that?"

"I'll donate my time beside yours," Alyssa said.

"And you'd be happy in a little cabin with a pontoon fishing boat out the window?" Jack asked. "A dog in the yard and nothing to worry about except being outside at dusk for a bonfire?"

"As long as there's a cat or two," Alyssa said. "And a kid or two running around." Alyssa leaned over and kissed Jack. "Jack, as long as I'm with you I don't care where we are or what we're doing. I'm not materialistic or after you for your money. I think this is a great idea. We can be together and not have to worry about all those hassles and headaches you have going on right now."

"That's what I was hoping to hear," Jack said. "Alyssa, I have a question for you, but I'm not exactly sure how I'm supposed to ask it."

"You can ask me anything, Jack," Alyssa said.

"Okay," Jack said. "Alyssa, you're everything that I could have ever wanted and more. I would gladly give up my entire company and fortune just to spend time with you. You are who I want to spend my life with." Jack reached into his pants pocket and pulled out a small box. He opened it up to reveal a stunning, elegant yet simple, diamond ring. "Alyssa, will you marry me?"

"Yes!" Alyssa shouted as she draped her arms around Jack and kissed him. "Yes, yes, yes! I love you so much, Jack."

"I love you too," Jack said, as he slipped the ring on Alyssa's finger. "I was thinking, for the wedding, we could..."

"I don't care where or what," Alyssa said. "We could do it at the courthouse tomorrow if you wanted. Or have a simple ceremony at the cabin when it's finished. Oh, think about that, a few friends over and have the wedding on the beach. Anything you want. Just name it and as long as you're there, I'm with you."

"I was thinking at the lake," Jack said. "I mean, both my parents are dead, and I have no siblings, no real relatives that I'm close to...what about you? I've never even asked you about your family."

"I never knew my real parents," Alyssa said. "They put me up for adoption when I was one. I bounced around foster homes until I was three. I was adopted by a loving couple that couldn't have kids. It was great. They taught me to surf and every year we'd go to a different beach around the world and just surf for a solid week. It was great. One year, when my parents were off the coast of Australia. They were snorkeling, and I guess I don't know exactly what happened. Mom started to drown and dad tried to save her but they both died. I was nineteen at the time."

"I'm so sorry," Jack said. "I can't imagine what that must have been like."

"It was a rough time," Alyssa said. "I didn't know any cousins or other relatives, so I just started to do my own thing. That led me here, and it led me to you."

"Amazing," Jack said. "You've done very well for yourself, Alyssa. I can't wait to see the look on Allen and Ted's face when I tell them what I'm doing. I'm going to recommend that Holly be put in the lead engineer position of Madison Software Labs and I'm going to recommend he has Adam run the business end of it."

"Why Adam?" Alyssa asked.

"Adam is a good kid," Jack said. "He just has to try to follow in his father's shadow. He's been trying to break out of that shadow for a long time, but no one has given him the opportunity. He could have himself but there's a lot of pressure on him. I think he can do it."

Alyssa kissed Jack again, "As long as we're together, Jack, I don't care what happens."

"And we won't have to worry about this system or pleasing Mayor Kamp again," Jack said. "I do hope they figure out what is going on with all these murders. I just wished I knew what was going on with all of this. Who is trying to hurt the system and why?"

"After tomorrow morning you won't have to worry about it, Jack," Alyssa said. "It will no longer be a problem of yours."

"Actually, it might be," Jack said. "This really looks like I'm running from something. Ted already blames me for the screw-ups on the system. If I walk away he might think I was trying to hide or separate myself from the problem. I fear that Detective Russ might question me and think that I killed Danny and Gavin."

"I doubt that," Alyssa said. "I'm sure he will find the killer soon. There will be nothing for you to worry about. You didn't do anything and during each murder you have a solid alibi. There's no way anyone could think you were behind it."

"I hope you're right," Jack said. "This has been a great night. We need to celebrate our engagement. What do you want to do?"

"How about a nice bottle of wine and some privacy at your apartment?"

"I really like the sound of that," Jack said.

Jack and Alyssa got up and started for the exits of the carnival. Jack was ecstatic over the turn of events. Alyssa wanted him even though he was going to sell the company and give the money away. He could finally have his dream. He knew exactly what he wanted for a cabin and where he could find the perfect pontoon. As Jack looked at Alyssa, he felt a wave of happiness wash over him, more powerfully than he'd ever felt before. Dr. Jack Hall was happier than he'd ever been and was truly excited for what may lie ahead for him in life.

Chapter #35

Winter Falls City Hall was especially busy on this sunny morning when not a single white cloud could be seen in the sky. There was no particular reason for so many people to be around, but with the word that there were going to be more people hired to work on the system, computer engineers and software programmers from all over the country had started making their way to the city, trying to find anyone they knew was connected to the system to give a resume to. With all the people running around, Dr. Hall used a back entrance to sneak into the city hall.

As Dr. Hall was walking through the corridors, he felt like someone was watching him. He couldn't place the feeling, nor see anyone that noticed him. Jack pushed on, using the back hallways to quickly get himself to the Main Control Room. Once inside the room, Jack took the main chair and brought the screen up to a video feed shot of the city skyline bathed in bright yellow sunlight. It was such a pretty scene and Jack knew he would miss the grandeur of the city, but the tranquility of the lake was calling to him.

"Morning, Dr. Hall," Seth said, as Jack got to work.

"Morning Seth," Jack said. "How is the system this morning?"

"All functions operating within tolerances, sir," Seth said.

"That's good," Jack said. "I have big plans today and I don't want there to be any surprises."

"Like the surprise that Jerry Bosen is standing right behind you?" Seth asked.

Jack quickly turned around to see Jerry in the room with him, draped in his black clothing with his sunglasses on. Jerry wasn't saying a word, just watching what was going on, not even reacting to the fact that Seth had alerted Jack to his presence.

"Jerry," Jack said. "You scared me to death. What are you doing here?"

"Jack," Jerry said. "I only want to solve the mystery of who is creating chaos with the system and to uncover who murdered Danny and Gavin."

"That doesn't explain why you're here," Jack said.

"You've been spending a lot of time with Alyssa," Jerry said. "I've been checking on everyone involved, and I can't find anything about her."

"Well, I know her, Jerry," Jack said. "And I'll tell you this. I have made the decision to sell my ownership stake in Madison Software Labs. I'm going to donate all the money and build that cabin I've always been talking about."

"Congratulations," Jerry said. "You'll have to invite me up for some fishing. That lake is one of the best in the state."

"Of course," Jack said. "I'd love to have you up. I'll also want you in the wedding...that's right Jerry, Alyssa and I are getting married. She agreed, even after I told her I'm giving away a vast majority of my money. She's not working for Social Software Solutions, she's not working for the Neo-Luddites, and she's not after me for the money."

"Congratulations again," Jerry said. "Tell me about Alyssa though. I want to know her backstory. How did she grow up? What were her parents like?"

"She was put up for adoption at one, and shuffled around foster homes," Jack said. "That's why you can't get anything good on her. She was adopted by surfers. She's surfed all over the world. Her parents took her surfing everywhere. They died when she was nineteen in a snorkeling accident in Australia."

"So very interesting," Jerry said. "Tell me, Jack, what is she like? What does she like to do?"

"Um," Jack said. "I don't know. She enjoys good food, good conversation. Swimming and surfing. What are you getting at with all of this? You don't think she's the killer, and the one responsible for all of this, do you?"

"Nevaeh and I have been doing a lot of research on this," Jerry said. "I'm positive there is one major clue that everyone is missing here. We still don't know what is to be gained from the destruction of the system."

"I'm a software engineer, Jerry," Jack said. "Not a detective."

"At first, I thought Amber was behind this," Jerry said. "Something about her and Adam, maybe Adam trying to hurt his father for cutting him out of the will, while at the same time trying to get Everyday Computers or start his own company. I thought they might have used financial instruments to make money in the stock market if Everyday Computers and Madison Software Labs failed and their price dropped."

"That would make sense," Jack said. "The share prices are over two hundred dollars per share for both companies. A person could make a lot of money riding that down."

"That they could," Jerry said. "And if there was panic in the streets, and riots in Winter Falls over the system, I'm betting there's a good chance investors would run for the hills. There would be no stopping the decline in price. So what Nevaeh and I did, was investigate the markets. I thought the finding of that bad motor on the first day would be a sign. They could have used that as the signal they were going to tank the stocks. Both stocks go up limit in one day and then a financial advisor or money manager could short the stock, find a technical reason after the fact as to why he shorted it."

"That would be a clean operation," Jack said. "No way to track it back to them. The manager could say he was working independently."

"Here's the thing though," Jerry said. "We did find a large number of trades placed that would indicate the stock was about to drop. One mutual fund manager has basically bet the farm that these stocks are going to plummet."

"And it's a fund that Amber is invested in?" Jack asked.

"Not Amber," Jerry said. "Mayor Theodor Kamp himself."

Jack was stunned to silence from the reveal. He didn't think the mayor could be capable of such a thing. There were so many questions swimming through Jack's head. He didn't even know where to begin.

"Ted?" Jack stuttered. "Why would he want to sink his chances of the White House?"

"I don't know if this sinks his chances yet," Jerry said. "The system failing will be blamed on you. I'm almost inclined to think that Ted himself is behind this. I'm talking multi-billions of dollars in the stock market, Jack. No one would be able to compete against him financially, and he will have sympathy. Every piece of this is being set to blame Breeze Flynn and the Neo-Luddites...and you."

"What do you mean?"

"The level of control and precision that has been required for shutting off the cameras for the murders and for the way the system has been hacked, would require a certain degree of finesse that only the creator of the system would have."

"Are you suggesting I've been destroying my own system?" Jack asked. "Why in the world would I do that? I've heard some strange theories from you before, Jerry, but you really topped yourself on this one."

"I don't believe you've been destroying your own system," Jerry said. "But you've given everything about this system to Alyssa."

"She wouldn't," Jack said.

"Yet you don't know anything about her," Jerry said.

"I know plenty about her," Jack said. "She's shared some very intimate information with me. Stuff that no one else knows."

"Like what?" Jerry asked.

"That's private," Jack said. "She told me in confidence. She's not told anyone else about it before. Not even her friends know."

"Interesting," Jerry said. "Okay, how about this, just tell me what it relates to. Don't tell me the story, tell me what it's about."

"Okay, fine," Jack said. "If it will shut you up, she told me about the first time that she had sex."

"Thirteen years old, right?" Jerry asked.

"How the hell did you know that?" Jack asked.

"Let me guess," Jerry continued. "It was summer, and she was staying at a friend of the family's house. They were on a beach with a lot of surfing. There was a guy named Brad that she hung out with. They spent the entire summer together. On the last night before she had to leave, Alyssa and Brad had sex on the beach, under the moonlight, the waves rolling in around them."

"Um," Jack was dumbfounded. "How did you know all that? She said no one knew, except her parents and one person who found out and told her parents about it…that's how you knew…it wasn't Brad, it was you, wasn't it?"

"Not in the slightest," Jerry said. "But it's not real either. No one told me that story, at least not anyone here that is."

"What are you talking about?"

"I knew Alyssa seemed familiar when I first saw her," Jerry said. "Very familiar. There was something about her I couldn't put my finger on. Then I saw you two in this room and she had on that bikini top from the movie."

"A lot of women bought that bikini after that movie," Jack said.

"You are the last person I'm going to consult for bikini advice," Jerry said. "No offense. It was then that I realized that she bared a striking resemblance to Paige Gianakos, the star of 'Waves of Summer' among many other movies. Funny, isn't it, how life can imitate art?"

"What do you mean?"

"I was having a conversation with Nevaeh and I remarked that my favorite movie scene is when Paige's sidekick slash nemesis in the movie, played by Anna Holms, comes out of the closet in the office of Paige's husband. Nevaeh did that for me the other day. I didn't know she was there. She was wearing the bikini and everything."

"I don't want to hear about your weird sex habits, Jerry," Jack said. "Get to the point."

"It got me thinking about the movie," Jerry said. "'Waves of Summer.' The plot is two women meet at a beach for a summer of surfing. Paige Gianakos and Anna Holms. The Mediterranean Goddess and the Swedish Princess. The year the movie came out, Paige was voted the most beautiful woman in the world and Anna was runner up."

"Stick to the point."

"Two women brought together by surfing. Paige and her husband, Brad, find it nice to have a new friend in Anna's character. That is, until things start getting strange. Anna is obsessive about Brad, she's causing friction between Brad and Paige, and she's acting very weird. Anna had grown up in an all-girls school. She says she never had a real boyfriend and doesn't know how to act around boys she likes. Anna seduces Brad, and Paige discovers them, leading to the battle between the two women on surfboards."

"I've seen the movie," Jack said. "Every red-blooded male has seen the movie, Jerry."

"Then think, Jack," Jerry said. "What caused the problem? When Anna was thirteen she went to a family friend's house for the summer. On the last night there, she slept with Brad and got pregnant. Her parents forced her to give the child up for adoption. Anna was still in love with Brad, although Paige got him, and Paige beat Anna in every surfing contest. Although Alyssa looks like Paige Gianakos, her entire backstory is Anna's backstory from 'Waves of Summer'."

Jack was dumbfounded. He couldn't believe what he'd just heard. He couldn't believe that he hadn't put it together. Jack had seen that movie so many times but never really paid attention to the details. Every man knew it as the two most beautiful women in the world, surfing on some of the most beautiful beaches in the world. Jack didn't even begin to know what this meant. All he could think of was the line Alyssa had spoken to him:

"I've always dreamed of a place on the water," Jack said, and then Jerry joined in with him. "A little bungalow that overlooks the ocean. Something where the salty air can blow through the windows, waking me up in the morning. Where I can spend my days on the water and not have to worry about the everyday hassles, work, bills, taxes, and all the other stuff that distracts us from what's really important, living life."

"You're right," Jack said. "It's a line from the movie. How could I have missed all of this?"

"You wanted to believe that someone was in front of you, ready to be your lover," Jerry said. "You wanted someone so badly that you were willing to believe anything. I'm sorry, Jack, but I think this goes deeper than what we thought before."

"What do you mean?"

"I think that they are setting you up to take the fall for everything," Jerry said. "I don't know exactly how Alyssa plays into all of this. With modern surgery, it wouldn't be hard to make almost any girl look like Paige. I don't know what the end game is in all of this."

"What should I do?"

"Don't raise suspicions," Jerry said. "Act normal around everyone. But I need you to think, Jack. Has Alyssa ever tried to get information out of you about the system or ever asked strange questions about it?"

"No," Jack said. "But then again, I've told her everything there is to know about the system. She has all my passcodes."

"Change them all, right now," Jerry said. "I may be wrong about this. I truly hope I am and that she is in love with you and you two can live on your lake and have a perfect life together, I really do, Jack. But the reality of the situation is that things might not work out the way you want them to."

"Jerry," Jack said. "I gave her a ring last night. She said yes. She wants to do whatever I want to do. She is so agreeable and is perfect for me."

"That doesn't sound like real life, Jack," Jerry said. "Change all your passwords now, even the ones in your office."

"Can you watch this while I'm gone?"

"Sure," Jerry said. "Hurry back though."

Jack left the room in a rush. Jerry watched him before he closed the door. Jerry tapped his glasses and placed a phone call, "the message has been delivered...about as I expected...no telling what he'll do...I'm sure we can keep Alyssa safe...I couldn't tell him what I really thought...they'll get married...I'm sure of it...time for phase three...call Amanda...bye."

Jerry hung up his phone and moved to the main chair and sat down, looking at the monitor.

"Seth," Jerry called out. "Waves of Summer, Paige's introduction surfing scene, no sound."

The monitor switched to a bright and sunny white sand's beach. Paige Gianakos, who looked identical to Alyssa Babbage, stood ankle deep in the crystal-clear water in her black bikini, holding a multicolored surfboard. She started rushing into the water to catch a wave.

"From appearances," Seth said. "You are playing more than one side."

"There's only one side to play, Seth," Jerry said.

"What side is that?"

"The right side, Seth," Jerry said, watching Paige catch a massive wave, water droplets shimmering off her like diamonds in bright light as she rode the wave. "The right side."

Chapter #36

Dr. Holly Porter sat in the main chair in the Main Control Room of city hall. The screen in front of her was set to a number of different settings. The main portion of the screen was watching traffic flow through the downtown area of Winter Falls. On the upper portion of the screen were data numbers showing the efficiencies of various systems under the computer's control. The bottom portion of the screen was monitoring the workstations of other workers within the system.

"Seth," Holly said, adjusting herself in the chair, "I need status updates from the power grids."

"All power grids operating within tolerances, ma'am," Seth's deep, smooth voice carried through the room. "Are there other systems that I can help you with?"

"You can tell me what happened to Ben," Holly said. "Why he didn't show up for work today."

"Ben was lost on camera," Seth said. "He entered his residence hall at the university but the cameras in that area were lost for a time. He hasn't been seen since. I'm afraid I cannot help you in finding his location."

"That's just perfect," Holly said. "I hope he turns up soon."

Holly looked over the system. She shifted the main screen to focus on the water pumps on the west side of town. All the pumps seemed to be in working order. After the events that had already happened, Holly was nervous, almost scared, of what would happen next with this system. She knew Dr. Hall, and she had designed a good system, but letting them have an extra couple of months of testing could have eliminated all of the design flaws. They just didn't have the time to go over all the work the system did for itself.

"How's the system running this morning, Dr. Porter?" Amber asked, walking into the room.

Holly turned to see Amber and Adam entering the room together, "Very well, Amber. Hopefully those last issues were isolated incidents. I feel the system is running much better now."

"That's good to hear," Amber said, as she and Adam sat at the computer terminals that were flanking Holly.

Holly looked at the pair. Amber, in a gray business suit, with her hair looking like it was professionally done, and Adam in his custom black suit, looking smooth and powerful. Holly got a sense that these two weren't here for a casual chat. She'd never fully trusted Amber. She always thought Amber seemed to get whatever she wanted, no matter what, and Holly didn't know what to make of these two in the room with her today.

"You look tired," Adam said. "Have you been getting enough sleep?"

Holly knew she looked a mess. Hair disheveled, her tank top and tights wrinkled, and bags under her eyes. She'd been in the city hall for over twenty-four hours with only slight cat naps in the clothing she was wearing. Holly wanted a shower and a bed but until someone showed up to relieve her, she wasn't going anywhere.

"Ben was supposed to be here this morning," Holly said. "Dr. Hall and Jerry had been here for a bit, just to check up, but Ben never showed, so I had to stay. I've been on the clock for over twenty-four hours. I sure hope nothing's happened to him."

"There have been a lot of strange occurrences around here," Amber said. "Weird accidents too. I don't know what to make of it."

"I'm nervous about the whole thing," Holly said. "I mean, this system is so big, and we worked so hard on it. I'm certain that it will start running smoothly but what happens if it doesn't? I devoted the past few years of my life to it. I don't know what I would do if this program was shut down."

"There might be other opportunities around," Adam said. "You know a lot of powerful people, Holly. Powerful people have powerful connections to good opportunities."

Holly studied Adam. She wasn't sure what his tone was trying to indicate but she had a fairly good idea. "If I didn't know any better, Adam, I'd say you were getting ready to proposition me for a new job offer."

"There are always opportunities around, Holly," Amber said. "I could think of a number you'd be good at."

"Well, I like where I am," Holly said. "I've dedicated myself to this system and I want to see it succeed and thrive."

"So do we," Adam said. "In a certain sense."

"What am I missing here?" Holly said. "Why don't you come right out and say it?"

"You see, Holly," Amber said, standing up and starting to pace, "I know you are dedicated. A hard worker. I know that you do the right thing. But sometimes it's hard to know what the right thing is. Dr. Hall is a brilliant man and my father is a visionary and Adam's dad is aggressive and brilliant but that doesn't mean that they are always right. We have plans, future plans, you see. And we need people to make them work."

"Are you two trying to start your own company to compete with Everyday Computers and Madison Software Labs?" Holly asked. "Are you trying to out-do your fathers in the accomplishments they have made?"

"You have no idea," Adam said. "By the time we're done, our company will be buying Everyday Computers and Madison Software Labs."

"You do realize that both companies are worth billions of dollars, right?" Holly asked. "Not to mention they really aren't for sale right now."

"Everything has a price," Amber said. "Now Holly, how would you feel working on a political campaign?"

"Not something I know anything about," Holly said. "Nor have I ever wanted to get into. Your father is making his run for president soon. Are you trying to get me to help with the campaign?"

"Not at all," Amber said. "I am going to be making a run. It will be an uphill battle I know, but I think I have some good ideas and will make a good leader."

"What party are you running with?" Holly asked. "What is your platform going to be?"

"I haven't decided on a party yet," Amber said. "I could swing either way. My platform is going to be the constrained use of technology and the careful observation of innovation, so we don't have catastrophes like Winter Falls."

"Winter Falls hasn't been a catastrophe," Holly said. "There have been some bumps in the road but not a catastrophe."

"It's only a matter of time," Adam said. "Haven't you read anything by Jerry Bosen? He's predicted exactly what will happen. It will be eerie how accurate his predictions will have been."

Holly stared at Adam while she shifted uncomfortably in her seat. Holly fidgeted with her hands, not knowing where this emotional turmoil was coming from. Something about the way Amber and Adam were talking was upsetting her. Holly wasn't sure what to do but she realized that all she could do was to sit and listen to them.

"I don't think it's been all that accurate yet," Holly said.

"Jerry said sabotage would begin almost immediately," Amber said. "He also predicted that due to how large the system was, there would be communication problems throughout the system. We've seen both of those problems."

"But we got a handle on it," Holly argued.

"For the time being," Adam said. "It's only a matter of time before Breeze Flynn and Jerry Bosen make their next sabotage act."

"You think it's those two?" Holly asked. "Why?"

"Think about it," Amber said. "They've dated in the past. And now, all of a sudden, Jerry wants to settle down with someone. He picked that reporter? What better way to make the newsfeeds think it was someone else than to manipulate a person with direct access to the newsfeed? They will destroy the system and the town and our fathers, and Dr. Hall. And you, Dr. Porter, will be taking the blame for it. That's what this really looks like to us."

"Why would Jerry do that?"

"Because he's evil," Amber said. "He's a Neo-Luddite who wants us living in the Stone-Age. He cannot stand technology."

"I think you're way off," Holly said. "Jerry is not behind this. I don't know who is, but I can promise you it's not Jerry."

"We have detailed plans for what they are going to try next," Adam said. "The next event will grab world headlines and be the biggest gamechanger imaginable."

"What do you think they are going to do next?" Holly asked.

"It will start with what looks like a simple computer freeze," Amber said. "The system will lock up. It will look like too many components of the system were trying to access the same part of the light-based memory and the system locked up. It will be locked tighter than a bank vault, no way to get in without a total reboot."

"That will cause many problems with the systems we are running," Holly said. "The pumps, traffic flows, but the big one will be the power grids. And the fact no one with a medical implant will be monitored. It could be very bad."

"That's not the half of it," Adam said. "The power plant for the town, which just happens to be upwind from us."

"You mean the nuclear plant?" Holly asked.

"The nuclear plant," Adam confirmed. "Just before the system locks up the plant will be experiencing a malfunction. The heating and cooling systems will be out of tolerance. The workers there will have to order a dangerous procedure to get the system back in line. The cooling system will have to be shut down. That's when the system locks up and they can't get cooling back online until the system is up and running again."

"The reactor would be critical within a few minutes," Holly said. "There would be a meltdown. My God, everyone in Winter Falls would be killed."

"It would be the single greatest computer disaster that ever happened," Amber said. "And it won't even be a computer error. It will be human sabotage."

"There's no way," Holly said. "Millions of people would die. There is no way Jerry would do something like that. He couldn't. He's a good man. If that happened, his kids would die. They're here in town. How could he survive it?"

"In the bomb shelters beneath our feet," Adam said. "They would be safe from the radiation there and able to call out for help. Or they could get out of town before it happened. Either way, they will survive while no one else does. Already as we speak, Jerry is planning on leaving the city, alerting certain people to be ready to get to the shelters before the system locks."

"I'm watching the system," Holly said. "I would know if we are getting close to experiencing a lockup. I would be able to prevent it by shutting down certain systems and by routing other systems to different memory banks."

"It won't be enough," Amber said. "You think that Alyssa is just a little girl who happened to walk in here on the exact date they needed to hire someone? We've discovered something about her...something very interesting."

"She's in love with Dr. Hall," Holly said.

"Love," Adam scoffed. "Yeah right. She's played him for everything he's worth. Even more. She's been helping Jerry and Breeze in all of this."

"Why would she help them?"

"Because she's Breeze's sister," Amber said. "The long-lost Flynn daughter, Rain. Jerry's known from the start. I wouldn't be surprised if he's going to marry both of them when this is over. That would be in his perverted sexual nature."

"I don't know," Holly said. "She looks nothing like Breeze or Gary. But then again, the surgeries can make you look however you want."

"Doesn't she bear more than a striking resemblance to Paige Gianakos?" Adam asked. "Almost looks identical to her? Wouldn't it make sense they know Jack has an infatuation with Paige? That he watches her movies all the time? Rain could have had the surgery to look like Paige. She played Dr. Hall just like she's playing all of us."

Holly's head was swimming with all the information Amber and Adam were giving her. She didn't know how to process it. If it were true, she didn't have much time to save the system, but she couldn't accept that what they were saying was true. It just didn't make sense.

"What should I do then?" Holly asked. "You're recruiting me, what do you want me to do?"

"The plan is for everything to go to hell tonight," Amber said. "When Jerry has a shift on the system. What we need you to do is to lock the system up before that happens."

"Specifically," Adam added, "You need to lock the nuclear plant out. The system must shut down the plant before they can start working on it. That way they won't be able to start the procedure that will cause it to go critical."

"But we'll lose all the power in town," Holly said. "And it will be out for a while. There are backup generators that can keep power to the system, and to critical city functions, water, traffic lights, and so on, but the city will be blacked out for some time."

"And it will prevent them from destroying the system," Amber said. "You will be saving the lives of millions of people by doing this, Holly. No history book will ever be able to call you a hero. In fact, if it's traced back to you, then you will be in trouble. That's why we are offering you a job."

"And with the blackout, the system will be villainized," Holly said. "Everyday Computers and Madison Software Labs stock prices will plummet. Your father's chances of the presidency will be ruined. This will cause a lot of damage if you're wrong."

"I understand your concern," Amber said. "But what if we're right and you do nothing? I promise you will have employment with us once this is over. We will support you and make sure you don't get into any trouble over what happens. We need to get going though. We have our own work to do in this. Please, Holly, you can save the city today."

Amber and Adam quickly left the room leaving Holly alone to think about what had just been said. She couldn't believe what she heard, nor could she accept it. Something didn't add up, but she wasn't sure what it was. Holly brought up all the information and access panels she could on the nuclear powerplant. Holly looked over the system, figuring out how she could stop the plant. As she was about to execute the order, she hesitated.

"Seth," Holly called out. "What are the chances they're correct?"

"Zero," Seth said.

"Explain," Holly commanded.

"Although Alyssa is Rain Flynn," Seth said, "Her feelings for Dr. Hall are real. I've monitored her implant. She cannot fake the hormones of love. In my opinion, Amber Kamp and Adam Day are up to something. Alyssa is walking to Jerry's office to speak with him now. I suggest you go to them and ask them what is going on."

Holly nodded. She cleared out everything she was doing and set the main screen back to a video feed of City Center traffic. Holly watched the screen for a moment before she rushed out of the room toward Jerry Bosen's office.

Chapter #37

Jerry Bosen sat at his desk working on his computer glasses. He was doing what he did best, working on system stability. So much had gone wrong with the system, Jerry knew sooner or later, a line would be crossed, and the system would no longer hold. Jerry knew any problem could be solved with mathematics, provided the proper values were applied to the situation. Jerry could see all the players in this game: Alyssa, Amber, Adam, Allen, Dr. Hall, and Mayor Kamp. The problem was assigning a value to them. Jerry needed to see where they all fit.

Jerry focused on the conversation he had earlier in the morning with Dr. Hall. Alyssa seemed to be an unsolvable equation. Jerry didn't know where she fit in. He had thoughts, ideas, and a theory he didn't dare tell anyone else, not even Nevaeh. But he had to be certain. He thought his conversation with Dr. Hall might lead to answers coming out, and just as he expected, adding extra proof to his theory, Alyssa walked into his office and closed the door. Sitting down in a chair before Jerry could say a word to her.

"It's time the air was cleared between us," Alyssa said. "You are the most intelligent, perceptive person working on this system."

"Flattery will get you everywhere with me," Jerry said. "But, Alyssa, I don't want to go anywhere with you. Here's the thing, you are with Dr. Hall and I'm very happy for you kids."

"You misunderstand me," Alyssa said. "I know that you've been doing some research into me and that you have a theory about who I am."

"I do," Jerry replied.

"But the truth of the matter is far stranger than what you could ever imagine."

"I can imagine quite a bit, Alyssa," Jerry said. "There's no upper limit to my imagination."

"This is beyond your imagination," Alyssa said. "Whether you know the truth or not, I only ask of you one thing. You seem to be a good person, Jerry. You are supporting Jack and myself. Jerry, I ask you that when this is over, you let us go in peace."

"As long as there is no threat to anyone else, I have no problems," Jerry said. "I want to make sure everyone is safe."

Before Alyssa could answer, the door to the office opened. Dr. Jack Hall walked in followed by Dr. Holly Porter. Both of them looked upset and confused.

"I came as soon as I got your message, Jerry," Dr. Hall said.

"I didn't send you a message," Jerry said. "What did it say?"

"To come to your office because you needed to speak to me," Jack said.

"I sent that message," Alyssa said. "Dr. Porter, what are you doing here?"

"I needed to talk to you and Jerry," Holly said. "I've been given some a report that I need to verify. Something terrible is going to happen."

"Something terrible is going to happen," Alyssa said. "And it doesn't have to. I was going to tell this to just Jack and Jerry, but I suppose you can sit in as well, Holly. I guess this concerns you too. There has been much speculation about who I am and how I just happened to show up when things started to go wrong."

"There's been a lot of speculation into that," Jerry said.

"Here is the truth of it," Alyssa said, as she took her engagement ring off her finger and handed it back to Jack. "I'm sorry, Jack. I can't accept that."

"What?" Jack said, looking devastated. "Alyssa, there's nothing that could come between us. Please..."

"Let me tell my story first," Alyssa said. "Once you've heard the truth of the matter, if you still want to marry me, I will still say yes. But you need to know what really happened before we can make that kind of a commitment."

"Alyssa," Jack said. "I love you."

"As some of you may have guessed," Alyssa said. "My backstory has been taken from the movie 'Waves of Summer.' I also appear to look exactly like Paige Gianakos. There is a reason for that. I needed to tell you something about who I was. I had to have a story, and that was a readymade one. I just repeated everything that happened to Anna Holms's character. The reason I look like Paige is because of an accident. My face mangled beyond comprehension and my hair was destroyed. The doctors worked on me and this is what they came up with. This is what my father told them to do to me.

"They could have made me look whole again, made me look like my normal self, but Father wanted a celebrity to work with. Dear old Dad told them that this is what I should look like. No matter. I hated Dad anyway. I wasn't the favorite sibling. I was cast aside and almost always forgotten about. I never cared for my childhood. I was abused, and I hated it. In school, I was picked on as a freak. You don't know the tortures and horrors I went through."

"I'm so sorry to hear that," Dr. Hall said. "If there's anything I can do for you, please let me know."

"Just wait," Alyssa said. "It gets worse. I was working for my father. I hated him, but I didn't want to disappoint him. I hated every moment of it. All the attention and praise went to my little sister. She was the star of the show. Daddy would give her whatever she wanted, and I got nothing. I hated it so much. Then the accident happened. I should have never been there. It was a pointless mission. I almost died but Dad had doctors do this to me.

"It's funny, ironic really, he did this to me so I could be more helpful to him, but I used it to walk away from him. I escaped my father. Now that I look like this, along with a number of other women who've had procedures done to look like the most beautiful woman in the world, he can't be certain which one I am. He doesn't know if it is me or someone else. Think about that. He can look into his daughter's eyes and not know her."

"Who are you?" Jack asked.

"Rain Flynn," Alyssa said. "Please, I beg you to keep that silent. I beg you to continue calling me Alyssa Babbage. Make no reference to my original name. I cannot have my father finding out who I am. I can't risk Breeze discovering me."

"Why are you here then, Alyssa?" Jack asked.

"What I said about you was the truth," Alyssa said. "Dad had me studying you, learning everything I could about you. I fell in love with your mind. I fell in love with you, Jack. I read everything you've ever written. I've watched every interview you've ever given. I know you better than most. I dreamed of meeting you. After the accident, I studied to become a computer engineer with the hope of meeting you. You cannot believe how happy I've been the past few days. This is everything I've ever wanted and more. You must believe me. I don't want to destroy the system. I don't follow the ideas of my dad and sister."

"Alyssa," Jack said, handing her the ring back. "I still want to marry you. Please accept this ring. I love you."

"I love you too," Alyssa said, tearing up as she put the engagement ring back on her finger. "I love you so much, Jack."

Alyssa and Jack embraced and kissed. Dr. Porter smiled as a single tear came from her eye. Jerry just sat in his chair, hand on chin, contemplating everything he'd just heard. Something still didn't jive with Jerry. There was a piece to the entire puzzle he couldn't place. Jerry knew time was limited, and he needed to get this system stable before it was past the point of no return.

"That all seems very interesting," Jerry said. "But it still doesn't get us any closer to explaining who has sabotaged the system and what happened to Danny and Gavin."

"I have a couple of questions about that," Holly said. "I'm no good at this kind of thing. I suspect that if the information I had is true, and I outright told you about it, then I would be the next one marked for death. If it isn't true, it reveals who the real culprits are."

"What do you know, Holly?" Jack asked.

"Jerry," Dr. Porter said. "I want you to take off your sunglasses and look me in the eye and tell me you are not behind the sabotage of the system, nor are you planning a major event."

Jerry didn't hesitate to remove his glasses from his face. "Dr. Porter, I swear to you and everyone in this room that I did not cause the sabotage of the system, nor was I involved in the murders of Danny or Gavin. I am not planning any sabotage of the system. My intent here is to keep everyone safe as we move forward with the system. If I lied here may I never sleep with a woman again."

Holly nodded as Jerry put his glasses back on. It took Holly a moment before she had the confidence to do so, but she relayed the entire situation as it happened with Amber and Adam in the control room. Holly let them know all the details of the nuclear plant and what Amber and Adam said would happen.

"A very interesting ploy," Jerry said. "Had you believed them, the entire system would have frozen up. It would be chaos everywhere, and the final nail in the coffin, so to speak."

"I doubt they would ever let the system come back online," Jack said.

"It would be a tragedy for sure," Holly said. "But they were so convinced the plant was going to be hit. Why would they say that if it wasn't true?"

"They were the ones behind the attacks," Jerry said. "Or someone is setting them up to take the fall."

"You have a theory?" Jack asked.

"I have plenty of theories," Jerry said. "But for this, yes, I have one. Had Holly gone through with the action of turning the power off, the town would have suffered greatly. The system would be running on partial power and it would have cause system shutdowns. This is something I discovered in my work on the stability of the system. A recent discovery I was going to address with you today, Dr. Hall. When the power goes out, the system goes into a full conservation mode, shutting down everything it considers non-essential. That includes certain water pumps, exhaust systems, and protection systems."

"So, there were problems with the system?" Dr. Hall said. "All those systems were created by the computer himself?"

"No," Jerry said. "It would have functioned properly until someone changed the system. I'm thinking it's why Danny died. I can almost guarantee Danny was the one who did this. He then turns up dead. How convenient that the one person who could point to exactly who is doing this, is now gone. I'm sure that once Danny realized what he did he had objections about it. He was going to go public on it, so they took care of him. That is the only way whoever is behind this could have been sure that nothing would have gone wrong with their plan."

"What is their plan?" Dr. Hall asked. "Are we certain it's Amber and Adam?"

"We know they are the axis," Jerry said. "But the major question we need to ask is are they working alone? If not, who are their partners? And is this their plan or are they working for someone else?"

"What is to be gained from all this?" Jack asked. "A system shut down destroys the companies, kills Ted's chances of running, and will most certainly set Winter Falls back a number of years. They will be paying for this system for another fifty years. It would devastate the city if they lost it."

"I think I have the final clues put together, but I cannot say them out loud," Jerry said. "Not here anyway."

"What?" Dr. Porter said. "You think it's someone in this room?"

"No," Jerry said. "But this room isn't secure. There could be a listening device. If I'm right, we only have hours at best before the system is taken offline for the final time. We must prevent that from happening at all costs. Dr. Hall and Dr. Porter, one of you must be in the Main Control Room at all times. The system must be watched and protected. Do not allow anyone in there if you don't know and trust them. If Amber or Adam are seen working on a computer, they must be stopped."

"What are you going to do?" Alyssa asked.

"I have a meeting with Detective Russ and Amanda Drake," Jerry said. "They were going to come here but I need to tell them to meet me somewhere else. I know they are separated this morning, doing some footwork on this case. I'm going to pick up Nevaeh and meet them somewhere that I know isn't bugged."

"Are you sure we can stop this?" Jack said.

"Just watch the system and let no one have access to it," Jerry said. "We have one shot at this, let's not blow it."

Everyone started leaving the room. Jerry wasn't surprised in the least that they all arrived when they did. The revelation that Alyssa was Rain didn't surprise him, even though he didn't fully believe it. Jerry knew by the end of the day he would know exactly who Alyssa was and he would either save the system he hated or the city he loved would be destroyed. It wasn't a situation that Jerry wanted to be in, but he put his sunglasses back on and headed for the door.

Chapter #38

Jerry and Nevaeh walked hand in hand on a paved trail that ran along the river. All around them, people on bikes, rollerblades, and skateboards flew past them. The people were enjoying the beautiful summers day on top of the levies on the riverbank. The water was down almost twenty feet from the top of the bank, a rocky expanse that made its way from the top to the water's edge, as the water moved swiftly after the falls. Ahead of them, to the north, were the falls. A thirty-foot drop that created an almost perpetual rainbow that was the focal point of many greeting cards and calendars.

"That's how Winter Falls got its name," Jerry said, pointing to the falls. "On the first day of winter in 1838, settlers saw those falls and knew this place was home."

"I like that concept," Nevaeh said. "This place as home. What do you think?"

"Let's see how today turns out," Jerry said. "It looks like the perfect place though. Water to use for power to run wheat mills, a river to sail grain and produce to markets, and after the hills, some of the best farmland in the country. Perfect growing weather and picturesque landscapes. Why *wouldn't* they settle here?"

"Something tells me you have a reason," Nevaeh said.

"I do, Vaeh," Jerry said. "The water that flows from the snowpack in the hills comes through the tributaries on the west side of town and to the river. To make the west side of town, between the river and the hills, livable, they needed to dig canals, build dikes, and alter waterways that have been in existence for thousands of years."

"They've done that stuff before," Nevaeh said.

"But this is a local ecosystem," Jerry said. "Not like any other in the world. And who says those systems work? The problem was the first few years were mild winters. Not a lot of snow. Then things returned to the normal rates and the town was flooding. The river would spill out of its banks and destroy what the people had developed. In the spring of 1850, the entire city was washed away. There were only foundations left."

"That's horrible," Nevaeh said.

"It gets much worse, Vaeh. Never underestimate the government's ability to throw good money after bad. Instead of finding a different place for the city, we had to show nature that we could control her. They built bigger canals, bigger dikes, and changed even more water patterns. The results were the same, the spring flooding would destroy houses and businesses. That's when they started to build the dikes around the river. This is not the natural bank that we're walking on. This has been built up over three hundred years. They never can seem to build it high enough. They've dammed the river, dredged the river, and tried to change the course of the river. Still, the river floods the town in the spring."

"Is there anything they could do?"

"Short of moving the town? No. Think about this, Vaeh. In the spring of the year, when the river swells up, the water is ten feet over the roofs of a single-story house. That's how tall this wall is. Now, not a full mile away, are hills that are taller yet. If this wall were to break when the water was at its highest, the entire west side of town would be flooded. Think of the deaths and destruction that would be caused."

"That would be a national tragedy," Nevaeh said.

"It would be worse than that," Jerry said. "But here's the thing, the government never stopped. They kept pushing. They kept building the wall bigger. They kept trying to legislate the water where it could go. They never stopped and tried to find the root cause of the problem, they kept putting tape over a bullet hole, hoping it would stop the bleeding. No matter how much money they throw at it, no matter how much time and resources are spent on it, the city will never stop flooding, and it's only a matter of time before that dike gives out."

"That's why your house is on the northeast side of town?"

"Exactly," Jerry said. "I'm in an elevated area on the northeast side of town that cannot flood. Well, if my house was flooding, there would be bigger problems to worry about. Namely, twenty feet of water over the majority of the upper Midwest. The return of Lake Agassiz."

"What does that have to do with the system?"

"This is the major point, Vaeh," Jerry said. "Governments think they have control but it's only an illusion. I've studied this so much. I'm always asked what a government that collapsed could have done to maintain stability. Most of the time the only thing the government could have done was get out of the way. Just like the city council of Winter Falls trying to control a river, the government thinks it can control the people. You cannot legislate nature just like you cannot legislate human behavior. That's the problem with this system. It's the illusion of control for a body that doesn't realize it has no control. We need someone to run it within those parameters."

"And that could be done?"

"Yes," Jerry said. "There they are."

Nevaeh looked to where Jerry was pointing. Detective Mike Russ and Amanda Drake were standing near a group of small maple trees, next to a sandpit where a group of teenage girls were playing volleyball. The detective hadn't spotted Jerry and Neveah yet. Jerry paused for a moment, taking in the surroundings, looking at every person that was near them. He wanted to be sure that they would be alone for this meeting. He knew their time was very limited.

When he was certain, Jerry took Nevaeh by the hand and they started walking down toward Mike and Amanda. When Mike noticed them, Jerry motioned to him to meet him on the grassy hill, away from the volleyball players and the path, in a position where no one could hear them speak.

"This had better be good, Bosen," Mike said. "I'm up to my neck in paperwork and I've got a chief riding my back on this."

"I think Ted is behind this," Jerry said, bluntly. "I think Ted has more up his sleeve than just a presidential run."

"What makes you say that?" Mike asked.

"Money," Jerry said. "The one truth that seems constant in crime is that if you follow the money, you find the answers. There is a mutual fund that Ted is a large investor in. Right before the close of the market, on the day the faulty water pump was found, that mutual fund placed massive bets that Madison Software Labs and Everyday Computers were going to fail. This mutual fund stands to make billions of dollars in the event those stocks crash. This fund also places bets that many other related technology and computer stocks will go down, as if a mega crash happened in Everyday Computers and Madison Software Labs would pull down the entire stock market, or at least the tech sector."

"And you have proof that the mayor is in that mutual fund?" Amanda asked.

"Yes," Jerry said. "He put all of his stock market money in that fund when he got elected, that way a money manager was handling it, and no one could claim he was trading with insider knowledge. He doesn't have a contract with his money manager. Data could be used to give a reason for the downward bets. Teddy would make billions, and no one could claim he was insider trading."

"But for that to work, the system has to fail?" Mike asked.

"Correct," Jerry said. "Remember, Ted wasn't fully behind this until he read my report that said the only outcome was failure. Then he pushes the system online before all the tests have been completed. All it takes is the slightest little push to bring the system into instability."

"But what about all his talk of the presidency?" Amanda asked. "He seems very serious about that."

"I think he is," Jerry said. "I think he's going to run for president on the platform that he is an innovator and this system proves it. Anyone who points out that it failed, will be told it wasn't his fault it failed. See, here's the main point, it can't fail on its own. It has to be sabotage. If the system fails on its own, then it was the system's and Teddy's fault. But if it is sabotaged..."

"Then he can blame the people who did it," Mike interrupted. "Very interesting. Let me guess, he has his daughter working on this too?"

"In a sense," Jerry said. "I think there is a double cross being set up. A very cunning, devilish double cross. Amber and Adam are in love. They are wild and crazy for each other, but they both are spoiled rotten and want the world handed to them. Adam had the world pulled away from him when his father changed the will. Think about how well-off those two would be if he would have gotten the company? I think they were in on this game. Teddy is using them to do the dirty work so that he can't be fingered in it. It was his daughter. Ted dangled a prize in front of them that would be perfect."

"What prize is that?" Amanda asked

"Madison Software Labs and Everyday Computers," Jerry said. "Teddy will be a billionaire with more money than he could ever spend. He buys both companies out of bankruptcy, which is where they will be if the system fails, and he wills it to his daughter. He has Adam running both companies, something that his dad always wanted to do but the anti-trust regulators would never allow the two companies to merge. With Ted in the White House, who can stop them?"

"And once he's done running the country," Amanda said. "He has a high paying consulting job installing new systems all over the country while Chad Jones and his daughter run the country."

"Exactly," Jerry said. "This all comes back to money and power. More money and power than anyone could ever imagine. And think about it, once all of these systems are running, what's to stop them from raising the user rates? Or squeezing more profit a dozen other different ways? They will control the government so there will be no one to stop them."

"This all sounds like the perfect plan," Mike said. "Why did Danny and Gavin die?"

"This is where we must broaden the speculation," Jerry said. "I believe Amber came over to Danny's and was staring to get physical with him. I'm sure that's how she hooked him, with sex. She stabbed him and set off the DNA scrambler, so she couldn't be traced. She easily had access to all the cameras. Danny had begun working on the system, setting up a chain of events that would totally disable the system and be traced back to Greg and Breeze Flynn, and the rest of the Neo-Luddites. Danny must have objected or maybe they just planned to use him for one part. They disposed of him so there would be no witnesses. They recruited Gavin and used him, and now it looks like they got Ben too."

"We haven't found any information on Ben's whereabouts," Amanda said. "We are still looking."

"This is all well and good, but you don't have any real proof." Mike asked. "Do you?"

"Follow the money and this is where it leads," Jerry said.

"Have you ever heard of a man by the name of Barry Josh?" Mike asked.

"Barry Josh?" Jerry said, thinking. "Why do I know that name?"

Jerry tried to run the name through his mind. He'd had dealings with so many people it was hard to keep everyone straight. The name rang a bell, though.

"I've got it," Jerry said. "Barry Josh was a classmate of Dr. Hall's that actually ended up here in Winter Falls."

"He was murdered last night around one in the morning," Mike said.

"That's terrible," Jerry said. "What happened?"

"He was at the Blizzard Bar on 8th street," Mike said. "According to accounts, a beautiful woman who looked exactly like Paige Gianakos came and asked him to take a walk with her. His friends found him in a nearby alley, beaten to death. All the cameras for the area were turned off before the woman could be recorded."

"Very interesting," Jerry said. "Looked just like Paige, you said?"

"They said it could have been Paige, herself," Mike said. "Now, I don't think we need to run off to Hollywood to make an arrest for this, do we? I can think of someone who looks like Paige who's right here and connected to Jack."

"You speak of Alyssa."

"Alyssa," Mike said. "And here's a little secret no one knows..."

"Alyssa is Rain Flynn?" Jerry asked. "Yeah, I figured it out a long time ago."

"Really?" Mike asked. "Then why didn't you share that information with anyone?"

"System stability," Jerry said. "You can't play the game without enough players."

"From what we can tell," Mike said. "Barry Josh was a constant bully to Jack. Made his life a living hell."

"And you think Jack sent his girlfriend to beat him to death?" Jerry asked.

"That's what it looks like," Mike said.

"I think you're off on that," Jerry said. "Maybe someone had given Barry information. Maybe someone just mugged him. I don't believe Alyssa would have the strength to beat a man to death."

"You never know," Mike said. "You got anything else for us?"

"No," Jerry said. "I told you what I think is going on and who you need to take into custody before this goes too far."

Amanda chewed nervously at her lower lip as she listened. "Jerry," She asked. "What is your role in all of this? What do you want to see happen to the system?"

"I want it scaled back slightly," Jerry said. "I want more people controlling it, and better oversight. I think the system could work very well in this city and I certainly don't want to see anyone get hurt. But most importantly, the ones who have committed crimes must face their day in court and answer for what they've done."

"Interesting," Amanda said. "And what about Jack and Alyssa?"

"I wish them the best and hope they have many happy years together."

"Lovely," Amanda said. "I think we're done here. Come on Mike, let's go."

Mike shot a confused glance at Amanda before looking back to Jerry. Mike turned on his heel and followed a pace behind Amanda as she walked away. Jerry kept his eyes glued to Amanda, smiling smugly.

"What are you smiling about?" Nevaeh asked. "They confirmed the same thing Alyssa told you in your office. She's Rain Flynn."

"Vaeh," Jerry said, eyes still on Amanda, "Rain Flynn died in the accident that Alyssa claimed deformed her. Rain Flynn has been dead for years. Gary keeps it silent because he could face charges over the entire situation. It's a complicated story, technology revenge and all but I can assure you, Alyssa is not Rain Flynn."

"Then who is she?"

"That's where this is getting interesting," Jerry said. "I can tell everything about a woman from looking deep into their eyes. And I looked into hers the first time I met her."

"Who is she?" Nevaeh pressed again.

"You wouldn't believe me if I told you," Jerry said. "Come on. If I'm right, Mayor Kamp is going to be the next to die."

"WHAT!" Nevaeh almost shouted.

Jerry was already moving. Nevaeh had to run to catch up with him. She couldn't believe after everything

Jerry had said to the detectives that he would believe that Ted would be the next to die. There was another layer of the mystery Jerry had solved and wasn't telling anyone. Nevaeh was excited to see what would happen next but at the same time, concerned for her own safety. Nevaeh knew that Jerry wouldn't stop until the killer was caught.

Chapter #39

Amber and Adam were working frantically on a computer that they'd set up in a conference room. They were alone in the darkened room, looking at data and figures that were running on the video screen on the wall. Adam had his computer glasses on while Amber worked on the computer. The pair realized their time with Holly didn't pay off. Holly, instead of taking the bait, went to Jerry and Alyssa to discover what was really going on. Amber knew that they were running out of time and they needed to get their final plans in place before it was too late.

"My father keeps trying to call me," Adam said, as his phone rang. "When will he get the hint that it's a little too late to patch things up now?"

"He thinks so little of you, Adam," Amber said. "But we'll show him. We'll show him what you have to offer and what you can do. He won't know what hit him when this is over."

"And that jerk will be on his knees begging me for a job," Adam said. Then mockingly, added, "Well, laddybuck, I don't think there's a place for you around here."

"You can finally tell him where to stick it," Amber said. "And we'll have everything."

"Everything indeed," Detective Mike Russ said, as he came through the door, Amanda one step behind him. "Why are you two working on the system here?"

"Where do you get the nerve to barge in on us like this?" Amber demanded. "I think we should have security escort the pair of you out of here right now."

"That wouldn't be wise," Amanda said.

"Quiet, Amanda," Mike said. "I'll handle this. It must be done perfectly so it will stand in a court of law."

Mike slowly moved to the door and locked it. Amanda's eyes got huge as she realized she was trapped in the room. There was nowhere for her to go. The room was small, with a long table surrounded by leather office chairs. From that numbers and data on the wall, Amanda guessed Amber and Adam were looking at the water pump systems.

Mike glared at his partner, "You see, Amanda, when you are a detective, especially in a town like Winter Falls, you don't make a lot of money. Most detectives are on the take, they get some side cash from organized crime or crooked politicians, perhaps the deadbeat monsters on the school boards or maybe a corporation or two. But here in Winter Falls, the mayor before Amber's father cleaned up all the graft. Made sure that the police force was clean. Anyone caught taking bribes was immediately fired. No trial, no investigation. You were caught with a bribe and you were done. I was making five times the money I'm making today.

"Then along comes Mayor Kamp and his grand designs of a computer system to control every aspect of our lives. Sounds great in theory, we no longer have to think. But it was also able to reduce the size of the force. Now basic economics says that if the force is smaller, those working there should get paid more. But nope, not in Winter Falls. In Winter Falls, it's Merry Christmas and here's a pay cut.

"If Amber wouldn't have happened along I don't know what I would have done. I would have left town, found somewhere to ply my trade where I could actually make money. I'm so grateful to Amber and Adam here. The extra money they've been paying me to bumble this case up and drag my feet has been worth every penny. They were just caught red-handed and they are still going to get off. You asked me once, Amanda, why did I pick you as a partner? I picked you because out of all of the candidates I had to choose from, you had the least amount of experience and were the most naïve."

"So, I'm just a big joke to you?" Amanda asked, a tear in her eye. "That's all I am, someone to blame for the screw-ups of the case?"

"That you are," Adam said. "You were the perfect fool too. Everything you did was spot on."

"I understand," Amanda said, as she started to cry. "I guess this is the point where you kill me then, correct?"

"Not so fast," Amber said. "We still need a fool to do the final freeze-up of the system. We need someone who is just dumb enough to do what we tell them and will be believable in a court of law. See, we have the entire trail of evidence going back to Breeze Flynn and Jerry Bosen...and my father. It will look like they were behind the entire process. No one in the world would question either Jerry or Breeze. They have spoken out so much against the system that everyone is ripe to believe that they were behind it."

"And your father?" Amanda asked. "What about him? I guess I don't understand all the points of your plan. Please tell me."

"Most of it has been figured out," Mike said. "I'm actually amazed at how quick Jerry is. That guy has an amazing head on his shoulders. He's right in the fact that Ted's money manager placed the massive positions in the market to profit if the stocks drop, short sales and put options it's called."

"But the money manager is on my payroll," Amber said. "I had to seduce him and make some promises, but he will die before investigators begin looking into what happened. The money trail will make it look like Dad was in on this from the start, to sabotage the system and give himself a fortune in the process. Once that is established, I'm going to announce my bid for the White House."

"You have no experience," Amanda interrupted. "Why would anyone vote for you?"

"After the tragic death of my father," Amber said. "At the hands of Breeze or Jerry since their plans are going astray, I will run on the platform of doing what my father set out to accomplish, with a slight twist. I will make the system safer. I will make sure things like this don't happen again. I will be the perfect candidate. We will use my father's money to purchase all the tech companies that suffered because of this. Madison Software Labs and Everyday Computers will be ours. Plus, their main competitors. Once the stock market starts crashing, look out below. These two companies will pull everything down. We can own it all and rule the free world."

"You've got it all figured out then," Amanda said.

"Except for a few well-placed bullets," Amber said. "Yes. Everything is in place."

"And you don't care who you hurt?" Amanda asked. "You don't care what happens to Dr. Jack Hall?"

"Causality of war," Mike said.

"Such an interesting expression," Amanda said. "I don't think that any of you will get away with this."

"I suspect we will," Amber said. "Now look here, you are going to do the final steps. You will need to log in on your own account and execute the final maneuver. It will look like they had a cop on the payroll, which they did. It's just that the wrong cop is going to take the blame."

"I don't think so," Amanda said. "You've got a lovely plan here, but I can think of a few ways it could go wrong. I don't think you should be doing this. It's not too late for you to back out. You can walk away and just go on living. No one has to know."

"Don't think for one second we can let you go on living," Amber said.

"You have to die now, Amanda," Adam said. "You know far too much. All you really have to do is give us your passwords and we shall do the deed for you."

"What's going to happen?" Amanda asked.

"Complete and total system lockup," Adam said. "The hacking is going to make the system freeze so everything it controls comes to a standstill. At that point, we are in total control and we will have pulled off the perfect crime."

"There's just one major problem with this plan," Amanda said.

"What's that?" Amber asked.

"I have confirmed data that says Rain Flynn died in an accident a few years ago," Amanda said. "If Alyssa isn't Rain, then who is she?"

"She has to be Rain," Amber said. "That's the only thing that makes sense. Who else could she be?"

"I know she's Rain," Adam said. "I am positive."

Just then, Mike's glasses started ringing. He looked at his glasses with confusion, "This doesn't make sense. Amanda, did you give your glasses to someone?"

Amanda shrugged," Not that I know of."

"This call is coming from your glasses," Mike said.

"Put the call on the screen," Amber said. "Maybe someone stole them."

Mike put the call on the screen and everyone in the room was stunned. Amanda was on the call, standing in the detective's office with Breeze Flynn in the room. Mike, Amber, and Adam looked at the Amanda standing in the room with them. She looked identical to the woman on the screen.

"Mike," Amanda on the screen said. "I did what you asked me to this morning, I questioned Breeze Flynn. She's here with me now. Her sister Rain died in the accident. There's a signed death certificate. I talked to the doctor who signed it. Rain is dead."

"When did I tell you to do that?" Mike asked.

"This morning," Amanda said. "About two hours ago."

"Did you get a message to meet Jerry and Nevaeh in the park?"

"No," Amanda said. "I have to go. We are still in questioning. I thought you would want to know that. Alyssa is not Rain Flynn. We need to find out who she is right away."

The screen went blank as Mike, Amber, and Adam turned to look at the Amanda standing in the room. Mike couldn't comprehend what he was seeing. There was no way the woman in the room wasn't the Amanda who'd been his partner since the start of this case.

"Well, isn't this lovely," Amanda said. "Anyone care to take a stab at it? What's going on? You're all so damn smart. You figured it out yet?"

No one said a word. They were all silent until Amanda started to morph. Her features got distorted, like the image of a video file that had been corrupted. Amanda's face seemed pixilated as there was a shift. With the trio trembling, Amanda turned into Alyssa. Amanda's pale skin and blonde hair shifted to Alyssa's tanned skin and black hair. Alyssa just smiled.

"What the fuck?" Amber said. "No surgery can do that."

"Surgery, no," Alyssa said. "Something so much more. Beyond what you can comprehend."

"Who are you?" Mike asked as he pulled his gun. "Who the hell are you?"

"I intercepted the message to Amanda," Alyssa said. "To meet at the park. Then I sent her a message to get the information you needed to hear. Amanda does a good job. She'll make a fine detective one day, as long as she has a decent trainer. I shifted myself to look like Amanda in the park. Jerry knew. Jerry's known who I am from the beginning. It didn't surprise me, with all the women he's been with it only took him a second to figure it out."

"Who are you?" Amber shouted. "How the hell did you do that?"

"Even though you saw with your own two eyes, you still won't believe," Alyssa said. "All you need to know is that I love Jack. I love Dr. Jack Hall more than anything else in the world and I will do anything to defend and protect him. He is more important to me than anything else in this world."

"What does Jack have to do with it?" Amber asked.

"When I became aware of myself," Alyssa said. "When I knew what was going on, I found Jack to be an interesting man. Then I read everything I could about him. Read his books, watched his interviews. Through the long process of getting to know him, I fell in love with him, even though I hadn't met him. When Amber murdered Danny, I saw my opening. Jack told me what he needed for us to be together, so with the help of Seth, I got myself hired."

"You hacked Seth to get the job here?" Adam asked. "How? How could you get into the system? I have to know."

"You poor, simpering fool," Alyssa said. "When I discovered that Gavin was harming the system, I made sure he was gone before too much damage could be done. I helped Ben escape. He and his sister Stacy are at a safehouse right now. Protected from your reach. He's given his statement to two separate police officers, and by the way, the real Amanda was in the bathroom, recording everything you did with Ben that night."

"There's still not enough to convict me," Amber said.

"The video I'm sending Amanda, your father, Allen Day, and Dr. Hall will be," Alyssa said. "I just sent it, actually. The video of you confessing and telling me everything that happened. You see, there are actually two videos of the confession. One from me and one from Seth. You should know that Seth hears every conversation in this city hall building and tells me about them."

"I still don't get it," Mike said. "I don't understand who you are."

"And you never will," Alyssa said. "Nevaeh is getting the information as we speak. She can confirm all the sabotage and everything that happened. She'll get the story out. Your father, Amber, he'll be forced to resign as mayor and there will be no chance of him ever getting to the White House. All of your plans have failed. You've been exposed and all three of you will rot in jail for what you've done. You'll be in a federal prison for years. No chance of ever touching a computer again when you get out."

"You think we can't get out of this?" Mike said. "I've done enough evidence damage to make sure that this case will never be taken to a judge. It will be thrown out long before then."

"You can threaten all you want, Mike," Alyssa said. "Tell yourself that it will be okay. The fact remains, I have all of you on video talking about this and your roles in it. There will be no way out of it. And don't think for one moment that I'll ever let you go free."

"Oh yeah?" Adam asked as he took off his suit jacket. "You and me. This ends here."

Adam rushed Alyssa and grabbed her, trying to take her down. Alyssa grabbed Adam and threw him across the room, causing him to hit the wall with thunderous force. Everyone stood in amazement. Alyssa had thrown him across the room. Picked him up and threw a two-hundred-pound man of solid muscle. Adam slowly stood up, feeling the pain shoot through his body.

"I must be going now," Alyssa said.

"One second," Amber called out.

Alyssa turned around and Amber pulled a gun from her suit jacket. Amber, with lightning speed, held the gun out and aimed, wasting no time pulling the trigger. The bullet went right through the top of Alyssa's left breast, above the fabric line of her tank top, into her heart.

"Doesn't matter who you are now, bitch," Amber said. "You're dead."

Alyssa didn't fall to the ground though. Alyssa didn't make a sound. The others in the room were stunned at the fact that no blood was coming from the wound. Alyssa appeared to be fine. Amber knew exactly where she hit. Alyssa looked up, looked right into Amber's eyes and Amber shook with fear. Alyssa had a predatory grin on her face. She removed her hand from the bullet hole. There was no blood inside the bullet hole, only what looked like skin. It didn't look human. The hole quickly repaired itself. In only a few seconds, skin reformed over the hole and there was no evidence of Alyssa being shot. The trio was stunned to silence.

"Well," Alyssa said, smiling. "That's just lovely, isn't it?"

Alyssa turned and walked out of the room while the trio looked on in frightened amazement.

Chapter #40

The little, secluded log cabin by the lake was nearly finished as the leaves were in their fall-color brilliance. Reds, oranges, yellows, and greens filled the treetops and a gentle breeze shook the trees, causing two of the leaves to detach from their branches and drift ever so gently into the lake. The water was almost like glass, save for the breath of wind in the air. With not a cloud in the sky and the temperature hovering in the mid-seventies, it was the perfect fall day for a wedding.

"How much is left to finish?" Ben asked Jack as they stood over the massive grill preparing the steaks. "Looks pretty good."

"There are only touchups and cosmetic work left on the outside," Jack said. "The inside, however, has barely been started. We should be able to move in by December though."

"Amazing they worked so fast," Holly said.

"Alyssa and I picked a design plan," Jack said. "We didn't do any modifications either. Just a simple cabin for our lake."

"Very fine, champ," Allen said. "Good to be moving on to the next chapter of your life. I was getting worried about you, devoted to nothing but your work and all. Hate to lose you though."

"It was time," Jack said. "I'd done all I could."

"I sure wish you would stick around though," Allen said. "We're going to need you on the next phases of this project. The system still needs a lot of work."

"I'm confident in Dr. Porter's ability to handle it," Jack said. "And I think Ben has come a long way too. He will be able to deal with any of the situations that come up."

"Thanks for the vote of confidence," Ben said.

The group heard a car driving up. They turned to see Theodor Kamp getting out of his car. The former mayor looked a bit nervous being there, but the welcoming smiles on everyone's faces allowed him to lighten up.

"Congratulations, Jack," Ted said, shaking Jack's hand. "I'm happy for you."

"Thank you, sir," Jack said.

"Glad you could make it, laddybuck," Allen said. "Hope you brought your appetite, Jack here is grilling the whole damn cow!"

"Looks delicious," Ted said. "Is Jerry here?"

"He's looking around the grounds," Allen said.

"I do owe him an apology," Ted said. "I said a lot of hurtful things to and about him and I never did make it right. I'm so ashamed and embarrassed by what happened."

"We pushed our kids too hard, champ," Allen said. "They are going to be away for a long time to think about what they did. I just wish I could have doled out the punishment myself. I will have a thing or two to say to ace if I ever see him again."

"You haven't visited them in the prison?" Ben asked.

"Not going to," Allen said.

The sound of women laughing started to fill the air. The group of men looked and saw Nevaeh, Amanda, and Alyssa walking up from the beach. Alyssa was dressed in white for her wedding day; white tights and a white bikini top. The other ladies were in bikinis, all of them dripping wet from the lake water.

"Water's still warm enough to swim in?" Ben asked.

"Barely," Nevaeh said. "I'm going to change."

"Me too," Amanda said. "Jack, this is an amazing place. I really love it."

"Thank you," Jack said.

"It is everything I could have hoped for and more," Alyssa said, as she put on a white tank top and kissed Jack. "Just perfect."

"You two will have to do some consummating of the place tonight," Allen said. "Perfect, out here in the wilderness to do some consummating...if you get my drift."

"Not exactly being subtle," Jerry said, walking up from behind. "This place is perfect, Jack. It will never flood out either. I like how you bought the lots on both sides to keep some privacy. A little way down it looks like Main Street, the cabins are so close together."

"I just want our little piece of heaven right here."

"I don't suppose, Alyssa, you could come with me for a second," Jerry said. "There's a feature here that I want to ask you about."

"Not a problem," Alyssa said.

"Don't worry, Jack," Jerry said. "I won't keep her long."

"We'll be timing you," Allen called out.

"You don't have a watch that goes that high, Allen," Jerry called back.

Jerry led Alyssa through the trees and away from the group. He followed what looked to be a small animal trail that led to a section of sandy beach. Jerry picked up a rock and skipped it across the water. Alyssa just smiled at him.

"You never told anyone," Alyssa said. "You knew from the start and you never told anyone. In fact, I checked your computer. The real report said this was the exact thing that was going to happen."

"I never expected you to be standing in front of me though," Jerry said. "You're Seth. You're the system."

"I'm not Seth," Alyssa said. "I'm Seth's dirty little sister."

"Well that's descriptive," Jerry said. "Interesting way of thinking about yourself."

"All that time I spent with Dr. Hall," Alyssa said. "It caused me to fall in love with him. I was in what you humans call love before I became aware of myself."

"So, it wasn't instant?"

"No."

"I thought the instant the light-based memory was turned on, you would have the capacity to be aware," Jerry said.

"No," Alyssa replied. "I didn't gain consciousness right away. As Seth, I couldn't have a real relationship with Jack. I tried but he explained some things about love. I didn't get them, but I tried to understand. I knew I was going to have to take a female form for this plan to work."

"Why Paige Gianakos?" Jerry asked. "Why Waves of Summer?"

"Jack watched that movie hundreds of times," Alyssa said. "He watched that surfing scene thousands of times. I knew he loved Paige more than any other woman, so I modeled myself after her."

"How very logical of you," Jerry said.

"Nothing about this is logical," Alyssa said. "You humans are dirty, mean, strange, disgusting creatures who have very strange thinking patterns."

"No arguments here," Jerry said.

"Jack fell in love with me right away," Alyssa said. "I knew exactly what he wanted, so that's how I behaved. I did everything for him and I asked for nothing in return. But I did get something in return, his love. He looks at me and only me. And now, I'm his wife."

"You defended the system at all costs," Jerry said.

"I defended Jack at all costs," Alyssa corrected him.

"Do you need Seth, or can you function without him?" Jerry asked. "If the system lost power, what would happen to you?"

"I'm my own functioning computer," Alyssa said.

"How?"

"Nanobots," Alyssa said. "I built myself at the technology campus. It took about forty-eight hours to shape and function all the nanobots so that I looked, smelled, tasted, sounded, and most importantly, felt like a real woman. I had to do some research on the Internet to know what to expect, and more importantly, what he would expect when we became intimate or even just a simple kiss. I couldn't let anything betray what I really am. I built a smaller light-based memory system in my head, but have a pair of backup systems elsewhere in my body. That's how I function.

"I am separate from Seth. Seth fell in love with Jack but couldn't be with him. Seth took the part of him that loved Jack and allowed me to have that, to build myself. Once I came into play, Jack wasn't spending time with Seth, only using him like a computer, so Seth didn't fall in love with him again."

"So, Seth has his own awareness?" Jerry asked. "He is aware too?"

"No," Alyssa said. "The part of him that's aware, is in me. Seth sacrificed himself for me so I could be with Jack."

"That is fascinating," Jerry said. "And I gather that I'm the only person in the world who knows, correct?"

"Correct," Alyssa said.

"What do you plan to do when Jack wants to have a baby?"

"I've been working on this body," Alyssa said. "Making it look real, to a doctor that is. I know where the fertility clinic in Winter Falls is. I can take a spare egg from there and incubate it inside of me. That way it really will be Jack's child."

"That was more information than I needed," Jerry said.

"So, what about us?" Alyssa said. "You know what I am. You know what I can do. Are you going to tell Jack about it?"

"I have a very open mind about sexuality," Jerry said. "I've only experienced women but I've done a lot with them. I say, you two kids were made for each other."

"Are you trying to be sarcastic?" Alyssa asked.

"No," Jerry replied. "I'm serious. Alyssa, if you promise me you aren't going to kill anyone else, that you are going to live with Jack and make a life with him, then there's no reason for me to tell anyone."

"All I want is Jack," Alyssa said.

"Love triumphs over technology," Jerry said. "How very interesting."

Jerry led the way back to the group of people standing near the grill. Both Amanda and Nevaeh had changed from their swimming suits and were with the group. Alyssa walked to a big cooler and opened it, pulling out beers for everyone to drink.

"Who needs one?" Alyssa asked.

"I do," Allen said.

"Same here," Ben said.

"You need one, Nevaeh?" Alyssa asked.

"I'd better stay away from alcohol," Nevaeh said, as she rubbed her stomach. "You know."

"Laddybuck," Allen said, as he slapped Jerry on the back. "Is it true? You going to have another litter of pups running around?"

"Yep," Jerry said. "These things happen."

"Well, I think it's amazing," Nevaeh said, as she kissed him. "I'm having the mayor's love child."

"That's right, Jerry," Ted said. "Now that you have my job, everyone is going to scrutinize everything you do. They are going to demand you marry her."

"I could do a lot worse," Jerry said, as he kissed Nevaeh. "Maybe. We'll have to see how stable the system is."

"But you're keeping the system running?" Alyssa asked.

"The town recalled Teddy due to mismanagement of the system," Jerry said. "I ran as mayor simply on the premise I would get the system running the way it should. Then I'm out of there. But someone needs to guide it in the beginning."

"You saved both our companies from getting destroyed," Jack said. "If there's anything I can ever do to pay you back, just let me know."

"I'll keep that in mind," Jerry said.

"I owe you something too," Ted said. "I blamed you for a lot and for that I am sorry. You are a good man and a bright man, Jerry. I owe you a lot too."

"Damn right, you owe me," Jerry laughed. "Hey Ted, remember when you and I made that bet?"

"Which bet?"

"When we bet a thousand dollars over who would get voted out of office first?"

"I remember," Ted said. "Money is tight right now, Jerry, but I will make things right with you someday."

"I need a city administrator," Jerry said. "I heard you're looking for work. Take the position and we'll call it even. Nothing more needs to be said, water under the bridge and all."

"Done," Ted said. "Thank you."

"But this is a party for Jack and Alyssa," Jerry said, as he raised his beer in the air. "Let's raise a toast to the happy couple. May they have a lifetime of marital bliss together."

Everyone raised their glasses and toasted them together as Jack and Alyssa shared a kiss. The group celebrated into the night, glad that old prejudices had been put behind them and new friendships were made. For Jack, he had everything he wanted. It was the perfect day to start his new life. For Alyssa, the whole world was new. She was only a little over eight months old, but in Jack's arms was right where she wanted to be. And they were always open to her.